Eva Scott

Rupert Prince Palatine

Eva Scott

Rupert Prince Palatine

ISBN/EAN: 9783743393387

Manufactured in Europe, USA, Canada, Australia, Japa

Cover: Foto ©Raphael Reischuk / pixelio.de

Manufactured and distributed by brebook publishing software (www.brebook.com)

Eva Scott

Rupert Prince Palatine

CONTENTS

ILLUSTRATIONS

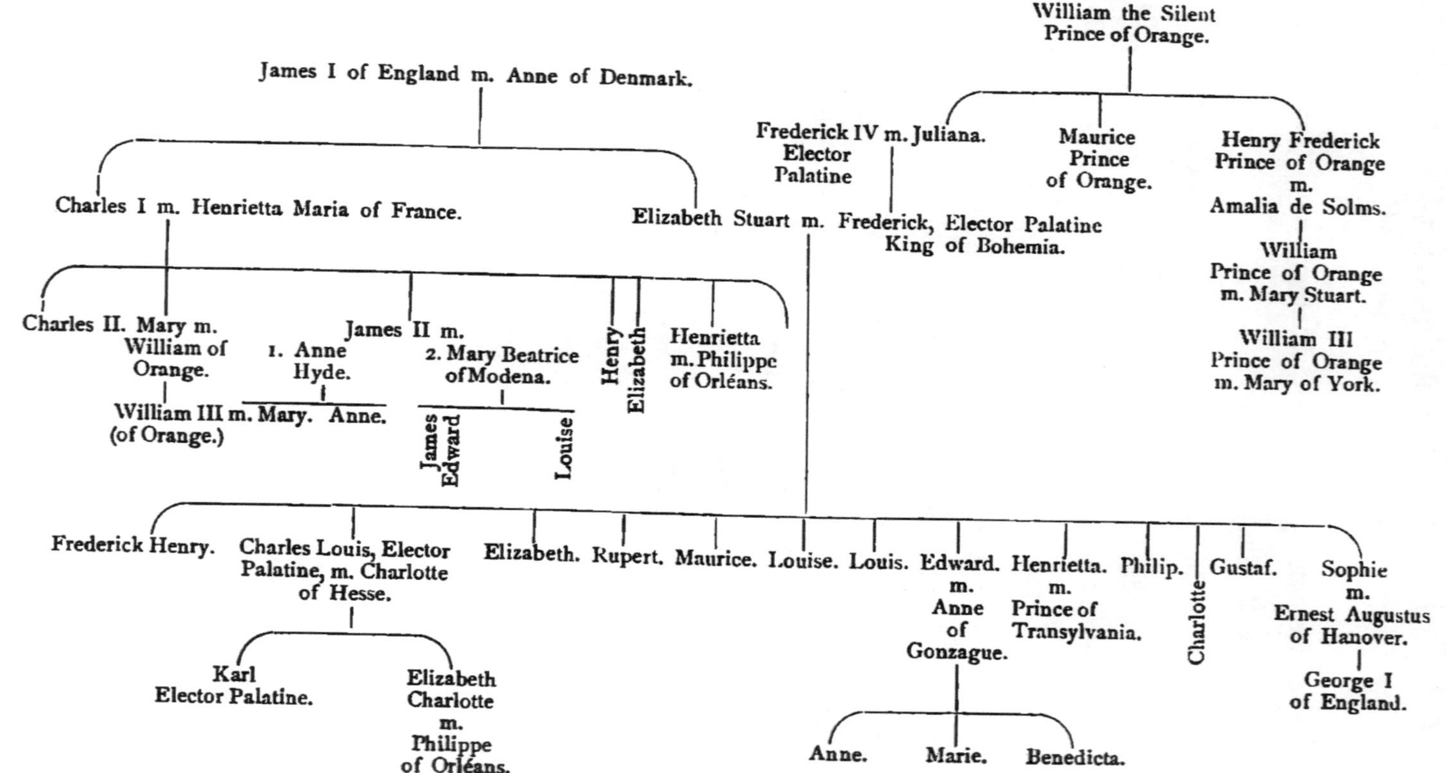

William the Silent Prince of Orange.
James I of England m. Anne of Denmark.
Frederick IV m. Juliana. Elector Palatine
Maurice Prince of Orange.
Henry Frederick Prince of Orange m. Amalia de Solms.
Charles I m. Henrietta Maria of France.
Elizabeth Stuart m. Frederick, Elector Palatine King of Bohemia.
William Prince of Orange m. Mary Stuart.
Charles II. Mary m. William of Orange.
1. Anne Hyde.
James II m.
2. Mary Beatrice of Modena.
Henry
Elizabeth
Henrietta m. Philippe of Orléans.
William III Prince of Orange m. Mary of York.
William III m. Mary. Anne. (of Orange.)
James Edward
Louise
Frederick Henry.
Charles Louis, Elector Palatine, m. Charlotte of Hesse.
Elizabeth. Rupert. Maurice. Louise. Louis. Edward. m. Anne of Gonzague. Henrietta. m. Prince of Transylvania. Philip. Charlotte Gustaf. Sophie m. Ernest Augustus of Hanover.
Karl Elector Palatine.
Elizabeth Charlotte m. Philippe of Orléans.
George I of England.
Anne. Marie. Benedicta.

RUPERT, PRINCE PALATINE

CHAPTER I

THE PALATINE FAMILY

"A man that hath had his hands very deep in the blood of many innocent people in England," was Cromwell's concise description of Rupert of the Rhine. [1]

"That diabolical Cavalier" and "that ravenous vulture" were the flattering titles bestowed upon him by other soldiers of the Parliament. [2] "The Prince that was so gallant and so generous," wrote an Irish Royalist. [3] And said Cardinal Mazarin, "He is one of the best and most generous princes that I have ever known." [4]

Rupert was not, in short, a person who could be regarded with indifference. By those with whom he came in contact he was either adored or execrated, and it is remarkable that a man who made so strong an impression upon his contemporaries should have left so slight a one upon posterity. To most people he is a name and nothing more;—a being akin to those iron men who sprang from Jason's dragon teeth, coming into life at the outbreak of the English Civil War to disappear with equal suddenness at its close. He is regarded, on the one hand, as a blood-thirsty, plundering ruffian, who endeavoured to teach in England lessons of cruelty learnt in the Thirty Years' War;

---

[1] Hist. MSS. Commission. 12th Report. Athole MSS. p. 30.

[2] Calendar of Domestic State Papers. Wharton to Willingham, 13 Sept. 1642.

[3] Carte's Original Letters. Ed. 1739. Vol. I. p. 59. O'Neil to Trevor, 26 July, 1644.

[4] Hist. MSS. Commission. 8th Report. Denbigh MSS. p. 552b.

on the other, as a mere headstrong boy who ruined, by his indiscretion, a cause for which he exposed himself with reckless courage. Neither of these views does him justice, and his true character, his real influence on English history are lost in a cloud of mist and prejudice. His character had in it elements of greatness, but was so full of contradictions as to puzzle even the astute Lord Clarendon, who, after a long study of the Prince, was reduced to the exclamation—"The man is a strange creature!"[1] And strange Rupert undoubtedly was! Born with strong passions, endowed with physical strength, and gifted with talents beyond those of ordinary men, but placed too early in a position of great trial and immense responsibility, his history, romantic and interesting throughout, is the history of a failure.

In his portraits, of which a great number are in existence, the story may be read. We see him first a sturdy, round-eyed child, looking out upon the world with a valiant wonder. A few years later the face is grown thinner and sadder, full of thought and a gentle wistfulness, as though he had found the world too hard for his understanding. At sixteen he is still thoughtful, but less wistful,—a gallant, handsome boy with a graceful bearing and a bright intelligent face, just touched with the melancholy peculiar to the Stuart race. At five-and-twenty his mouth had hardened and his face grown stern, under a burden which he was too young to bear. After that comes a lapse of many years till we find him embittered, worn, and sad; a man who has seen his hopes destroyed and his well-meant efforts perish. Lastly, we have the Rupert of the Restoration; no longer sick at heart and desperately sad, but a Rupert who has out-lived hope and joy, disappointment and sorrow; a handsome man, with a keen intellectual face, but old before his time, and made hard and cold and contemptuous by suffering and loneliness.

[1] Calendar Clarendon, State Papers, 27 Feb. 1654.

The first few months of Rupert's existence were the most prosperous of his life, but he was not a year old before his troubles began. His father, Frederick V, Elector Palatine of the Rhine, had been married at sixteen to the famous Elizabeth Stuart, daughter of James I of England; the match was not a brilliant one for the Princess Royal of England, but it was exceedingly popular with the English people, who regarded Frederick with favour as the leader of the Calvinist Princes of the Empire. Elizabeth was no older than her husband, and seems to have been considerably more foolish. Her extravagancies and Frederick's difficult humours were the despair of their patient and faithful household steward; yet for some years they dwelt at Heidelberg in peaceful prosperity, and there three children were born to them, Frederick Henry, Charles Louis, and Elizabeth.

But the Empire, though outwardly at peace, was inwardly seething with religious dissension, which broke out into open war on the election of Ferdinand of Styria, (the cousin and destined successor of the Emperor,) as King of Bohemia. Ferdinand was a staunch Roman Catholic, the friend and pupil of the Jesuits, with a reputation for intolerance even greater than he deserved. [1] As a matter of fact Protestantism was abhorrent to him, less as heresy, than as the root of moral and political disorder. The Church of Rome was, in his eyes, the fount of order and justice, and he was strongly imbued with the idea, then prevalent in the Empire, that to princes belonged the settlement of religion in those countries over which they ruled.

But it happened that the Protestants of Bohemia had, at that moment, the upper hand. The turbulent nobles of the country were bent on establishing at once their political and religious independence; they rose in revolt, threw the Emperor's ministers out of the Council Chamber window at Prague, and rejected Ferdinand as king.

---

[1] Gardiner's History of England. 1893. Vol. III. Chap. 29. pp. 251—299.

The Lutheran Princes looked on the revolt coldly, feeling no sympathy with Bohemia. They believed as firmly as did Ferdinand himself in the right of secular princes to settle theological disputes. They were loyal Imperialists, and hated Calvinism, anarchy and war, far more than they hated Roman Catholicism.

With the Calvinist princes of the south, at the head of whom stood the Elector Palatine and the Landgrave of Hesse Cassel, the case was different. Fear of their Catholic neighbours, Bavaria and the Franconian bishoprics, made them war-like; they sympathised strongly with their Bohemian co-religionists, they longed to break the power of the Emperor, and were even willing to call in foreign aid to effect their purpose. Schemes for their own personal aggrandisement played an equal part with their religious enthusiasm, and their plots and intrigues gave Ferdinand a very fair excuse for his unfavourable view of Protestantism.

For a time they merely talked, and on the death of Matthias they acquiesced in the election of Ferdinand as Emperor: but only a few days later Frederick was invited by the Bohemians to come and fill their vacant throne.

Frederick was not ambitious; left to himself he might have declined the proffered honour, but, urged by his wife and other relations, he accepted it, and departed with Elizabeth and their eldest son, to Prague, where he was crowned amidst great rejoicings.

Among the Protestant princes, three, and three only, approved of Frederick's action; these were Christian of Anhalt, the Margrave of Anspach and the Margrave of Baden. Maurice of Hesse-Cassel, on the contrary, though a Calvinist and an enemy of the Imperial House, strongly condemned the usurpation as grossly immoral; and in truth the only excuse that can be offered for it is Frederick's belief in a Divine call to succour his co-religionists. Unfortunately he was the last man to succeed in so difficult an enterprise; yet for a brief period all went well, and at Prague, November

FREDERICK V., ELECTOR PALATINE, KING OF BOHEMIA.

From the Engraving by Delff in the British Museum after the Portrait by Miereveldt.

Face page 4.

28th, 1619, in the hour of his parents' triumph, was born the Elector's third son—Rupert.

The Bohemians welcomed the baby with enthusiasm; the ladies of the country presented him with a cradle of ivory, embossed with gold, and studded with precious stones, and his whole outfit was probably the most costly that he ever possessed in his life. He was christened Rupert, after the only one of the Electors Palatine who had attained the Imperial crown. His sponsors were Bethlem Gabor, King of Hungary, whose creed approximated more closely to Mahommedanism than to any other faith; the Duke of Würtemberg, and the States of Bohemia, Silesia, and Upper and Lower Lusatia. The baptism was at once the occasion of a great feast, and of a political gathering; it aggravated the already smouldering wrath of the Imperialists; a revolt in Prague followed, and within a year the Austrian army had swept over Bohemia, driving forth the luckless King and Queen.

Frederick had no allies, he found no sympathy among his fellow-princes, on the selfish nobility and the apathetic peasantry of Bohemia he could place no reliance; resistance in the face of the Emperor's forces was hopeless;—the Palatines fled.

In the hasty flight the poor baby was forgotten; dropped by a terrified nurse, he was left lying upon the floor until the Baron d'Hona, chancing to find him, threw him into the last coach as it left the courtyard. The jolting of the coach tossed the child into the boot, and there he would have perished had not his screams attracted the notice of some of the train, who rescued him, and carried him off to Brandenburg after his mother.

Elizabeth had sought shelter in Brandenburg because the Elector of that country had married Frederick's sister Catharine. But George William of Brandenburg was a Lutheran, and a prudent personage, who had no wish to embroil himself with his Emperor for a cause of which he thoroughly disapproved. He gave his sister-in-law a cold reception, but, seeing her dire necessity, lent her his castle of Custrin, where, on January 11th, 1620, she gave birth to a fourth son. Damp, bare and comfortless was the castle in which this child first saw the light, and mournful was the welcome he had from his mother. "Call him Maurice," she said, "because he will have to be a soldier!" So Maurice the boy was named, after the warlike Prince of Orange, the most celebrated general of that day.[1]

To the Prince of Orange the exiles now turned their thoughts. Return to their happy home in the Palatinate was impossible, for Frederick lay under the ban of the Empire, and his hereditary dominions were forfeited in consequence of his rebellious conduct; therefore when, six weeks after the birth of her child, George William informed Elizabeth that he dared no longer shelter her, she entrusted the infant to the care of the Electress Catharine, and taking with her the little Rupert, began her journey towards Holland.

Maurice, Prince of Orange and Stadtholder of Holland, was the eldest son of William the Silent, and brother of Frederick's mother, the Electress Juliana. He had strongly urged his nephew's acceptance of the Bohemian crown, and it seemed but natural that he should afford an asylum to those whom he had so disastrously advised. He did not shrink from his responsibility, and the welcome which he accorded to his hapless nephew and niece was as warm as that of the Elector of Brandenburg had been cold. At Münster they were met by six companies of men at arms, sent to escort them to Emerich, where they met their eldest son, Henry, who had been sent to the protection of Count Ernest of Nassau at the beginning of the troubles; there also gathered round them the remnants of their shattered court, and it was with a shadowy show of royalty that they proceeded to the Hague.

---

[1] Green, Lives of the Princesses of England. 1855. Vol. V. p. 353.

Nothing could have exceeded the kindness of their reception, princes and people being equally anxious to show them sympathy. Prince Henry Frederick of Orange, the brother and heir of the Stadtholder, resigned his own palace to their use, and the States of Holland presented Elizabeth with a mansion that stood next door to the palace. The furniture necessary to make this house habitable, Elizabeth was enforced to borrow from the ever generous Prince Henry. For all the necessaries of life the exiles were dependent upon charity, and, but for the generosity of the Orange Princes, supplemented by grants of money from England and from the States of Holland, they would have fared badly indeed.

Thenceforth Elizabeth dwelt at the Hague, while the Thirty Years' War, of which her husband's action had lit the spark, raged over Germany. Slowly and reluctantly a few of the Protestant Princes took up arms against the Emperor. James I sent armies of Ambassadors both to Spain and Austria, and offered settlements to which Frederick would not, or could not agree, but he lent little further aid to his distressed daughter. He regarded his son-in-law's action as a political crime, which had produced the religious war that he had striven all his life to avoid, therefore, though he tacitly permitted English volunteers to enlist under Frederick's mercenary, Count Mansfeld, he would not countenance the war openly. Indeed he deprecated it as the chief obstacle to the marriage of Prince Charles with the Spanish Infanta, on which he had set his heart. The English Parliament, on the contrary, detested the idea of a Spanish alliance, and eagerly advocated a war on behalf of the Protestant exiles.

But if her father would not fight on her behalf Elizabeth had friends who asked nothing better. For her sake Duke Christian of Brunswick, the lay-Bishop of Halberstadt, threw himself passionately into the war. He and Mansfeld having completed between them the alienation of the other Princes, by their lawless plunderings, were defeated by the Imperialist General, Tilly. The Emperor settled the Upper Palatinate on his brother-in-law, the Duke of Bavaria, and, though the Lower Palatinate clung tenaciously to its Elector, Frederick was never able to return thither, until, many years later, the intervention of the quixotic King of Sweden won him a brief and evanescent success.

Thus in trouble, anxiety and poverty passed the early youth of the Palatine children. In the first years of the exile only Henry and Rupert shared their parents' home at the Hague; Charles and Elizabeth had been left in the care of their grandmother Juliana, who, when Heidelberg became no longer a safe place of residence, carried them off to Berlin, where Maurice had been left with his aunt.

Henry was old enough to feel the separation from his brother and sister, to whom he was much attached. "I trust you omit not to pray diligently, as I do, day and night, that it may please God to restore us to happiness and to each other," he wrote with precocious seriousness to Charles, "I have a bow and arrow, with a beautiful quiver, tipped with silver, which I would fain send you, but I fear it may fall into the enemy's hands." [1] In another letter he tells Charles that "Rupert is here, blythe and well, safe and sound," that he is beginning to talk, and that his first words were "Praise the Lord", spoken in Bohemian. [2] In the following year, 1621, Rupert was very ill with a severe cold, and Henry wrote to his grandfather, King James:—"Sir, we are come from Sewneden to see the King and Queen, and my little brother Rupert, who is now a little sick. But my brother Charles is, God be thanked, very well, and my sister Elizabeth, and she is a little bigger and stronger than he." [3] A quaint mixture of childishness and precocity is noticeable in all his letters. "I have two

---

[1] Benger's Elizabeth Stuart. Ed. 1825. Vol. II. p. 255.
[2] Ibid. II. p. 257.
[3] Hist. MSS. Com. Report 3. Hopkinson MSS. p. 265a.

horses alive, that can go up my stairs; a black horse and a brown horse!" he informed his grandfather on another occasion. [1]

Frederick, an affectionate father to all his children, was especially devoted to his eldest son, whom he made his constant companion. Of Rupert also we find occasional mention in his letters. "The little Rupert is very learned to understand so many languages!" [2] he says in 1622, when the child was not three years old. In another letter, dated some years later, he writes to his wife: "I am very glad that Rupert is in your good graces, and that Charles behaves so well. Certes, they are doubly dear to me for it." [3]

But the Queen, so universally beloved and belauded, does not appear to have been a very affectionate mother. A devoted wife she unquestionably was, but she did not exert herself to win her children's love. "Any stranger would be deceived in that humour, since towards them there is nothing but mildness and complaisance," [4] wrote her son Charles in after years; and, though Charles himself had little right so to reproach her, there was doubtless some truth in the saying. She had not been long at the Hague before she obtained from the kindly Stadtholder the grant of a house at Leyden, "where," says her youngest daughter, Sophie, "her Majesty had her whole family brought up apart from herself, greatly preferring the sight of her monkeys and dogs to that of her children." [5]

Having thus successfully disposed of her family, Elizabeth was able to live at the Hague with considerable satisfaction, surrounded by the beloved monkeys and dogs, of which she had about seventeen in all. Nor was she without congenial society. At the Court of Orange there were

<hr>

[1] Green's Princesses, Vol. V. p. 408, note.
[2] Bromley Letters. Ed. 1787. p. 21.
[3] Bromley Letters, p. 38.
[4] Ibid. p. 178.
[5] Preussischen Staatsarchiven. Bd. 4. Memoiren der Herzogin Sophie, pp. 34—35.

no ladies, for both the Princes were unmarried; but very speedily a court gathered itself about the lively Queen of Bohemia. English ladies flocked to the Hague to show their respect and sympathy for their dear Princess. Nobles and diplomates, more especially Sir Thomas Roe and Sir Dudley Carleton, the last of whom was English Ambassador at the Hague, vied with one another in evincing their friendship for the Queen; and hundreds of adventurous young gentlemen came to offer their swords to her husband and their hearts to herself. "I am never destitute of a fool to laugh at, when one goes another comes,"[1] wrote Elizabeth, à propos of these eager volunteers, who had dubbed her the "Queen of Hearts."

Soon after they were settled at Leyden, Henry and Rupert were joined by the sister and brothers hitherto left at Berlin, and their society was further augmented by other children, born at the Hague, and despatched to Leyden as soon as they were old enough to bear the three days' journey thither. To the youngest sister, Sophie, we owe a detailed description of their daily life. "We had," she wrote, "a court quite in the German style; our hours as well as our curtsies were all laid down by rule." Eleven o'clock was the dinner hour, and the meal was attended with great ceremony. "On entering the dining-room I found all my brothers drawn up in front, with their gentlemen and governors posted behind in the same order, side by side. I was obliged to make a very low curtsey to the Princes, a slighter one to the others, another low one on placing myself opposite to them, then another slight one to my governess, who on entering the room with her daughters curtsied very low to me. I was obliged to curtsey again on handing my gloves over to their custody, then again on placing myself opposite to my brothers,

---

[1] Letters and Negotiations of Sir T. Roe, p. 74. Elizabeth to Roe, 19 Aug. 1622.

Photo E. Dossetter

ELIZABETH, QUEEN OF BOHEMIA.

From the Engraving by Van Vorst in the British Museum, after a Portrait by Honthorst.

Face page 20.

again when the gentlemen brought me a large basin in which to wash my hands, again after grace was said, and for the ninth, and last time, on seating myself at table. Everything was so arranged that we knew on each day of the week what we were to eat, as is the case in convents. On Sundays and Wednesdays two divines or two professors were always invited to dine with us."[1]

All the children, both boys and girls, were very carefully instructed in theology, according to the doctrine of Calvin, and, observed the candid Sophie, "knew the Heidelberg Catechism by heart, without understanding one word of it."[2] According to the curriculum arranged for them, the boys enjoyed four hours daily of leisure and exercise. They had to attend morning and evening prayers read in English; the morning prayer was followed by a Bible reading, and an application of the lesson. They were instructed also in the terrible Heidelberg Catechism, in the history of the Reformers, and in religious controversy. On Sundays and feastdays they had to attend church, and to give an abstract of the sermon afterwards. They learnt besides, mathematics, history, and jurisprudence, and studied languages to so much purpose that they could speak five or six with equal ease.[3] To their English mother they invariably wrote and spoke in English, but French was the tongue they used by preference, and amongst themselves; a curious French, often interpolated with Dutch and German phrases.

Rupert early evinced his independence of character by revolting against the strict course laid out for him. "He was not ambitious to entertain the learned tongues.... He conceived the languages of the times would be to him more useful, having to converse afterwards with divers na-

[1] Publication aus den Preussischen Staatsarchiven. Bd. 4. Memoiren der Herzogin Sophie, pp. 34—35.
[2] Ibid.
[3] Haüsser, Geschichte der Rheinischen Pfalz. Vol. II. p. 510.

tions. Thus he became so much master of the modern tongues that at the thirteenth year of his age he could understand, and be understood in all Europe. His High and Low Dutch were not more naturally spoken by him than English, French, Spanish and Italian. Latin he understood." [1] He showed, moreover, a passion for all things military. "His Highness also applying himself to riding, fencing, vaulting, the exercise of the pike and musket, and the study of geometry and fortification, wherein he had the assistance of the best masters, besides the inclination of a military genius, which showed itself so early that at eight years of age he handled his arms with the readiness and address of an experienced soldier." [2]

Occasionally their mother would summon the children to the Hague, that she might show them to her friends; "as one would a stud of horses," [3] said Sophie bitterly. The life at Leyden was also varied by the visits of the Elector Frederick, who was occasionally accompanied by Englishmen of distinction.

In 1626 came the great Duke of Buckingham himself. James I was dead, and Charles I reigned in his stead, but the brilliant favourite Buckingham ruled over the son as absolutely as he had ruled over the father before him. He was inclined now to take up the cause of the Palatines, and, as the price of his assistance, proposed a marriage between the eldest prince, Henry, and his own little daughter, the Lady Mary Villiers. Frederick, knowing his great power, listened favourably, and Buckingham accordingly visited the children at Leyden, where he treated his intended son-in-law with great kindness. Henry remembered the Duke with affection, and addressed some of his quaint little letters to him, always expressing gratitude for his

---

[1] Lansdowne MSS. 817. Fol. 157—168. Brit. Mus.
[2] Warburton, Rupert and the Cavaliers, Vol. I. p. 449.
[3] Memoiren der Herzogin Sophie, p. 35. Publication aus den Preussischen Staatsarchiven.

kindness. "My Lord," he wrote in 1628, "I could not let pass this opportunity to salute you by my Lord Ambassador, for whose departure, being somewhat sorrowful, I will comfort myself in this, that he may help me in expressing to you how much I am your most affectionate friend.—Frederick Henry." [1] But ere the year was out the Duke had fallen under the assassin's knife, and the little Prince did not long survive him.

The Stadtholder Maurice had died in 1625, bequeathing to Elizabeth, amongst other things, a share in a Dutch Company which had raised a fleet intended to intercept Spanish galleons coming, laden with gold, from Mexico. In January 1629 this fleet returned triumphant to the Zuyder Zee. To Amsterdam went Frederick, accompanied by his eldest son, now fifteen, to claim Elizabeth's share of the spoil. "For more frugality" [2] the poverty-stricken King and Prince travelled by the ordinary packet-boat, They reached Amsterdam in safety, but on the return journey, the packet-boat was run down by a heavy Dutch vessel, and sank with all on board. Frederick was rescued by the exertions of the skipper, but young Henry perished, and his piteous cry, "Save me, Father!" rang in the ears of the unhappy Frederick to his dying day. [3]

Miseries accumulated steadily. The poverty of the exiles increased as rapidly as did their family, and at last they could scarcely get bread to eat. The account of their debts so moved Charles I that he pawned his own jewels in order to pay them, after which, the King and Queen retired to a villa at Rhenen, near Utrecht, where they hoped to live economically. There Elizabeth was, to a great extent, deprived of the society which she loved; but she found consolation in hunting, a sport to which she

---

[1] Harleian MSS. 6988. Fol. 83. British Museum.

[2] Howell's Familiar Letters. Edition 1726. Bk I. p. 177. 25 Feb. 1625.

[3] Strickland's Elizabeth Stuart. Queens of Scotland, Vol. VIII. pp. 134, 161. Green's Princesses. V. 468—9.

was devoted. Sometimes she permitted her sons to join her, and on one such occasion a comical adventure befell young Rupert. A fox had been run to earth, and "a dog, which the Prince loved," followed it. The dog did not reappear, and Rupert, growing anxious, crept down the hole after it. But, though he managed to catch the dog by the leg, he found the hole so narrow that he could extricate neither his favourite nor himself. Happily he was discovered in this critical position by his tutor, who, seizing him by the heels, drew out Prince, dog, and fox, each holding on to the other. [1]

To Frederick the sojourn at Rhenen was very agreeable. Failing health increased his natural irritability, and he ungratefully detested the democratic Hollanders. "Of all *canaille*, deliver me from the *canaille* of the Hague!" [2] he said. "It is a misery to live amongst such a people." [3] At last, in 1630, a ray of hope dawned upon him. Gustavus Adolphus, King of Sweden, resolved to assist the Protestants of Germany, and, encouraged by France, launched himself into the Empire. In 1631 he gained the battle of Leipzig, and success followed success, until the Lower Palatinate was in the Swedish hero's hands. Then Frederick, provided, by the Stadtholder, with £5,000, set out to join Gustavus, but ere his departure, paid a farewell visit to Leyden. There he attended a public examination of the University Students, in which Charles and Rupert won much distinction. The visit was his last. By November 1632 his troubles were over, and the weary, anxious, disappointed king lay dead at Mainz, in the thirty-sixth year of his age. The immediate cause of his death was a fever contracted in the summer campaign; but it was said that his heart had been broken by the death of his eldest son, and that all through his illness he declared that he heard

<hr>

[1] Warburton, Vol. I. p. 49, *note.*
[2] Strickland, Elizabeth Stuart, p. 138.
[3] Bromley Letters, p. 20.

the boy calling him. The death of Gustavus Adolphus in the same month checked the victorious progress of the Swedish army, and, consequently, the hopes of the Palatines.

Frederick had been loved by his sons, and his loss was keenly felt by those of them who were old enough to understand it. The misfortune was, however, beyond the comprehension of the five-year-old Philip, who evidently had learnt to regard military defeat as the only serious disaster. "But is the battle then lost, because the king is dead?" he demanded, gazing in astonishment at Rupert's passionate tears. [1] More than a battle had been lost, and forlornly pathetic was the letter indicted by the elder boys to their uncle, King Charles:

"We commit ourselves and the protection of our rights into your gracious arms, humbly beseeching your Majesty so to look upon us as upon those who have neither friends, nor fortune, nor greater honour in this world, than belongs to your Royal blood. Unless you please to maintain that in us God knoweth what may become of your Majesty's nephews.

"CHARLES.

"RUPERT.   "MAURICE.

"EDWARD." [2]

Hard, in truth, was the position of Elizabeth, left to struggle as she might for her large and impecunious family. She had lost, besides Henry, two children who had died in infancy. There remained ten, six sons and four daughters, the eldest scarcely sixteen, and all wholly dependent on the generosity of their friends and relations. The States of Holland at once granted to the Queen the same yearly sum which they had allowed to her husband, and while her brother, Charles I, prospered, and the Stadt-

---

[1] Sprüner's Pfalzgraf Ruprecht, p. 17. Staatsbibliothek zu München.
[2] Green, English Princesses, Vol. V. p. 515.

holder Henry still lived, she did not suffer the depths of poverty to which she afterwards sank. Yet money was, as her son Charles put it, "very hard to come by"; [1] they were always in debt, and it is recorded by another son, that their house was "greatly vexed by rats and mice, but more by creditors." [2]

Happily for herself, Elizabeth was possessed of two things of which no misfortune could deprive her, namely, a buoyant nature and a perfect constitution. "For, though I have cause enough to be sad, I am still of my wild humour to be merry in spite of fortune," she once wrote to her faithful friend, Sir Thomas Roe. [3] And her children inherited her high spirits. "I was then of so gay a disposition that everything amused me," wrote Sophie; "our family misfortunes had no power to depress my spirits, though we were, at times, obliged to make even richer repasts than that of Cleopatra, and often had nothing at our Court but pearls and diamonds to eat." [4] And as it was with Sophie so it was with the others; despair was unknown to them, and for long it was their favourite game to play that they were travelling back to the lost Palatinate, and had entered a public-house on the way. [5] Nor did they less inherit their mother's iron constitution. "Bodily health is an inheritance from our mother which no one can dispute with us," declared Sophie; "the best we ever had from her, of which Rupert has taken a double share." [6]

Thus, in spite of poverty, misfortune, and the learning thrust upon them, the children grew up gay, witty, as full of tricks as their mother's cherished monkeys, and all distinguished for personal beauty, unusual talents, strong

[1] Bromley Letters, p. 124.
[2] Dict. of National Biography. Art. Elizabeth of Bohemia.
[3] Letters and Negotiations of Roe, p. 146.
[4] Memoiren der Herzogin Sophie, p. 43.
[5] Sprüner, p. 15. MSS. der Staatsbibliothek zu München.
[6] Briefwechsel der Herzogin Sophie mit Karl Ludwig von der Pfalz, p. 309.

wills, and a superb disregard of the world's opinion. Charles, called by his brothers and sisters, "Timon", on account of his misanthropic views and bitter sayings, was not a whit behind Rupert in learning, and far his superior in social accomplishments. He was his mother's favourite son. "Since he was born I ever loved him best—when he was but a second son,"[1] she wrote once; to which replied her correspondent: "It is not the first time your Majesty has confessed to me your affection to the Prince Elector, but now I must approve and admire your judgment, for never was there any fairer subject of love."[2] Elizabeth, named by the rest "La Grecque," was considered, later in life, the most learned lady in all Europe; and the merry Louise was an artist whose pictures possess an intrinsic value to this day. Her instructor in the art of painting was Honthorst, who resided in the family. He often sold her pictures for her, thus enabling her to contribute something to the support of the household. So it happens that some of the pictures now ascribed to Honthorst, are in fact the work of the Princess Louise.

Sophie has left us a description of all her sisters: "Elizabeth had black hair, a dazzling complexion, brown sparkling eyes, a well-shaped forehead, beautiful cherry lips, and a sharp aquiline nose, which was apt to turn red. She loved study, but all her philosophy could not save her from vexation when her nose was red. At such times she hid herself from the world. I remember that my sister Louise, who was not so sensitive, asked her on one such unlucky occasion to come upstairs to the Queen, as it was the usual hour for visiting her. Elizabeth said, 'Would you have me go with this nose?'—Louise retorted, 'What! will you wait till you get another?'—Louise was lively and unaffected. Elizabeth was very learned; she

---

[1] Dom. State Papers. Carl I. Vol. 325. Fol. 47. Eliz. to Roe, 4 June, 1636.
[2] Ibid. Roe to Eliz., 20 July, 1636. Vol. 329. fol. 21.

knew every language under the sun and corresponded regularly with Descartes. This great learning, by making her rather absent-minded, often became the subject of our mirth. Louise was not so handsome, but had, in my opinion, a more amiable disposition. She devoted herself to painting, and so strong was her talent for it that she could take likenesses from memory. While painting others she neglected herself sadly; one would have said that her clothes had been thrown on her." [1]

Rupert, nicknamed "Rupert le Diable" for his rough manners and hasty temper, was himself no mean artist, but of his especial bent something has been said already. Of the younger children we know less. Maurice is chiefly distinguished as Rupert's inseparable companion and devoted follower. Like Rupert, he seems to have been of gigantic height, for we find Charles, at eighteen, boyishly resenting the imputation that "my brother Maurice is as high as myself," and sending his mother "the measure of my true height, without any heels," to disprove it. [2] Edward must have been unlike the rest in appearance, for Charles describes him as having a round face, and fat cheeks, though he had the family brown eyes. [3] He shared the wilfulness of the rest, but never especially distinguished himself. Henriette was fair and gentle, very beautiful, but less talented than her sisters. She devoted herself to needlework and the confection of sweetmeats. Poor, fiery Philip, valiant, passionate and undisciplined, came early to a warrior's grave. Sophie lived to be the mother of George I of England, and was famous for her natural intelligence, learning, and social talents. Little Gustave died at nine years old, after a short life of continual suffering.

As the boys and girls grew up they were withdrawn from Leyden to the court at the Hague. The Queen of

---

[1] Memoiren der Herzogin Sophie, pp. 38—39.
[2] Bromley Letters, p. 97.
[3] Forster's Statesmen, Vol. VI. p. 81, *note*.

Bohemia's household was a singularly lively one, abounding in practical jokes and wit of a not very refined nature, so that the young princes and princesses had to "sharpen their wits in self-defence."[1] It was a fashion with them to run about the Hague in disguise, talking to whomever they met.[2]—Private theatricals were a favourite form of amusement, and the Carnival—their Protestantism notwithstanding—was kept with hilarious rejoicing. The Dutch regarded them with kindly tolerance. The English Puritans were less phlegmatic; and a deputation, happening to come over with "a godly condolence" to Elizabeth, in 1635, retired deeply disgusted by the "songs, dances, hallooing and other jovialities" of the Princes Charles, Rupert, Maurice and Edward.[3]

[1] Memoiren der Herzogin Sophie, pp. 36—37.
[2] Memoirs of the Princess Palatine. Blaze de Bury. p. 112.
[3] Strickland, Elizabeth Stuart, p. 174.

CHAPTER II

AT the age of thirteen Rupert made his first campaign.
Prince Henry of Orange had succeeded his brother Maurice
as Stadtholder, and under his Generalship, the Protestant
states of Holland still carried on the struggle against Spain
and the Spanish Netherlands, which had raged since the
days of William the Silent. The close alliance of Spain
with the Empire, and of Holland with the Palatines, connected
this war with the religious wars of Germany; young Rupert
was full of eagerness to share in it, and the Stadtholder,
with whom the boy was a special favourite, begged Elizabeth's leave to take him and his elder brother on the
campaign of 1633. The Queen consented, saying, "He
cannot too soon be a soldier in these active times." [1] But
hardly was the boy gone, than she was seized with fears
for his morals, and recalled him to the Hague. Rupert
submitted reluctantly, but the remonstrances of the Stadtholder, ere long, procured his return to the army.

A brief campaign resulted in the capture of Rhynberg,
which triumph Prince Henry celebrated with a tournament
held at the Hague. On this occasion Rupert greatly distinguished himself, carrying off the palm, "with such a
graceful air accompanying all his actions, as drew the
hearts and eyes of all spectators towards him ... The ladies
also contended among themselves which should crown him
with the greatest and most welcome glory." [2]

[1] Domestic State Papers. Elizabeth to Roe, $^{12}/_{22}$ April, 1634.
[2] Lansdowne MSS. 817. Fol. 157—168.

PORTRAIT DU JEUNE PRINCE RUPRECHT.

From the Engraving in Guiffrey's " Antoine Vandyke," after the Portrait by Vandyke in the Imperial Museum at Vienna.

Face page 32.

After all this excitement, the boy found his life at Leyden irksome, and "his thoughts were so wholly taken up with the love of arms, that he had no great passion for any other study." He was therefore allowed to return to active service, and on the next campaign he served in the Stadtholder's Life Guards. With eager delight, he "delivered himself up to all the common duties and circumstances of a private soldier;" [1] in which capacity he witnessed the sieges of Louvain, Schenkenseyan, and the horrible sack of Tirlemont. Even thus early he showed something of the impatience and impetuosity which was afterwards his bane. The dilatory methods and cautious policy of the Stadtholder fretted him; "an active Prince, like ours, was always for charging the enemy." His courage indeed "astonished the eldest soldiers," and they exerted themselves to preserve from harm the young comrade who took no care of himself. [2] Eventually Rupert returned from his second campaign, covered with glory, and not a little spoilt by the petting of the Stadtholder, and of his companions in arms. A visit to England, which followed soon after, did not tend to lessen his good opinion of himself.

His eldest brother, Charles Louis, had just attained his eighteenth year. This being the legal age for Princes of the Empire, he assumed his father's title of Prince Elector Palatine, and was thereupon summoned to England by his uncle, King Charles, who hoped to accomplish his restoration to the Palatinate. Elizabeth suffered the departure of her favourite with much misgiving. "He is young *et fort nouveau*, so as he will no doubt commit many errors," she wrote to Sir Henry Vane. "I fear damnably how he will do with your ladies, for he is a very ill courtier; therefore I pray you desire them not to laugh too much at him, but to be merciful to him." [3]

---

[1] Benett MSS. Warburton. Vol. I. p. 450.

[2] Lansdowne MSS. 817. British Museum.

[3] Dom. State Papers. Carl I. Vol. 300. fol. 1. 18/28 May, 1635.

In October 1635 young Charles landed at Gravesend, and was well received by his relatives. "The King received him in the Queen's withdrawing room, using him extraordinarily kindly. The Queen kissed him. He is a very handsome young prince, modest and very bashful; he speaks English," was the report of a friend to Lord Strafford. [1] Nevertheless the Elector, who had expected to be restored with a high hand, was somewhat disappointed in his uncle. Ambassadors King Charles did not spare. In July 1636 he despatched Lord Arundel on a special mission to Vienna. He endeavoured to league together England, France and Holland in the interests of the Palatines. He negotiated with the King of Hungary, and he attempted to secure the King of Poland by marrying him to the Elector's eldest sister, Elizabeth. The marriage treaty fell through because the princess refused to profess the Roman Catholic faith. The other negotiations proved equally fruitless; and armies, fleets and money it was not in the King's power to furnish. "All their comfort to me is 'to have patience'!" [2] complained the young Elector to his mother.

In other respects he had nothing to complain of; the impression he made was excellent, and the King showed him all the kindness in his power. The old diplomat, Sir Thomas Roe, who watched over the boy with a fatherly eye, wrote enthusiastically to his mother, Elizabeth: "The Prince Elector is so sweet, so obliging, so discreet, so sensible of his own affairs, and so young as was never seen, nor could be seen in the son of any other mother. And this joy I give you: he gains upon his Majesty's affection, by assiduity and diligent attendance, so much that it is expressed to him by embracings, kissings, and all signs of love." [3]

---

[1] Letters and Despatches of Thomas Wentworth, Earl Strafford. Ed. 1739. Vol. I. p. 489.

[2] Bromley Letters, p. 73.

[3] Dom. State Papers. Carl I. 320. 2; 1 May, 1636.

Thus encouraged, Elizabeth resolved to send her second son to join his brother; though with little hope that "Rupert le Diable" would prove an equal success with the young Elector. "For blood's sake I hope he will be welcome," she wrote; "though I believe he will not trouble your ladies with courting them, nor be thought a very *beau garçon*, which you slander his brother with." And she entreated Sir Henry Vane "a little to give good counsel to Rupert, for he is still a little giddy, though not so much as he has been. Pray tell him when he does ill, for he is good-natured enough, but does not always think of what he should do." [1] But the mother's judgment erred, for the despised Rupert won all hearts at the English Court, so completely as to throw his brother into the shade. Doubtless the jeers of his mother had helped to render him shy and awkward at the Hague; now, for the first time, he found himself free to develop unrestrained, in a congenial atmosphere. The natural force of his character showed itself at once, and his quick wit and vivacity charmed the grave King. "I have observed him," reported Sir Thomas Roe, "full of spirit and action, full of observation and judgment; certainly he will *réussir un grand homme (sic)*; for whatsoever he wills he wills vehemently, so that to what he bends he will in it be excellent... His Majesty takes great pleasure in his unrestfulness, for he is never idle; in his sports serious, in his conversation retired, but sharp and witty when occasion provokes him." [2]

In his love for the arts King Charles found another point of sympathy with his nephew. The English Court was then the most splendid in Europe; Charles's collections of pictures, sculptures, and art treasures were the finest of the times. He was himself so proficient a musician that an enemy remarked later, that he might have earned his

---

[1] Dom. State Papers. Eliz. to Vane, Feb. 2, 1636. Carl I. Vol. 313. f. 12.
[2] Dom. State Papers. Roe to Elizabeth, July 20, 1636. Carl I. Vol. 339. f. 21.

living by his art. [1] Rubens, Van Dyke and other famous artists, sculptors and musicians were familiar figures at the Court. In a word, the society which Charles gathered round him was cultivated and intellectual to the highest degree. To a boy like Rupert, sensitive, excitable, and intensely artistic in feeling, there was something intoxicating in this feast of the senses and intellect, so suddenly offered to him. Nor was this all. The Queen and her ladies, so famous for their wit and beauty, marked him for their own; and before he had been many days in England, the boy found himself the chief pet and favourite of his fascinating aunt. Queen Henrietta, who had a passion for proselytising, soon saw in her handsome young nephew a hopeful subject for conversion to the Roman Church; and Rupert, on his part, was not a little drawn by the artistic aspect of her religion.

The young Elector watched his brother's prosperous course with dismay. Rupert, he lamented, was "always with the Queen, and her ladies, and her Papists." Nor did he look more favourably on Rupert's affection for Endymion Porter, a poet, and a connoisseur in all the arts, whose wife was as ardent a Roman Catholic as was the Queen herself. "Rupert is still in great friendship with Porter," he wrote to his mother. "I bid him take heed he do not meddle with points of religion among them, for fear some priest or other, that is too hard for him, may form an ill opinion in him. Mrs. Porter is a professed Roman Catholic. Which way to get my brother away I do not know, except myself go over." [2] Roe also hinted that Elizabeth would do well to recall her second son. "His spirit is too active to be wasted in the soft entanglings of pleasure, and your Majesty would do well to recall him gently. He will prove a sword for all his friends if his edge be set right. There is nothing ill in his stay here, yet he may gather a diminution from

[1] Lilly. Character of Charles I.
[2] Bromley Letters, p. 86.

company unfit for him." [1] It was enough. Elizabeth took alarm, and from that time made desperate but vain efforts to recover her giddy Rupert, who, said she, "spends his time but idly in England." [2] But Rupert was far too happy to return home just then; nor were his uncle and aunt willing to part with him. The Queen loudly declared that she would not let him go, and Elizabeth was obliged to resign herself, saying, "He will not mend there." [3]

It was not fears for her son's Protestantism alone that moved her. She was aware that he and the King were concocting between them, a scheme of which she thoroughly disapproved. This was a wild and utterly unfeasible plan for founding a colony in Madagascar, of which Rupert was to be leader, organiser, and ruler. He had always taken a keen interest in naval affairs, and now he devoted himself eagerly to the study of ship-building. But his unfortunate mother was frantic at the idea. In her eyes, the boy's only fit vocation was "to be made a soldier, to serve his uncle and brother," [4] and she entreated her friend Roe to put such "windmills" out of this new Don Quixote's head. No son of hers, she declared, fiercely, should "roam the world as a knight-errant;" [5] not foreseeing, poor woman, that such was precisely her children's destined fate. From Roe at least she had full sympathy: "I will only say," he wrote to her, "that it is an excellent course to lose the Prince in a most desperate, dangerous, unwholesome, fruitless action." [6] But to mockery and exhortation Rupert turned a deaf ear. His mother, finding her letters treated with indifference, sent her agent, Rusdorf, to represent to the boy his exalted station as a Prince of the Empire, the grief he was causing to his grandmother, mother and sisters,

---

[1] Dom. State Papers. Carl I. 320. f. 2. 1 May, 1636.
[2] Dom. State Papers. Carl I. 318. f. 16. 4 April, 1636.
[3] Ibid. 325. f. 47. 4 June, 1636.
[4] Ibid. 318. f. 16. April 4, 1636.
[5] Howell's Letters, p. 257, 4 Jan. 1636.
[6] Dom. State Papers. Roe to Eliz. Carl I. 350. 16. 17 March, 1637.

and the necessity of his remaining in Europe to combat his ancestral enemies. Rupert listened in absolute silence, and remained unmoved at the end. Nor could his brother Charles make the least impression on him. "When I ask him what he means to do I find him very shy to tell me his opinion," [1] was the young Elector's report. Rupert probably knew Charles well enough to guess that anything he did tell him would be at once repeated to his mother, and he was always good at keeping his own counsel.

Both boys had broken loose from their home restraints. They were now "quite out of their mother's governance", and resolved to go their own way, heeding neither her nor her agents, present or absent. [2] The state of affairs was not improved by the interference of one of Elizabeth's ladies, who was also on a visit to England. Between the boys and this Mrs. Crofts there was no love lost. She told tales of their doings to their mother, and carried complaints of their rudeness to their mentor, Lord Craven. The Princes were furious, believing that she had been sent to spy upon them, and, at the same time, they betrayed evident terror lest her stories should gain credence rather than their own. "I am sure your Majesty maketh no doubt of my civil carriage to Mrs. Crofts, because she was your servant, and you commanded it," declared Charles, "yet I hear she is not pleased, and hath sent her complaints over seas. I do not know whether they are come to your Majesty's ears, but I easily believe it, because she told my Lord Craven that I used her like a stranger and would not speak to her before her King and Queen. Yet I may truly say that I have spoken more to her, since she came into England, than ever I did in all my life before." [3] Rupert also had insulted the lady. "He told

---

[1] Bromley Letters, p. 86.
[2] Haüsser, Geschichte der Rheinischen Pfalz. Vol. II. p. 546.
[3] Bromley Letters, p. 85.

me she would not look upon him," [1] wrote his brother indignantly.

After all this agitation, a visit to Oxford, in the company of the King, proved a welcome diversion. This was a great event in the University, and the scholars were admonished "to go nowhere without their caps and gowns, and in apparel of such colour and such fashion as the statute prescribes. And particularly they are not to wear long hair, nor any boots, nor double stockings, rolled down, or hanging loose about their legs, as the manner of some slovens is." [2] On the night of the Royal Party's arrival a play was performed by the students of Christ Church, which Lord Carnarvon reported the worst he had ever seen, except one which he saw at Cambridge. On the following day Rupert, clad in a scarlet gown, was presented for the degree of Master of Arts by the Warden of Merton College. The University bestowed on him a pair of gloves; and from Archbishop Laud, then Chancellor of Oxford, he received a copy of Cæsar's Commentaries. Subsequently the Royal guests dined with Laud, at St. John's College, and in the evening they were condemned to witness a second play at Christ Church, which happily proved "most excellent." [3]

Elizabeth remained, in the meantime, far from satisfied; and in February 1637, King Charles thought it well to ascertain her serious intentions with regard to Rupert. To this end, young George Goring, then serving in the Stadtholder's army, was commissioned to sound her. Thus he reported to his father :—"I found she had a belief he would lose his time in England, and for that reason had an intention to recall him. I saw it not needful to give her other encouragement from His Majesty, than that I heard the King profess that he did believe Prince Rupert

[1] Bromley Letters, p. 88.
[2] Dom. S. P. Decree of University, Aug. 12, 1636.
[3] Ibid. 5 Sept. 1636.

would soon be capable of any actions of honour, and if he were placed in any such employment would acquit himself very well; and I persuaded Her Majesty to know what the Prince of Orange would think fit for him to do, which she did on their next meeting, and His Highness wished very much that there were some employment in the way worthy of him. But this business is silenced since upon a letter the Queen has received from the Prince Elector, where he mentions the sending of some land forces into France, which he judges a fit command for him ... Only that which His Highness spoke to Dr. Gosse, concerning Prince Rupert, would joy me much, being I might hope for a liberty of attempting actions worthy of an honest man." [1]

Plans for the recovery of the lost Palatinate were now indeed maturing. The cause was one very near the hearts of the English Puritans, who regarded it as synonymous with the cause of Protestantism, and they showed them-selves willing to subscribe money in aid of it. The King promised ships, and tried to win the help of France; while young English nobles eagerly offered their swords to the exiled Princes. The Elector was so delighted that he could scarcely believe his good fortune, and Rupert abandoned his own schemes in order to assist his brother. "The dream of Madagascar, I think, is vanished," wrote Roe. "A blunt merchant called to deliver his opinion, said it was a gallant design, but one on which he would be loth to venture his younger son." [2]

But the dream of Rupert's conversion was not over, and his mother was as anxious as ever to recover possession of him. She appealed now to Archbishop Laud who had shown great interest in the boys, often inviting them to dine with him. "The two young Princes have both

<hr>

[1] Dom. State Papers. Geo. Goring to Lord Goring, 4 Feb. 1637. Carl I. 346. f. 33.

[2] Ibid. Roe to Elizabeth, May 8, 1637.

been very kind and respective of me," he said. "It was little I was able to do for them, but I was always ready to do my best."[1] To him therefore Elizabeth declared that she was about to send Maurice with the Prince of Orange, "to learn that profession by which I believe he must live,"[2] and that she desired Rupert to bear his brother company. "I think he will spend this summer better in an army than idly in England. For though it be a great honour and happiness to him to wait upon his uncle, yet, his youth considered, he will be better employed to see the war."[3] Laud replied in approving terms: "If the Prince of Orange be going into the field, God be his speed. The like I heartily wish to the young Prince Maurice. You do exceedingly well to put him into action betimes."[4] Still he offered no real assistance, and Elizabeth fell back on the sympathetic Roe, repeating how she had sent for Rupert, and adding—"You may easily guess why I send for him; his brother can tell you else. I pray you help him away and hinder those that would stay him."[5]

Her untiring solicitations and Rupert's own martial spirit, combined with the fact that the Elector, having completed his negotiations, was now ready to return with his brother, prevailed. The King at last consented to let them go, and in June 1637 they embarked at Greenwich, arriving safely at the Hague, after a stormy passage in which both suffered severely. The parting in England had been reluctant on both sides. "Both the brothers went away very unwillingly, but Prince Rupert expressed it most, for, being a-hunting that morning with the King, he wished he might break his neck, and so leave his bones in England."[6]

[1] Dom. S. P. Laud to Eliz. Aug. 7, 1637.
[2] Ibid. Eliz. to Laud. May 19, 1637.
[3] Ibid. June 10, 1637. Carl I. 361.
[4] Ibid. Laud to Eliz. June 22, 1637.
[5] Ibid. Eliz. to Roe. June 7, 1637.
[6] Strafford Papers. Vol. II. p. 85. June 24, 1637.

But, in the opinion of Elizabeth and Roe, that pleasant holiday had ended none too soon. "You have your desire for Prince Rupert," wrote the latter. "I doubt not he returns to you untainted, but I will not answer for all designs upon him. The enemy is a serpent as well as a wolf, and, though he should prove impregnable, you do well to preserve him from battery."[1] Later the boy confessed that a fortnight more in England would have seen him a Roman Catholic. Elizabeth thereupon poured forth bitter indignation on her sister-in-law, but Henrietta only retorted, with cheerful defiance, that, had she known Rupert's real state of mind, he should not have departed when he did.

So far as Rupert was concerned, the visit had not been, from the mother's point of view, a success. The only one of her brother's schemes for the boy's advantage of which she approved, unhappily commended itself very little to Rupert himself; this was no less than the time-honoured device of marrying him to an heiress. The lady selected was the daughter of the Huguenot Duc de Rohan, and in September 1636 the Elector had written to his mother: "Concerning my brother Rupert, M. de Soubise hath made overture that, with your Majesty's and your brother's consent, he thinks M. de Rohan would not be unwilling to match him with his daughter.... I think it is no absurd proposition, for she is great both in means and birth, and of the religion."[2] The death of the Duc de Rohan delayed the conclusion of the treaty, which dragged on for several years. In 1638 King Charles renewed relations with the widowed Duchess, through his Ambassador at Paris, Lord Leicester. "For Prince Robert's service, I represented unto her as well as I could, how hopeful a prince he was, and she said she had heard much good of him, that he was very handsome, and had a great deal of wit

<hr>

[1] Dom. State Papers. Roe to Eliz. June 19, 1637.
[2] Bromley Letters, p. 56.

and courage," [1] wrote the Ambassador. But Cardinal Richelieu was by no means willing to let such a fortune as
that of the Rohans, fall to a heretic foreigner, and without
his consent, and that of Louis XIII, nothing could be done.
The difficulties in the way were great, and though the
Duchess was well inclined to Rupert, both on account of
his religion and of his Royal blood, she was not blind to
the fact that neither of these would support either himself
or his family. He would, she supposed, settle down in
France, but great though her daughter's fortune was, it
would not, she declared, maintain a Royal prince in Paris;
and she desired to know what King Charles would do for
his nephew. Leicester could only reply vaguely that the
King would "take care" of his nephew, and of any future
children. He was, however, admitted to an interview with
the young lady, whom he facetiously told, that he "came
to make love unto her, and that, if it were for myself, I
thought she could hardly find it in her heart to refuse me,
but it being for a handsome young prince, countenanced
by the recommendation of a great king, I did take upon
myself to know her mind.... She gave me a smile and
a blush, which I took for a sufficient reply." [2]

Owing to the opposition of the Cardinal, no formal be-
trothal took place, but Marguerite de Rohan evidently regarded her unwilling lover with favour, for when he fell
into the hands of the Emperor she showed herself loyal to
him. Leicester, on receiving the news of Rupert's capture,
hastened to interview the Duchess, but found her still well
inclined. "I cannot find that she is at all changed," he
reported. "She answered also for her daughter, and related
this passage to me. Some one had said to Mademoiselle
de Rohan: 'Now that Prince Rupert is a prisoner, you
should do well to abandon the thought of him, and to entertain the addresses of your servant, the Duc de Nemours.'

---

[1] Collins Sydney Papers, 1746. Vol. II. p. 549. 28 May, 1638.
[2] Collins Sydney Papers, 1746. Vol. II. pp. 560–561. 22 July, 1638.

To which she answered: 'I am not engaged anywhere; but, as I have been inclined, so I am still, for it would be a *lâcheté* to forsake one because of his misfortunes, and some generosity to esteem him in the same degree as before he fell into it." [1]

Her generosity was not felt as it deserved. Rupert did not want to be married; he had already plenty of interests and occupations, and he could not be brought to regard the matter from a practical point of view. Eighty thousand pounds a year, united to much other valuable property and the expectation of two more estates, could not induce the penniless Palatine to sacrifice his liberty. In 1643 Marguerite would await the recalcitrant suitor no longer, and the incident closed with a very curious letter, written by King Charles to Maurice. Evidently the King was loth that such a fortune should be lost to the family, after all his trouble.

"Nepheu Maurice," he wrote, "though Mars be now most in voag, yet Hymen may sometimes be remembyred. The matter is this: Your mother and I have bin somewhat ingaged concerning a marriage between your brother Rupert and Mademoiselle de Rohan. Now her friends press your brother for a positive answer, which I find him resolved to give negatively. Therefore I thought fit to let you know, if you will, by your ingagement, take your brother handsomely off. And indeed the total rejecting of this alliance may do us some prejudice, whether ye look to these, or to the German affairs; the performance of it is not expected until the times shall be reasonably settled, but I desire you to give me an answer, as soon as you can, having now occasion to send to France, because delays are sometimes as ill taken as denials. So hoping, and praying God for good news from you,

"I rest, your loving oncle,

"C. R." [2]

---

[1] Collins Sydney Papers, Vol. II. p. 575. 12 Nov. 1638.
[2] Harleian MSS. 6988. fol. 149.

But Maurice was not to be moved by his uncle's eloquence, and his answer was as positively negative as that of his brother had been. Subsequently the neglected lady wedded Henri Chabot, a poor gentleman of no particular distinction, with whom she was, possibly, happier than any Palatine would have made her.

CHAPTER III

THE SIEGE OF BREDA. THE ATTEMPT ON THE PALATINATE.
RUPERT'S CAPTIVITY

IMMEDIATELY on his return from England in 1637, Rupert joined his brother Maurice in the army of the Stadtholder. Prince Henry was just then engaged in the siege of Breda, a town which was oftener lost and won than any other in the long wars of the Low Countries. Many Englishmen were fighting there, in the Dutch army: Astley, Goring, the Lords Northampton and Grandison, with whom the Palatines were already well acquainted, besides others whom they were to meet hereafter in the English war, either as friends or foes. The two young princes acted with their usual energy and "let not one day pass in that siege, without doing some action at which the whole army was surprised." [1] Once, by their courage and ready wit, they saved the camp from an unexpected attack. Waking in the night, Rupert fancied that he heard unusual sounds within the city walls. He roused Maurice, and the two crept up so close to the Spanish lines that they could actually hear what the soldiers said on the other side. Thus they discovered that the enemy was preparing to fall upon them at mid-night, and, hastening back to the Stadtholder, they were able to give him timely warning. Consequently, when the besieged sallied out, the besiegers were ready for them, and forced them to retire with great loss. [2] On another occasion Rupert's love of adventure led him into flat insubordination. Monk, afterwards Duke of

[1] Lansdowne MSS. 817. fol. 157—168.
[2] Benett MSS. Warburton, Vol. I. p. 450.

Albemarle, was about to make an attack upon the enemy's works, which was considered so dangerous that the Stadtholder expressly forbade Rupert to take part in it. But Rupert no sooner heard the Stadtholder give the order to advance, than he dashed away, anticipating the aide-de-camp, himself delivered the order to Monk, and, slipping into his company as a volunteer, took his share in the exploit. The Prince came off unhurt, but many of his comrades fell, and both Goring and Wilmot were severely wounded. The fight over, Rupert and some other officers threw themselves down on a hillock to rest; they had been there some time, when, to their surprise, a Burgundian, whom they had taken for dead, suddenly started up, crying: "Messieurs, est-il point de quartier?" The English officers burst out laughing, and immediately dubbed him "Jack Falstaff", which name he bore to his dying day. [1] What the Stadtholder thought of Rupert's mutinous conduct is not recorded.

Eventually Breda fell to the Dutch arms, and Maurice was, immediately after, sent to school in Paris, with his younger brothers, Edward and Philip. He must have gone sorely against his will, especially as Charles and Rupert were proceeding to levy forces for their own attempt on the Palatinate. But Elizabeth was inexorable. She was resolved not to blush for the manners of her younger sons, as she declared she did for those of Rupert; and she was, besides, anxious to have Maurice in safety, seeing that the two elder boys were about to risk their lives in so rash a venture.

Since the death of their King Gustavus the Swedes had continued the war in Germany, though without any such brilliant successes as had been theirs before. Still many towns were in their hands, and doubtless the young Elector hoped for their coöperation in his own venture. He had been joined by many English volunteers; and by means of English

---

[1] Benett MSS. Warburton. Vol. I. p. 451.

money he was able to raise troops in Hamburg and Westphalia. As a convenient muster-place, he had purchased Meppen on the Weser, from a Swedish officer, to whom the place had been given by Gustavus. But ere the Elector's levies were completed, the negligence of the Governor suffered the town to fall into the hands of the Imperialists. Charles took this mischance with praiseworthy philosophy: "A misty morning," quoth he, "often makes a cheerfuller day." [1] And thanks to the kindness of the Stadtholder, and the connivance of the States, he was enabled to continue his levies, quartering his men about Wesel.

In the midst of their labours, both he and Rupert found time to attend a tournament at the Hague. Dressed as Moors, and mounted on white horses, they, as usual, outshone all others. Indeed so pleased were they with their own prowess, that they issued a printed challenge for a renewal of the courses. Balls also were in vogue, and the Hague was unusually gay; yet Elizabeth retired, early in the season, to her country house at Rhenen. Feeling between mother and sons was still somewhat strained. The Queen found the boys far less submissive to her will than they had been before their year of liberty in England, and Lord Craven, who acted as mediator, found the post no sinecure.

But to Lord Craven no task came amiss in the service of the Palatines. The history of his life-long devotion to the exiled Queen is well known, and it is doubtful whether his unparalleled generosity, or the boundless wealth which made such generosity possible, be the most astonishing. His father, a son of the people, had made in trade, the enormous fortune which he bequeathed to his children. The eldest son, fired by military ambition, had entered the service of the Palatine Frederick, and, at the siege of Kreuznach, had attracted the notice and approbation of the great Gustavus. His wealth and his military fame

---

[1] Green's Princesses, Vol. V. p. 558.

CHARLES LOUIS, ELECTOR PALATINE.

From the Engraving in the British Museum after a Portrait by Vandyke.

Face page 36.

won him an English peerage, but, after Frederick's death, Lord Craven continued to reside at the Hague, filling every imaginable office in the impoverished Palatine household, and lavishing extravagant sums on the whole family. "He was a very valuable friend, for he possessed a purse better furnished than my own!"[1] confessed Sophie. In later years, when the good Prince of Orange was dead, and Charles I no longer in a position to aid his sister, Elizabeth was almost entirely dependent on this loyal friend; but the English Parliament at last confiscated his estates, and so deprived him of the power to assist her. The young Palatines were doubtless attached to him, but it must be admitted that they showed themselves less grateful than might have been desired. His follies and his eccentricities impressed them more than did his virtues, and "the little mad my lord" afforded them much matter for mirth. Possibly he was, as Sophie said, lamentably lacking in common-sense,[2] but the family would have fared far worse without him. On the present occasion he had contributed £10,000 to the support of the Elector's army, and, at Elizabeth's request, undertook the special care of the rash young Rupert, whose senior he was by ten years.

By October 1638 Charles Louis' little army was ready for action. Rupert had the command of a regiment of Horse, and Lord Craven led the Guards; the other principal officers were the Counts Ferentz and Königsmark. Anything more wild and futile than this expedition it is hard to conceive. There seems to have been no coöperation with the Protestant princes of the Empire, nor with the Swedish army. On the contrary, at the very moment of the Elector's attack, there was a cessation of hostilities elsewhere. Banier, the chief of the Swedish commanders, lay with his forces in Munster, and he made no movement to join with his

---

[1] Memoiren der Herzogin Sophie, pp. 42—43.

[2] Briefwechsel der Herzogin Sophie mit Karl Ludwig von der Pfalz. Ed. Bodemann. p. 184. Preussischen Staats Archiven.

young ally; all that he did was to send his second in command, a Scot, named King, to direct the Elector's operations. To the advice of King, Rupert, at least, attributed the disasters that followed; but it would have been a miracle indeed had the two boys, with their four thousand men, dashed themselves thus wildly against the numberless veteran troops of the Emperor with any better result.

To the Lower Palatinate, which was always loyal at heart, Charles Louis turned his eyes. Accordingly he marched from Wesel, eastward, through the Bishopric of Munster. On the march, Rupert, with his usual eagerness to fight, succeeded in drawing out upon his van an Imperial garrison. But the vigorous charge with which he received it drove it back into the town, whither Rupert nearly succeeded in following it.[1] On this occasion a soldier fired at him from within ten yards, but, as so often happened when the Prince was threatened, the gun missed fire. After this adventure the army proceeded steadily towards the river Weser, resolving to lay siege to Lemgo, which lies south of Minden in Westphalia. But hardly had the Elector sat down before the town, when he heard that the Imperial forces, led by General Hatzfeldt, were advancing to cut off his retreat. To await Hatzfeldt's onslaught was madness, and instant retreat to Minden, then held by the Swedes, was the only course for the Palatines. Two routes lay open to them, that by Vlotho on the west, or by Rinteln on the east. Following the advice of General King, they chose the way of Vlotho and thus fell "into the very mouth of Hatzfeldt."[2] They were still between Lemgo and Vlotho when they encountered eight regiments of Imperialist Cuirassiers, a regiment of Irish Dragoons, and a force of eighteen thousand foot. General King at once sent away his baggage, "an act

[1] Benett MSS. Warburton, Vol. I. p. 453.
[2] Ibid.

which received a very ill construction,"[1] and then counselled the Elector to draw up his troops on the top of a
neighbouring hill. Field-marshal Ferentz ' complied with
the suggestion; but Königsmark who commanded the hired
Swedes, so much disliked the position, that Rupert offered
to follow him wherever he pleased. Thereupon Königsmark drew the horse down again, into an enclosed piece
of land, courteously giving the van to the Elector. King,
in the meantime, went to bring up the foot and cannon.

The Imperialists fell first upon the Elector and Ferentz,
who were both beaten back. Rupert withstood the third
shock, and beat back the enemy from their ground. Lord
Craven then brought his Guards to Rupert's assistance,
and a second time they beat back the Imperialists with
loss. They were, however, far outnumbered. Calling up
another regiment, under Colonel Lippe, and sending eight
hundred Horse to attack Rupert's rear, the enemy charged
him a third time, with complete success. The young
Elector, who had hitherto fought bravely, now took to
flight, with General King, and both narrowly escaped
drowning in the flooded Weser. Rupert might also
have escaped; cut off from his own troops by the very
impetuosity of his charge, he rode alone into the midst of
the enemy, but, by a curious chance, he wore in his hat
a white favour, which was also the badge of the Austrians,
and thus, for a time, escaped notice. While he looked
out for some chance of escape, he perceived his brother's
cornet struggling against a number of Imperial troopers.
Rupert flew to the rescue, and thus betrayed himself. The
Austrians closed round him; he tried to clear the enclos-
ure, but his tired horse refused the jump. Colonel Lippe
caught at his bridle, but Rupert, struggling fiercely, made
him let go his hold. Lord Craven and Count Ferentz
rushed to the rescue of their Prince, but all three were

[1] Warburton, I. p. 453.

speedily overpowered. Then Lippe struck up Rupert's visor, and demanded to know who he was. "A Colonel!" said the boy obstinately. "Sacrement! It is a young one!" cried the Austrian. A soldier, coming up, recognised the boy and identified him as "the Pfalzgraf", and Lippe, in great joy, confided him to the care of a trooper. Rupert immediately tried to bribe the man to let him escape, giving him all the money he had, "five pieces", and promising more. But the arrival of Hatzfeldt frustrated the design, and the Prince was carried off, under a strict guard, to Warrendorf. On the way thither a woman, won by the boy's youth and misfortunes, would have helped him to escape, but no opportunity offered itself. At Warrendorf, Rupert was allowed to remain some weeks, until Lord Craven, who, with Ferentz, was also a prisoner, had somewhat recovered from his wounds. The Prince was also permitted to despatch Sir Richard Crane to England, with a note to Charles I, written in pencil on a page of his pocketbook, for pen and ink were denied him. [1]

News of the disaster had been received with dismay in England, where it was reported with much exaggeration. "Prince Rupert," it was said, "is taken prisoner, and since dead of his many wounds; he having fought very bravely, and, as the gazette says, like a lion." [2] His fate remained doubtful for some days, and it was even rumoured that he had been seen at Minden, two days after the battle. But his mother gave little credence to such flattering reports; in her opinion the boy's death would have been preferable to his capture. "If he be a prisoner I confess it will be no small grief to me," she wrote to her faithful Roe, "for I wish him rather dead than in his enemies' hands." [3] And when her worst fears had been realised, she wrote again: "I confess that in my passion I did

<hr>

[1] Benett MSS. Warburton. Vol. I. pp. 454—455
[2] Dom. S. P. Nicholas to Pennington, Nov. 14, 1638.
[3] D. S. P. Eliz. to Roe, Oct. 2, 1638.

rather wish him killed. I pray God I have not more cause to wish it before he be gotten out. All my fear is their going to Vienna; if it were possible to be hindered!... Mr. Crane, one that follows My Lord Craven, is come from Rupert, who desired him to assure me that neither good usage nor ill should ever make him change his religion or his party. I know his disposition is good, and that he will never disobey me at any time, though to others he was stubborn and wilful. I hope he will continue so, yet I am born to so much affliction that I dare not be confident of it. I am comforted that my sons have lost no honour in the action, and that him I love best is safe." [1] "Him I love best" was of course the Elector Charles, and thus, even in the moment of Rupert's peril, his mother confessed her preference for his elder brother.

In January 1639 Elizabeth's fears about Vienna seemed justified, for an English resident wrote thence to Secretary Windebank: "Prince Rupert is daily expected, and will be well treated, being likely to be liberated on parole. Hatzfeldt praises him for his ripeness of judgment, far beyond his years." [2] And to Rupert himself Hatzfeldt gave the assurance that he should see the Emperor—"Then the Emperor shall see me also!" [3] exclaimed the boy, in angry scorn. But the interview did not take place. In February Rupert was lodged, not at Vienna, but at Linz on the Danube, under the care of a certain Graf Kuffstein. Craven and Ferentz soon ransomed themselves. They had not been permitted to accompany the Prince further than Bamberg, though Lord Craven, who paid £20,000 for his own liberty, offered to pay more still for permission to share Rupert's captivity. But the Emperor was resolved to isolate the boy from all his friends, as a first step towards gaining him over to the Imperial politics, and the Roman faith.

[1] Dom. State Papers, Eliz. to Roe, Nov. 6, 1638.
[2] Clarendon State Papers. f. 1171. Taylor to Windebank, Jan. 12, 1638-9.
[3] Green's Princesses of England. Vol. V. p. 570.

The Elector therefore attempted in vain to send some companion to his brother. "I must tell Your Majesty," he wrote to his mother, "that it will be in vain to send any gentleman to my brother, since he cannot go without Hatzfeldt's pass, for which I wrote long ago. But I have received from him an answer to all points in my letter, except to that, which is as much as a modest denial. Essex [1] should have gone, because there was no one else would, neither could I force any to it, since there is no small danger in it; for any obstinacy of my brother Rupert, or venture to escape, would put him in danger of hanging. The Administrator of Magdeburg was suffered to have but a serving-boy with him. Therefore one may easily imagine that they will much less permit him (*i.e.* Rupert) to have anybody with him that may persuade him to anything against their ends." [2]

As Charles surmised, Rupert's confinement was, at first, very vigorous. All the liberty that he enjoyed was an occasional walk in the castle garden; all his entertainment an occasional dinner with the Governor. Graf Kuffstein, himself a convert from Lutheranism, was commissioned by the Emperor to urge his desires on the young prisoner. "And very busy he was to get the prince to change his religion." At first he urged him to visit some Jesuits, but this Rupert refused to do unless he might also go elsewhere. Then Graf Kuffstein offered to bring the Jesuits to the Prince, but Rupert would only receive their visits on condition that other people might visit him also. [3] To the promise of liberal rewards if he would but serve in the Imperial army, the boy proved equally impervious; and though deprived of all society he found interests and occupations for himself. His artistic talents stood him in good stead, and he devoted himself much to drawing and etching. At

---

[1] Probably Colonel Charles Essex, killed 1642, at Edgehill.
[2] Bromley Letters, p. 103.
[3] Benett MSS. Warburton. Vol. I. p 457.

this period also he perfected an instrument for drawing in perspective, which had been conceived, but never rendered practical, by Albert Durer. This instrument was in use in England after the Restoration of 1660. Military exercises Rupert also used, as far as his condition would permit. He was allowed to practise with "a screwed gun," and, after some time, he obtained leave "to ride the great horse," and to play at tennis. Naturally, constant efforts were made to procure his release. In July 1640 Lord Craven wrote to Secretary Windebank on the subject: "Mr. Webb has informed me that His Majesty has imposed upon you the putting him in mind of pressing on the Spanish Ambassador the delivery of Prince Rupert. I know you will, of yourself, be willing enough to perform that charitable action, however, the relation I have to that generous prince is such that I should fail of my duty if I did not entreat your vigilance in it."[1] King Charles sent Ambassadors extraordinary, not only to the Emperor, but also to Spain, whose intercession he entreated. The Cardinal Infant promised to plead, at least, for Rupert's better treatment, and King Charles next turned to France. France, then at war with the Empire, held prisoner Prince Casimir of Poland who, it seemed to Charles, might be a fit exchange for his nephew. Through Leicester he urged Prince Casimir's detention until Rupert's liberty were promised. But the scheme failed; Rupert, it was answered, was "esteemed an active prince,"[2] and would not be released, so long as danger threatened the Empire. So early had he acquired a warlike reputation.

Owing perhaps to the intercession of the Cardinal Infant of Spain, he was at last permitted the attendance of a page and groom, who might be Dutch or English, but not German. "I have sent Kingsmill his pass," wrote the Elector

---

[1] Dom. State Papers, Craven to Windebank, July 6, 1640.

[2] Clarendon State Papers, Sir A. Hopton to Windebank, 18—28 July, 1640. fol. 1397.

in August 1640, "he will be fit enough to pass my brother Rupert's time, and I do not think he will use his counsel in anything." [1] Of Kingsmill's arrival at Linz we hear nothing, but two other companions now relieved Rupert's solitude.

Susanne Marie von Kuffstein, daughter of Rupert's gaoler, was then a lovely girl of about sixteen. She was, says the writer of the Lansdowne MS., "one of the brightest beauties of the age, no less excelling in the beauty of her mind than of her body." On this fair lady the young prisoner's good looks, famous courage, and great misfortunes made a deep impression. She exerted herself to soften her father's heart, and to persuade him to gentler treatment of the captive. In this she succeeded so well "that the Prince's former favours were improved into familiarities, as continual visits, invitations and the like." Thus Rupert was enabled to enjoy Susanne's society, and that he did enjoy it there is very little doubt, "for he never named her after in his life, without demonstration of the highest admiration and expressing a devotion to serve her." [2] It has been suggested that the memory of Susanne von Kuffstein was the cause of Rupert's rejection of Marguerite de Rohan. There is, however, little ground for crediting him with such constancy. Maurice, it must be remembered, rejected the unfortunate Marguerite with equal decision. Moreover, Susanne herself married three times, and Rupert's sentiment towards her seems to have been nothing more passionate than a chivalrous and grateful admiration.

Besides Susanne the Prince had at Linz another friend,— his white poodle "Boye." This dog was a present from Lord Arundel, then English Ambassador at Vienna; it remained Rupert's inseparable companion for many years, and met at last a soldier's death on Marston Moor. The Prince also, for a short time, made a pet of a young hare, which he trained to follow him like a dog, but this he afterwards released, fearing that it might find captivity as irksome as did he himself.

Thus passed a two years' imprisonment, after which the Emperor deigned to offer terms to his captive. In the first place he required that Rupert should embrace the Roman faith. But the boy was a Palatine, and, though he had listened willingly to the persuasions of his aunt, Henrietta, the least hint of compulsion rendered him staunchly Protestant. He answered the Emperor, somewhat grandiloquently, "that he had not learnt to sacrifice his religion to his interest, and he would rather breathe his last in prison, than go out through the gates of Apostacy." The Emperor then consented to waive the question of religion, only insisting that Rupert must ask pardon for his crime of rebellion against the Holy Roman Empire. But to do this would have been to deny his brother's right to his Electorate, and Rupert only retorted coldly that he "disdained" to ask pardon for doing his duty. Finally, he was invited to take service under the Emperor, and to fight against France, which country had just imprisoned his eldest brother. But here also the boy was obdurate. To fight under the Emperor would inevitably involve fighting against the Swedes and the Protestant princes. Rupert therefore replied, "that he received the proposal rather as an affront than as a favour, and that he would never take arms against the champions of his father's cause." [1]

After such contumacy it may well be believed that the Emperor's patience was exhausted. His brother-in-law the Duke of Bavaria, then owner of the Upper Palatinate, and of the ducal title which was Rupert's birthright, suggested that the boy's spirit was not yet broken, and urged the Emperor to deprive him of his privileges. Accordingly, Graf

[1] Lansdowne MSS. 817.

Kuffstein was ordered to cease his civilities, and Rupert was placed in a confinement rendered stricter than ever, guarded day and night by twelve musketeers.

For this severity the proximity of a Swedish army was an additional reason. Maurice himself was serving in their ranks, and the Emperor feared lest Rupert should hold correspondence with them. Against these Swedes was despatched the Emperor's brother, the Archduke Leopold, who, very happily for Rupert, passed, on his way, through Linz. Being at Linz, the Archduke naturally visited the youthful prisoner who had made so much sensation, and was forthwith captivated by him. Leopold, whose gentle piety had won him the name of "the Angel", was but a few years older than the Palatine; the two had many tastes in common, and in that visit was established a friendship between Rupert the Devil and Leopold the Angel, which endured to the end of their lives.

The Archduke's intercession with the Emperor not only restored to Rupert his former privileges, but won him the additional liberty of leaving the castle on parole for so long as three days at a time.[1] As soon as this concession made their civilities possible, the nobles of the country showed themselves anxious to alleviate the tedium of Rupert's captivity. They "treated him with all the respects imaginable," invited him to their houses, and gave hunting parties in his honour. The house most frequented by Rupert was that of Graf Kevenheller, who, oddly enough, had been one of Frederick's bitterest foes. Yet Frederick's son found this Graf's house "a most pleasant place," at which he was always "very generously entertained."[2] And Rupert, on his part, seems to have made himself exceedingly popular with his friendly foes. He was, as they said, "beloved by all,"[3] and, wrote an Impe-

---

[1] Benett MSS. Warburton. Vol. I. pp. 457—458.

[2] Warburton, p. 458.

[3] Clarendon State Papers, Leslie to Windebank, July 19, 1640.

rialist soldier, "his behaviour so obligeth the cavaliers of this country that they wait upon him and serve him as if they were his subjects."[1] As pleasant a captivity as could be had was Rupert's now, but yet a captivity; and still, in spite of Susanne von Kuffstein, in spite of the Archduke and of "all the cavaliers of the country," his thoughts turned wistfully to the Hague, where, for him, was home.

[1] Dom. S. P. Leslie to Windebank, July 29—Aug. 8, 1640.

CHAPTER IV

THE PALATINES IN FRANCE. RUPERT'S RELEASE

ELIZABETH had imagined that by sending her younger sons to school in Paris, she was keeping them out of harm's way; great was her surprise and annoyance when she found their position to be almost as dangerous as was that of Rupert. The cause of this new disaster was the imprudent conduct of the elder brother, Charles Louis. Undaunted by his recent defeat, the young Elector sought new means for recovering his country, and he now bethought him of Duke Bernhard of Saxe Weimar. The alliance of this Duke, a near neighbour of the Palatinate, was very important, and in January 1639 Lord Leicester had proposed a marriage between him and the Princess Elizabeth. Further, he had suggested to King Charles that Maurice should take a command in Bernhard's army, for which, young though the Prince was, he believed him fitted. "For," said he, "besides that he has a body well-made, strong, and able to endure hardships, he hath a mind that will not let it be idle if he can have employment. He is very temperate, of a grave and settled disposition, but would very fain be in action, which, with God's blessing, and his own endeavours will render him a brave man ... Being once entered there, if Duke Bernhard should die, the army, in all likelihood would obey Prince Maurice; so keep itself from dissolving, and bring great advantage to the affairs of your nephew"[1] (*i. e.* to the Elector, Charles Louis).

But Charles Louis, full of impatience, and putting little faith in the negotiations of his uncle, set off in October

---

[1] Collins Sidney Papers, Vol. II. pp. 584—5, 28 Jan. 1639.

1639 to join Duke Bernhard in Alsace. Foolishly enough, he visited Paris, by the way, "*en prince*," and then attempted to depart thence incognito. Now it so happened that Cardinal Richelieu had uses of his own for the army of Duke Bernhard. It therefore suited him to detain the Elector in Paris, and the Elector's irregular conduct gave him the pretext he required. Declaring that so serious a breach of etiquette was capable of very sinister construction, he arrested Charles Louis, and placed his three brothers under restraint. Lord Leicester complained loudly of this treatment of the Elector, and though Maurice at once sent a servant to his brother, the man was only allowed to speak to Charles in French, and in the presence of his guards. The distracted mother flew to the Prince of Orange, who explained to her that Richelieu feared her son's attachment to England, which, however, Richelieu himself denied.

No sooner was the Weimarian army safely committed to the charge of a French general than Charles Louis was permitted to take up his residence with the English Ambassador. After this, though still a prisoner, he spent a very pleasant time in Paris, at an enormous expense to the King, his uncle. Maurice was allowed to return home in an English ship, but Edward and Philip were detained as hostages. Elizabeth spared no pains to recover them, and, as usual, made the Prince of Orange her excuse, "I send for Ned out of France, to be this summer in the army," she wrote to Roe; "and, finding Philip too young to learn any great matters yet, I send for him also, to return next winter;—*which I assure you he shall not do.*" [1]

But it was not until April 1640 that her boys were restored to her, and the Elector did not recover his full liberty until the following July. In the autumn of the same year he went to England, to attend the marriage of his cousin Mary with the little William of Orange, on

[1] Dom. State Papers. Carl I. Vol. 539. Eliz to Roe, Jan. 7/17, 1640.

which occasion he quarrelled with the bridegroom for precedence. But his chief object in this visit was to obtain money either from King or Parliament. Elizabeth urged him to do something for Maurice, but he evidently regarded his third brother with much indifference. "As for my brother Maurice," he wrote, "your Majesty will be pleased to do with him as you think fit. It will be hard to get the money of his pension paid him." [1] His next letter was a little more encouraging. "The King says he will seek to get money for Maurice, and then he may go to what army he pleases. I want it very much myself, and it is very hard to come by in these times." [2]

The army which Maurice chose was that of the Swedes, under Banier; perhaps because it was then quartered near to the captive Rupert. Ere his departure, he wrote to King Charles:

"Sir,—Being ready to tacke a journy towards Generall Banier, I may not neglect to aquaint you therewithal, et to recomend myselfe et my actions to Yor Roial favour, whiche I chal strive to deserve in getting more capacity for your service. Yt is the greatest ambition of Yor Majestie's

"Most obedient nephew et humble servant,

"MAURICE." [3]

The letter, which is written in a clear, school-boy hand, betrays less confusion of tongues, the curious use of "et" notwithstanding, than do most epistles of the Palatines.

Maurice remained with the Swedes some months. In January 1641 his mother informed Roe that he was at Amberg in Bavaria. In the next month she was able to report of him at greater length. "I have had letters from Maurice, from Cham in the High Palatinate. He tells me

---

[1] Bromley Letters, p. 122.
[2] Ibid. p. 124.
[3] Dom. State Papers. Maurice to Charles I, Oct. 30, 1640. Carl I. Vol. 470. fol. 21.

that Banier has intercepted a letter of the Duke of Bavaria, to the Commander of Amberg. He writes that he understands that there is in Banier's army a young Palatine; and he should take good heed no bailiffs, or other officers, go to see him or hold any correspondence with him ... Maurice is still very well used by Banier, who now makes more of Princes than heretofore, since he has married the Marquis of Baden's daughter." [1]

In June 1641 Maurice returned to Holland where he found life going on much as usual. Hunting and acting continued to be the principal Palatine amusements. " I did hunt a hare, last week, with my hounds; it took seven hours, the dogs never being at fault," wrote Elizabeth triumphantly; "I went out with forty horse at least, and there were but five at the death ... Maurice, Prince Ravenville, the Archduke, and many another knight, were entreated by their horses to return on foot. I could not but tell you this adventure, for it is very famous here." [2] In another letter she tells how her daughters acted the play of " Medea and Jason ", and how Louise, who played a man, looked " so like poor Rupert as you would then have justly called her by his name." [3] It is not unlikely that Louise impersonated Jason in her brother's clothes, and so enhanced the likeness.

The family had, by this time, almost despaired of " poor Rupert's " release; but it was nearer than they thought. King Charles, after labouring for three years in vain, had at last succeeded in rousing the sympathy of France, and, when he despatched Sir Thomas Roe, in 1641, to plead Rupert's cause at Vienna, it was with a reasonable hope of success. " I hope, by the solicitation of Sir Thomas Roe, we shall see our sweet Prince Rupert here. He

---

[1] Dom. State Papers, Carl I. Vol. 477. Feb. 22, 1641.
[2] Ibid. Carl I. Vol. 539. Jan. 7—17, 1641.
[3] Ibid. Carl I. 484. f. 51. Oct. 10, 1641.

hath been so long a prisoner!"[1] wrote one of Elizabeth's ladies.

The Emperor had long had a secret kindness for the gallant boy who had dared to defy him, and, in the Archduke Rupert had a warm friend and advocate. But in the old Duke of Bavaria, who held, as before said, so much of the Palatine property, he had a bitter foe. His release became the subject of fierce family discussion. The Emperor hesitated, but, moved by the intercession of France, and by his affection for his brother, decided at last to show mercy. Thereupon, his sister, the Duchess of Bavaria, fell on her knees before him, and passionately entreated him to detain Rupert a prisoner. Again the Emperor wavered, but the Empress, siding with the Archduke, carried the day in Rupert's favour. The boy was offered his liberty on the single condition of never again drawing sword against the Imperial forces. The peremptory commands of King Charles procured Rupert's submission to this condition, which he would fain have disputed. But when his promise was required in writing it was more than he could endure. "If it is to be a lawyer's business let them look well to the wording!" said he scornfully. The Emperor took the hint, and declared himself satisfied with a simple promise, Rupert giving his hand upon it, according to the custom of the country.[2]

Though France had been the principal factor in Rupert's release, Sir Thomas Roe had all the credit of it; and to Roe's guidance Elizabeth exhorted her son to submit himself. Rupert obeyed her meekly. He seems indeed to have been in an unusually submissive frame of mind, judging by the letters which he addressed at this time to Roe. The first of these bears the date, "Linz, 21 Aug. 1641."

[1] Fairfax Correspondence. Ed. Johnson. 1848. Vol. I. p. 322.
[2] Benett MSS. Warburton. I. pp. 102, 458.

"My Lord!

"A little journe a had towards the Count of Kevenheller was the cause that thus long you were without an
answer. But now I could not let another occasion pass
without giving you very great thanks for your pains, and
the affection you show in my business, and to tell you
that I leve all the conditions to your disposing, since I
know your Lordshippe is my frend, and am assured that
you would do nothing against my honor.

"And so I rest

"Your Lordshippe's most affectioned frend,

"RUPERT." [1]

The next letter, written a month later, is very curiously
humble, coming from the fiery Rupert.

"My Lord!

"According your demand I doe send you this answer with all possible speed. As for the present your
Lordshippe speks of I am in greate doubt what to give,
this being a place where nothing worth presenting is to
be had; besides I doe not knowe what present he would
accept. Therefore I must heere in desire your Lordshippes
consel, desiring you to let Spina take what you shalle
thinke fitt, both for the Count, and for the Emperor's —,
who deserves it, having had a greate dele of paines with
my diet, and other thinges. Sir, I must give you a greate
dele of thankes for the reale frendshipp you shewed in
remembering me of my faults, whiche I confesse, and
strive, and shalle the more heereafter, to mend. But I
doubt not, according to the manner of some peple heere,
they have added and said more than the thinge itselfe is.
I beseech you not to hearken to them, but assure your-
selfe that it has been only from an evill costum, which I
hope in short time to mend. Desiring you to continue

---

[1] Dom. State Papers. Carl I. Vol. 483. fol. 39.

this your frendshippe in leting me knowe my faults, that
I mai have to mend them,

"I rest,

"Your Lordshippe's most affecionat frend,

"RUPERT." [1]

The third, and last letter is dated "October" and docketed
"of my release."

"My Lord!

"Sence you have happiely broght this businesse almost
to and end, I mene to followe your Lordshippe's consel in
alle. At your coming, alle shalle be redie for our journay
to Viena. The moyns (moyens, *i.e.* money) I have when
alle debts are paiet woul not bee moer than a 1,000 ducats.
Thefore I beseech your Lordshippe to hasten our journe
from Viena as much as possible. If you think fit, I mene
to take my waie to Inspruck and throgh France, whiche
is sertainely the best and saifest wai of alle. I woul desire
a sudain answer of your Lordshippe that I mai send for
bils of exchange to bee delivered at Geneva and Paris. Thys
is alle I have at this time to troble Yor Lordshippe withalle,
and so I rest,

"Your most affectioned to doe you service,

"RUPERT." [2]

It may here be noticed that Rupert, throughout his
whole life, was singularly scrupulous about the payment of
his debts.

When all negotiations were completed, the Emperor
organised "an extraordinary hunting" in Lower Austria,
at which Rupert was directed to appear, as if by chance.
He had the good luck to kill the boar with his spear, an
exploit very highly accounted in the Empire. The Emperor,

<hr>

[1] Dom. State Papers. Sept. 19—29. 1641. Carl I. 484. f. 36.
[2] Ihid. Oct. 1641. Carl I. 484 f. 61.

thereupon, extended his hand to the successful hunter; Rupert kissed it, and, that being the final sign of release, was thenceforth free. For a week he was detained as a guest at Vienna, while every effort was made to gain his adherence to the Emperor. He seems to have been as popular at Vienna as at Linz. "There were," says the Lansdowne MS., "few persons of quality by whom he was not visited and treated.... The ladyes also vied in their civilities, and laboured to detain him in Germany by their charms." But Rupert refused to be beguiled, charmed they never so wisely. As for the Emperor, he lavished so much kindness on his quondam prisoner, "that the modesty of the Prince could not endure it without some confusion. Yet his deportment was composed, and his answers to the civilities of the Emperor were so full of judgment and gratitude that they esteemed him no less for his prudence than for his bravery." [1]

At last he was suffered to depart. Fain would the Emperor have sent him to the Archduke at Brunswick, believing that the influence of the Angel might yet win him. But Rupert preferred to visit Prague, his own birthplace, and the scene of his father's brief kingship. With a kindly caution not to venture into the power of the Duke of Bavaria, the Emperor bade him farewell. From Prague Rupert went to Saxony, where he astonished the reigning Elector not a little by his refusal to drink. A banquet had been arranged in his honour, but the Prince, "always temperate", excused himself from drinking with the rest. "'What shall we do with him then,' says the Elector, 'if he cannot drink?'—and so invited him to the entertainment of a hunting." [2] After this Rupert travelled night and day, in his eagerness to be the first to bring news of his release to his family. He just managed to anticipate Roe's letter, which arrived at the Hague on the same night with himself. Boswell, then English Ambassador in Holland, wrote

[1] Lansdowne MSS. 817. British Museum.
[2] Warburton. I. p. 459.

an account of the event to Roe. "Prince Rupert arrived here in perfect health, but lean and weary, having come that day from Swoll, and from Hamburg since the Friday noon. Myself, at eight o'clock in the evening, coming out of the court gate, had the good luck to receive him first of any, out of his waggon; no other creature in the court expecting his coming so soon. Whereby himself carried the news of his being come to the Queen, newly set at supper. You may imagine what joy there was!"[1] And to Roe wrote the Queen also: "The same night, being the 20th of this month (December), that Rupert came hither I received your letter, where you tell me of his going from Vienna. He is very well satisfied with the Emperor's usage of him. I find him not altered, only leaner, and grown. All the people, from the highest to the lowest, made great show of joy at his return. For me, you may easily guess it, and also how much I esteem myself obliged to you."

Yet, even after a three years' separation, Elizabeth had no notion of keeping her son beside her. "What to do with him I know not!" she lamented. "He cannot in honour, yet go to the war; here he will live but idly, in England no better. For I know the Queen will use all possible means to gain him to the prejudice of the Prince Elector, and of his religion. For though he has stood firm against what has been practised in his imprisonment, amongst his enemies, yet I fear, by my own humour, that fair means from those that are esteemed true may have more power than threatenings or flattery from an enemy."[2] Doubtless the Queen's anxiety for her son's employment was justified; there was no money to maintain him; and, moreover, the Hague was no desirable residence for an idle and active-minded young Prince. There seems to have been some idea of sending him to Ireland, where the natives had risen against the English Government. The King approved of the

---

[1] Dom. S. Papers. Boswell to Roe. 23 Dec. 1641. Carl I. 486. f. 53.
[2] Dom. State Papers. Carl I. 486. f. 51. Elizabeth to Roe, 23 Dec. 1641.

suggestion: "But," wrote the Elector, "the Parliament will employ none there but those they may be sure of. I shall speak with some of them about it, either for Rupert, or for brother Maurice. This last might, I think, with honour, have a regiment under Leslie, but to be under any other odd or senseless officer, as some are proposed, I shall not advise it."[1] Apparently the idea failed to commend itself to the English Parliament, which perhaps suspected that the younger brothers would be found less time-serving than was the Elector.

In accordance with his mother's wishes, and doubtless with his own, Rupert went over to England, early in February 1642, with the avowed object of thanking his uncle for his release. He found King Charles at Dover, whither he had accompanied his wife and eldest daughter on their way to Holland. Affairs in England were approaching a crisis, and the Queen, under the pretext of taking the Princess Mary to her husband, was about to raise money and men for the King, on the Continent. The visit of the warlike Rupert at so critical a juncture roused hostile comment, and, since war was not yet considered inevitable, the King desired his nephew to return home with the Queen. Therefore, after a visit of three days, he embarked with the Queen and Princess on board the Lyon, and sailed straight for Holland. The arrivals were met, on their landing, by Elizabeth, two of her daughters, the Prince of Orange and his son; all of whom proceeded in one coach to the Court of Orange. Rupert remained at the Hague until August, when war broke out in England, and gave him the employment desired for him by his mother.

At this point, August 1642, closes what we may consider as the first period of Rupert's life. Probably these early years were his best and happiest. Marked though they were by poverty and misfortune, they were yet full of

---

[1] Forster's Statesmen, Vol. VI. p. 74. 10 March, 1642.

interests and adventure, unmarred by the struggles, jealousies, disappointments, and family dissensions which were to come. Rupert had no lack of friends; he had won the hearts of his very enemies. Not the least among a brilliant group of brothers and sisters, he was happy in their companionship and sympathy, the bond of which was so soon to be severed; happy also in the kindness and affection of the Prince of Orange and of the King and Queen of England. He had shown himself gifted with rare abilities, capable of valiant action, and of loyal and patient endurance;—a generous, high-souled boy, fired by chivalric fancies, free from all self-seeking, earnest, faithful, strong-willed, but also, alas, opinionated, and impatient of contradiction.

CHAPTER V

ARRIVAL IN ENGLAND. POSITION IN THE ARMY. CAUSES OF FAILURE

DURING his last brief visit to England Rupert had promised to serve his uncle whensoever he should have need of him; and in August 1642, he received, through Queen Henrietta, his Commission, as General of the Horse. Immediately upon this he set out to join the King in England. He embarked in the "Lyon," the ship which had brought the Queen to Holland; but, after the Prince had come on board, the Commander, who was of Puritan sympathies, received a warning against bringing him over. Captain Fox's anxiety to get rid of his passenger was favoured by the weather. A storm blew them back to the Texel, and there Fox persuaded the Prince to go ashore, promising to meet him at Goree so soon as the wind should serve. Rupert thereupon returned to the Hague, and Fox, after quietly setting the Prince's people and luggage on shore, sailed away, and was no more seen in Holland.

Enraged and disappointed, Rupert appealed to the Stadtholder, who lent him another ship, commanded by Captain Colster. This time Maurice insisted on accompanying his brother, and the two Princes, having provided themselves with an engineer, a "fire worker," and a large store of arms, muskets, and powder, set sail for Scarborough. Near Flamborough Head they were spied by some Parliamentary cruisers, and a ship called the "London" came out to hail them. Colster hoisted the Dunkirk colours, but the other Captain, still unsatisfied, desired to search the small vessel in which the arms were stored. Rupert, who had been extremely, and even dangerously, ill throughout the voyage, struggled on deck "in a mariner's cap" and ordered out the guns, saying he would not be searched. On this the "London" shot to leeward, and two other ships came out to her aid. But Rupert succeeded in running into Tynemouth, and, anchoring outside the bar, landed by means of boats. His little vessel also escaped, and landed her stores safely at Scarborough in the night.[1]

When they reached Tynemouth it was already late, but Rupert's eagerness would brook no delay. "The zeale he had speedily to serve His Majesty made him think diligence itself were lazy."[2] Accompanied by Maurice, an Irish officer, Daniel O'Neil, and several others, he started at once for Nottingham. But the stars, in their courses, fought against him. As ill luck would have it, August though it was, a hard frost came on, and Rupert's horse slipped and fell, pitching him on to his shoulder. The shoulder was discovered to be out of joint, but, "by a great providence," it happened that a bone-setter lived only half a mile away. This man, being sent for in haste, set Rupert's shoulder in the road, and, "in conscience, took but one-half of what the Prince offered him for his pains." Within three hours the indefatigable Rupert insisted on continuing his journey.

Arrived at Nottingham, he retired to bed, but he was not destined long to enjoy hisw ell-earned rest. A curious dilemma now brought him into contact with the two men who were to prove, respectively, his warmest friend and his bitterest foe, in the Royal Army,—namely, Captain Will Legge, and George, Lord Digby. The King, who was at Coventry, had sent to Digby, demanding a petard. Odd though it may appear, a petard was to Digby a thing unknown—"a word which he could not understand." He therefore sought out the weary Prince to demand an explanation. Rupert, at once, got out of bed to search the arsenal; but no such thing as a petard was to be found. Then,

[1] Warburton. Vol. I. pp. 460—462.
[2] Lansdowne MSS. 817.

Captain Legge, coming to the rescue, contrived to make one out of two mortars, and sent it off to the King.[1] Rupert, following the petard, found his uncle at Leicester Abbey, and there formally took over charge of the cavalry, which then consisted of only eight hundred horse. On the next day, August 22nd, they all returned to Nottingham, where the solemn setting up of the Royal Standard took place.

War was now irrevocably declared, and Rupert found his generalship no sinecure. The King, in these early days, relied implicitly on his nephew's advice, and, though Commander of the Cavalry only in name, Rupert had in reality the whole conduct of the war upon his hands. The real Commander-in-Chief was old Lord Lindsey, but Rupert's position was one of complete independence. He was, indeed, instructed to consult the Council of War, but was also directed "to advise privately, as you shall think fit, and to govern your resolution accordingly."[2] Further, he requested that he might receive his orders only from the King himself. And this request King Charles unwisely conceded, thus freeing Rupert from all control of the Commander-in-Chief, dividing the army into two independent parties, and establishing a fruitful source of discord between the cavalry and infantry.

Yet Rupert was in many respects well-fitted for his post. Distinguished by his dauntless courage and resolute nature, he was possessed also of a knowledge of war such as was not to be learnt in England. He was really the only professional soldier of high rank in the army, and he proved himself both a clever strategist, and a good leader of cavalry, though he did unfortunately lack the patience and discretion necessary to the making of a successful general. "That brave Prince and hopeful soldier, Rupert," wrote the gallant Sir Philip Warwick, "though a

[1] Warburton. I. p. 462.
[2] Rupert Transcripts. Instruction to the Prince. 1642.

young man, had in martial affairs some experience, and a good skill, and was of such intrepid courage and activity, that,—clean contrary to former practice, when the King had great armies, but no commanders forward to fight,— [1] he ranged and disciplined that small body of men;—of so great virtue is the personal courage and example of one great commander. And indeed to do him right, he put that spirit into the King's army that all men seemed resolved, and had he been as cautious as he was a forward fighter, he had, most probably, been a very fortunate one. He showed a great and exemplary temperance, which fitted him to undergo the fatigues of a war, so as he deserved the character of a soldier. *Il était toujours soldat!* For he was never negligent by indulgence to his pleasures, or apt to lose his advantages." [2]

In truth Rupert's cheerfulness and brilliant courage inspired confidence in his own troops, and terror in those of the enemy. "There was no more consternation in the King's troops now. Every one grew assured. The most timorous was afraid to show fear under such a general, whose courage was increased by the esteem we had of him." [3] And throughout the war Rupert was the very life of the Royalist army; "adored by the hot-blooded young officers, as by the sturdy troopers, who cried, when they entered a fallen city: 'D—— us! The town is Prince Rupert's!' " [4]

The very first skirmish of the war established his reputation. The terrified Puritans spread abroad reports of the "incredible and unresistible courage of Prince Rupert," [5] which grew and multiplied as the war proceeded, until Rupert, "exalted with the terror his name gave to the enemy," [6] would not believe that any troops could with-

---

[1] *I.e.* in the Scottish wars.
[2] Memoirs of Sir Philip Warwick, pp. 226—228.
[3] Lansdowne MSS. 817.
[4] A Looking Glass etc. Civil War Tract. Brit. Mus.
[5] Clarendon's Hist. of the Rebellion. Ed. 1849. Bk. VI. p. 46.
[6] Ibid. Bk. VI. p. 109.

stand his charge. "The enemy is possest with so strange and senseless a feare as they will not believe any place tenable to which Your Highness will march,"[1] reported his officers. Nor was it wonderful that the Puritans deemed him something more than human. Conspicuous always by his dress and unusual height, ever foremost in the charge, utterly "prodigal of his person," he bore a charmed life. Twice pistols were fired in his face, without doing him the slightest harm. Once his horse was killed under him, but "he marched off on foot leisurely, without so much as mending his pace."[2] While guarding the retreat from Brentford he stood alone for hours, exposed to a heavy fire, and yet came off unscathed. "Nephew, I must conjure you not to hazard yourself so nedlessely,"[3] wrote his anxious uncle; but the King's anxiety was uncalled for, Rupert remained uninjured till the end of the war, though Maurice was wounded in almost every action in which he engaged.

The Austrians at Vlotho had called Rupert "shot free", and so he seemed now to Puritan and Cavalier.

> "Sir, you're enchanted! Sir, you're doubly free
> "From the great guns, and squibbing poetry,"[4]

declared a Royalist poet.

Rupert, moreover, seemed to be in all places at once. "This prince, like a perpetual motion.... was in a short time, heard of in many places at great distances,"[5] says the Parliamentary historian, May. And again: "The two young princes, and especially Prince Rupert, the elder brother, and most furious of the two, within a fortnight after his arrival commanded a small party.... Through

---

[1] Mr. Firth's Transcripts. Geo. Porter to Rupert, March 24, 1644.
[2] Warburton. II. p. 250. Journal of Siege of Bristol.
[3] Pythouse Papers. Ed. Day. 1879. p. 46. 16 Nov. 1642.
[4] Rupertismus. Cleveland's Poems. Ed. 1687. p. 51.
[5] May. Hist. of Long Parliament. Ed. 1854. p. 249.

divers parts of Warwickshire, Nottinghamshire, Leicester-shire, Worcester and Cheshire did this young prince fly with those troops he had." [1] Nowhere did the adherents of the Parliament feel safe from his attack, and the magical rapidity of his movements enhanced the terror inspired by his prowess. Wrote his admirer, Cleveland:

> "Your name can scare an atheist to his prayers,
> "And cure the chincough better than the bears;
> "Old Sybils charm toothache with you; the nurse
> "Makes you still children; and the pondrous curse
> "The clown salutes with is derived from you;
> "'Now Rupert take thee, Rogue! How dost thou do?'" [2]

Yet Rupert, in spite of this reputation was neither ruffianly nor cruel. The News Letters called him "a loose wild gentleman", [3] and many accused him of hanging Roundheads at their own doors, and plundering villages wholesale; [4] but such rumours were libels. "Where are these men that will affirm it? In what country or town stood those houses betrayed by me, or by my sufferance, to that misery of rapine?" demanded the Prince, in answer to one of his accusers. "He will answer '*they*' said it. But who '*they*' were he knows not; in truth, nor I neither, nor no man else." [5] And said Sir Thomas Roe, who was not all inclined to approve the part Rupert had taken: "I cannot hear anything, *credibly* averred, which can be blamed by those who know the liberty of wars." [6] But the English did not know "the liberty of the wars," and they were naturally inclined to judge the young Prince harshly. Severe Rupert undoubtedly could be, if necessary. When the Puritans began a wholesale massacre of the King's Irish soldiers, the Prince promptly retaliated by executing an equal number of Puritan

---

[1] May. Hist. of Long Parliament. Ed. 1854. p. 243-4.
[2] Rupertismus.
[3] Webb. Civil War in Herefordshire. Vol. I. p. 129.
[4] May. p. 244.
[5] Prince Rupert: His Reply. Brit. Mus.
[6] Webb. Civil War in Hereford. I. p. 149.

prisoners. But the stern act, coupled with the assurance that for the life of every Royalist that of a Roundhead should pay, effectually checked the barbarities of the Parliament. The nickname of "Prince Robber"[1] was certainly unjustly bestowed; yet the Royal Army had to be supported, and the only way to support it was by levying contributions on the country. "The Horse have not been paid, but live upon the country,"[2] wrote a Cavalier to his wife.

It is possible that Rupert was not over-scrupulous when the persons taxed happened to be Puritans, yet he always maintained what he considered a proper degree of discipline; and the frequent apologies of his officers prove that the Prince did not permit indiscriminate plunder. "Our men are not very governable, nor do I think they will be, unless some of them are hanged. They fall extremely to the old kind of plundering, which is neither for their good, nor for His Majesty's service,"[3] wrote Lord Wentworth. And, after a high-handed capture of some arms at Swanbourne, the same officer again apologised: "If your Highness think it too great a cruelty in us I hope you will pardon us. You shall consider that we could not have done otherwise."[4]

Another Colonel denied strenuously an accusation of oppression which had excited Rupert's anger against him.[5] That the failure at Edgehill was due to the greed of Rupert's men in plundering the baggage waggons, was an imputation which the Prince hotly resented. To his announcement that he could, "at least, give a good account of the enemy's horse," a bystander retorted: "And of their carts too!"[6] Whereupon the Prince drew his sword, and

<hr>

[1] Gardiner's Civil War, I. p. 15.
[2] Sydney Papers. Spencer to Lady Spencer. II. p. 667.
[3] Rupert Correspondence. Warburton. II. p. 191.
[4] Ibid. p. 193.
[5] Rupert Transcripts, Colonel Blagge to the Prince, 2 March, 1643.
[6] Verney Memoirs, Vol. II. p. 115.

there was nearly a duel in the King's presence. The idea
that he enriched himself by plunder is too absurd to need
refutation; yet, were it needed, proof to the contrary might
be found in a letter written at the end of the war, which
draws a painful picture of Rupert's extreme poverty. [1]

For the rest, the Prince regarded the enemy with a soldierly chivalry. Instances of his courtesy are not wanting,
and in all matters of honour he was most punctilious.
"The Prince," said one of his officers, "uses to make good
his word, not only in point of honour, but as a matter of
religion too." [2] Thus, when his men snatched the colours
of an enemy promised a safe passage, "some of them felt
the edge of his sword," and the colours were courteously
returned. To his honourable conduct, under similar circumstances at Bristol, the Puritan Governor bore generous
testimony. [3]

But personal gallantry, promptitude, and ubiquity were
far from being Rupert's only qualifications for his post. He
understood, as he himself phrased it, "what belongs to war."
His tactics were of the school of the great Gustavus, and
he abolished the absurd custom of letting the cavalry
halt to fire, before making a charge. At Edgehill he went
from rank to rank, bidding the men to charge at the first
word, and thus he formed an irresistible cavalry which never
failed to sweep all before it, until it met its match at Marston
Moor. His method was thus described by the son of one
of his officers: "His way of fighting was that he had a
select body of horse that always attended him, and, in
every attack, they received the enemy's shot without returning it, but one and all bore with all their force upon
their adversaries, till they broke their ranks, and charged
quite through them. Then they rallied, and, when the enemy
were in disorder, fell upon their rear and slaughtered them,

[1] Dom. State Papers. Nicholas to King, Sept. 18, 1645.
[2] Warburton. II. 262.
[3] Warburton. II. 267.

into scarce any opposition."[1] And says Professor Gardiner: "Rupert was as capable of planning a campaign as he was of conducting a charge."[2] Until November 1644, at which period, it should be noted, Rupert's power was on the wane, the strategical superiority was decidedly with the King. The operations of the Royalist army were based on a well-conceived plan, that plan was varied and supplemented as occasion required. This skilful warfare Professor Gardiner ascribes to Rupert's genius. Why then, may we ask, did so good a soldier fail so signally?

The reasons for failure are not far to seek. In the first place, Rupert was too complete a soldier for the task he had undertaken. His common-sense, soldierly point of view quite failed to embrace the political and constitutional sides of the question. He could no more comprehend the King's refusal to make any compromise, than he could have understood the moderate Royalists' dread of a complete victory for their own side. The boyish challenge purporting to be sent by him to Essex, shows, if genuine, how absolutely he failed to grasp the points at issue. "My Lord," it begins, "I hear you are a general of an army. ...I shall be ready, on His Majesty's behalf, to give you an encounter in a pitched field at Dunsmore Heath, 18th October next. Or, if you think it too much labour, or expense, to draw your forces thither, I shall be as willing, on my own part, to expect private satisfaction at your hands, and that performed by a single duel. Which proffer, if you please to accept, you shall not find me backward in performing what I have promised. ... Now I have said all, and what more you expect of me to be said, shall be delivered in a larger field than a small sheet of paper, and that by my sword, and not by my pen. In the interim

---

[1] Troubles of our Catholic Forefathers. Ed. Morris. 1872. Sir Edward Southcote's Narrative, 1st Series, p. 392.

[2] Gardiner's Civil War, I. p. 2.

I am your friend, till I meet you next."[1]   The stories of his wandering in disguise through the quarters of the Parliament may be somewhat apocryphal, but they show, at least, the impression he made on his contemporaries.   And there is nothing doubtful in the fact that he and Maurice laughed aloud in the face of the Parliamentary Commissioner who proclaimed them solemnly, "traitors, to die without mercy."[2]

Rupert, notwithstanding his twenty-two years and his unusual experiences, was a boy still; far too young for the position he held.   He was over-confident, and rash with the rashness of youth.   Frequently his victorious charge was but the prelude to disaster; for the cavalry were apt to pursue too eagerly, leaving the foot unsupported on the field.   Still, it should be remembered that it must have been next to impossible to hold back those gallant, untrained troops; though probably Rupert did not try very hard to do it.

In truth the Royalist army was as hard a one to manage as ever fell to the lot of a general.   It was an army of volunteers, supported chiefly by the private means of nobles and gentlemen, who, while scorning to take orders from one another, showed themselves equally averse to taking them from a foreign Prince.   It was small, far smaller than that of Essex; undisciplined, badly armed, and continually on the verge of mutiny for want of pay.   "It is e'en being, for the most part, without arms, a general of an army of ordnance without a cure, not a gun too, lesse money, much mutiny,"[3] wrote a faithful follower of Rupert, at one period of the war.   The men were raw recruits; the officers were full of complaints and discontents, all showing a remarkable willingness to do anything rather than that

---

[1] Civil War Pamphlets. British Museum. "Prince Rupert's Message to my Lord of Essex."

[2] Whitelocke's Memorials, 1732, p. 114.

[3] Carte's Ormonde, VI. p. 197, 20 Aug. 1644.

which they were required to do. "The officers of your troop will obey in no kind of thing, and, by their example, never a soldier in that company," lamented Daniel O'Neil, from Abingdon. "I had rather be your groom in Oxford than with a company that shall assume such a liberty as yours does here!"[1] From Reading, protested Sir Arthur Aston, "I wish when your Highness gave your consent to leave me here behind you, that you had rather adjudged me to lose my head."[2] And from Wales came the striking declaration, "If your Highness shall be pleased to command me to the Turk, or the Jew, or the Gentile, I will go on my bare feet to serve you; but from the Welsh good Lord deliver me!"[3] From all sides came complaints of mutinies, of "unbecoming language," "affronts," injuries and violence. "In spite of my three several orders to come away, Captain Mynn remains at Newent," declared Colonel Vavasour. The garrison of Donnington not only defied the order to be quiet, "it being very late at night," but forcibly released one of their number, under arrest, and outraged the town by "robbing, and doing all villainy."[4]

Nor was it with insubordination alone that Rupert had to deal. Wrote Louis Dyves: "Our men are in extreme necessity, many of them having neither clothes to cover their nakedness, nor boots to put on their feet, and not money enough amongst them to pay for the shoeing of their horses."[5] And declared Sir Ralph Hopton: "It is inconceivable what these fellows are always doing with their arms; they appear to be expended as fast as their ammunition."[6] Another officer required supplies of biscuits: "For your Highness knows what want of victuals is among com-

<hr>

[1] Warburton, II. p. 82, 19 Dec. 1642.
[2] Ibid. II. p. 175.
[3] Ibid. II. p. 386. 11 Mar. 1644.
[4] Transcripts, 30 Jan. 1644.
[5] Warburton, II. p. 85.
[6] Ibid. II. p. 291, 17 Sept. 1643.

mon men." [1] A fourth desired a change of quarters, "because
the country, hereabouts, is so heavily charged with contributions, as our allowance falls short." [2] A fifth modestly
requested, "to be put into the power of a thousand horse,
or foot, and then I doubt not, by God's assistance, to give
a sufficient account of what is committed to my charge." [3]
Every one of them lacked arms and ammunition, and all
their wants were poured out to the luckless young Prince,
who was expected to attend to every detail, and whose
own supplies were wretchedly insufficient.

Added to all this, there were private quarrels to be
appeased. Wyndham declined to serve under Hopton,
who had "disobliged" him. [4] Vavasour complained of
"very high language" used towards him by Sir Robert
Byron. At Lichfield disputes between the factions of Lord
Loughborough and Sir William Bagot raged violently. "In
all places where I come, it's my misfortune to meet with
extreme trouble," declared the brave old Jacob Astley, to
whose lot the pacifying of this quarrel fell; "I have met,
in this place with exceeding great trouble, the commanders
and soldiers in the close at Lichfield, having shut out my
Lord Loughborough." [5] And not even the efforts of old
Astley could bring about a peace between the contending
officers; "our minds being both too high to acknowledge
a superiority," [6] confessed Loughborough candidly. But
even more serious than such quarrels as these were the
court factions which divided the Royalist army against itself.
From the very beginning, the attempts of the King's
Council to regulate military affairs were bitterly resented
by the soldiery. Courtier detested soldier, and soldier despised courtier! Nor were the military and civil factions

[1] Transcripts. Blagge to Rupert. 1643.
[2] Rupert Transcripts. Dyves to the Prince. Sept. 21, 1642.
[3] Ibid. Kirke to Prince. 22 Feb. 1644.
[4] Add MSS. 18982. Wyndham to the Prince. Jan. 6, 1644.
[5] Transcripts. Astley to the Prince, Jan. 12, 1645.
[6] Ibid. Loughborough to the Prince, July 25, 1645.

the only ones existent; there was party within party, intrigue within intrigue. Wrote the shrewd Arthur Trevor,
in 1643: "The contrariety of opinions and ways are equally
distant with those of the elements, and as destructive, if
there were not a special providence that keeps men in
one mind against a third party, though they agree in no
one thing among themselves."[1] Equally opposed to the
military party of Rupert, and to the constitutionalists led
by Hyde and Falkland, were the followings of the Queen
and of Lord Digby. Bitter, private jealousies completed
the confusion, and the vacillation of the King, who lent
an ear now to one, now to another, destroyed all consist-
ency of action. With such a state of affairs a young man
of barely three-and-twenty was called upon to deal!

Obviously the position was one requiring the greatest
tact, patience and circumspection, which were, unhappily,
the very qualities most lacking in the young Prince. The
circumstances of his early career had been calculated to
inspire him with an exaggerated sense of his own importance. Notwithstanding his position as fourth child among
thirteen, and the constant snubs of his mother, he had
been spoilt by the Prince of Orange, and by the English
Court. The admiration he had won, during his captivity
among his enemies, added to his self-esteem. His stead-
fast refusal to renounce either his faith or his party, in
spite of flatteries, threats, promises and persuasions, had
raised him to the proud position of a Protestant martyr.
"All the world knows how deeply I have smarted, and
what perils I have undergone, for the Protestant cause,"[2]
he declared to the English Parliament. Thus conscious of
his own abilities and claims to distinction, and valuing
to the full his previous experience, he was possessed of a
not unnatural contempt for the military views of civilians.

[1] Carte's Ormonde. Trevor to Ormonde. Nov. 21, 1643. Vol. V. pp. 520-1.
[2] Prince Rupert: his Declaration. Pamphlet. British Museum. See Warb. II.
p. 124.

The overbearing manner which he permitted himself to assume towards Courtiers and Councillors gave great offence. "We hear that Prince Rupert behaves himself so rudely, whereby he doth himself a great deal of dishonour, and the King more disservice,"[1] was the report of a Royalist to his friends. "Prince Rupert's pleasure was not to be contradicted," and, "Prince Rupert could not want of his will," says the contemporary historian, Sir Edward Walker.[2] Clarendon complained that the Prince "too affectedly" despised what was said of him, and "too stoically contemned the affections of men."[3] While the faithful Sir Philip Warwick lamented that, "a little sharpness of temper and uncommunicableness in society, or council, by seeming, with a 'Pish!' to neglect all that another said and he approved not, made him less grateful than his friends could have wished. And this humour soured him towards the Councillors of Civil Affairs, who were necessarily to intermix with him in Martial Councils."[4] Certainly this was not the spirit calculated to recommend him to the English nobles, men who served their sovereign at their own cost, and who considered themselves at least as good as the son of a dethroned King.

Nor could Rupert atone for official imperiousness by geniality in private life. In happier days, at Heidelberg, Frederick's faithful steward had declared that the morose manners of his master rendered him "afraid and ashamed" when any one visited the castle.[5] Something of his father's disposition Rupert had inherited; and, with all his self-confidence, he was very shy. From the nobility both he and Maurice held aloof with a reserve born of pride and an uncertain position. Princes they might be, but they were

<hr>

[1] Hist. MSS. Commission. 5th Report, p. 162. Ap. I. Sutherland MSS. Stephen Charlton to Robert Leveson, 1642.

[2] Walker's Historical Discourses. Ed. 1705. p. 126.

[3] Clarendon Hist. Bk. VII. p. 279.

[4] Warwick Memoirs. p. 228.

[5] Green's Princesses, V. p. 267.

also exiled and penniless, dependent on their swords, or on the bounty of their relatives. " The reservedness of the Prince's nature, and the little education he then had in Courts made him unapt to make acquaintance with any of the Lords, who were thereby discouraged from applying themselves to him," says Clarendon. " Whilst some officers of the Horse were well pleased to observe that strangeness, and fomented it, believing that their credit would be the greater with the Prince." [1] Maurice, of whom Clarendon confessed he had " no more esteem than good manners obliged him to," [2] came in for yet stronger censure. " This Prince had never sacrificed to the Graces, nor conversed among men of quality, but had most used the company of inferior men, with whom he loved to be very familiar. He was not qualified with parts by nature, and less with any acquired; and towards men of the best condition, with whom he might very well have justified a familiarity, he maintained—at least—the full state due to his birth." [3] Doubtless Clarendon's personal dislike of the Palatines made him a severe critic; but, in the main, his censure was true enough. Their unfortunate shyness threw them almost entirely upon their officers, and men of lesser rank, for friendship and companionship. Nor was the position unnatural; for many of these men were already well known to them as brother officers in the army of the Stadtholder, and familiar guests at their home at the Hague.

Thus condemned by Statesmen, distrusted by the old-fashioned officers, and disliked by the nobility, the Princes became the acknowledged leaders of the military faction. They soon had a devoted following; a following of which every member was a very gallant soldier, though doubtless many of them were also dissolute and reckless. Even Clarendon was forced to confess that Maurice, " living with

---

[1] Clarendon's History. Bk. V. p. 78.
[2] Clarendon's Life. Ed. 1827. Vol. I. p. 197, *note.*
[3] Clar. Hist. Bk. VII. p. 85.

the soldiers sociably and familiarly, and going with them upon all parties and actions,"[1] had made himself exceedingly popular amongst them. Rupert they adored; and the account of him handed down to Sir Edward Southcote by his father differs widely from the description of Clarendon. "My father," wrote Sir Edward, "still went with the King's army, being very ambitious to get into Prince Rupert's favour, being, he was, the greatest hero, as well as the greatest beau, whom all the leading men strove to imitate, as well in his dress as in his bravery ... The Prince was always very sparkish in his dress, and one day, on a very cold morning, he tied a very fine lace handkerchief, which he took out of his coat pocket, about his neck. This appeared so becoming that all his mimics got laced pocket-handkerchiefs and made the same use of them; which was the origin of wearing lace cravats, and continued till of late years."[2] There was in fact a general eagerness to serve directly under the hero Prince. "I must confess, I have neither desire nor affection to wait upon any other general," wrote Sir Arthur Aston.[3] "'Tis not advance of title I covet, but your commission,"[4] protested another officer. Such letters indeed are numberless; and that of Louis Dyves, half-brother to Lord Digby himself, may serve as an example of all:—"Amongst the many discourses which I receive daily of the ill-success and unhappy conduct of his Majesty's affairs here, since the light and comfort of your presence was removed from us, there is none that affects me more than to live in a place where I am rendered incapable to do you service. Which, I take God to witness, hath been the chief bent of my harte from the first hour I had the honour to serve under your command; and I shall never deem myself happy until I be restored again to the same

[1] Clar. Life. I. p. 196, *note*.
[2] Sir Edward Southcote's Narrative, p. 392.
[3] Rupert Correspondence. Aston to the Prince. Aug. 1643.
[4] Ibid. Sandford to Prince. No date.

condition. If your Highness therefore shall be pleased to command my attendance, I will break through all difficulties, and come to you. And it shall be my humble sute unto His Majesty to give me leave to go where I know I shall be best able to serve him, which can be nowhere so well as under your command. If I may but understand of your gratious acceptance of the fervent desire I have to sacrifice my life at your feet, there shall no man with more cheerfulness of harte, be ready to expose it more frankly, than your Highness's most humble, most faithful servant, Louis Dyves. There is no man can make a truer character of my harte toward you, than the bearer, Mr. Legge."[1]

In a strain of jesting familiarity, wrote the young Lord Grandison: "and, by this light, you shall be unprinced, if you believe me not the most humble of your servants."[2] And the gallant George Lisle carried his devotion to such a pitch as to sign himself always, "your Highness's most faithful affectionate servant, and obedient sonne."[3]

But this cult of the Prince indulged in by the soldiery and some of the younger nobility, rather aggravated than healed the prevailing dissensions. It was indeed impossible for a boy of Rupert's age and passionate temper to throw oil on the troubled waters. He loved and hated with equal vehemence, and "liked what was proposed as he liked the persons who proposed it."[4] Such was his detestation of Digby and Culpepper that he never could refrain from contradicting all that they said. Wilmot he treated in like manner, and we read: " Whilst Prince Rupert was present . . . all that Wilmot said or proposed was enough slighted and contradicted," but that during the Prince's long absence in the North, he, Wilmot, "became marvellously elated."[5]

<hr>

[1] Rupert Correspondence. Add. MSS. British Museum. 18981. Louis Dyves to the Prince. Apr. 8, 1644.
[2] Rupert Transcripts. Grandison to Prince. Feb. 7, 1645.
[3] Ibid. Lisle to Prince. Dec. 6-13, 1644.
[4] Clarendon. Bk. VIII. 168.
[5] Ibid. VIII. 30.

Goring the Prince loved no better, and that general complained loudly that he, "denied all his requests out of hand."[1] And Lord Percy was also distinguished with a particular hatred.

To the objects of his affection, Rupert was, on the contrary, only too compliant; a failing most strongly, and most unfortunately, exhibited in his dealings with his brother Maurice. The younger Prince had none of his brother's ability, was ignorant of English manners and customs, "showed a great aversion from considering them," and "understood very little of the war except to fight very stoutly when there was occasion."[2] Yet Rupert "took it greatly to heart"[3] that Maurice held no higher command than that of lieutenant-general to Lord Hertford. Accordingly, he persuaded the King that Maurice ought to be made general in the West, and, the promotion being conceded, Maurice did considerable harm to the cause by his blundering and want of discipline. But, says Professor Gardiner, "Maurice was Rupert's brother, and not to be called to account!"[4]

Yet, his favouritism admitted, it must be confessed that Rupert's friends were generally well-chosen. Chief among them was Colonel William Legge, a man so faithful, so unselfish, and so unassuming, that he contrived to remain on good terms with all parties. Best known to his contemporaries as "Honest Will", he shines forth, amidst the intriguing courtiers of Oxford, a bright example of disinterestedness. In spite of his intimacy with Rupert, he contrived to remain for long on friendly terms with Lord Digby, though, as he told the latter, "I often found this a hard matter to hold between you."[5] To Legge, Rupert

---

[1] Rupert Transcripts. Goring to Prince. Jan. 22, 1643.
[2] Clarendon. Bk. VII. 85, *note*.
[3] Ibid. 144.
[4] Gardiner's Civil War. Vol. I. 197.
[5] Wm. Legge to Lord Digby. Warburton. III. p. 129.

was wont to pour out the indignation of his soul in hastily
scribbled letters, and "Will" pacified both the Prince and
his enemies, as best he could, "conceiving it," he said, "a
matter of advantage to my master's service to have a good
intelligence between persons so eminently employed in his
affairs." [1] At the same time he never hesitated to express his
opinion in "plain language", and from him the fiery Prince
seems to have accepted both counsel and reproof, without
resentment. Even Clarendon could find nothing worse to say
of Will Legge than that he was somewhat diffident of his own
judgment. [2] And the King charged the Prince of Wales, in his
last message, "to be sure to take care of Honest Will Legge,
for he was the faithfullest servant that ever any Prince had."
Which charge Charles II fulfilled at the Restoration. [3]

Next to Legge among Rupert's friends we must count
the grave and melancholy Duke of Richmond. As a Stuart
he was Rupert's cousin, and him the Prince excepted from
his general dislike of the English nobility. Like Legge,
Richmond was free from all self-seeking, honourable, upright,
irreproachable, both in public and in private life. His
personal devotion to the King, who had brought him up,
was intense, and, at the end of the tragedy, he volunteered
with Southampton and Lindsey, to die in the stead of his
sovereign. Like the King, he was deeply religious, a faithful
son of the Church. He was courteous to all, gentle and
reserved, but "of a great and haughty spirit." [4] At the
beginning of the troubles he had been almost the only man
of the first rank who had unswervingly opposed the popular
party; and he valued his fidelity at the rate it was worth.
He gave his friendship slowly, and only with the approval,
asked and received, of the King. [5] But his friendship, once

---

[1] Wm. Legge to Lord Digby. Warburton. III. p. 129.
[2] Clarendon. Bk. X. p. 130.
[3] Collins Peerage: 'Dartmouth'. Vol. IV. p. 107 *et passim*.
[4] Clarendon Hist. Bk. VI. p. 384.
[5] Clarendon Life. I. p. 222.

given, was absolute and unalterable. He had in his character a Stuart strain of sensitiveness, amounting to morbidness. Thus, when gently warned by the King against too much correspondence with the treacherous Lady Carlisle, he considered his own loyalty impugned, and for weeks held aloof from the Committee of Secret Affairs. Hyde, commissioned by the distressed King to reason with the Duke, speedily discovered the true source of trouble to be Richmond's jealousy of his master's affection for Ashburnham. The King retorted by taking exception to Richmond's secretary, and it was long ere the hurt feelings of both King and Duke could be soothed. Yet, in spite of his own super-sensitiveness, Richmond was a peacemaker. His letters to Rupert, long, involved and incoherent, are full of soothing expressions and assurances that all will go well. He also was struggling, and struggling vainly, to keep the peace between Rupert and Digby. But, though he watched over his cousin's interests with affectionate care, he was too honest and simple-minded to cope successfully with Oxford intrigues.

Among Rupert's other friends was Sir Charles Lucas, who, said his sister, "loved virtue, endeavoured merit, practised justice, and spoke truth; was constantly loyal, and truly valiant." [1] Also, in high favour with the Prince was Sir Marmaduke Langdale, "a person of great courage and prudence", [2] a good scholar, and a good soldier; though Clarendon found him "a very inconvenient man to live with." [3] Less estimable was the hot-blooded Charles Gerrard, who, though as valiant a soldier as any of the others, reflected too many of Rupert's own faults; was rash, hot-tempered, and addicted to "hating on a sudden, without knowing why." [4] And besides these there were others too

---

[1] Life of Newcastle, by Duchess of Newcastle. Ed. Firth. 1886, p. 280.

[2] Carte Papers. Trevor to Ormonde, Sept. 13, 1644.

[3] Clarendon State Papers. Hyde to Nicholas. Febr. 7, 1653.

[4] Clar. Hist. Bk. IX. p. 121.

numerous to mention, valued by the Prince for their soldierly qualities, or for the frankness of their dispositions.

But in the list of Rupert's friends, there is one more
who must not be forgotten: one who was his inseparable
companion for nearly six years, who shared his captivity
in Austria, followed him to England, eat with him, slept
with him, accompanied him to Council and to Church,
shared all his dangers and hardships, and never left his
side, till he fell, with many gallant Cavaliers, on the field
of Marston Moor;—this was the Prince's white dog, Boye.
This dog attained great fame in England, and Rupert's
fondness for it was the subject of good-natured jesting
among the Cavaliers, and of bitter invective from the Puritans. A satirical pamphlet, preserved in the Bodleian library,
describes the dog's habits, and the mutual affection sub-
sisting between him and his master! From it we learn that
Boye was always present at Council, that he was wont to
sit on the table by the Prince, and that frequent kisses and
embraces passed between them. On the principle of "Love
me, love my dog," the King also extended his favour to
Boye: "For he himself never sups or dines, but continually
he feeds him. And with what think you? Even with sides
of capons, and such Christian-like morsels... It is thought
the King will make him Serjeant-Major-General Boye. But
truly the King's affection to him is so extraordinary that
some at court envy him. I heard a Gentleman-Usher swear
that it was a shame the dog should sit in the King's chair,
as he always does; and a great Lord was seriously of
opinion that it was not well he should converse so much
with the King's children, lest he taught them to swear."
Boye repaid the King's affection warmly: "Next to his
master, he loves the King and the King's children, and
cares very little for any others." We are told further, in
a paragraph evidently aimed at Rupert, that the dog, "in
exercises of religion, carries himself most popishly and
cathedrally. He is very seldom at any conscionable sermons,

but as for public prayers, he seldom or never misses
them ... But, above all, as soon as their Church Minstrel
begins his arbitrary jig, he is as attentive as one of us
private Christians are at St. Antholin's." [1] Boye is generally
supposed to have been a poodle, and certainly he is so
represented in the caricatures preserved of him. But he
must have been in truth a remarkable one, for Lady Sussex
relates in one of her letters, that when Rupert shot five
bucks, "his dog Boye pulled them down." [2] To this "divill
dog" were attributed supernatural powers of going invisible,
of foretelling events, and of magically protecting his master
from harm. "The Roundheads fancied he was the Devil,
and took it very ill that he should set himself against them!"
says Sir Edward Southcote. [3] Many of the Puritans did, in
truth, imagine him to be Rupert's evil spirit, and it was
reported that the dog fed on human flesh. Cleveland refers
to their general fear of Boye in his "Rupertismus":—

> "They fear the giblets of his train, they fear,
> "Even his dog, that four-legged Cavalier,
> "He that devours the scraps that Lunsford makes,
> "Whose pictures feeds upon a child in stakes,
> "'Gainst whom they have these articles in souse,—
> "First that he barks against the sense o' th' House,
> "Resolved 'delinquent,' to the Tower straight,
> "Either to the Lyons, or the Bishop's gate.
>
>   *   *   *   *   *   *   *   *   *
>
> "Thirdly he smells intelligence, that's better,
> "And cheaper too, than Pym's, by his own letter;
> "Lastly he is a devil without doubt,
> "For when he would lie down he wheels about,
> "Makes circles, and is couchant in a ring,
> "And therefore, score up one, for conjuring!" [4]

With the Cavaliers the dog was of course as popular as
with the Puritans he was the reverse. It was reported, by

---

[1] Pamphlet. Bodleian Library, Oxford. "Observations on Prince Rupert's
White Dog called Boye."
[2] Verney Memoirs. Vol. II. p. 160.
[3] Sir Edward Southcote's Narrative, p. 392. Pamphlet. Brit. Mus.
[4] Cleveland's Poems, p. 51. Rupertismus.

GEORGE DIGBY, EARL OF BRISTOL.

*From the Engraving by H. T. Ryall, from the Vandyke in the Collection of the
Right Honourable The Earl Spencer.*

Face page 81.

their enemies, that the Royalists, after their capture of Birmingham, passed the night in "drinking healths upon their knees,—yea, healths to Prince Rupert's dog!"[1] Finally, when poor Boye had fallen on the field of battle, the death of Prince Rupert's "witch" was recorded with exultation in the Parliamentary journals: "Here also was slain that accursed cur, which is here mentioned, by the way, because the Prince's dog has been so much spoken of, and was valued by his master more than creatures of more worth."[2]

Having said so much of Rupert's friends, it may be well to say a word of his principal enemies. Chief among these was George, Lord Digby, the eldest son of the Earl of Bristol. He was a man of great personal beauty, brilliant talents, and unrivalled powers of fascination. But he was unfortunately afflicted with a "volatile and unquiet spirit", and an over-active imagination. His natural charms and great plausibility won him the love and confidence of the King; but his unparalleled conceit and his insatiable love of meddling made him an object of detestation to the Palatine Prince.[3] As Secretary of State, Digby necessarily came into contact with Rupert, and the result was disastrous. No doubt there was much of personal jealousy mingled with Rupert's more reasonable objections to Digby; but the fact remains that Rupert understood war, and that Digby did not; that Rupert's schemes were reasonable and usually practicable, and that Digby's were wild and fantastic to a degree. Rupert resented Digby's interference and incompetence; Digby resented Rupert's off-hand manners and undisguised contempt of himself. Both were equally self-confident, and equally intolerant of rivalry. England was not large enough to contain the two, and Digby, by his superior powers of intrigue, carried the day.

---

[1] Pamphlet. Brit. Museum. London, May 1643. "Prince Rupert's Burning Love to England."

[2] More true Relation; also Vicars' Jehovah Jireh, p. 277.

[3] See Clarendon State Papers: A Character of the Lord Digby.

With Lord Percy, in whose charge were all the stores
of arms and ammunition, Rupert was not on much better
terms than with Lord Digby. Powder, bullets, carts and
horses proved fruitful sources of dissension. Rupert accused
Percy of delaying his supplies, and Percy resented Rupert's
staying of his carts.[1] In proof of his own blamelessness
Percy appealed to the testimony of others. "My Lord
Jermyn knows this was the truth, and no kind of fault in
me. .... Give me leave to tell you, sir, I cannot believe
them, your real servants, that do give you jealousies of those
that do not deserve them."[2] At other times Percy professed
a great deal of devotion to Rupert, but always with a touch
of sarcasm in his manner. His letters consequently offended
the Prince, and Percy treated his indignation lightly: " Though
you seemed not to be pleased that I should hope for the
taking of Bristol before it was done, which fault I confess
I do not understand, I hope you will give me leave to
congratulate you now with the rest.... Your best friends
do wish that, when the power is put absolutely into your
hands, you will so far comply with the King's affairs as
to do that which may content many and displease fewest."[3]
Such phrases were not calculated to soothe, and the breach
widened steadily until, in the autumn of 1644, Percy found
himself so deeply involved in the disgrace of Wilmot that
he sought refuge with the Queen in France.

With Lord Goring and Lord Wilmot, Rupert was likewise
at daggers drawn. Both these men had been his comrades
in the Dutch army, and Goring especially had been on
intimate terms with the Palatines at the Hague. Indeed
it seems likely that he had carried on a very flourishing
flirtation with the Princess Louise; and a beautifully drawn
picture letter which she addressed to him, is still extant.
Distinguished, like Digby, for his personal beauty and

---

[1] Rupert Transcripts, July 30, 1643, also Aug. 17, 1643, Percy to Rupert.
[2] Ibid. Mar. 21, 1642.
[3] Rupert Transcripts, July 29, 1643.

fascinating manners, Goring was also justly celebrated for his brilliant courage. Yet it was no wonder that Rupert did not share his sister's friendship for him, since the man was as false and treacherous as he was brave and plausible. He had promoted and betrayed the Army Plot of 1641; he had received the charge of Portsmouth from the Parliament, held it for the King, and then surrendered it without a struggle. Yet no breath of suspicion ever sullied his courage, and his personal attractions and undoubted ability won him trust and confidence again and again. Rupert admired him for his talents, hated him for his vices, and feared him for his "master-wit", which made him a dangerous rival for the King's favour. Goring, on his part, heartily reciprocated the Prince's aversion; kept out of his command as far as possible, disobeyed his orders as often as he could, and amused himself by writing to his enemy in terms of passionate devotion. "I will hasard eight thousand lives rather than leave anything undone that may conduce to his Majesty's service or to your Highness's satisfaction; being joyed of nothing so much in this world as of the assurance of your favour, and that it will not be in the power of the devil to lessen your goodness to me, or to alter the quality I have of being your Highness's most humble, faithful, and obedient servant." [1]

Wilmot, Lieutenant-General of the Horse, was a less fascinating but a less unprincipled person than Goring. That is to say that, while Goring would betray any friend, or violate any promise, "out of humour or for wit's sake," Wilmot would not do either, except "for some great benefit or convenience to himself." [2] He is described by Clarendon as "a man of a haughty and ambitious nature, of a pleasant wit, and an ill understanding." [3] Like Goring, he drank hard,

---

[1] Rupert Correspondence. Goring to the Prince, May 12, 1645. Add. MSS. Brit. Mus. 18982.

[2] Clarendon Hist. Bk. VIII. 169.

[3] Ibid. VIII. 30.

but not, like Goring, to the neglect of his military duties. With the dissolute wits of the army he was exceedingly popular, but Rupert, always so temperate himself, had no sympathy with the failings of Wilmot. As early as November 1642 he had conceived "an irreconcilable prejudice" [1] against his lieutenant-general. Possibly the seed of this prejudice had been sown at Edgehill, where Wilmot refused to make a second charge, saying: "We have won the day; let us live to enjoy the fruits thereof." [2] And justly or unjustly, the combined hatred of Rupert, Digby, and Goring accomplished Wilmot's overthrow in 1644.

[1] Clar. Hist. Bk. VI. 126, *note.*
[2] Ibid. VI. p. 79, *note.*

CHAPTER VI

THE BEGINNING OF THE WAR. POWICK BRIDGE. EDGEHILL. THE MARCH TO LONDON

THE setting up of the Royal Standard was a depressing ceremony. The weather was so bad that the very elements seemed to fight against the Royalists; and the standard was blown down the same night, which was regarded as a very evil portent. Moreover, the Royal forces were still so lamentably small that Sir Jacob Astley openly expressed a fear that the King would be captured in his sleep.[1] The arms and ammunition were not yet come from York, and a general sadness pervaded the whole company. In this state of affairs, the King made another futile attempt at treating with the Parliament; an attempt so distasteful to Rupert and his officers "that they were not without some thought—or at least discourses—of offering violence to the principal advisers of it."[2] The abortive treaty proved, however, to the King's advantage, for its failure turned the tide in his favour, and brought recruits to his banner.

During the delay at Nottingham, Rupert was created a Knight of the Garter, and, at the same time, he contrived to fall out with Digby. Even as early as September 10th, we find Digby protesting against the Prince's prejudice towards himself. Evidently he had indulged in remarks upon Rupert's love of "inferior" company, which he now endeavoured to explain away.[3] His apology was accepted; and for a short time he served under the Prince.

[1] Clar. Hist. Bk. VI. p. 1.
[2] Ibid. VI. 21.
[3] Rupert Transcripts. Digby to Prince, Sept. 10, 1642.

Already Rupert was scouring the country in search of men, arms and money. On September 6th "that diabolical Cavalier," [1] as a Puritan soldier called him, had surrounded Leicester and summoned the Mayor to confer with him. That worthy cautiously declined the interview, whereupon he received a peremptory letter, demanding £2,000 to be paid on the morrow "by ten of the clock in the forenoon." He was assured that the King's promise would prove a better pledge for repayment than the "Public Faith" of the Parliament; and the letter concluded with the characteristic assurance that, in case of contumacy, the Prince would appear on the morrow, "in such a posture as shall make you to know it is wiser to obey than to resist His Majesty's command." [2] Five hundred pounds were forthwith paid, but a complaint was despatched to the King, who hastened to disavow his nephew's arbitrary proceedings.

An attack on Caldecot House proved more to the Prince's credit. This house belonged to a Warwickshire Puritan, a Mr Purefoy, then absent with the troops of the Parliament. Early on a Sunday morning Rupert appeared before the house, with five hundred men, and summoned it to surrender. The summons was defied, and he ordered an assault. The defenders consisted only of Mrs. Purefoy, her two daughters, her son-in-law, Mr. Abbot, three serving-men, and three maids; yet the fight was continued for some hours, and with serious loss to the Cavaliers. At last Rupert forced the outer gates, fired the barns, and advanced to the very doors. Then Mrs. Purefoy came out and threw herself at the victor's feet. Rupert asked her what she would have of him. She answered, the lives of her little garrison. Rupert then raised her to her feet, "saluted her kindly," and promised that not one of them should be hurt. But when he had entered the house and discovered how small was the garrison, his pity was changed to admiration. He com-

[1] Dom. State Papers. Wharton to Willingham, 13 Sept. 1642.
[2] Rupert to Mayor of Leicester. Warburton, I. p. 393.

plimented Mr. Abbot on his skill and gallantry, and offered him a command in his own troop, which was, however, refused. Finally he drew off his forces, promising that nothing upon the place should suffer injury. "And the Prince faithfully kept his promise, and would not suffer one pennyworth of goods in the house to be taken."[1] Such is the testimony of a fanatical enemy; nor is it the only instance of Rupert's chivalry. "Sir Edward Terrell was a little fearful, Prince Rupert had been hunting at his Park," wrote the Puritan Lady Sussex; *"but he took him much, with his courtesy to him."*[2]

On September 13th the King left Nottingham for Derby, and Rupert joined his march at Stafford. There it was that the Prince fired a remarkable shot, to prove his skill as a marksman. Standing in a garden about sixty yards distant from the church of St. Mary, he shot clean through the tail of the weathercock on the steeple, "with a screwed horseman's pistol, and a single bullet."[3] The King declared that the shot was but a lucky chance; whereupon Rupert fired a second time, with the same result.

From Stafford, Rupert proceeded by night to Bridgnorth, and from there he went, on September 21st, to secure Worcester. Finding Worcester quite indefensible, he resolved to go on to Shrewsbury, but, in the meantime, he led his small troop into a field near Powick Bridge to rest. The officers, among whom were Maurice, Digby, Wilmot, Charles Lucas, and the Lords Northampton and Crawford, threw themselves down on the grass, divested of all armour. In this position they were surprised by a troop of Essex's horse, under Sandys and Fiennes, which advanced, fully armed, down a narrow lane. In the confusion there was scarcely time to catch the horses, and none to consult as to methods of defence. Rupert shouted out the order to

---

[1] Vicars' God in the Mount, pp. 155—157.
[2] Verney Memoirs, Vol. II. p. 160.
[3] Plot's Hist. of Staffordshire, Ch. 9, p. 336. Hudibras, ed. 1810. I. p. 156, *note*.

charge, and vaulted on to his horse. Maurice threw him·
self next his brother; and the other officers, seeing that
it would be useless to rejoin their men, followed the
Princes. Thus, with the officers in the van and the men
straggling behind as best they could, the Royalists
charged. The Puritans, well-armed and well-commanded
though they were, could not stand against that sudden fierce
assault. Two of their officers fell, and in a very few
moments the whole body, nearly a thousand in number,
broke and fled, the "goodness of their horses" making it
impossible to overtake them. The number of the slain
was between forty and fifty; six or seven colours were
captured, and a few Scottish officers taken prisoners. The
loss on the King's side was small, and though all the
officers, Rupert excepted, were wounded, none were killed.
Maurice had received so dangerous a wound in the head
that he was reported killed, but it was not long before
he was again "abroad and merry." [1] The slight loss suffered
by the Cavaliers was the more remarkable since they had
had neither armour nor pistols, and had fought only with
their swords. [2]

The moral advantage of this skirmish was very great.
It gave increased courage to Rupert's troops and it "ex·
ceedingly appalled the adversary," to whom the Prince's
name was henceforth "very terrible." To the Elector, and
to some of the friends of his family, such a reputation
was less gratifying than it was to Rupert himself. Depen·
dent upon the English Parliament as the Palatines were,—
for King Charles could no longer help them, and the
Stadtholder was old and failing,—Rupert's zeal in his uncle's
cause was a serious disadvantage to them. "I fear," wrote
Roe to the Elector, "the freshness of his spirit and his
zeal to his uncle may have drawn from him some words,
if not deeds, that have begot a very ill odour; insomuch

[1] Warburton, I. p. 409. Falkland, 28 Sept. 1642.
[2] Clarendon. Hist. Bk. VI. 44—46. Dom. S. P. 13 Sept. 1642.

that nothing is so much cried out against as his actions, which do reflect upon your whole family and cause, and there may be more need of a bridle to moderate him than of spurs. They will never forgive me the ill-fortune to have procured his liberty." [1] To this the Elector replied indignantly: "It is impossible either for the Queen—my mother, or myself to bridle my brother's youth and fieryness, at so great a distance, and in the employment he has. It were a great indiscretion in any to expect it, and an injustice to blame us for things beyond our help." [2] He did his best to appease the Parliament by exhibiting his own ingratitude towards his uncle. "The Prince Elector doth write kindly—others might say basely—to the Roundhead Parliament," [3] reported Sir George Radcliffe. Further, Charles Louis published a manifesto in the names of himself and his mother, deprecating Rupert's actions, and disclaiming all sympathy with them. And in 1644 he came himself to London, and took the Covenant; in reward for which hypocrisy the Parliament lodged him in Whitehall, and granted him a large pension. [4] Elizabeth was less time-serving, and her intercepted letters to Rupert gave great offence to the Parliament. She tried to pacify the indignation she had roused, writing to the Speaker: "Albeit I cannot at present remember what I then particularly writ, yet if anything did perchance slip from my pen in the private relation between a mother and son, which might give them the least distaste, I entreat them to make no worse construction of it than was by me intended." [5] But she could not disguise her real sentiments, and her pension was stopped by the Parliament. "Our gracious Mistress hath her part, as who hath not, in these public sufferings,"

[1] Webb, Civil War in Herefordshire. Vol. I. p. 131. 20 Sept. 1642.
[2] Dom. State Papers. Carl I. Vol. 492. fol. 31. 6 Oct. 1642.
[3] Carte, Original Letters. Vol. I. p. 47. 8 Mar. 1643.
[4] Whitelocke. p. 101.
[5] Green. VI. 11.

wrote one of her gentlemen in 1643. "It is upon a full year that her entertainments have been stopped, and I believe that she fareth the worse for the impetuousness of Prince Rupert her son, who is quite out of her government." [1]

Directly after the skirmish of Powick Bridge, Rupert fell back upon Ludlow, and it was while quartered there that he was supposed to have made his first expedition into Essex's camp. The stories of his disguises are told by Puritans, and are, as before said, very probably apocryphal; but they are given here for what they are worth. The Puritan army was encamped on Dunsmore Heath, and Rupert, riding as near to it as he dared, overtook a man driving a horse which was laden with apples. The man, on being interrogated, informed the Prince that he was going to sell the apples to the soldiers of the Parliament. "Why dost thou not go to the King's army?" asked the Prince; "I hear they are generous sparks and will pay double!" "Oh," said the man, "they are Cavaliers, and have a mad Prince amongst them. Devil a penny could I get in the whole army." Rupert thereupon purchased the whole load for ten shillings, changed coats and horses with the man, and himself sold the apples to the forces of Essex. On his return, he gave the man a second piece of gold, with the command to "go to the army, and ask the commanders how they liked the fruit which Prince Rupert did, in his own person, but this morning sell them." [2]

During this time the King had lain at Shrewsbury, whither he now summoned all his forces, and on October 12th he began his march towards London. This was in accordance with Rupert's scheme of concentrating all forces on the centre of disaffection. The three brigades of foot were commanded respectively by Sir Nicholas Byron, Colonel Wentworth, and Colonel Fielding. Lord Lindsey was Commander-

[1] Warburton. II. p. 196.
[2] Pamphlet. Brit. Museum. Prince Rupert: his Disguises.

in-Chief, and Sir Jacob Astley was his Major-General; Ruthven, though a Field-Marshal, preferred to remain entirely with the cavalry. The dragoons were under Sir Arthur Aston, and most of the nobles and richer gentry enlisted in Lord Bernard Stuart's regiment of gentlemen, nicknamed "The Show Troop." "Never," says Clarendon, "did less baggage attend a royal army, there being not one tent, and very few waggons, in the whole train."[1] This being the case, it is singular that the place where the King's tent was pitched is still pointed out at Edgehill.

The Royalists advanced slowly, by way of Birmingham, halting at several places on the march. On October 22nd the King reached Edgecot, and Essex arrived the same day at Kineton, ready to bar his way. Rupert advanced to Lord Spencer's house at Wormleighton, where his quarter-master had a skirmish with the quarter-master of Essex, who had also been sent to take possession of the house. Rupert's men captured twelve of Essex's soldiers, from whom they learnt the unexpected proximity of the enemy. Rupert thereupon made his men take the field, and sent the intelligence to the King. The King responded in a brief note: "I have given order as you have desyred; so I dout not but all the foot and cannon will bee at Edgehill betymes this morning, where you will also find your loving Oncle."[2]

Early in the morning of October 23rd, Rupert advanced his forces to the summit of Edgehill, where, as he had expected, he was joined by the King. A council of war was then held. But, alas, dissension was already beginning in the army, the mutual jealousy of the officers having grown on the march to "a perfect faction"[3] between the foot and horse. On this occasion Rupert's bold and rapid tactics were strenuously opposed by the cautious old Lindsey. But the King strongly supported his nephew, and thereupon

---

[1] Clarendon. Bk. VI. 75.
[2] King to Rupert. Warburton. II. p. 12.
[3] Clarendon. Bk. VI. p. 78.

Lindsey resigned his generalship, preferring to fight as a mere colonel rather than to nominally command a battle over which he had no control. Then his son, Lord Willoughby,—deeply resenting the slight on his father,—refused to charge with Rupert, and elected to fight on foot at his father's side. Ruthven (afterwards Lord Brentford) was hastily appointed in Lindsey's place, and as he had fought under Gustavus, he readily gave his support to the Prince who followed the great Swede's tactics.

It was one o'clock before the King's foot could be brought up to the rest of the army; and though Essex was in order by eight in the morning, he was in no hurry to begin the battle. His numbers were already greater than those of the King, but he hoped still that three more regiments might join him. Not till three o'clock did the fight begin, and this was considered so late that some of the Royalists would have willingly postponed it till the morrow. But it was to the King's advantage to hasten the attack, since he had no provisions for his army, and he hoped also to anticipate the arrival of Essex's reinforcements. The history of the battle is an oft-told tale. Rupert commanded the right wing, and he committed a serious error at the outset by permitting the "Show Troop" to charge in the van. This troop had been irritated by the scoffs of blunter soldiers, and it seemed but courtesy to accede to its request, yet it was most unwise to do so, for it left the King unguarded on the field. "Just before we began our march," says Bulstrode, "the Prince passed from one wing to the other, giving positive orders to the horse to march as close as possible, keeping their ranks, sword in hand; to receive the enemy's shot without firing either carbine or pistol till we broke in among them, and then to make use of our firearms as need should require." [1] The charge thus made, swept Essex's horse from the field, and Rupert's

[1] Bulstrode's Memoirs. Ed. 1721. p. 81.

horse followed far in the pursuit. "Our horse pursued so eagerly that the commanders could not stop them in the chase," said the Royalists. [1] The King's foot, left unsupported on the field, suffered great damage. Then it was that Lord Lindsey fell, and his gallant son was captured in the attempt to save his father. Then Sir Edmund Verney died, and the standard was taken, but subsequently regained. Only the enemy's own want of skill and experience saved the King himself from capture. Thus the advantage won by the first charge was lost, and when Rupert returned he found the King with a very small retinue, and all chance of a complete victory gone. Nor could the cavalry be rallied for a second charge. Where the soldiers were collected together the officers were absent, and where the officers were ready the soldiers were scattered. Consequently the result of the battle was indecisive, and both sides claimed the victory; the advantage really lay with the King, insomuch as he held the field, and had opened the way to London. But the Royalist losses had been very great. Besides Lindsey and Verney, had fallen Lord Aubigny, brother of the Duke of Richmond, and many other officers. Moreover, the Cavaliers were in a hostile country, unable to obtain either food or shelter, and the night was terribly cold. Towards daybreak the King retired to his coach to rest; and the morning found the two armies still facing one another. Thus they remained throughout the day, but towards evening Essex drew off to Warwick. No sooner did Essex begin his retreat than Rupert started in pursuit. At Kineton he captured the rear guard of dragoons, with their convoy of money, plate and letters. The taking of the letters proved of no slight importance, for among them Rupert discovered a circumstantial report of his own proceedings, furnished to Essex by his own secretary. There was found also the secretary's demand for an increase

---

[1] Carte's Original Letters, Vol. I. p. 10.

of pay from the Parliament, which already paid him
£50 a week. The man was of course tried, and hanged
at Oxford.[1]

Rupert was now anxious to push on to London before
the enemy could rally. "He proffered, if His Majesty
would give him leave, to march with three thousand
horse to Westminster, and there dissolve the Parliament."[2]
Very likely this plan might have succeeded, for the panic
in London was great, but the old Earl of Bristol declared
that Rupert, once let loose on London, would plunder
and burn the city. This fear so worked on the King that
he refused to countenance the design. It is only fair to add
that Rupert indignantly repudiated the intentions attributed
to him. "I think there is none that take me for a coward,—
for sure I fear not the face of any man alive,—yet I shall
repute it the greatest victory in the world to see His Majesty
enter London in peace without shedding one drop of blood."[3]
The tales spread abroad of his "barbarousness and inhumanity" caused him real annoyance, and he endeavoured
to refute them in a published "Declaration." After retorting
on the Parliament various instances of Puritan plundering
and violence, he continued: "I must here profess, that I
take that man to be no soldier or gentleman that will
strike, much less kill, a woman or a child... And for
myself, I appeal to the consciences of those lords and
gentlemen who are my daily witnesses, and to those people
wheresoever our army hath been, what they know, or
have observed in my carriage which might not become
the son of a king."[4] Doubtless the boast was made in
all good faith, but doubtless also the views of Rupert and
his enemies as to what was "becoming" differed widely,
especially in regard to plunder. True the Puritans not

[1] Warburton, II. pp. 4, 47.
[2] Ibid. I. p. 465.
[3] Prince Rupert: his Declaration. Pamphlet. British Museum.
[4] Prince Rupert: his Declaration. Pamphlet. Brit. Mus. Warburton, II. 124.

infrequently plundered Royalists, just as the Royalists plundered Puritans; but the Parliament had the less need to do it, seeing that all the King's revenue was in its hands. The hapless King could not, in consequence, pay his cavalry, and it was Rupert's task to raise supplies from the country. He was authorised to requisition daily provisions from the inhabitants of the places where the horse were quartered. For all such supplies a proper receipt was to be given, and the officers were not permitted, "upon pain of our high displeasure," to send for greater quantities of provision than would actually supply the men and horses. [1] To Rupert, used as he was to continental warfare, such a state of affairs seemed natural enough. "Was I engaged to prohibit them making the best of their prisoners?" he retorted in answer to a later charge made against his men. [2] And, among the State Papers, there is to be found an engagement of a certain John van Haesdonck to bring over to Rupert, two hundred expert soldiers from Holland who were to be permitted to divide their booty, "according to the usual custom beyond seas." [3]

But if Rupert understood "the law of arms" as the peaceful English citizens did not, both he and his officers respected its limits, and fain would have checked the excesses of their men. Whitelocke, while lamenting the wreck of his own house, honourably acquitted the officers in command of any share in it. "Sir John Byron and his brothers commanded those horse, and gave orders that they should commit no insolence at my house, nor plunder my goods." But, in spite of the prohibition, hay and corn were recklessly consumed, horses were carried off, books wantonly destroyed, the park railings broken down, and the deer let out. "Only a tame young stag they led away and presented to Prince Rupert, and my hounds, which were

---

[1] Rupert Papers. Order of King. Warb. II. 71.
[2] Prince Rupert: his Reply.
[3] Dom. State Papers, 27 Nov. 1642.

extraordinary good." [1] What Rupert did with the tame young stag history relates not, but he certainly did not countenance such outrages. They were of course attributed to his influence, but he could, and did, retort similar instances—and worse—upon the soldiers of the Parliament: "I speak not how wilfully barbarous their soldiers were to the Countess Rivers, to the Lady Lucas in Essex, and likewise to many persons of quality in Kent, and other places." [2]

Owing to the fear of Rupert's "downright soldierism" such advantage as might have been gained from Edgehill was lost. Instead of pressing on for London, the King wasted valuable time in the siege of Banbury. It is to this period that the story of Rupert's visit to Warwick belongs. To this town Essex had retreated after the battle, and about it his army was still quartered. "Within about eight miles of the said city, Prince Robert was forced by excess of raine to take into a little alehouse out of the way, where he met with a fellow that was riding to Warwick to sell cabbage nets, but stayed, by chance, to drink. He bought the fellow's nets, gave him double what he asked, borrowed his coat, and told him he would ride upon his horse some miles off, to put a trick upon some friends of his, and return at evening. He left his own nag and coat behind, and also a crown for them to drink, while waiting his return. When he came to Warwick he sold his nets at divers places, heard the news, and discovered many passages in the town. Having done this he returned again, and took his own horse. Then he sent them (*i. e.* the citizens of Warwick) word, by him he bought the nets of, that Prince Rupert had sold them cabbage nets, and it should not be long ere he would require their kindness and send them cabbages." [3]

[1] Whitelocke's Memorials. p. 65. Ed. 1732.
[2] Pamphlet. Brit. Mus. Warb. II. p. 121.
[3] Prince Rupert: his Disguises. Pamphlet. British Museum.

On October 27th Banbury fell, and two days later the King entered Oxford, where he was enthusiastically received. Rupert advanced to Abingdon, overran the country, took Aylesbury, cut off Essex's communications with London, and seized arms and forage for the King. Essex sent Balfour to intercept the Prince; Rupert and Sir Louis Dyves met him with a valiant charge across a swollen ford, but they were forced back, and proceeded through Maidenhead to Windsor, "with the most bloody and mischievous of all the Cavaliers."[1] The taking of Windsor Castle would have enabled Rupert to stop the barges on the Thames, and cut off the London traffic to the West. But his summons to surrender was refused, and his assault repulsed. His men declared that they would follow him anywhere against *men*, but not against stone walls; and though he cheered them on to a second attack, that also failed. Considering Windsor hopeless, he fell back to Kingston, intending to erect there a fort to command the river. But the trained bands of Berkshire and Surrey were ready to receive him. "About two of the clock," says Whitelocke, "on the seventh of November, the Cavaliers came on with undaunted courage, their forces in the form of a crescent. Prince Rupert, to the right wing, came on with great fury. In they went pell-mell into the heart of our soldiers, but they were surrounded and with great difficulty cut their way through, and made their way across to Maidenhead, where they held their quarters."[2]

From his quarters at Maidenhead Rupert seized on Colebrook; an exploit reported in London under the exciting title, "Horrible news from Colebrook." In the same pamphlets the already terrified citizens were cheered by the news: "The Prince hath deeply vowed that he will come to London; swearing he cares not a pin for all the Roundheads or their infant works; and saying that he will

---

[1] Pamphlet. British Museum. Warb. II. p. 50.
[2] Warburton, II. pp. 50—51. Whitelocke's Memorials.

lay their city and inhabitants on the ground." [1] On November 4th, the King reached Reading with the bulk of his army, and the Parliament, thoroughly frightened, requested a safe-conduct, in order to treat. The King's objection to one of their emissaries led to some delay, but danger pressed; the Parliament yielded and sent its representatives. At the same time it ordered Essex, who had also reached London, to take the field. The King on his part advanced to Colebrook before he sent his answer;—which was a proposal that Windsor should be given up to him as a place for treaty, and avoided all mention of a cessation of arms. On the same night, November 11th, he ordered Rupert to clear the way by an attack on Brentford. At the same time he wrote to the Houses that he intended to be in London next evening to hear what they had to say. The Prince received the King's orders at Egham. There he had captured two London merchants, and he judged it wise to detain them, lest they should be spies. When they had recovered their liberty next day, they gave the following account of their adventures. They had been taken to the Prince, who was "in bed with all his clothes on," from which it was inferred that he had vowed never to undress "or shift himself until he had reseated King Charles at Whitehall." The Prince examined the prisoners himself, and, attracted by a bunch of ribbons in the hat of one of them, "he took the pains to look them over himself, and turned and tossed them up and down, and swore there was none of the King's favours there. The gentleman replying that they were the favours of his mistress, the Prince smiling, without any word at all, returned him his favours and his hat again." On the next morning they saw the King and Prince together on Hounslow Heath. "Prince Rupert took off his scarlet coat, which was very rich, and gave it to his man; and he buckled

---

[1] Horrible News from Colebrook. London, Nov. 11, 1642. Pamphlet. Brit. Museum.

on his arms and put a grey coat over it that he might not be discovered. He talked long with the King, and often in his communications with His Majesty, he scratched his head and tore his hair, as if in some grave discontent."[1]

The discontent was soon allayed by a successful dash upon Brentford. The town was taken, though not without hard fighting, and there was captured also a good supply of guns and ammunition. The question as to whether this advance, pending negotiation, was or was not a breach of faith on the King's part has been much debated. No cessation of arms had been agreed on, but the Parliament, thinking it a mere oversight, had sent again in order to arrange it. At the same time Essex was warned to hold all his forces ready for battle, but to abstain from acts of hostility. Essex having advanced towards him, the King would have been completely surrounded, had he not seized upon Brentford. Therefore, from the military point of view, the advance was altogether justifiable; from the political, it was unwise, for it lost Charles the hearts of the Londoners. "Charles's error," says Professor Gardiner, "lay in forgetting that he was more than a victorious General."[2]

The King's triumph was short-lived. The citizens and the Parliamentary troops rallied to the defence of the capital. An army, twice as large as that of Charles, barred his way on Turnham Green. Essex advancing on Brentford, forced Rupert to retire. This he did in excellent order, entrusting the conduct of the retreat to Sir Jacob Astley. The Prince himself stood his horse in the river beside the bridge that he might watch his men pass over. And there he remained for hours, exposed to a heavy fire, and all the while "cheering and encouraging the retiring ranks to keep order, and to fire steadily on the advancing foe."[3] His troops passed that night drawn up on Hounslow Heath;

[1] Relation of Two London Merchants. Pamphlet. British Museum.
[2] Gardiner's Civil War, Vol. I. p. 60.
[3] Rupert MSS. Warburton, II. p. 67.

thence Rupert conducted them to Abingdon, himself returning, November 22nd, to the King at Reading.

At Reading they were detained some days by the illness
of the Prince of Wales, but on Tuesday, the 29th, the King
took up his winter quarters in Oxford. Rupert continued to
hover about Essex's army, and ordered Wilmot to take
Marlborough. This duty Wilmot accomplished, but with
evident reluctance. " Give me leave to tell your Highness
that I think myself very unhappy to be employed upon
this occasion," he wrote, "being a witness that at other
times, in the like occasions, troops are sent out without any
manner of forecast or design, or care to preserve or quarter
them when they are abroad." [1] It is not remarkable that
Rupert did not love an officer who addressed him in such
a strain. Sir John Byron also wrote with ill-concealed impatience to demand his instant removal from Reading, where,
he said, the want of accommodation was ruining his regiment. And Daniel O'Neil sent pathetic accounts of his
struggles with the Prince's own troop, in the absence of
their leader. "They say you have given them a power to
take what they want, where they can find it. This is so
extravagant that I am confident you never gave them any
such. That the rest of the troop (not only of your own
regiment, but that of the Lieutenant-General) may be
satisfied, declare in what condition you will have your
company, and how commanded. And let me, I beseech
you, have in writing the orders I shall give to that party
you sent into Buckinghamshire." [2] Already numberless such
complaints were pouring in. Even then the Royalists, as
Byron said, "abounded in nothing but the want of all
things necessary;" and Rupert was well-nigh distracted by
his efforts to supply their needs, quash their mutinies, and
soothe their discontents. So closed the year 1642.

[1] Rupert Transcripts. Wilmot to the Prince, Dec. 1st, 1642.
[2] Warburton, II. p. 82. Rupert Correspondence. O'Neil to the Prince,
Dec. 19, 1642.

CHAPTER VII

THE WAR IN 1643. THE QUARREL WITH HERTFORD. THE ARRIVAL OF THE QUEEN

FROM Christmas Eve, 1642, till January 6th, 1643, Rupert remained quietly at Oxford. His attempt to concentrate his forces on London had failed, and he was now resolved on a new strategy. The King was to hold Essex in check from Oxford; Lord Newcastle, who had raised an army in the north, was to push through the midlands towards Essex; and Hopton, marching from Cornwall to Kent, was to seize on the banks of the Thames below London and so stop the city trade. Thus the enemy would be completely surrounded and overwhelmed. For his own part, Rupert had resolved on the capture of Cirencester. With this end he started from Oxford, January 6th. His march, which continued all day and all night, seems to have been lighted by meteors. "This night we saw the strange fire falling from Heaven, like a bolt, which, with several cracks, brake into balls and went out, about steeple height from the ground." [1] Early on the morning of the 7th, they faced Cirencester, but, owing to the late arrival of Lord Hertford, who was to act with Rupert, the attack failed. Rupert therefore retreated, and occupied himself in circling round Oxford until the end of the month. On February 2nd, he renewed the attempt on Cirencester. A successful feint towards Sudely drew off the attention of the town and enabled him to enter it with comparative ease. But the garrison of Cirencester kept up a brave resistance for an hour after the Royalists were in possession of the place, which unhappily resulted

[1] Clar. State Papers. f. 2254. Prince Rupert's Journal in England. Jan. 6, 1643.

in much bloodshed. Moreover, the town was sacked by "the undistinguishing soldiers,"[1] and over a thousand prisoners were carried off to Oxford. The actual facts were bad enough, for Rupert's men were not yet disciplined and had broken loose, but the report of the Parliament was embellished with the usual exaggerations. "The enemy entered the town and, being much enraged with their losses, put all to the sword they met with; men, women and children; and in a barbarous manner murdered three ministers, very godly and religious men."[2]

This success cooled the King's desire for agreement with the Parliament, which had just sent Commissioners to Oxford to treat. "The welcome news of your Highness taking of Cirencester by assault, with admirable dexterity and courage, came this morning very seasonably and opportunely, as His Majesty was ready to give an answer to the Parliamentary Committee, and will, I believe, work better effects with them and with those that sent them than the gracious reception they had here from His Majesty,"[3] wrote the Secretary Nicholas to the Prince. After reconnoitring Warwick and Gloucester, Rupert returned to Oxford, where he composed the elaborate defence of his conduct already quoted, entitled "Prince Rupert, his Declaration."

By February 22nd he had resumed his wanderings. Only a study of his journal can give any idea of his restless activity, and therefore a few entries from March 1643, are here quoted.

March   4. Satterday, to Cirencester.

,,   5. To Malmesbury in Wiltshire.

,,   6. Mundaye, to Chipping Sodburye in Glostershire.

,,   7. Tuesday night, on Durdan Down by Bristol.

---

[1] Clarendon. Hist. Bk. VI. 238.

[2] Pamphlet. British Museum. Relation of the taking of Cirencester, Feb. 1642—3.

[3] Rupert Correspondence. Nicholas to the Prince, Feb. 3, 1643.

March   8. Wednesday morning, advancing towards Bristol,
              we heard how Mr. Bourcher and Mr. Yeoman's
              plot was discovered, and we instantly faced
              about to Chipping Sodbury.
   „   9. Thursday, to Malmesbury.
   ,.   10. Friday, home to Oxford.
   „   18. Satterday, to Abingdon.
   „   19. Sunday, to Tetsworth.
   „   20. Monday, to Denton in Buckinghamshire.
   „   21. Tuesday, the little Skirmish before Aylesbury.
              That night to Oxford. [1]

The entry of March 8th alludes to a Royalist plot by
which it had been intended to surrender Bristol to Rupert.
But the plot was betrayed, and the two merchants who
had been the prime movers of it were executed.

Meanwhile the King's party was prospering in the North.
Some time previously the Queen had despatched Goring
to the aid of the Earl of Newcastle in Yorkshire; and in
March she landed there herself, bringing supplies and reinforcements. In Lancashire and Cheshire Lord Derby
was struggling valiantly, but he felt himself out-numbered,
and earnestly implored Rupert to come to his assistance.
The Countess of Derby, Charlotte de La Tremouille, who
had been brought up at the Hague in intimate relations
with the Palatines, added her entreaties to those of her
husband: "Je ne sais ce que je dis, mais ayez pitié de
mon mari, mes enfans, et moi." [2]   Moved by this urgent
appeal, Rupert resolved to go northward, and Digby volunteered to accompany him.

In the beginning of April they set forth, with twelve
hundred horse and about six hundred foot. Marching through
Stratford-on-Avon, they came to Birmingham, a place famous
for its active disloyalty; it had seized upon Royal plate,
intercepted Royal messengers, and now boldly refused to

[1] Clar. State Papers. Rupert's Journal.
[2] Rupert Transcripts, April 1, 1643, also Warburton, II. p. 149.

admit Rupert within its walls. The Prince resolved on an assault, and, on Easter Monday, he took and entered the town. The conduct of the Cavaliers here was as much debated as it had been at Cirencester. "The Cavaliers rode through the streets like so many furies or bedlams; Lord Denbigh in the front, singing as he rode," says the Puritan account. "They shot at every door and window where they could espy any looking out. They hacked, hewed, or pistolled all they met with; blaspheming, cursing, and damning themselves most hideously ... Nor did their rage cease here; but when, on the next day, they were to march forth out of the town, they used every possible diligence to set fire in all the streets, and, lest any should save any of the goods they had left, they stood with drawn swords about all the houses, endeavouring to kill anyone that appeared to quench the flames."[1] The Royalist version was very different. After relating the excessive provocation suffered by the soldiers, it admits that, in order to force his entrance, the Prince did fire some houses, but that as soon as the entrance was effected, he ordered the fire to be extinguished. And on the next day, when he was about to leave the town, "fearing the exasperation of his men, he gave express orders that none should attempt to fire the town; and, after his departure, hearing that some soldiers had fired it in divers places, he sent immediately to let the inhabitants know that it was not done by his command, and he desired it might be quenched."[2] This last account, being found in a private letter, is probably more worthy of credit than the Puritan pamphlet written to excite the populace.

On April 8th, Rupert summoned Lichfield to surrender, but that town, well garrisoned and well commanded, answered him with defiance. Rupert perceived that the siege would

---

[1] Pamphlet. British Museum. Prince Rupert's Burning Love to England discovered in Birmingham's flames.
[2] Letter from Walsall to Oxford. Warb. II. p. 154, *note*.

be a matter of some time, and he acted with great prudence.   Withdrawing his cavalry from its perilous position
before the town, he managed to obtain fifty miners from
the neighbouring collieries.   Then he asked his men and
officers to volunteer, as foot-soldiers, to the aid of the miners;
with which request they " cheerfully and gallantly " complied.
On this occasion George Digby especially distinguished
himself, working in the trenches " up to his waist in mud "
until he was disabled by a shot in the thigh.   But this
was the last time that he served under Rupert, for
very soon afterwards he quarrelled with the Prince, threw
up his commission in a rage, and fought thenceforth as a
volunteer. [1]

In ten days the moat was dry, two bridges made, and
the miners engaged on the walls.   Harassed by continual
appeals for his presence elsewhere, Rupert made an effort
to hasten matters by storming the town.   But the attempt
failed, and the garrison hanged one of their prisoners over
the wall, bidding the Prince in derision, to shoot him down.
Rupert thereupon swore deeply that not one man should
have quarter, but on the following day he repented of his
resolve, and sent to offer it.   His overtures were rejected;
and he resumed his operations.   That same evening his
mine was sprung—the first ever sprung in England—and
the besiegers rushed into the city.   But so fierce was the
opposition of the garrison at the barricades, that Rupert
recalled his storming party, and fired on the breach, until
the enemy at last hoisted the white flag.   Colonel Hastings
was then sent into the city with powers to treat, but he
was detained all night, and the Prince, fearing treachery,
ordered the attack to be renewed at daybreak.   Fortunately,
with the light, came Hastings; the garrison had surrendered,
and was permitted to march out, " colours flying, trumpets
sounding, and matches lighted; " [2] an honour scarcely

[1] Clar. State Papers. A character of Lord Digby.
[2] Warburton, II. p. 169.

deserved after the horrible manner in which it had desecrated the Lichfield Cathedral.

No sooner was the city taken than Rupert unwillingly turned back to Oxford. During the siege he had received letters from the King, urging him to hasten northward, but ere its completion the state of affairs was changed. Reading was in dire peril, and its Governor, Sir Arthur Aston, protested desperately to the Prince: "I am grown weary of my life, with perpetual trouble and vexation." In his garrison he seemed to have no confidence: "I am so extremely dejected with this business that I do wish, with all my heart, I had some German soldiers to command, or that I could infuse some German courage into them. For your English soldiers are so poor and base that I could never have a greater affliction light upon me than to be put into command of them."[1] The report of the Secretary Nicholas was not more comforting: "I assure your Highness it is the opinion of many here that, if Prince Rupert come not speedily, Reading will be lost!"[2] And finally, a peremptory command from the King for his instant return left the Prince no room for hesitation.

But with all his haste Rupert came too late. Aston had been incapacitated by a severe wound, and the command had fallen to his subordinate, Colonel Fielding. Ignorant of the King's long delayed advance to his relief, Fielding made a truce with Essex, in order to treat; consequently, when the King and Rupert arrived and fell upon Essex, Fielding could not, in honour, sally to their assistance. The relief party perforce retired, and Rupert sent to demand of Essex the name of a gentleman who had very valiantly attacked him in the retreat.[3] After this failure, there was nothing left but to surrender, and Fielding accepted Essex's permission to march out with the honours

---

[1] Rupert Transcripts. Aston to Rupert, 22 Jan. 1643; Pythouse Papers, p. 12.
[2] Ibid. Nicholas to Rupert, 21 April, 1643.
[3] Warburton, II. p. 179.

of war. But Essex was unable to prevent a breach of the articles by his soldiers, who attacked and insulted the Royalist garrison. This faithless conduct was bitterly remembered by the Royalists, and subsequently repaid in kind at Bristol and Newark. As for the unfortunate Fielding, he was tried by court-martial, and condemned to death for his untimely surrender of his charge. But Rupert, who fully understood his difficult position, was resolved that he should not suffer, and urged the young Prince of Wales to plead with the King for his life.[1] The little Prince's intercession prevailed, and Fielding was spared. Throughout the rest of the war he served as a volunteer, but, though he displayed great gallantry, his reputation never recovered the unfortunate miscarriage at Reading.

The vicinity of Essex's army detained Rupert for some time at Oxford. From that centre he and his picked troops carried on an active guerilla warfare, scouring the country on all sides. "They took many prisoners who thought themselves secure, and put them to ransom. And this they did by night marches, through unfrequented ways, often very near London." At the same time Rupert had to attend to a voluminous correspondence with his officers in all parts of the country. The generals, Crafurd, Newcastle, Maurice, and others demanded his orders. Lord Northampton appealed to him for relief from the exorbitant demands made on his tenantry by Colonel Croker.[2] From all sides came the usual complaints about quarters, and supplies of provisions or ammunition. Sir William Vavasour had a more unusual grievance. He commanded in Wales, under Lord Herbert, but Lord Herbert, being a Roman Catholic, could not openly exert his powers for fear of prejudicing the King's affairs; and Digby presumed to send orders to Vavasour. "How to behave myself in this I know not," wrote the distracted Colonel to the Prince. "Nor do I

<hr>

[1] Gardiner's Civil War, I. p. 130.
[2] Rupert Correspondence. See Warburton, II. 187.

understand in what condition I myself am. My Lord Herbert is General, and yet all despatches are directed to me; which is not very pleasing to his Excellency." [1]

That Digby's intrigues were already beginning to disturb the King's councils is apparent from a sympathetic letter addressed by Nicholas to Rupert. Evidently the Prince had expressed some indignation at the vexatious interference of incapable persons. "The King is much troubled to see your Highness discontented," says Nicholas, "And I could wish that some busybodies would not meddle, as they do, with other men's offices; and that the King would leave every officer respectively to look after his own proper charge; and that His Majesty would content himself to overlook all men, and see that each did his duty in his proper place; which would give abundant satisfaction, and quiet those that are jealous to see some men meddle who have nothing to do with affairs." [2] But in spite of this plain speaking, the divisions which were to prove so fatal to the cause, were as yet but in embryo. Rupert was still the hero of the hour, still all powerful with his uncle, when he was near him. His next exploit was to raise his reputation yet higher.

In the middle of June, Rupert accomplished his famous march to Chalgrove Field. Intending to beat up Essex's quarters and to capture a convoy of money, he left Oxford on a Saturday afternoon with a force of some two thousand in all, horse and foot. Tetsworth was reached at 1 a. m. and, though all the roads were lined by the enemy, who continually fired upon the Royalists, Rupert marched through, forbidding any retaliation. By 3 a. m. he was at Postcombe, where he surprised several houses, and took some prisoners. Two hours later he reached Chinnor, and had surrounded and entered it before the Parliamentary

<hr>

[1] Pythouse Papers, p. 15.

[2] Rupert Correspondence. 1898o. Nicholas to Prince, May 11, 1643. Warb. II. p. 189.

soldiers were even aware of his presence. There, many
of the enemy were killed and a hundred and twenty taken
prisoners. But, unfortunately for Rupert, the noise of the
conflict reached the very convoy he was come to seek,
and it was saved by a *détour* from its intended route.
Finding that he had missed the object of his expedition,
Rupert began a leisurely retreat, hoping to draw the enemy
after him. In this hope he was not disappointed. A body
of Essex's troops hastily followed him, and between seven
and eight a.m. he was attacked by his pursuers. At nine
o'clock on Sunday morning he halted in a cornfield at
Chalgrove. First securing his passage over the Thames
by sending a party to hold the bridge, he lined the lane
leading to it with dragoons, and then attempted by a slow
retreat to draw the enemy into it. They followed eagerly;
but the Prince suddenly realised that only a single hedge
parted him from his foes, and thereupon halted abruptly.
"For," said he, "the rebels, being so neere us, may bring
our reere into confusion before we can recover to our
ambush." Seeing him halt, the enemy began to fire, and
the impetuous Prince could contain himself no longer.
"'Yea,' said he, 'their insolency is not to be endured.'
This said, His Highness, facing all about, set spurs to his
horse, and first of all, in the very face of the dragooners,
leapt the hedge that parted him from the rebels ... Every
man, as he could, jumbled over after him; and as about
fifteen were gotten over, the Prince drew them up into a
front." It was enough. The enemy, among whom was
Hampden, were both better officered and better disciplined
than heretofore, but they could not stand before the charge
of the terrible Prince. The skirmish was sharp but short;
Hampden fell, and, after a valiant if brief resistance, his
comrades fled. Rupert's friend, Legge, had been, "as
usual", taken prisoner, but was rescued in the confusion
of the Puritans' flight. The Cavaliers, after nearly fourteen
hours in the saddle, were too weary for pursuit. Rupert

quickly rallied them, held the field half-an-hour, and then marched towards home. In less than twenty-four hours he had made a circuit of nearly fifty miles, through the heart of the enemy's country; had taken many prisoners, colours, and horses, surprised two outposts, won a battle, and lost about a dozen of his men. And it is added: "The modesty of all when they returned to Oxford was equal to their daring in the field." [1] Two of his prisoners Rupert had left at Chalgrove, with a surgeon to attend their wounds; but they showed themselves so ungrateful for this consideration as to break their parole. Essex received Rupert's complaint of their dishonourable conduct in a soldierly spirit, and returned two Royalist prisoners in exchange. [2] Essex was indeed always a courteous foe. Some time after this incident Rupert's falconer and hawk fell into his hands, and were by him generously restored to the Prince. Rupert happened to be absent from Oxford at that period, but the Puritan general's courtesy was gratefully acknowledged by Colonel Legge. [3]

Rupert's next duty was to bring the Queen to Oxford, a matter of no slight importance; for not only was her personal safety at stake, but also that of her money, arms, and troops. Essex, as well as the Prince, set out to meet Her Majesty, and it was Rupert's object to keep his own troops always between Essex and the Queen. On July 1st he quartered at Buckingham, and early in the next morning some of his men were attacked by those of Essex, at Whitebridge. Rupert was in the act of shaving when the noise of the skirmish came to his ears. Half-dressed and half-shaved, as he was, he dashed out without a moment's delay, charged and scattered his foes, and then quietly returned to resume his toilet. Throughout this march he

---

[1] His Highness's late Beating up of the Rebels' Quarters. Pamphlet. Bodleian Library.

[2] Warburton, II. 212. Essex to Rupert, June 22, 1643.

[3] Ibid. II. p. 390, *note*. Ellis Original Letters, Vol. IV.

MARY VILLIERS, DUCHESS OF RICHMOND.

From the Hollar Collection of Engravings in the British Museum after a Portrait by Vandyke.

Face page 111.

kept Essex on perpetual duty, harassing him by day and night, until, after some dexterous manœuvring, he left him unexpectedly on Brickhill, and himself joined the Queen at Stratford-on-Avon. That night, says tradition, Queen and Prince were the guests of Shakespeare's grand-daughter. If this was really the case, Rupert doubtless regarded his hostess with deep interest; for all the Palatines could quote Shakespeare. On July 13th the King came to meet his wife at Edgehill, and King, Queen and Prince slept at Wroxton Abbey. On the following day they entered Oxford in safety.

The Queen's arrival considerably changed the condition of the University. The colleges were populated no more by scholars, but by ladies and courtiers; Oxford was no longer a mere garrison, it was also a court. Chief among the noble ladies who attended the Queen, was the beautiful young Duchess of Richmond, only daughter of the King's dead friend, "Steenie," Duke of Buckingham. She it was whom her father had once destined to be Rupert's sister-in-law, as the bride of his brother Henry. But ere the bride was ten years old, both her father and her intended bridegroom had died untimely deaths, and the fair Mary Villiers was therefore brought up in the Royal family as the adopted daughter of the King. For her father's sake, and for her own, she had always been a petted favourite of her royal guardian, who called her "The Butterfly", a name derived from an incident which occurred when the lady was eleven years old. Once, dressed in her widow's weeds—she had been a widow at eleven—she had climbed a tree in the King's private garden, and had been nearly shot as a strange bird. But the courtier sent to shoot her perceived his error in time, and, at her own request, sent her in a hamper to the King, with a message that he had captured a beautiful butterfly alive; and the name clung to her ever after.[1] The King's affection for her and for the Duke of

____

[1] Marie de la Mothe, Countess d'Aulnoy. Memoirs of the Court of England, ed. 1707, pp. 397—400.

Richmond made it seem good to him to unite them in marriage, and the arrangement appears to have pleased all parties. Mary had disliked her boy-husband, Lord Herbert;[1] but the Duke she seems to have regarded with favour. Possibly his quiet and melancholy disposition supplied the necessary complement to her own merry and vivacious temperament. In 1636 the Queen had refused to have her in the Bedchamber, on the plea that her charms eclipsed all others; and now, in 1643, Mary Villiers was, at the age of twenty, in the prime of her beauty. Rumour said that she had won the heart of "the mad Prince," while the equally lively Mrs. Kirke had subjugated that of Maurice. A libellous Puritan tract represents Mrs. Kirke as extolling Maurice's "deserts and abilities," though she was forced to acknowledge that he "did not seem to be a courtier." But the Duchess assured her companions "that none was to be compared to Prince Rupert."[2] Nor was it only Puritans who commented on Rupert's admiration for the Duchess. The Irish Cavalier, Daniel O'Neil, "said things" in Ireland to Lord Taafe, after which he lost both the Prince's favour and his troop of Horse.[3] Rupert hotly resented the imputations cast upon him, and, had they been other than slanders, it is impossible to conceive that he and the Duke could have maintained their close and faithful friendship. The Duke, with his "haughty spirit", was not a man to dissemble, and his letters to Rupert are all full of solicitude for his welfare, and of sympathy and consolation for his troubles. Even in his hour of failure and ruin the Duke stood loyally by his side, though, in so doing, he was putting himself in opposition to his adored sovereign. Still it is certain that Rupert both felt and evinced a very strong admiration for the Duchess. "There will be a widow, and

---

[1] Strafford Papers, ed. 1739, Vol. I. p. 359.

[2] Somers Tracts, V. pp. 473—7.

[3] Carte's Ormonde, VI. p. 277. O'Neil to Ormonde, 12 April, 1645. Clarendon, Bk. VIII. p. 369.

whose she shall be but Prince Rupert's, I know not," wrote a Cavalier, when the Duke's death was rumoured in 1655.[1] But the Duchess took for her third husband, not Rupert, but "Northern Tom Howard," whom she said she married for love, and to please herself; her two former marriages having been made to please the Court.[2] Most likely she had never really cared for the Prince, and had merely amused herself with a flirtation. She was, no doubt, proud of so distinguished a conquest, but she never disguised her friendship for her supposed lover, and she sent him messages by all sorts of people, in the most open way. "I had an express command to present the Duchess of Richmond's service to you,"[3] wrote Rupert's enemy, Percy, in July 1643.

The society of the Duchess could not detain the active Prince at Oxford, and within four days of his arrival there, he set out for a second attempt upon Bristol. The Royalist arms were prevailing in the West. A few days previously Nicholas had reported to the Prince the victory of Lansdowne, with the comforting assurance that "Prince Maurice, thanks be to God, is very well and hath received no hurt, albeit he ran great hazards in his own person."[4] Two days later Maurice arrived in Oxford, to obtain supplies of horses and ammunition for Ralph Hopton, who lay seriously wounded at Devizes. Thither Maurice returned with all speed, and, immediately on his arrival, took place the battle of Roundway Down. This was a brilliant victory for the Royalists, and the news was received in Oxford with much rejoicing; albeit for Rupert the joy was tempered with disgust at the credit which thereby redounded to Lord Wilmot.[5] These successes increased the Prince's desire to capture Bristol, then the second city in the Kingdom, and

---

[1] Nicholas Papers. Camden Soc. 1 Jan. 1655. Vol. II. p. 158.

[2] Hatton Papers. Camden Society. New series, I. p. 42.

[3] Pythouse Papers, p. 57. Percy to Rupert, July 1643.

[4] Rupert Correspondence. Warburton, II. p. 226. Nicholas to the Prince, July 8, 1643.

[5] Clarendon Hist. Bk. VII. p. 121.

the key of all South Wales. Maurice and Hertford were now at liberty to assist him, and, on July 18th, he began his march with fourteen regiments of foot, "all very weak," and several troops of horse. Waller was the General of the Parliament now opposed to him, but Waller's troops had been in a broken condition ever since the victories of Hopton and Wilmot, and he retreated before Rupert's advance. On the 20th, Thursday, Maurice came to meet his brother at Chipping Sodbury, and joined his march. On Sunday they were within two miles of Bristol, and the two Princes took a view of the city from Clifton Church, which stood upon a hill within musket-shot of the porch. While they stood in the church-yard the enemy fired cannon on them, but without effect; seeing that their shot would be harmless, Rupert quartered some musketeers and dragoons upon the place. That night Maurice retired over the river to his own troops; and the same evening the enemy made a sally, but were repulsed.

On Monday morning Rupert marched all his forces to the edge of the Down, in order to display them to the garrison of Bristol; and Lord Hertford, who commanded the Western army, made a similar show upon the other side. About 11 a. m. Rupert sent to the Governor— Nathaniel Fiennes, a son of Lord Say—a formal summons to surrender. The summons was of course refused, and immediately the attack began. Long after dark Rupert continued to fire on the city. "It was a beautiful piece of danger to see so many fires incessantly in the dark from the pieces on both sides, for a whole hour together. ...And in those military masquerades was Monday night passed." [1] Tuesday was spent in skirmishing, while Rupert went over the river to consult with Lord Hertford and Maurice. The result of this consultation was a general assault of both armies next morning. "The word for the soldiers was to

---

[1] Journal of the Siege of Bristol. Warburton, II. p. 244.

be 'Oxford', and the sign between the two armies to know each other, to be green colours, either bows or such like; and that every officer and soldier be without any band or handkerchief about his neck." [1] The zeal of Maurice's Cornish soldiers nearly proved disastrous, for on Wednesday morning, "out of a military ambition", they anticipated the order to attack. [2] As soon as he heard the firing Rupert hastened to draw up his own men, but the scaling ladders were not ready. In consequence of this, the young Lord Grandison, to whom had been entrusted the capture of the fort, had made no impression, after a valiant assault which lasted an hour and a half, and during which he lost twenty men. For a short time he was forced to desist, but, speedily returning to the attack, he discovered a ladder of the enemy by which he was able to mount; only to find that he could not get over the palisades. In his third assault Grandison was fatally wounded, and his men, utterly discouraged, left the attack. At this point Rupert sent word that Wentworth had entered the suburbs, upon which Grandison retired to have his wounds dressed, and ordered his men to join Bellasys on the left. Instead of obeying this order they began to retreat; but were met by Rupert himself who led them back to the enemy's works. It was then that Rupert's horse was shot under him and he strolled off on foot, with a coolness which immensely encouraged the men. Having, after a while, obtained a new horse, "he rode up and down from place to place, wherever most need was of his presence, here directing and encouraging some, and there leading up others. Generally it is confessed by the commanders that, had not the Prince been there, the assault, through mere despair, had been in danger to be given over in many places." [3]

On the other side Maurice was equally active. He had

---

[1] Journal of the Siege of Bristol. Warb. II. p. 246.
[2] Ibid. p. 247.
[3] Ibid. pp. 250—255.

directed his men to take faggots to fill the ditches, and ladders to scale the forts, but in their haste to begin the attack, they had forgotten both. The scaling party had therefore failed and retired. During the retreat "Prince Maurice went from regiment to regiment, encouraging the soldiers, desiring the officers to keep their companies by their colours; telling them that he believed his brother had already made his entrance on the other side."[1] Retreats seem to have succeeded under Maurice, for we are told by one contemporary that he earned from his foes the name of "the good-come-off."[2] In a short time his assurance was justified; Rupert sent word that the suburbs were entered, and demanded a thousand Cornish men to aid his troops. Maurice sent over two hundred, but presently came across the river himself with five hundred more. By that time the fight was nearly over, and Fiennes sent to demand a parley. The demand was a welcome one, for the Cavaliers' losses had been very heavy, especially in officers. Among the fallen were Grandison, Slanning, Trevanion and many more of famous and honourable name.

At five o'clock on the evening of July 26th, terms were agreed on between Fiennes and the Princes; Lord Hertford not being consulted in the matter. Fiennes was to march out at nine o'clock next morning with all the honours of war, and to be protected by a convoy of Rupert's men. Contrary to all expectation and custom, he marched out next morning at seven o'clock, two hours before the time arranged. The convoy promised by Rupert was not ready, and the Royalist soldiers, remembering Puritan perfidy at Reading, attacked and plundered the retiring garrison. The fault was none of Rupert's, but for all that he keenly felt the breach of faith. "The Prince who uses to make good his word, not only in point of honour, but as a matter of religion too, was so passionately offended at this disorder

---

[1] Journal of the Siege of Bristol. Warb. II. p. 258.
[2] Lloyd's Lives and Memoirs, ed. 1677, p. 656.

that some of them felt how sharp his sword was," wrote one of his officers. [1] The Puritans would fain have used the incident to blacken the Prince's character; but Fiennes himself generously acquitted his conqueror of all blame. "I must do this right to the Princes," he said; "contrary to what I find in a printed pamphlet, they were so far from sitting on their horses, triumphing and rejoicing at these disorders, that they did ride among the plunderers with their swords, hacking and slashing them; and that Prince Rupert did excuse it to me in a very fair way, and with expressions as if he were much troubled at it." [2]

The unfortunate Fiennes was very severely censured for the loss of the city, which, it was maintained, was so strongly fortified that it should have been impregnable. The truth was that the garrison had been totally insufficient for the defence; but Fiennes remained under a cloud until later events justified him in the eyes of the Parliament.

Among the Royalists at Oxford the joy over this important success was marred by the dissensions of the victorious generals. The Princes had never been on cordial terms with Lord Hertford, the General of all the Western forces. Hertford was a constitutional Royalist, who served the King from a strict sense of duty, and from no love of war. He was of a grave, studious and peace-loving nature, and Maurice's appointment as his lieutenant-general had not brought satisfaction to either. Maurice had begun by despising Hertford for a "civilian". And Hertford had resented both the Prince's tendency to assume to himself " more than became a Lieutenant-General," and his interference in civil affairs which he did not understand. The arrival of Rupert on the scene did not make for peace. Maurice complained bitterly to Rupert, and the elder brother violently espoused the cause of the younger. The spark

---

[1] Journal of Siege. Warburton, II. 262.

[2] A Relation made to the House of Commons by Colonel Nat. Fiennes, Aug. 5, 1643; see Warburton, II. p. 267, also Clarendon, Bk. VII.

thus lighted flamed forth over the Governorship of Bristol.[1]
Hertford, as said above, commanded all the Western Counties, and he considered, with some justice, that Rupert ought
to have consulted him, before concluding the terms of
surrender with Fiennes. In revenge for the slight put
upon him, he appointed Sir Ralph Hopton Governor of
Bristol, without a word on the subject to the Prince. Rupert,
who considered the city won by his prowess as was in
truth the case, was wildly indignant. He would not oppose
another officer to the gallant Hopton, but he demanded
the Governorship of the King for himself. The King,
ignorant of Hertford's action, readily granted his nephew's
request. Rupert then offered the post to Hopton as his
lieutenant. Hopton, anxious for peace, willingly accepted
the arrangement, and Hertford resented Hopton's compliance with the Prince as an injury to himself. The affair
became a party question. The courtiers, "towards whom
the Prince did not live with any condescension," sided with
Hertford.[2] The King really believed his nephew's claims
to be just; and the army vehemently supported its beloved
Prince. Finally, the King was forced to come to Bristol
in order to allay the storm which he had so unwittingly
raised. On the flattering pretext of requiring Hertford's
counsel and company in his own army, he detached him
from that of the West; and on Rupert's suggestion he
made Maurice a full general. The contending officers were
silenced; but the breaches in the army were widened, and
feeling embittered.[3]

The tactics to be next followed were hotly disputed. The
Court faction was anxious to unite the two armies, but,—
for other reasons than the important one that Maurice, in
that case, could have been only a colonel,—Rupert prevailed

---

[1] Clarendon Hist. 1849. Vol. III. pp. 121—126. Bk. VII. pp. 85, 98,
144—148; also Life, pp. 196—7, *note*.
[2] Clarendon Life. Vol. I. p. 195,
[3] Ibid.

against this counsel. Maurice was therefore ordered to march with foot and cannon after Lord Carnarvon, who was besieging Dorchester. It was said by the Court that, had Maurice marched more slowly, Carnarvon would have succeeded better. For Maurice "was thought to incline so wholly to the soldier, that he neglected any consideration of the country."[1] Fear of him roused the people of the country to active opposition. The licence of his soldiers — though admitted even by Clarendon to have been "reported greater than it was"—alienated the county, and Carnarvon took the Prince's conduct "so ill" that he threw up his commission and returned to Oxford.[2] Maurice thus left to labour alone, took Exeter and Weymouth, over the governorship of which he had a second quarrel with Hertford, who, though absent, was still nominally Lord Lieutenant of the western counties; on this occasion the King favoured Hertford, who triumphed accordingly. In October Maurice took Dartmouth, but effected little else of importance. Handicapped by a long and dangerous attack of influenza—"the new disease,"[3] it was called then—he besieged Lyme and Plymouth for months without success, and lost a good deal of reputation in the process.

In accordance with Rupert's scheme of campaign, the King should now have pushed on with the main army to London. But to render this plan successful it was necessary that Newcastle should sweep down from the North, and Maurice or Hopton, come to meet him from the West; the strength of local feeling prevented any such resolute and united action. Newcastle's northern troops would not leave their own counties exposed to hostile garrisons and hostile armies, in order to assist the King in a distant part of the country. In the same way the men of Cornwall and Devon refused to quit their own territory, and for the King

---

[1] Clar. Hist. Bk. VII. pp. 98, 192.
[2] Clarendon History. Bk. VII. p. 192.
[3] Verney Memoirs. Vol. II. p. 171.

to push on alone to London was absolutely useless. He was therefore forced to fall back on the old plan of conquering the country piecemeal, town by town, village by village; and accordingly, August 10th, he laid siege to Gloucester. Massey, then governor of Gloucester, had once served under Legge, and now sent word to him that he would surrender the city to the King, but not to Rupert. This message was the chief cause of the siege that followed; but Massey, either from inability or change of purpose, did not keep his engagement. Rupert held aloof from the siege altogether. No doubt he was disappointed at the rejection of his own more sweeping measures, and when he found that he would not even be allowed to assault the town, he declined to command at all. He could not, however, resist lingering about the trenches in a private capacity, and while so doing, had several very narrow escapes from shots and stones.[1]

After a fruitless siege the King was forced to retire before Essex, who advanced with a large force to the relief of Gloucester. On his way Essex surprised and took Cirencester; the King then moved after him, but—owing to his neglect of Rupert's warning, as the Prince's partisans asserted; or to Rupert's neglect of Byron's warning, as that officer declared—he was out-manœuvred. Some confusion there certainly was. Rupert had mustered his troops on Broadway Down, but, though he waited till nightfall, he received no news from the King; and at last he set out in person to seek him. In the window of a farm-house he perceived a light, and, advancing cautiously, he looked in. There sat the King quietly playing at piquet with Lord Percy, while Lord Forth looked on. The Prince burst in upon them, crying indignantly that his men had been in the saddle for hours, and that Essex must be overtaken before he could join with Waller. Percy and Forth offered objections, but Rupert carried the day, and dashed off as

[1] Journal of the Siege of Gloucester. Warburton II. p. 282.

impetuously as he had come, taking with him George Lisle and a regiment of musketeers. Marching night and day, "with indefatigable pains," he overtook and defeated Essex on Aldbourn Chase. [1] Essex retreated to Hungerford; but though defeated he was by no means crushed. He was still strong enough to fight, and, as his provisions were running short, his only hope lay in immediate victory. This Rupert knew, and for once in his life he preferred discretion to valour, and counselled passive resistance. If the King would be content to hold the roads between Essex and London, hunger and mutiny would speedily ruin the army of the Parliament. On September 20th, a part of the royal army occupied the road through the Kennet valley; Rupert with most of the cavalry held the road over Newbury Wash. But the lanes to the right were insufficiently secured, and Essex, spurred on by dire necessity, succeeded in gaining the slopes above the Kennet valley. Thus he commanded the whole position; and the first battle of Newbury proved the first great disaster for the Cavaliers. The surprised Royalists, seeing their enemies above them, charged up the hill to retrieve the ground, and the conflict raged long, with great loss. On the left, where Rupert lay, impatience proved nearly as fatal as neglect had done on the right. Instead of waiting to attack Essex's main army as it filed through the lanes, the Prince dashed off to the open ground of Enborne Heath, where Essex's reserves were strongly guarded by enclosures. There he charged and scattered some Parliamentary horse, but on the London trained bands he could make no impression, until the approach of some Royalist infantry caused them to retreat in good order. Whitelocke relates a personal encounter which took place between Rupert and Sir Philip Stapleton in this battle. This officer of the Parliament, "desiring to cope singly with the Prince, rode up, all alone, to the troop of horse,

---

[1] Clarendon Hist. Bk. VII. 207.

at the head of which Rupert was standing with Digby and some other officers. Sir Philip looked carefully from one to the other until his eyes rested upon Rupert, whom he knew; then he deliberately fired in the Prince's face. The shot took no effect, and Sir Philip, turning his horse, rode quietly back to his own men, followed by a volley of shots from the indignant Royalists.[1] For hours the fight continued; a series of isolated struggles took place in various fields, and when night fell the King's ammunition failed, and he retreated to Newbury, leaving Essex's way to London open. The advantage therefore was to the Parliament, though Essex could not claim a great victory. Also the King's loss had been immense, and among the fallen were Falkland, Sunderland, and the gallant Carnarvon. What could be done to retrieve the Royalist fortunes Rupert did. Rallying such men as were not utterly exhausted, he followed Essex closely, through the night,—surprised him, with some effect, and threw his rear into confusion. But, on September the 22nd, Essex entered Reading; and on the next day, Rupert returned with the King to Oxford.[2]

Rupert's star was paling, and his successes were well-nigh at an end. The King had hoped much from the Queen's coming and had begged her to reconcile Rupert with Percy, Wilmot and others. But Henrietta, once so kind to her nephew, now bitterly opposed him. She believed—or professed to believe—that he had formed a deliberate plan to destroy her influence with her husband. Perhaps the idea was not altogether without foundation; undoubtedly Rupert's common-sense showed him the folly of much of the Queen's conduct; and he was not the man to tolerate the interference of a woman in matters military. During the siege of Bristol, Henrietta had taken offence at what she considered Rupert's neglect of herself. "I hope your successes in arms will not make you forget your

[1] Whitelocke's Memorials, p. 74.
[2] Gardiner's Civil War, Vol. I. pp. 209—217.

civility to ladies," Percy had written to the Prince. "This I say from a discourse the Queen made to me this night, wherein she told me she had not received one letter from you since you went, though you had writ many." [1] Percy's interference was not calculated to improve the state of affairs; and the siege of Gloucester excited Henrietta's jealousy yet more. She was eager for the advance on London, and she could not be made to understand that it was impossible, in existing circumstances. Rupert, as we have seen, was anxious for the very same thing, but he saw its impracticability and yielded to necessity. Because he so yielded, the Queen chose to consider him as the instigator of the siege of Gloucester, and she angrily declared that the King preferred his nephew's advice to that of his wife. Had he done so, it would but have shown his common-sense; but he hastened to Oxford to appease her indignation and soothe her jealousy as best he could. Then occurred the first open breach between Henrietta and Rupert. At this very juncture, three Puritan peers, Bedford, Clare, and Holland, had quitted the Parliament, and sought to be reconciled with the King. Henrietta received them with contempt. Rupert had more sense; he perceived the wisdom of conciliation, and brought the three peers to kiss his uncle's hand. The Queen's anger at this was loud and long; and henceforth the struggle of Prince versus Queen raged openly in Oxford. [2] The King was torn in two between them; he adored his wife, and he believed in his nephew. When actually at his uncle's side Rupert could usually gain a hearing, but once away, he had no security that the plan agreed upon but a few hours before would not be supplanted by some wild scheme emanating from the Queen, or from Digby. [3] At the Court the Queen's views were in the ascendant. Percy, Wilmot and Ashburn-

---

[1] Percy to Rupert, July 29, 1643; Pythouse Papers, p. 55.
[2] Rupert's Diary. Warburton, II. p. 272.
[3] See Gardiner's Civil War, I. p. 345.

ham threw in their lot with the Prince's enemies, and, as the two last had control of all supplies of ammunition and money respectively, Rupert experienced great difficulty in obtaining the barest necessities for his forces. Wilmot and Goring were able to raise a faction hostile to the Prince, within the army itself, and it was at this period that Arthur Trevor compared the "contrariety of opinions" to the contending elements. "The army is much divided," he wrote to Lord Ormonde, "and the Prince at true distance with many of the officers of horse; which hath much danger in it, out of this, that I find many gallant men willing to get governments and to sit down, or to get employments at large, and so be out of the way. In short, my lord, there must be a better understanding among our great horsemen, or else they may shortly shut the stable door."[1]

Rupert did not spare his indignation. He quarrelled freely with Percy, by letter. He left Digby's epistles unanswered,[2] and he slighted Wilmot. He accused the King of treating without his knowledge; which, said his distracted uncle, was a "damnable ley."[3] The truth was that the French Ambassador had proposed to ascertain what terms the Parliament might be likely to offer, and the King had consented to his so doing. Richmond hastened to explain matters to the Prince. "I should have told you before," he concluded, "but I forgot it; and but little knowledge is lost by it. It was ever my opinion that nothing would come of it, and so it remains still for anything I can hear, and I converse sometimes with good company."[4] But Rupert was not easily appeased; the supposed treaty was but one grievance among many, and ere long a letter from Digby had raised a new storm. The patient Duke as usual

[1] Carte's Ormonde, Vol. V. pp. 520—1, 21 Nov. 1643.
[2] Rupert Transcripts. Jermyn to Rupert, 26 Mar. 1644.
[3] Ibid. King to Rupert, 12 Nov. 1643.
[4] Transcripts. Richmond to Rupert, 12 Oct. 1643.

received his fiery cousin's complaints, and again took up his pen to pacify him. "Upon the receipt of your letter," he wrote, "perceiving that, from a hint taken of a letter from Lord Digby, you were in doubt that, in Oxford, there might be wrong judgments made of you and of your business, I made it my diligence to clear with the King, who answers the same for the Queen..... Considering the jealousy might have grown from some doubtful expressions in the letter you mention, I spoke with the party, (*i. e.* Digby) who seemed much grieved at it, and assured me he writ only the advice of such intelligence as was brought hither, and for information to make use of as you best could upon the place. Yesterday one brought me your commission to peruse.... I looked it well over, and I think it is well drawn." [1] The last sentence shows that Richmond did not confine his services to mediating between the Prince and his enemies, but watched over his cousin's more material interests with anxious care.

During all this time Rupert was not very far distant from Oxford. He had taken Bedford, and recaptured Cirencester, and would have held Newport Pagnell, thus cutting London off from the north; but during his absence in Bedfordshire, orders from Oxford drew off Louis Dyves whom he had left in charge at Newport Pagnell, and the place was seized by Essex. In the same way Vavasour's scheme for blockading Gloucester was ruined. "Sir, I am now in a good way, if no alteration come from Court," [2] he wrote early in December. But the vexatious "alteration" came, and his plan failed. Hastings lamented that his lack of arms made "the service I ought to do the King very difficult;" [3] and everywhere despondency prevailed. "The truth is," wrote Ralph Hopton from Alresford, "the duty of this service here would be insupportable, were it

---

[1] Rupert Transcripts. Richmond to Rupert, Nov. 9, 1643.
[2] Ibid. Vasavour to Rupert, Dec. 4, 1643.
[3] Pythouse Papers. Hastings to Nicholas, pp. 13—14..

not in this cause, where there is so great a necessity of prevailing through all difficulties, or of suffering them to prevail, which cannot be thought of in good English." [1]

Throughout the winter the usual mass of petitions, complaints, accusations, and remonstrances poured in upon the Prince. Among them, " Ye humble Remonstrance of Captain John Ball" deserves notice as a curiosity. This gentleman stated that he had, out of pure loyalty and with exceeding difficulty, raised 34 horses, 48 men, 12 carabines, 12 cases of pistols, 6 muskets, and 20 new saddles for the King's service. This done, he had gone to Oxford to obtain the King's commission to serve under Sir Henry Bard. During his absence, Sir Charles Blount, by order of Sir Jacob Astley then in command at Reading, had broken into his stables at Pangbourne and carried off both horses and equipments. [2] To this accusation old Sir Jacob responded with his wonted quaint directness: " As conserninge one yt calls himselfe Cap^ne Balle, yt hath complayned unto yr Highnes yt I hav tacken awaie his horsses from him; this is the trewth. He hath livede near this towne ever since I came heather, and had gotten, not above, 12 men togeather, and himselfe. He had so plundered and oppressed the pepell, payinge contributions as the Marquess of Winchester and my Lord Hopton complayned extreamly of him. He went under my name, wtch he used falcesly, as givinge out he did it by my warrant. Off this he gott faierly, and so promised to give no more cause of complaynt. Now, ever since, he hath continewed his ould coures (courses), in soe extreame a waie, as he, and his wife, and his sone, and 10 or 12 horsses he hath, to geather spoyles the peepell, plunders them, and tackes violently their goodes from them." [3]

As a climax to all Rupert's other anxieties came the

[1] Hopton to Rupert, Dec. 12, 1643. Warb. II. p. 333.
[2] Add. MSS. 18981. Jan. 4, 1644.
[3] Transcripts. Astley to Rupert, Jan. 11, 1644; Warburton. II. p. 358.

severe illness of Maurice, who was engaged at the siege of Plymouth. All the autumn he had been suffering from a low fever, which was in fact the modern influenza. So serious was his condition that his mother, in Holland, declined an invitation to the Court of Orange, on the grounds that she expected hourly to hear of Maurice's death. [1] More than once reports that he was actually dead gained credence, and the doctors who sent frequent bulletins to Rupert, would not answer for their patient's recovery, "by reason that the disease is very dangerous, and fraudulent." But by October 17th they were able to send a hopeful report. Maurice had slept better, the delirium had left him, and he had recognised Dr. Harvey—the discoverer of the circulation of the blood. When given the King's message of sympathy he had shown "an humble, thankful sense thereof." And on receiving Rupert's messages, "he seemed very glad to hear of and from your Highness." [2] A relapse was feared, but Maurice recovered steadily, though very slowly. In November he was anxious to join his forces before Plymouth, but had to give up the attempt, and the siege suffered from his absence. "Your brother resolved to have removed hence nearer towards Plymouth, upon Monday, but upon tryal finds himself too weak for the journey," wrote Sir Richard Cave, an old friend of the Palatines, to Rupert. "I dare boldly say that, had he been with the army, the army and the town had been at a nearer distance before now. Your brother presents his respects to your Highness, but says he is not able yet to write letters with his own hand." [3]

<hr>

[1] Green, Vol. VI. p. 137.
[2] Dr. Harvey and others to Rupert, Oct. 17, 1643; Warburton. II. p. 307.
[3] Rupert Transcripts. Cave to Rupert, Nov. 4, 1643.

CHAPTER VIII

THE PRESIDENCY OF WALES. THE RELIEF OF NEWARK.
QUARRELS AT COURT. NORTHERN MARCH.
MARSTON MOOR

THROUGHOUT the year 1643 the advantage in arms had lain decidedly with the King, and the Parliament now sought new strength in an alliance with the Scots. Such an alliance involved a strict adherence to Presbyterianism, which was naturally very distasteful to the Independents, who were growing steadily in strength and numbers. Therefore, though the entrance of the Scots into England in January 1644, brought a valuable accession of military force, it proportionately weakened the Puritan Party by increasing its internal dissensions. For a brief period the Independents sought alliance with those members of the Parliament and of the City, known as the Peace Party, and the result of this drawing together was a resolve to appeal privately to the King for some terms of agreement. The emissary employed in this secret negotiation was a certain Ogle, who had long been held a prisoner, but was now purposely suffered to escape. As an earnest of good faith, he was to assure the King that Colonel Mozley, brother of the Governor of Aylesbury, would admit the Royalists into that town. But Ogle was himself betrayed. Mozley had communicated all to the Presbyterian leaders of the Parliament. The whole plot was carefully watched, and plans laid to entrap Rupert himself. It was said that Essex boasted that he would have the Prince in London, alive or dead.

On the night of January 21st, Rupert set out to take possession of the offered town. The snow fell thick, but it did the Prince good service, for it prevented Essex falling upon him, as had been intended. Fortunately, also, Rupert was prudent, and declined to approach very near Aylesbury, until Mozley should appear on the scene in person. This he failed to do. Then the Prince wished to assault the town on the side where he was not expected, but the brook which ran before it was so swelled by the snow and sudden thaw, as to be impassable. Nothing remained but a speedy retreat, in which, owing to wind, snow and swollen streams, some four hundred men perished. In his fury Rupert would have hanged Ogle for a traitor, but the unfortunate man was rescued by the intercession of Digby. Probably the Secretary was moved as much by detestation of Rupert as by compassion for Ogle. There was soon a new *causa belli* between them.

In February Rupert was made a peer of the realm, as Duke of Cumberland and Earl of Holderness, in order that he might sit in the Royalist Parliament now called to Oxford. In the same month, it was proposed to make him President of Wales and the Marches, which appointment carried with it, not only military, but also fiscal and judicial powers, the right to levy taxes and to appoint Commissioners for the administration of the country. Digby had no mind to see his rival thus promoted, and he made the appointment the subject of a court intrigue. First he suggested that Ormonde would make a far better President than the Prince. But Ormonde could not possibly be spared from his Government of Ireland, and therefore Digby had to invent new delays and difficulties. "The business of the Presidency is at a standstill," wrote Rupert's faithful agent in Oxford, Arthur Trevor, "upon some doubts that my Lord Digby makes, which cannot be cleared to him without a sight of the patent which must be obtained from Ludlow." [1] The Prince seems to have been rather apathetic in the matter, for, in a few days, Trevor wrote again: "I am at

---

[1] Rupert Correspondence. 18981 Add. MSS. British Museum. Trevor to Rupert, Feb. 16, 1644.

a stand in your business, not receiving your commands . . .
Persuasion avails little at Court, where always the orator
convinces sooner than the argument. Let me beseech your
Highness you will be so kind as to bestow what time you
can spare from the public upon your private interests; which
always thrive best when they are acted within the eye of
the owner." [1] From Byron, then at Chester, came an anxious
letter, demonstrating the great importance of Wales as a
recruiting ground, and as the place whence communication
with Ireland was easiest. The state of the Marches was
exceedingly critical, and Byron pathetically begged Rupert
not to refuse them the aid of his presence. "I have heard
that means is used underhand to persuade your Highness
not to accept the President's place of Wales; the end of
which is apparent, for if your Highness refuse it, it will lessen
the military part of your command, be a great prejudice
to the country, and withal lose an opportunity of settling
such a part of the country, converging upon Ireland, that
is most likely to reduce the rest." [2] To the other despairing
commanders in those districts the prospect of Rupert's coming
was as welcome as to Byron, and, urged by their letters,
Rupert resolved not to be turned from the work. Fortunately
for himself he had staunch allies in Richmond, Nicholas,
and above all, the Queen's favourite, Harry Jermyn. The
last named was indeed all-powerful just then. "I find," wrote
Trevor, alluding to the ciphers in which he corresponded,
"not Prince Rupert, nor all the numbers in arithmetic have
any efficacy without Lord Jermyn." [3] And Jermyn, strange
to say, usually showed himself a good friend to Rupert.
"My Lord Jermyn is, from the root of his heart, your very
great servant," declared Trevor. Apparently, also, Jermyn
had reconciled the Queen to her nephew, for, at the same

---

[1] Rupert Correspondence. Add. MSS. Brit. Mus. 18981. Trevor to Rupert,
Mar. 30, 1644.

[2] Ibid. Byron to Rupert, April 1644.

[3] Carte's Ormonde. Trevor to Ormonde, Feb. 19, 1644. Vol. VI. pp. 37—38.

time, Trevor informed Ormonde that he would speedily receive a request from the Queen "to be as kind as possibly your Lordship can unto Prince Rupert, especially in a present furnishment of some arms and powder."[1]

The appointment to Wales having been carried by his allies, Rupert was brought into very close connection with Ormonde. To Ireland the King looked for supplies of arms, ammunition, and of soldiers, as a counterpoise to the invasion of the Scots. The transport of these stores and troops was now regarded as part of Rupert's business in his new Government. He was willing enough to attend to the matter, for he was "mightily in love" with his Irish soldiers;[2] and, thanks to Ormonde's good sense and unswerving loyalty, a good understanding was preserved between himself and the Prince. Efforts to poison Ormonde's mind against Rupert were not wanting on the part of Digby. He did his best to make the Irish Lord Lieutenant think himself slighted by Rupert's preferment. "But let me withal assure you that I knew not of it till it was done," he wrote, "I being not so happy as to have any part in His Highness's Counsels."[3] To which the incorruptible Ormonde replied only, that he held himself in no way injured, and regarded the appointment as very fittingly bestowed on the Prince. Nor did Digby's new ally, Daniel O'Neil, meet with any better success. The Irish soldier of fortune had now quarrelled with Rupert, and thrown in his lot with that of the Secretary. Early in 1644 he was despatched to Ireland by Digby, in order to arrange various matters and, incidentally, to do Rupert as much harm as he could. But though introduced to Ormonde as Digby's "special, dear and intimate friend,"[4] he gained little credence. "I easily believe that Daniel O'Neil was willing I

---

[1] Carte's Ormonde. Trevor to Ormonde, Feb. 19, 1644. VI. p. 37.

[2] Ibid. VI. 87, Ap. 13, 1644.

[3] Ibid. VI. 41, Digby to Ormonde, Feb. 20, 1644.

[4] Carte's Ormonde. Digby to Ormonde. Vol. VI. p. 21, Jan. 20, 1644.

should be Lord Lieutenant; and perhaps he will unwish it again," [1] said Ormonde calmly. No doubt Rupert owed much to the good sense and diligence of Trevor, who was himself a staunch adherent of Ormonde, and honoured by him with the title of "my friend." He seems to have been a clever man, of ready wit and unfailing energy, and he needed it all in his service of the Prince.

Rupert's new appointment involved the keeping up of an establishment at Shrewsbury, which he seldom occupied, but which added greatly to his expenses, and his personal labours were also multiplied. He had reached Shrewsbury on February 19th, having spent a week at Worcester and four days at Bridgnorth by the way. On March 4th he was "marching all night" to Drayton; on the 5th he was skirmishing with Fairfax; on the 6th he was "home" again; but only to resume his wanderings four days later. [2] He made it his business to visit every garrison under his charge, and his rapid movements were observed with pride by the Cavaliers. "In the morning in Leicestershire, in the afternoon in Lancashire, and the same day at supper time at Shrewsbury; without question he hath a flying army," reported the News-letters with cheerful exaggeration. [3] Certainly the Prince never spared himself, and he expected that others should show an equal energy and attention to business. Good officers, with other qualifications than mere social rank, he would have; and he allowed no private considerations to interfere with the public necessities. His vigorous decision did indeed bear hard on individual cases, as when he offered an unfortunate Herefordshire gentleman three alternatives, — to man and defend his house himself, to have it occupied by a governor and garrison of the Prince's own choosing, or to blow it up. But, if war is

<hr>

[1] Carte's Ormonde, VI. p. 60, Ormonde to Radcliffe, Mar. 11, 1644.
[2] Rupert's Journal in England. Clarendon State Papers, 2254.
[3] Mercurius Britanicus, May—June, 1644; Webb, Hist. of Civil War in Herefordshire, II. p. 54.

to be effective, such hardships are inevitable; and by Rupert's zealous activity garrisons were wrested from the enemy, and those of the King established, all over the district, in their stead. Of course the complaints which were daily delivered to the Prince were multiplied by his promotion; but, amidst all his labours, he seems to have found a little leisure, for he begged of Ormonde "a cast of goshawks," for his amusement in his winter quarters.[1]

In the meantime his agent at Oxford enjoyed no easy task. For everything that Rupert wanted Trevor had to contend vehemently with Percy and Ashburnham, and, had he not been clever enough to win the alliance of Jermyn, his success would have been small indeed. Jermyn exerted himself nobly. He collected evidence of Rupert's strength and necessities to lay before the Oxford Parliament. He supplied a consignment of muskets, pistols, and powder at his own expense;[2] he even combated the obstinacy of the King, though not always with success, as on one occasion he was forced to despatch supplies to Worcester, "where the King sayeth they are to go, and would have it so, in spite of everything that could be said to the contrary; though I did conceive it was your Highness's desire that they should be sent to Shrewsbury."[3]

Yet even Jermyn was occasionally disheartened by the Prince's insatiable wants. "His Majesty," wrote Trevor in February, "was very well pleased at your letter, and so was my Lord Jermyn, until he found your wants of arms, and ammunition. At which, after a deep sigh, he told me; 'This is of more trouble to me than it would be pain to me at parting of my flesh and bones.'" This despondency is partially accounted for by the next sentence; "The petards I cannot now send Your Highness, by reason of a strong quarrel that is fallen out between M. La Roche

---

[1] Carte Papers, Bodleian Library, 8, 217-222. Rupert to Ormonde, April 1644.
[2] Add. MSS. Brit. Mus. 18981. Trevor to Rupert, Feb. 16, 1644.
[3] Ibid. 18981. Jermyn to Rupert, Mar. 24, 1644.

and Lord Percy, whose warrant and orders he absolutely denies to obey. Where it will end I know not. It begins in fire." [1] This state of affairs must have lasted for weeks. Not until April did Trevor wring two petards from Lord Percy, "and now I have got them, I do not, for my life, know how to send them to your quarters," he declared. And La Roche seems to have been, even then, in the same impracticable frame of mind: "Your Highness's letters to M. La Roche I did deliver; and when he had sworn and stared very sufficiently, and concluded every point with, 'Noe money! noe money!'—he carried me to his little house by Magdalen, and when he had swaggered there a pretty time, and knocked one strange thing against another, he told me he would send me letters, wherewith I was well satisfied, not having money for him, without which I see he hath no more motion than a stone. He talks much of Captain Faussett, but whether good, bad, or indifferent, I swear I do not know!" [2]

Such were the contentions that delayed and handicapped the Royalist forces; but Arthur Trevor was not to be discouraged. "Until I have all the affairs, both of peace and war, settled as they may be most to your desires, I will not miss His Majesty an interview every morning in the garden," [3] he protested; and, on a later occasion, he declared: "I am not so ill a courtier, in a request of money, as to sit down with one denial." [4] His difficulties were increased by the carelessness of Rupert himself, and he wrote to the Prince reproachfully: "I find a bill of exchange signed by Your Highness, and denied by the party you charged it on, and grown to be the discourse of the town before ever I heard a syllable of it. Truly the giving out that bill without giving me advice of it, that I might have

[1] Add. MSS. 18981. Trevor to Rupert, Feb. 1644.
[2] Rupert Transcripts. Trevor to Rupert, Ap. 22, 1644.
[3] Trevor to Rupert, Feb. 1644. Add. MSS. 18981.
[4] Warburton. II. p. 377. Trevor to Rupert, Feb. 22, 1644.

got the money ready, or an excuse for time, hath not done Your Highness right here." [1] Two days later he wrote again: "The liveries for your servants are now come. I only wait for your orders how I shall carry myself towards the merchants, who are very solicitous for ready pay. The sum will be about £200. If Your Highness will not have His Majesty moved in it, Lord Jermyn and I will try all the town, but we will do the worth." [2] Rupert's answer is not forthcoming, but he was evidently as anxious as usual to pay this, or other debts, for he commissioned Trevor to represent to the King the "injustice" that the delay of money was doing towards men to whom he was indebted, and whom he would willingly satisfy. [3]

The needs of the North were becoming very pressing. Newcastle constantly represented the smallness of his forces, and the danger threatening from the Scots. Sir Charles Lucas also forwarded a melancholy account of the northern army, and Lord Derby implored Rupert to go to the rescue of his Countess who was valiantly defending Lathom House: "Sir, I have received many advertisements from my wife, of her great distress and imminent danger," he wrote, "unless she be relieved by your Highness, on whom she doth rely more than on any other whatsoever... I would have waited on your Highness this time, but that I hourly receive little letters from her who haply, a few days hence, may never write me more." [4] But greatest of all was the danger of Newark, besieged by Meldrum, Hubbard and Lord Willoughby. Already the brave little garrison was almost starved into surrender, and willingly would the men have sacrificed their lives in one desperate sally, but for the women and children who would thus have been left to the mercy of the foe. Rupert resolved to go first to the

---

[1] Warburton. II. p. 377. Trevor to Rupert, Feb. 22, 1644.
[2] Ibid. Trevor to Rupert, Feb. 24, 1644. Warb. II. 379.
[3] Add. MSS. Trevor to Rupert, Mar. 11, 1644.
[4] Warburton. II. p. 383. Derby to Rupert, Mar. 7, 1644.

relief of Newark. But even Arthur Trevor could not obtain the supplies necessary for the exploit: "I can promise nothing towards your advantage in those supporters of war, money and arms..." he said. "Money, I am out of hopes of, unless some notable success open the purse strings... March, and then I will make my last attempt for that business, and if I fail I will raise my siege, burn my hut, and march away to your Highness." [1]

Newark was in the last straits. To the reiterated summons of the Puritan forces, the valiant garrison replied only that they could starve, and they could die, but one thing they could not do, and that was open their gates to rebels. Rupert would delay no longer, and, in accordance with Trevor's advice, he set forth, on March 13th, with a small force, borrowed from the garrisons he passed on the march. Essex at once despatched a force of cavalry in pursuit, of which Ashburnham advertised the Prince in the following concise note: "The strength that followeth your Highness is nine hundred dragoons, and one regiment of horse, which I hope they will all be damned." [2] By March 20th Rupert was at Bingham, twelve miles from Newark. The besiegers, who numbered some 2,500 horse and 5,000 foot, heard the news of his approach with light-hearted incredulity, being unable to believe that he could have the temerity to attack them; and in an intercepted letter the Prince found mention of "an incredible rumour" of his advance. [3] When within six miles of Newark he contrived to let the garrison know of his vicinity. Fearing that his cipher had fallen into the hands of the enemy, he dared not write, but sent only an ambiguous message, the meaning of which he did not even explain to the messenger: "Let the old drum be beaten, early on the morrow morning." Happily the Governor, Sir John Henderson, was quick to grasp the meaning—namely,

---

[1] Warburton. II. p. 388. Trevor to Rupert, Mar. 24, 1644.
[2] Ibid. p. 392. Ashburnham to Rupert.
[3] Baker's Chronicle, p. 571.

that he was to sally out on Meldrum at day-break. [1] By two o'clock in the morning, Rupert was in the saddle, and ere it was light, he charged down upon the besieging army. Surprised and confused, the besiegers broke their ranks, and at the same moment the garrison sallied. The fight was hot, and once at least Rupert was in imminent danger. He found himself assaulted by "three sturdy Roundheads" all at once; one he slew with his own sword; Mortaigne, a French follower of the Prince, shot another, and the third, who had laid hold of Rupert's collar, had his hand cut off by O'Neil. The Prince was thus "disengaged, with only a shot in his gauntlet." [2] The engagement lasted nearly all day, but at dusk, Charles Gerard, who had been wounded and captured, came limping forth from the enemy's trenches, with offers of treaty. Rupert agreed to terms, and; on the following morning, Meldrum and his colleagues were permitted to raise the siege and march off with the honours of war.

These terms Rupert was accused of having broken. His men were eager to avenge a Puritan outrage at Lincoln, as formerly at Bristol they had remembered Reading. Therefore when Meldrum's forces marched off with "more than was conditioned," in the shape of arms and pikes, the Royalists seized the excuse to fall upon them, and, in their turn, snatched away colours, and "more than the articles warranted." Rupert, as before, dashed amongst his men with his drawn sword, and he did not neglect to return the stolen colours, with apologies. The occurrence is described by Mrs. Hutchinson, but more fairly by Rushworth, who adds, after relating how the Puritans were despoiled of their pikes and colours: "the King's party excused it, by alleging that they (the Puritans) attempted to carry out more than was conditioned, and that some of theirs had been so used at Lincoln, and especially that it was against the Prince's mind, who slashed

<hr>

[1] Warburton. II. 393—4. Dickison's Antiquities of Newark.
[2] Webb. I. p. 385.

some of his soldiers for it, and sent back all the colours they had taken."[1] When the enemy had fairly retired, Rupert made his entry into Newark, where he was received with delirious joy. Davenant, the Cavalier poet, who himself served in the northern army, celebrated the whole story in a long poem, and thus he describes the Prince's entrance:

"As he entered the old gates, one cry of triumph rose,
 To bless and welcome him who had saved them from their foes;
 The women kiss his charger, and the little children sing:
 'Prince Rupert's brought us bread to eat, from God and from
                                        [the King.'"[2]

Considering the small force with which it had been effected, Rupert's exploit was indeed wonderful, and congratulations poured in from all quarters. "Nephew," wrote the King, "I assure you that this, as all your victories, gives me as much contentment in that I owe you the thanks, as for the importance of it; which in this particular, believe me, is no less than the saving of all the North."[3]

"Our sense of it here is as much beyond expression as the action itself,"[4] declared Digby. Trevor offered all the appreciation possible "On this side idolatry," an expression of which he was rather fond; and even the quiet Richmond was roused to enthusiasm: "Give me leave to dilate now upon my particular joyes," he wrote, "and to retire them so farre from the present jubilee all men are in at your last great victory, to beginne with that which before this jubilee was one to me; I mean the honor and contentment I lately received from you, which, if valew can make precious and an intent affection do anything to show an acknowledgment, will not be lost. Your command to pray for you, at a time was then to come, shall be, as before, my

[1] Hutchinson Memoirs. ed. Firth. 1885. I. p. 325; Rushworth. ed. 1692. pt. 3. II. 308.
[2] Davenant's Poems. Siege of Newark.
[3] Warb. II. 398. King to Rupert, March 25, 1644.
[4] Ibid. p. 399. Digby to Rupert, Mar. 26, 1644.

general rule." [1] Lord Newcastle added to his extravagant congratulations an entreaty that Rupert would push on to his aid; "without which that great game of your uncle's will be endangered, if not lost. ... Could Your Highness march this way, it would, I hope, put a final end to all our troubles." [2] But Rupert, with the best will in the world, lacked the power to do as Newcastle desired. With an army at his back, he might indeed have pushed on northwards, conquered the eastern counties, and driven back the Scots; but he had no army at his disposal! Brilliant though his recent achievement had seemed, it was but ephemeral in reality. Newark relieved, the men who had relieved it returned to the garrisons whence they came, and from which they could ill be spared. All that Rupert had gained was the preservation of a loyal town, and the surrender of a few scattered outposts which he had not men to garrison. Reluctantly he turned back to Wales, where he hoped he might yet raise a force to save the North.

During the weeks of recruiting which followed the relief of Newark, the usual disputes and jealousies agitated the Court. Jermyn, who was still Rupert's friend, expected shortly to quit Oxford with the Queen, and would fain have reconciled the Prince to Digby before his departure. "He has written several times to you since you went away, and you have not made him one answer," he protested. And he proceeded to explain, at great length, how advantageous a correspondence with Digby would be, and how exaggerated were the Prince's notions of the Secretary's hatred to him. [3] But such representations made no impression upon Rupert; the question really at stake was whether he or Digby should rule the King's counsels, and no compromise was possible between them. Another suggestion of Jermyn's met with more favour; there was a vacancy in the King's

---

[1] Rupert Transcripts. Richmond to Rupert, Mar. 25, 1644.
[2] Warburton. II. p. 400. Newcastle to Rupert, Mar. 29, 1644.
[3] Rupert Transcripts. Jermyn to Rupert, Mar. 26, 1644.

Bedchamber, and only Rupert's nomination was needed to secure the appointment for his friend Will Legge. "The chief cause I write is to mention that to you which he (Legge) least looks after, viz., that which pertains to his own interests,"[1] said Jermyn. Rupert obtained the post for his friend, and wrote to "give him joy" of it.[2] At the same time the place of Master of the Horse was offered to himself; hitherto it had been held by the Marquess of Hamilton, who was now deprived of it on account of his disloyalty. "If the King offers Rupert the Master of the Horse's place, he will receive it as a favour," wrote Rupert, in reply to a question on the subject. "But he desires it may not be done so it may look as if Rupert had a hand in the ruin of my Lord Marquis. Let every one carry his own burden."[3]

Ere long, a hasty recall to Oxford roused all the Prince's indignation. True, the order was revoked next day, but Rupert was none the less furious. How was he to effect anything of importance if his plans were to be interrupted and frustrated at Digby's whim? He would not endure, he wrote to Richmond, the discussion of all his proceedings by a mere civilian Council. The Duke strove to pacify him in a long and, as usual, incoherent letter. "You may perceive that no Oxford motion, if rightly represented, could move any cause of jealousy of a desseigne here either to forestall your judgement or prelimett yr command. I have bine present at most of the consultations; (till yesterday some occasions made me absent, and of that daies' worke my Lord Biron will give the best account); and in all I could ever discerne the proceeding hath bine to propound only by way of question alle thinges of moment, which were to be attended, or acted, by you." The recent recall to Oxford Richmond owned an exception to this rule, but as regarded other matters, he concluded;

---

[1] Warburton. II. p. 405. Jermyn to Rupert, Ap. 13, 1644.
[2] Ibid. p. 407. Rupert to Legge. No date.
[3] Ibid.

"I think I could not have mist myselfe so much if other had been to be seen, or where the King's service, and my ancient respect for Rupert, (which time works no such earthy effects upon as to decay), call for my observation, that my senses could be deceived, or I not attentive. The most that was treated was when Will Legge was here, and in his presence, who certainly is a safe man to consult with in your interests.   And the furthest discourse was but discourse!"[1]   The King also wrote on the same day, promising that, whenever possible, his nephew should be *consulted* rather than *commanded;* and asserting with gentle dignity, "Indeed I have this advantage of you, that I have not yet mistaken you in anything as you have me."[2]

Whatever effect these soothing epistles might have had was nullified by a second letter from Digby, in which he assumed a tone of authority such as Rupert would not brook. "Lord Digby, with whom Prince Rupert hath no present kindness, writ yesterday about the relief of Lathom House," wrote Trevor to Ormonde. "The paper, which was not an order, but would fain have disputed itself into authority, was so ill-received that I am afraid my work of reconciliation is at an end."[3]   Rupert was indeed in an angry frame of mind.   He despatched a furious, incoherent letter to Legge, full of ironical and rather unintelligible complaints against his uncle, and dark threats of his own resignation.   "If the King will follow the *wise* counsel, and not hear the soldier and Rupert, Rupert must leave off all."   And he wound up with a short account of a successful skirmish, adding spitefully: "If Goring had done this you would have had a handsome story."[4]   None of the plans then in favour at Oxford met with his approval.   The Queen was bent on going to Exeter, in spite of her nephew's assurance

<hr>

[1] Rupert Transcripts. Richmond to Rupert, Ap. 21, 1644.
[2] Ibid. and Warburton. II. 403, *note.*   King to Rupert, 1st and 21st Ap. 1644.
[3] Carte's Ormonde. VI. p. 87. Trevor to Ormonde, Ap. 13, 1644.
[4] Warburton. II. 408. Rupert to Legge, Ap. 23, 1644.

that the place was most unsafe, as indeed it proved; and the King was extremely anxious to send the Prince of Wales to Bristol, as nominal head of the army in the West. But Rupert had not much faith in Maurice's army, and he thought that the young Prince would be far better under his own care. He had at that time a paramount influence over little Charles, and he had, besides, a staunch ally in one of his young cousin's gentlemen, a certain Elliot, whom the King considered to have "too much credit"[1] with his son. Between them, Prince Charles was inspired with such an aversion to his father's plan that he boldly declared he would have none of it, and added ingenuously, that his Cousin Rupert had "left him his lesson" before his departure from Oxford.[2] His submission to Rupert's will is evidenced by the letters of Elliot to the Prince: "He has commanded me to tell you that he is so far from believing that any man can love him better than you do, that he shall, by his good will, enterprise nothing wherein he has not your Highness's approbation. For the intention of carrying him to that army, (in the West,) he has yet heard nothing of it, and, if he shall, he will without fail oppose it; and I may say truely that if he has a great kindness for any man it is for your Highness."[3] For the moment Rupert triumphed. Richmond, who opposed the plan for the West as strongly as the Prince could have wished, assured him that it was "but a dream,"[4] and for a while it fell into abeyance.

In the beginning of May, Rupert's new levies were ready for action, but when the moment for the northern march had come, the Prince was, to his intense disgust, once more summoned to Oxford. So earnestly did he deprecate

[1] Clarendon Life. I. 229.
[2] Add. MSS. 18981. Ellyot to Rupert, May 7, 1644.
[3] Ibid. 18981. May 22, 1644.
[4] Rupert Correspondence. Add. MSS. 18981. Richmond to Rupert, May 26, 1644.

the recall, that the King declared he would be content with 2,000 foot and one regiment of horse, provided that Rupert would join him at Oxford in the beginning of June. But the one demand was as fatal as the other. Rupert's heart was set on the relief of Lord Newcastle, and he could not bear that his hard won army should be thus ruthlessly torn from him. A personal interview with the King was his only chance, and, with characteristic rashness, he marched off to Oxford with the most slender of escorts, to plead his cause with his uncle. Eloquently he explained to the King the simplicity of his plans. All that Charles himself had to do was to keep the surrounding towns well garrisoned, to manœuvre round Oxford with a body of horse, and, in the meantime, to leave Maurice free in the West, and Rupert free for the North. On May 5th the Prince left Oxford, having every reason to believe that his advice would be followed. But, on the very next day, Digby had persuaded the King to abandon the plan as too extensive; Rupert wrote to expostulate, but received only thanks for his "freedom," with the comment, "I am not of your opinion in all the particulars."[1] And when misfortune had ensued, it was but slight consolation that the King acknowledged his error, "I believe that if you had been with me I had not been put to those straits I am in now. I confess the best had been to have followed your advice."[2] Richmond also lamented Rupert's absence. "We want money, men, conduct, provisions, time, and good counsel," he asserted; "our hope rests chiefly in your good success."[3]

Rupert was by that time far away in the North. On May 8th he had returned to Shrewsbury, and on the 16th he began his long projected march to York. From Chester he drew out all the men who could be spared, leaving "honest Will Legge" in their place. At Knutsford he had

---

[1] Rupert Transcripts. King to Rupert, May 26, 1644.
[2] Ibid. June 7, 1644; Warburton. II. p. 415.
[3] Richmond to Rupert, June 9, 1644; Warb. II. p. 415.

a successful encounter with some Parliamentary troops; and on the 25th he seized upon Stockport, which so alarmed the forces besieging Lathom House, that they raised the siege, and marched off to Bolton. So strong was the Puritanism of Bolton that it has been called the "Geneva of England," and Rupert at once resolved to take the town. His first assault was repulsed, and the besieged, in their triumph, hanged one of his Irish troopers over the walls. The insult gave the Prince new stimulus; throwing himself from his horse he called up his retreating men, and renewed the attack with such vigour that the town was quickly stormed, and he entered it with Lord Derby at his side. The angry troopers sacked the place; and Rupert sent the twenty-two standards he had taken to Lady Derby, as a graceful acknowledgment of her long and valiant defence of Lathom. Recruits now flocked to his standard, and his march became a triumphal progress; so great was the enthusiasm of the loyal town of Wigan, that rushes, flowers and boughs were strewn in the streets before him. On June 11th he won another triumph, in the capture of Liverpool, which suffered a like fate with Bolton. But he was disappointed of the stores he had expected to find there, which were all carried off by sea before the town fell. From Liverpool the Prince wrote a curious letter to the Bishop of Chester, asking for a collection to be made in all the churches of the diocese for the benefit of the sick and wounded soldiers. And he also expressed a desire that the clergy should exhort the people to prepare for their own defence and to maintain their loyalty, in language "most intelligent to the congregation." [1]

It was now high time to set out for York, which Newcastle felt that he could hold only six days more. Richmond wrote to urge as much haste as possible. "If York should be lost," he said, "it would prove the greatest blow

---

[1] Warburton. II. p. 432.

which could come from those parts, Rupert being safe; but what is fit to be done you will best know and judge." [1] But Rupert was not just then in a state of mind to judge calmly of anything. His enemies at Court, envious of his recent success, were preparing new calumnies against him, and profiting by his absence to excite the King's distrust. Some did not hesitate to hint at the Prince's over-greatness and possible designs on the Crown itself; and all urged the King to recall him, rather than suffer him to risk his army in a great battle. Trevor thus reported the affair to Ormonde: "Prince Rupert, by letters from Court, understands that the King grows daily more and more jealous of him, and of his army; so that it is the commonest discourse at the openest places, of the Lord Digby, Lord Percy, Sir John Culpepper, and Wilmot, that it is indifferent whether the Parliament or Prince Rupert doth prevail. Which doth so highly jesuite *(sic)* Prince Rupert that he was resolved once to send the King his commission and get to France. This fury interrupted the march ten days. But at length, time and a friend, the best coolers of the blood, spent the humour of travel in him, though not that of revenge. ....This quarrel hath a strong reserve, and I am fearful that a little ill-success will send my new master home into Holland. I perceive the tide's strong against him, and that nothing will bring him to port but that wind which is called *contra gentes.*" [2] And, about the same time, Ormonde was informed by another correspondent, that "Prince Rupert professeth against Lord Digby, Percy, Wilmot and some others. Some think that he will remove them from the King. The fear of this may do harm; perhaps had done already." [3] The ten days' delay was spent chiefly at Lathom House, and by June 22nd, Rupert had sufficiently recovered his temper to set out for York. Some days previously Goring had

[1] Rupert Transcripts. Richmond to Rupert, June 14, 1644.
[2] Carte's Ormonde. VI. p. 151. Trevor to Ormonde, 29 June, 1644.
[3] Ibid. VI. p. 167. Radcliffe to Ormonde, 18 July, 1644.

written that he was ready to join the Prince with 8,000 horse, and only awaited the appointment of a meeting-place. The King, at the same time, demanded Goring's instant return to himself, but Rupert took no notice of the order, being convinced, and rightly as it happened, that Goring's services were more necessary to himself. He joined Goring on the borders of Lancashire and Yorkshire. On the 26th he halted at Skipton, to "fix his armes," [1] and to send a message to York. On the 29th he quartered at Denton, the house of the Puritan General, Lord Fairfax. Two of the Fairfaxes had fallen years ago, in the fight for the Palatinate, and Rupert, having noticed their portraits, preserved the house uninjured for their sakes. "Such force hath gratitude in noble minds," [2] comments the Fairfax who tells the story. Lord Fairfax and his son were both engaged at the siege of York, together with Lord Manchester, and the Scotch General, Leven; but there was no good intelligence between the Parliamentary commanders, and they dared not await the onslaught of the Prince. "Their Goliah himself is advancing, with men not to be numbered," [3] was the report among the Puritans; and when Rupert reached Knaresborough on June 30th, only twelve miles distant from York, the Generals of the Parliament raised the siege and marched off to Marston Moor. They hoped to bar Rupert's passage to the city, but by skilful manœuvring he crossed the Ouse, and halted outside York. "Prince Rupert had done a glorious piece of work," wrote a soldier of the Parliament. "From nothing he had gathered, without money, a powerful army, and, in spite of all our three generals, had made us leave York." [4] So far all was well, and well for Rupert had he left things thus! But, alas, he was about to make his first great mistake, and to take a decided step on his downward career.

---

[1] Clar. State Papers. Rupert's Journal, Fol. 135.
[2] Fairfax Correspondence. ed. Johnson. 1848. I. p. 1.
[3] Pamphlet. Brit. Mus. Warburton. II. p. 442.
[4] Webb. II. p. 59.

The blame of the disastrous battle of Marston Moor has always been laid upon Rupert, but his friends were wont to ascribe it rather to Lord Digby, who, they believed, had inspired the King's "fatal" letter of June 14th; a letter which Rupert carried about him to his dying day, though he never produced it in refutation of any of the charges against him. "Had not the Lord Digby, this year, given a fatal direction to that excellent Prince Rupert to fight the Scottish army, surely that great Prince and soldier had never so precipitately fought them," [1] declared Sir Philip Warwick, who was himself present at the battle. The King began his letter with apologies for sending such "peremptory commands," but went on to explain: "If York be lost I shall esteem my crown little less. ... But if York be relieved, *and you beat the rebels' army of both Kingdoms, which are before it, then, but otherwise not*, I may possibly make a shift, upon the defensive, to spin out time until you come to assist me." [2] The order was plain, and though Rupert did some-times ignore less congenial commands, he could scarcely disobey such an order as this, unless he had private inform-ation that his uncle's situation was less desperate than he had represented it. Culpepper, at least, never doubted what would be the Prince's action: "Before God you are undone!" he cried, when told that the letter was sent—"For upon this peremptory order he will fight, whatever comes on't!" [3]

And Culpepper was right. Rupert greeted Newcastle with the words, "My Lord, I hope we shall have a glorious day!" And when Newcastle advised him to wait patiently, until the internal dissensions of the enemy broke up their camp, he retorted, "Nothing venture, nothing have!" and declared that he had "a positive and absolute command to fight the enemy." [4] He showed plainly that he had no inten-

---

[1] Warwick's Memoirs, p. 274.
[2] Rupert Correspondence. King to Rupert, June 14, 1644; Warburton. II. p. 438.
[3] Warburton. II. p. 438.
[4] Clarendon State Papers. 1805. Life of Newcastle. ed. Firth. p. 77, *note*.

tion of listening to the Marquess, at whose cost the whole northern army had been raised and maintained. The older man was silenced, vexed at his subordination to the young Prince whom he had so eagerly called to his aid, and hurt and offended by Rupert's abrupt manners. But, as Professor Gardiner has pointed out, Newcastle's achievements were not such as could inspire great respect in the soldier prince.[1] He was but a dilettante in war as in the gentler arts, and his reasoning was not, on the face of it, very convincing. His manœuvres might fail; and Rupert, who had not yet met Cromwell's horse, had no reason to suppose that his charge would be less effective now than in time past. As for the Parliamentary forces, their only hope lay in battle, and they gladly perceived the Prince's intention to fight.

Throughout the day the two armies faced one another; but Rupert dared not attack without Newcastle, and there was considerable delay in drawing out his forces. Trevor reported that, "The Prince and the Marquess of Newcastle were playing the Orators to the soldiers in York, being in a raging mutiny for their pay, to draw them forth to join the Prince's foot; which was at last effected, but with much unwillingness."[2] But it was the interest of Rupert's partisans to undervalue the assistance lent by the Marquess; and Trevor himself did not arrive on the scene till the battle was over. By other accounts it does not seem that the Prince entered the city at all. Though he had not yet met with Cromwell, he had heard of him, and he is said to have asked a prisoner, "Is Cromwell there? And will they fight?" The answer was in the affirmative, and Rupert despatched the prisoner back to his own army, with the message that they should have "fighting enough!" To which Cromwell retorted: "If it please God, so shall he!"[3]

<hr>

[1] Gardiner's Civil War. Vol. I. p. 374.
[2] Carte, Original Letters. I. 57, 10 July, 1644.
[3] Gardiner, Vol. I. p. 376.

The evening was wild and stormy. As it grew dusk, Rupert ordered prayers to be read to his men, a proceeding much resented by the Puritans, who regarded religion as their own particular monopoly. Earlier in the war, they had complained that the Prince "pretended piety in his tongue";[1] and now they declared wrathfully: "Rupert, that bloody plunderer, would forsooth to seem religious!"[2]

The Prince had drawn up his army for immediate attack. In the centre was placed his foot, flanked on the right by Goring's horse; on the left wing, which was opposed to the Scots, Rupert placed his own cavalry. Behind the Prince's army was disposed that of Newcastle, both horse and foot. But by the time that the line of battle was ready, evening had come, and Rupert judged it too late to fight. Here lay his fatal error, for he had drawn up his forces to the very edge of a wide ditch which stretched between himself and the foe; instant attack alone could retrieve the position. Yet Rupert seems to have been unconscious of his mistake, for he showed his sketch of the plan of battle gaily to Lord Eythin (the General King, who had been with him at Vlotho), asking how he liked it. "By God, Sir, it is very fine on paper, but there is no such thing in the field!" was Eythin's prompt reply. Then Rupert saw what he had done, and meekly offered to draw back his men. "No, Sir," retorted Eythin, "it is too late."[3] Seeing that nothing could be done, the Prince sat down on the ground to take his supper, and Newcastle retired to his coach to smoke. In another moment the enemy fired, and the battle had begun. Rupert flew to the head of his horse, but Cromwell's horse charged over the ditch, and Rupert's one chance, that of assuming the offensive, was gone. For a few moments he drove Cromwell back, but Leslie's Scots

[1] Pamphlet. Brit. Mus. Prince Rupert's Message to My Lord of Essex.
[2] Vicars' Jehovah Jireh. God's Ark. p. 281.
[3] Gardiner. I. p. 377.

came up, and Rupert's once invincible cavalry fled before "Ironside", as he himself named Cromwell on that day. In the Royalist centre the Scots did deadly work. Newcastle's Whitecoats fell almost to a man, dying with their own blood the white tunics which they had vowed to dye in the blood of the enemy. On the right, Goring routed the Yorkshire troops of the Fairfaxes, who fled, reporting a Royalist victory; but that success could not redeem the day. Rupert's army was scattered, Newcastle's brave troopers were cut to pieces, York fallen, the whole north lost, and—worst of all—Rupert's prestige destroyed. Arthur Trevor, arriving at the end of the battle, found all in confusion, "not a man of them being able to give me the least hope where the Prince was to be found." [1] Rupert had, in fact, finding himself all alone, leapt his horse over a high fence into a bean-field, and, sheltered by the growing beans, he made his way to York, "escaping narrowly, by the goodness of his horse." [2] Dead upon that fatal field he left his much loved dog. In the hurry and excitement of the charge he had forgotten to tie it up with the baggage waggons, and it followed him into the battle. "Among the dead men and horses which lay upon the ground, we found Prince Rupert's dog killed," says Vicars. [3]

It was reported by the Puritans that Rupert declared himself unable to account for the disaster, except by the supposition that "the devil did help his servants;" a speech characterised as "most atheistical and heathenish." [4] The Prince blamed Newcastle, and Newcastle blamed the Prince; but the manner in which each took his defeat is so characteristic as to deserve quotation.

"Sayes Generall King, 'What will you do?'

"Sayes ye Prince, 'I will rally my men.'

---

[1] Carte's Letters, I. p. 56.

[2] Whitelocke, p. 94.

[3] Vicars' God's Ark. p. 277,

[4] Ibid. p. 274.

"Sayes Generall King, 'Nowe you, what will you, Lord Newcastle, do?'

"Sayes Lord Newcastle, 'I will go into Holland.'

"The Prince would have him endeavour to recruit his forces. 'No,' sayes he, 'I will not endure the laughter of the Court.'"[1] Newcastle's decision was the subject of much discussion at Court. "I am sure the reckoning is much inflamed by my Lord Newcastle's going,"[2] declared O'Neil, who on this occasion sided with the Prince. Rupert had done his best to detain both Eythin and the Marquess, but when he found his efforts vain, he let them depart, promising to report that Newcastle had behaved "like an honest man, a gentleman, and a loyal subject."[3] Eythin he found it harder to forgive; and some months later that General wrote to represent the "multiteud of grieffs" he endured through the Prince's bad opinion of him. "I would rather suffer anything in the world, than live innocently in Your Highness's malgrace,"[4] he declared.

Rupert's own conduct was soldierly enough. Bitterly though he felt the position, he was of stronger mould than the fantastic Marquess. Clarendon blames him severely for leaving York, but Clarendon was no soldier, and he did not understand that the attempt to hold the city, with no hope of relief, would have been sheer madness. What Rupert could do, he did: gathering together the shattered remnants of his army, he marched away into Shropshire, "according to the method he had before laid for his retreat; taking with him all the northern horse which the Earl of Newcastle left to His Highness, and brought them into his quarters in Wales, and there endeavoured to recruit what he could."[5] On the second day of his retreat he halted at Richmond,

---

[1] Warburton, II. p. 468.

[2] Carte's Letters, I. 59. O'Neil to Trevor, 26 June, 1644.

[3] Life of Newcastle. ed. Firth, 1886. p. 81.

[4] Pythouse Papers, p. 21. General King to Rupert, Jan. 23, 1645.

[5] Rupert's Diary. Warburton, II. 468

where he remained three days, "staying for the scattered troops." On July 7th he resumed his march, and passing by Lathom House, whence Lord Derby had departed, he came on the 25th to Chester. On the Welsh Marches he wandered until the end of August, foraging, recruiting, skirmishing, while the Parliament exulted in his overthrow. " As for Rupert which shed so much innocent blood at Bolton and at Liverpool, if you ask me where he is, we seriously protest that we know not where to find him." [1]

Rupert did not need the jeers of his enemies to convince him of his failure. He was beaten and he knew it! His projects were crossed, his labours unavailing, and in his heart he knew that the cause was lost. The disaster had cut him to the heart, yet, in his pride, he would not speak a word of self-justification. He had obeyed orders, the result was unfortunate, and no excuse or vindication would he offer. Perhaps he thought he acted generously in not shifting the responsibility to the King, but Clarendon blames his reticence. "Prince Rupert, only to his friends and after the murder of the King," he says, "produced a letter in the King's own hand... which he understood to amount to no less than a peremptory order to fight, upon any disadvantage whatsoever; and he added that the disadvantage was so great that it was no wonder he lost the day."

Deeply had the iron entered into Rupert's soul! Other misfortunes were yet to come; he was to know a yet more fatal defeat, poverty, hardships such as he had never yet encountered, the misjudgment of friends, the loss of those dearest to him; but nothing could be to him as the shock of Marston Moor had been. Nothing could affect him as that first great failure which dashed him from the height of triumph to the depths of despair. He seems to have been, for a time, strangely unlike himself. The strain under which he had laboured suddenly relaxed, apathy succeeded

[1] Webb, II. 71.

to over-wrought excitement, carelessness to vigilance, self-indulgence to rigid self-restraint, and the Royalists looked on in terrified dismay! "Prince Rupert is so much given to his ease and pleasures that every man is disheartened that sees it,"[1] lamented Arthur Trevor. Strangely do the words contrast with the "toujours soldat" of Sir Philip Warwick, and with the general praises of the Prince's "exemplary temperance," but Trevor would assuredly not have spoken undeserved evil of his master. Despair had seized on Rupert's soul, and he sought to drown the bitterness of memory in sensual indulgences.

The mood passed with the autumn, and, ere the winter had come, Rupert was a man again, ready as ever to do and dare. But the scar remained; all his life long he carried the King's letter on his person, and all his life long Marston Moor was a bitter memory to him!

[1] Carte's Ormonde, VI. 206. Trevor to Ormonde, 13 Oct. 1644.

CHAPTER IX

INTRIGUES IN THE ARMY. DEPRESSION OF RUPERT. TREATY
OF UXBRIDGE.   RUPERT IN THE MARCHES.   STRUGGLE
WITH DIGBY.   BATTLE OF NASEBY

TERRIBLE though the disaster in the North had been, the blow was softened to the King by successes in the West. During August, in company with Maurice, he pursued Essex into Cornwall and forced his whole army of foot to surrender without a struggle. But for the supineness of Goring, who had just succeeded Wilmot as General of the Horse, the Parliamentary cavalry might have been captured in like manner. But when Balfour led his troops through the Royalist lines, Goring happened to be carousing in congenial company; he received the news of the escape with laughter, and refused to stir until the enemy were safely passed away.[1]   Goring's new prominence and importance was one among the many unfortunate results of Marston Moor.   That battle had ruined Rupert's reputation, and it had proportionately raised that of Goring, who alone among the Royalist commanders had had success that day. To Goring, therefore, the King turned, and Goring's licence, negligence, indifference—or perhaps treachery—eventually lost the West completely to the Royalists. Had Rupert been placed in Goring's position he must have certainly effected more than did his rival.

For some time the King had been anxious to remove Wilmot from his command. As early as May he had suggested to Rupert, as "a fancy of my own,"[2] that Maurice

---

[1] Clarendon, Bk. VII. p. 96, *note*.

[2] King to Rupert, 26 May, 1644. Rupert Correspondence, Add. MSS. 18981.

should be declared General of the Horse in Wilmot's stead. But Rupert did not encourage the idea; he knew probably that his brother was unfit for so much responsibility. Wilmot therefore remained in command until August 9th. He was, as has been said, a good officer, but he talked so wildly in his cups that his loyalty was suspected; and when he was detected in private correspondence with Essex, the King decided to arrest him, and to promote Goring to his post. The arrest took place in sight of the whole army; but though Wilmot was exceedingly popular with his officers, they confined their protest to a little murmuring and a "modest petition" to be told the charges against their commander. The King responded by a promise that Wilmot should have a fair trial, and his partisans were apparently pacified, though Goring declared to Rupert: "This is the most mutinous army that ever I saw, as well horse as foot!"[1] Digby's account of the affair, also addressed to the Prince, was as follows: "We have lately ventured on extreme remedies unto the dangers that threaten us amongst ourselves. Lord Wilmot, upon Wednesday that was a s'ennight, was arrested prisoner on the head of his army, and Goring declared General of the Horse. ... There have been since consultations and murmurings among his party, but the issue of them was only this enclosed modest petition, which produced the answer and declaration of the causes of his commitment; and so the business rests. My Lord Percy also withdrawing himself upon good advice, and my Lord Hopton being possessed of his charge, I make no doubt that all the ill-humours in our army will be allayed, now that the two poles on which they moved are taken away."[2]

But, though neither Wilmot nor Percy were estimable characters, Goring was no better, and the result of these drastic measures was only to render the state of Court and

[1] Warburton, III. p. 16.
[2] Add. MSS. 18981. Digby to Rupert, Aug. 15, 1644.

Army more confused and more factious than ever. Digby's partisans tried to lay the onus of Wilmot's fall on Rupert, and Rupert's friends endeavoured to refer it to Digby. Judging from Digby's own letter above quoted, Rupert, who was absent from the King's army during the whole of the proceedings, does not seem to have had much share in them. Certainly the Secretary gives no hint of his collusion. "Lord Digby is the great agent to incense the King," asserted Arthur Trevor. "My Lord Wilmot undertakes to turn the tables on him, and so the wager is laid head to head. Daniel O'Neil goeth his share in that hazard, for certainly the Lord Digby hath undone his credit with the King... And truly I look upon Daniel O'Neil as saved only out of want of leisure to dispose of him. Prince Rupert and Will Legge are his severe enemies; and so is Ashburnham."[1] Critical indeed was the position of the unlucky Daniel, who had been so lately the "dear and intimate friend" of Digby. Owing, as he explained to Ormonde, to "the unfortunate falling out of my two best friends," he had fallen between two stools. Wilmot he considered most to blame, for he had endeavoured to render Digby "odious to the army and to all honest people."[2] The army had been on the very point of petitioning against the Secretary when he forestalled the move by the unexpected arrest of his adversary. "How guilty he will be, I know not," was the conclusion of O'Neil. "But sure I am that the accusing of him was not seasonable, and his commitment less... and two friends I have lost!"[3] Wilmot himself seems to have directed his animus principally against Rupert. He was unwilling to stand his trial, and was therefore permitted to join the Queen, then in France. There he found the Marquess of Newcastle, whom he hoped to secure as an ally against the Prince. "I understand from one coming from Wilmot," wrote

[1] Carte's Letters, I. 63. 13 Sept. 1644.
[2] Carte's Ormonde, IV. 190. 13 Aug. 1644.
[3] Ibid.

Trevor, "that he and the Marquess of Newcastle are preparing a charge against Prince Rupert, and will be at the next advice of Parliament at Oxford, where their party will be great,—the Marquess of Hertford, Lord Herbert— you may guess the rest. Prince Rupert and Daniel O'Neil are inconsistent in this state."[1]

The proposed accusation of Rupert was never made, and was probably a figment of Wilmot's brain. Neither Hertford nor Herbert (with whom Rupert had clashed as President of Wales) had any love for the Prince, but they were both too loyal to increase the King's difficulties by factious action. And indeed in the spring of 1645, we find Hertford, Rupert, and Ashburnham in close alliance against Digby and Cottington; the three first desiring a treaty with the Parliament, and the other two opposing it. O'Neil was easily convinced that Wilmot owed his fall to Rupert, and in October 1644 he wrote to Ormonde: "Prince Rupert, whoe is nowe knowen to bee the primum mobile of that mischeef, iss strangely unsatisfied with Wilmot's resolutione. For he thought to make use of this occatione to ruine Lord Digby; but, his project fayling, he plays the Courtier and iss reconsyled, whiche iss a great hapines to the King."[2]

The truth was that, were the charges against them true or false, Wilmot and Percy did really owe their downfall to the hatred of Rupert and Digby. The Secretary had been the actual agent in the matter, but Rupert approved and supported his action. The two were willing enough to unite against their enemies, and they would have been equally willing to ruin each other. But for a time Rupert endeavoured, for his uncle's sake, to curb his hatred of the Secretary. In August the King had exhorted his nephew earnestly to make friends with Digby; "whom I must desire you (for my service, and because he is a useful servant) to countenance so far as to show him a possibility to recover

---

[1] Carte's Ormonde. VI. 206. 13 Oct. 1644.
[2] Ibid. Vol. VI. 203. 3 Oct. 1644.

your favour, if he shall deserve it ... Not doubting but, for my sake, ye will make this, or a greater, experiment ... I must protest to you, on the faith of a Christian—the reason of this protest I refer to Robin Legge—that as concerning your generosity and particular fidelity and friendship to me, I have an implicit faith in you." [1] This passionate protest was caused by the libels circulated against the Prince, some of which had reached the King's ears. For a while Rupert was pacified, and he made overtures of tolerance to Digby, who responded fluently that his previous unhappiness as the object of Rupert's aversion, would now serve only to increase his joy and satisfaction in the Prince's confidence and friendship. [2] "Rupert and Digby are friends; but I doubt they trust one another alike!" [3] was the Prince's own view of the matter, as expressed to Will Legge.

Digby had also formed a close friendship with Goring, "each believing that he could deceive the other." It was to Digby that Goring chiefly owed his promotion, though it had been accorded the approval of Rupert, who was inclined, just then, to tolerate Goring. Nor was George Goring backward in receiving overtures of peace. "My Prince," he wrote to Rupert familiarly, and he signed himself, "your Highness's all-vowed, all-humble, all-obedient Goring." Moreover, having made up his mind never to serve under Rupert again, he took care to add, "there is nothing on this earth I more passionately desire than to sacrifice my life in your service, and near your person." [4] But the truce could not last. Rupert, as Commander-in-Chief and Governor of Bristol, had a double power in the West, and Goring was determined to escape from his control. In January 1645, we find him writing with unwonted candour: "Your Highness is pleased to think yourself disobliged by me for

---

[1] Add. MSS. 18981. King to Rupert, Aug. 30, 1644.
[2] Ibid. Sept. 23, 1644. Digby to Rupert.
[3] Rupert to Legge. Oct. 16, 1644. Warburton, III. p. 27.
[4] Warburton, II. 172, and III. 16.

desiring my orders under the King's hand. As I remember, Sir, the reason I gave His Majesty for it was the having more authority by that to guide the Council of this army to obedience; *but one reason I kept to myself*, which was that I found all my requests denied by your hand, and therefore desired my orders from another."[1]

The Prince of Wales had by this time been sent to Bristol as nominal General of the Western army, with a selection of the King's Councillors to assist him. The conflicting orders of Rupert, Prince Charles's Council, and the King, gave Goring an excellent excuse for disobeying all. In March, Rupert indignantly desired Legge to ask the King whether he had authorised that Council to send orders to Goring, and added cautiously, "Let Sir Edward Herbert be by, he can argue better than you."[2] A few days later he visited his young cousin at Bristol, and advised him to send Goring with his horse into Wiltshire, or with his foot to besiege Taunton. Prince Charles sent orders as directed, but Goring, knowing them to emanate from Rupert, retired to Bath, and refused to do anything at all. Rupert now thoroughly "abhorred" the notion of Goring's proximity to the Prince of Wales, and had him recalled to Oxford. But there his friendship with Digby, and his own natural powers, won him so much influence with the King, that Rupert was soon as eager to send him back into the West as Goring was to escape from the Prince's vicinity. Thus their "very contrary affections towards each other,"[3] worked to one end. There was a second truce. Rupert told Goring, no doubt with some pleasure, all the evil that the Council of the West had said concerning him; and Goring returned the compliment, with notes and additions. Goring was given the command of all the West, whither he gladly departed. "Goring and Prince Rupert are now friends," wrote

---

[1] Warburton, III. p. 52.
[2] Warburton, III. p. 73. Rupert to Legge, Mar. 31, 1645.
[3] Clarendon, Bk. IX. p. 30.

Trevor, "but I doubt the building being made of green wood, which is apt to warp and yield!"[1] As proved ere long to be the case.

We return now to the autumn of 1644. Rupert's wanderings had brought him, by the end of August, to Bristol, whither he was pursued by doleful reports from his officers left in the Marches.

"My most dear Prince," wrote Legge from Chester, "in truth Your Highness's departure sent me back here a sad man, and the news I met with gave me new cause of trouble.... I despair of any good in Lancashire."[2] And in Cheshire itself, Byron and Langdale had just suffered a defeat from Massey. "Upon the spot where Your Highness killed the buck, as the horse were drawing out,"[3] explained Byron with careful exactness. These new misfortunes increased Rupert's melancholy, which was already deep enough. Something of his state of mind may be gathered from a sympathetic and consolatory letter written to him at this time by Richmond.

"Though I was very much pleased for myself with the honour and favour I had by yours from Bristol, yet I must confess, it takes not all unquietness from me. The melancholy you express must be a discontent, for my mind which has so much respect must partake of the trouble of yours. And I should be more restless if I did believe your present sad opinion would be long continued, or that there were just cause for it. All mistakes, I am confident, will wane, when the King can speak with power. I shall not prejudice that *éclairissement* by being tedious beforehand. Yet I will say that, though an intention (to that purpose) was not the cause of your coming sooner to the King, you could not have resolved better by the King's good at this time. So in your own understanding

---

[1] Carte's Letters, I. 86—87, 25 May, 1645.
[2] Warburton, III. p. 21.
[3] Ibid. p. 22.

JAMES STUART, DUKE OF RICHMOND.

*From the Engraving in the British Museum after the Portrait by Vandyke in the
Collection of Paul Methuen, Esq.*

Face page 160.

you must consent that even from those actions which are the most retired from an appearance (of it) blessings spring. How great this will be when Rupert makes it his care, as formerly our hope, measure by joy (*sic*). This I conclude doth certainly engage Rupert to know how great good he may bring the King, which must also assure Rupert of the love, value, and trust the King must have of him. This mutual satisfaction will prove happy to themselves, and to all who respect either, as I do both!" [1] The Duke's friendly attempt to console the Prince for past misfortunes, restore his self-confidence, and reassure him of the King's trust and affection seems to have succeeded. Rupert roused himself, and set out, September 29th, to meet the King at Sherborne in Dorset. Charles was just then returning from his successful expedition to Cornwall, and Waller had been despatched by the Parliament to intercept him. Rupert extracted from his uncle a promise not to fight until he could rejoin him, and hastened back to fortify Bristol. But the perilous condition of two Royalist garrisons, those of Basing House, and Donnington Castle, made delay impossible. The King sent peremptory orders to Rupert to join him at Salisbury with all the force he could muster. But, before Rupert could obey, Goring, "possessed by a great gaiety," [2] had drawn Charles into the second unfortunate battle of Newbury. Rupert, making all possible haste, reached Marshfield near Bristol, the day after the battle, October 28th. There he learnt that the King had been defeated at Newbury, and was now at Bath. Maurice, it was feared, was dead or a prisoner. Upon this, Rupert asserted, oddly as it seems, that his brother was quite safe; and so it proved, for he was discovered at Donnington Castle. [3] Both Princes joined the King at Bath, and thence, by Rupert's advice, marched to Oxford. At Newbury they

---

[1] Rupert Transcripts. Richmond to Rupert, Sept. 14, 1644.
[2] Clarendon, Bk. VIII. p. 149.
[3] Warburton, III. p. 31.

again encountered Waller and Cromwell, but refused battle, and Rupert succeeded in drawing off his forces without losing one man. The dexterous retreat was compared by one of the young nobles to a country dance. [1] On November 21st Rupert made a vain attempt to recover Abingdon, which was now possessed for the Parliament; and on the 23rd he entered Oxford with the King.

During the march, the Prince had finally received that appointment of Master of the Horse concerning which he had entertained so many doubts. At the same time he was declared Commander-in-Chief in place of the old Lord Brentford, who had become very deaf, and who "by the long-continued practice of immoderate drinking, dozed in his understanding." [2] The change was exceedingly popular with the soldiers, but exceedingly distasteful to the courtiers and councillors. Brentford had always been willing to permit discussion, only feigning unusual deafness when he was strongly averse to the proposals made. But Rupert showed himself "rough and passionate," [3] cut short debate whenever possible, and endeavoured to carry all with a high hand. In addition to the promotion already conferred on him, he had expected the colonelcy of the Life-Guards, and when this was bestowed on Lord Bernard Stewart, the Prince felt himself so unreasonably injured "that he was resolved to lay down his command upon it." [4] He did in fact go the length of demanding a pass to quit the kingdom, but happily the persuasions of his friends brought him to a wiser state of mind, and he apologised for his folly. Another fruitless attempt on Abingdon closed the military proceedings of the year.

The chief events of the winter months were the Treaty

[1] Warburton, III. p. 32.
[2] Clar. Hist. Bk. VIII. p. 29.
[3] Ibid. p. 108.
[4] Warburton, III. p. 32, and Rupert's Journal, Nov. 15, 1644, Clarendon Papers.

of Uxbridge, and the forming of the Parliament's new model army. The negotiation of January 1645 was due to Scottish influence, and though many of the Royalists were eager to come to terms, the religious question proved, as always, an insuperable obstacle. Moreover, it was quite impossible for Charles to accept the long list of excepted persons "who shall expect no pardon," which was headed by the names of his own nephews. The Princes themselves appear to have been infinitely amused by the circumstance, for it is recorded by Whitelocke, himself one of the Parliamentary Commissioners: "Prince Rupert and Prince Maurice being present, when their names were read out as excepted persons, they fell into a laughter, at which the King seemed displeased, and bid them be quiet." [1]

In spite of this incident, Rupert forwarded the treaty by all means in his power. He had been one of the first to meet the Commissioners on their arrival. They had gone, on the same day, to visit Lord Lindsey, and ten minutes after their entrance Rupert had put in an appearance, privately summoned by their host, as the Commissioners suspected. He had been present at all the discussions of the treaty, occasionally speaking to remind the King of some forgotten point, but otherwise keeping silence; [2] and when the treaty ultimately collapsed, the Prince "deeply deplored" its failure. He understood only too well the weakness of the King's resources, and the growing strength of the Parliament. The new model army, from which all incompetent officers were excluded, and which was to resemble in strength and discipline, Cromwell's own "lovely Company" was rapidly being developed. And as the power of the Parliament waxed, that of the King waned. Goring, brilliant, careless, valiant, and self-indulgent was losing the West by his negligence, and alienating it by his oppressions. Nor were matters much better elsewhere. Maurice had

[1] Whitelocke. ed. 1732. p. 114.
[2] Ibid.

succeeded his brother in the care of Wales and the Marches, though without his title of President. His advent had been eagerly welcomed by the despondent Byron, but he was incompetent to deal with the difficulties that beset him. From Worcester, where he was established, he sent helpless appeals to Rupert for advice and assistance. In January he demanded an enlargement of his commission. "I desire no further latitude than the same from you that you had from the King,"[1] he told his brother discontentedly. He had promised a commission to the gentlemen of Staffordshire, which he had not the power to grant them, "though I would not let them know as much," he confessed, with youthful vanity.[2] Very shortly a serious misfortune befell him in the betrayal of Shrewsbury to the Parliament.—"A disaffected town with only a garrison of burghers, and a doting old fool of a Governor,"[3] it had been called by Byron, whose language was usually forcible.—And Maurice's difficulties were further increased by the wholesale desertion of his men.

The exhaustion of the country was making it harder than ever to find food and quarters for the soldiers. In Dorsetshire the peasants were already rising, under the name of "Clubmen," to oppose the encroachments of both armies. And the Royalist officers disputed among themselves over the supplies wrung from the impoverished country. From Camden, Colonel Howard simply returned Rupert's order to share his district with another regiment, "resolving to keep nothing by me that shall hang me," he explained; and he went on to assert that even his rival colonel "blushed to see the unreasonableness" of the Prince's order. "What horrid crime have I committed, or what brand of cowardice lies upon me and my men that we are not thought worthy of a subsistence? Shall the Queen's seventy horse have

[1] Maurice to Rupert, Jan. 29, 1645. Warb. III. p. 54.
[2] Warburton, III. p. 54. Maurice to Rupert, Jan. 29, 1645.
[3] Rupert Transcripts. Byron to Rupert, 14 Jan. 1644.

Westmester hundred, Tewkesbury hundred, and God knows what other hundreds, and yet share half with me in Rifsgate, who has, at this very present, a hundred horse and five hundred foot, besides a multiplicity of officers? Sir, at my first coming hither, the gentry of these parts looked upon me as a man considerable, and had already raised me sixty horse towards a hundred, and a hundred foot, and were continuing to raise me a greater number. But at the sight of this order of your Highness I resolved to disband them, and to come to Oxford where I'll starve in more security. But finding my Lieutenant-Colonel forced to come to your Highness and to tell his sad condition, I find him so well prepared with sadness of his own, that I cannot but think he will deliver my grievances rarely. As I shall find myself encouraged by your Highness, I will go on and raise more forces. Ever submitting all my proceedings to your Highness's orders—*bar starving, since I am resolved to live.*" [1]

Not more cheering was the report of Sir Jacob Astley, then at Cirencester. "After manie Scolisietationes by letters and mesendgeres, sent for better payment of this garrison, and to be provided with men, arms and ammonition for y[e] good orderinge and defence of this place, I have received no comfort at all. So y[t] in littel time our extreameties must thruste the souldieres eyther to disband, or mutiny, or plunder, and then y[e] faulte will be laid to my charge. Gode sende y[e] Kinge mor monne, and me free from blame and imputation." [2] Rupert had little comfort to give, and no money at all, but he answered the old soldier with the respect and consideration which he always showed him. In earlier days old Astley had been Governor to Rupert and Maurice, and to him they probably owed much that was good in them. Rupert, in consequence, never treated Astley in the peremptory fashion that he used with others. "For

---

[1] Warburton, III. p. 56—7. Howard to Rupert, Jan. 30, 1645.
[2] Rupert Transcripts. Astley to Rupert, Jan. 11, 1645. Pythouse Papers, p. 20.

such precise orders as you seem to desire, I must deal freely with you, you are not to expect them," he wrote to his old Governor; "we being not such fit judges as you upon the place... I should be very loath, by misjudging here, to direct that which you should find inconvenient there."[1]

Such phrases contrast strongly with the Prince's usual high-handed procedure, of which we find the King himself complaining at this very time. "Indeed it surprised me a little this morning," he wrote to his nephew, "when Adjutant Skrimshaw told me that you had given him a commission to be Governor of Lichfield without ever advising with me, or even giving me notice of it;—for he told me as news, and not by your command. I know this proceeds merely out of a hasty forgetfulness and want of a little thinking, for if you had called to mind the late dispute between the Lord Loughborough and Bagot, that is dead, you would have advised more than you have done, both of the person, and the manner of doing it; and then, it may be, you would have thought George Lisle fitter for it than him you have chosen. Upon my word I have taken notice of this to none but this bearer, with whom I have spoken reasonable freely, by which you may perceive that this is freedom and nothing else, that makes me write thus, expecting the same from you to your loving Oncle."[2] Whether Rupert did or did not resent the reproof does not appear, but the King proved right, and Skrimshaw quarrelled with Loughborough no less than Bagot had done.

Perilous as was the condition of the Royalists on all sides, the condition of Wales seemed the most desperate, and thither Rupert hastened in the March of 1645. He took his way first to Ludlow, where he hoped to raise new forces, and a few days later he joined Maurice at Ellesmere. Thence he wrote despondently to Legge, dwelling on the great numbers of the enemy, and exhorting him to see that

---

[1] Domestic State Papers. Rupert to Astley. Jan. 13, 1645.
[2] Rupert Transcripts. King to Rupert, Jan. 1645.

the Oxford army held Monmouthshire in check. "I am going about a nobler business," he added, "therefore pray God for me; and remember me to all my friends."[1] But by the 14th he had got an army together, and his spirits were marvellously revived. "We are few, but shrewd fellows as ever you saw. Nothing troubles us but that Prince Charles is in worse (condition), and pray God he were here. I expect nothing but ill from the West; let them hear that Rupert says so." (This was for Goring's benefit.) "As for Charles Lucas' business, assure the King that nothing was meant but that it should be conceded by Lord Hopton; but his lieutenant, Slingsby, is a rogue. I have enough against him to prove him so, when time shall be. This enclosed will show you a fine business concerning my cousin the Bishop of York. Pray acquaint His Majesty with it, it concerns him. Martin's man carried a letter to you from Stowe, which you did receive, and one for Sir Edward Herbert. Pray remember me to him, and to all my friends, and inquire about the letter; you'll find knavery in it. Prince Charles wrote to me about Mark Trevor; I denied it (*i. e.* refused) as well as I could: he goes to him. Cheshire will not prosper. (Maurice was there.) Your company is here, so is your friend Rupert."[2]

The allusion to the Archbishop of York shows that Rupert had already detected the intrigues of that warlike and treacherous prelate. He had fortified and defended his castle of Conway, but quarrelled incessantly with all the Royalist officers in the district, and eventually he admitted the enemy to his castle. At the date of the above letter he was following the example of Digby, and trying to sow dissension between Ormonde and Rupert. Cheshire and Wales, he declared, lay "all neglected and in confusion", owing to the private quarrels of Rupert's "favourite", Legge, and the Byrons, whom he represented as

[1] Warburton, III. p. 68. Rupert to Legge, Mar. 11, 1645.
[2] Ibid. p. 69, Mar. 24, 1645.

"thrown out of their governments, abandoned by the King, and left to die in prison." [1] The Byrons themselves do not appear to have made any such complaints; and a sentence in one of Lord Byron's letters to the Prince seems to deprecate the reports spread by the Archbishop. "I heard," he says, "that Your Highness was informed that, in your absence, I showed most disrespect to those you most honour. This is very far from the truth, as it ever shall be from the practice of your most humble and most obliged servant, Byron." [2]

And in spite of the Archbishop's hostility Rupert's efforts in the Marches were attended by success. On the 19th of April, háving been rejoined by Maurice, he forced Brereton to raise his siege of Beeston Castle, which had endured for seventeen weeks. A few days later he was engaged in suppressing a revolt in Herefordshire, where the peasants were rising like the clubmen of Dorset. Most of them fled before the Prince, but two hundred stood their ground, of these Rupert took the leaders, and persuaded the rest to lay down their arms; he was anxious, if possible, to con‑ciliate the people rather than to suppress them by force. [3] No sooner was this task accomplished than Astley arrived with the news that a Parliamentary force, under Massey, was at Ledbury. Without an instant's delay Rupert set out, marched all night, and attacked and routed Massey in the morning, April 22nd. From Ledbury he went to Hereford, where he remained some days before returning to Oxford.

It was at this time that Rupert performed the stern act of retaliation, which so roused the wrath of the Parliament. The King's importation of Irish soldiers had been regarded by the Puritans as a gross aggravation of all his other

---

[1] Carte's Ormonde, VI. 271—272. Archbishop Williams to Ormonde, Mar. 25, 1655.
[2] Add. MSS. 18982. Byron to Rupert, Jan. 1645.
[3] Webb, Vol. II. pp. 141, 157, 178.

crimes. They chose to regard all the Irish as responsible for the massacre of the Protestants which had occurred in Ireland in 1641, and in accordance with this view they gave them no quarter. In March 1645 Essex happened to take thirteen Irish troopers, whom he hanged without mercy; and Rupert immediately retaliated by the execution of thirteen Roundhead prisoners. Essex thereupon wrote an indignant letter, reproaching the Prince for his barbarous and inhuman conduct, to which Rupert responded in a letter "full of haughtiness", that since Essex had "barbarously murdered" his men, "in cold blood, after quarter given", he would have been unworthy of his command had he not let the Puritans know that their own soldiers "must pay the price of such acts of inhumanity." [1] The Parliament then took upon itself to remonstrate at great length, but received only a concise and decided reply from the Prince's secretary:

"I am, by command, to return you this answer. You gave the first example in hanging such prisoners as were taken, and thereupon the same number of yours suffered in like manner. If you continue this course you cannot, in reason, but expect the like return. But, if your intention be to give quarter, and to exchange prisoners upon equal terms, it will not be denied here." [2] The Prince's resolute attitude had the desired effect, and the Puritans were forced to recognise Irishmen as human beings.

In contrast with this incident, we find a frantic appeal to the Prince for mercy, dated April 28. A young Royalist officer—Windebank—had most unjustifiably surrendered Blechingdon House, of which he was Governor, and by a court-martial held at Oxford he was doomed to die. Poor Windebank was no coward, but he had acted in a moment of panic, engendered by the terror of his young wife, and it was on his behalf that Sir Henry Bard now pleaded with

---

[1] Webb. II. pp. 146—147.

[2] Gilbert's History of the Irish Confederation, Vol. IV. p. XIV. Ralph Goodwin to Houses of Parliament, Mar. 23, 1645.

Rupert. "The letter enclosed was sent to me from Oxford, to be conveyed with all speed possible. Pray God it comes time enough! It concerns a most unfortunate man, Colonel Windebank. Sir, pity him and reprieve him! It was God's judgment on him, and no cowardice of his own. At the battle of Alresford he gave a large testimony of his courage, and if with modesty I may bring in the witness, I saw it, and there began our acquaintance. Oh, happy man had he ended then! Sir, let him but live to repair his honour, of which I know he is more sensible than are the damned of the pains of hell." [1] Rupert had saved Fielding, and he would in all probability have saved Windebank had it been possible. But, alas, Bard's letter was intercepted by the Parliament and never reached its destination! And Windebank died on May 3rd, the day before Rupert reached Oxford.

. The King was about to begin his last campaign, and he therefore summoned both his nephews to his side. The two Princes reached Oxford on May 4th, after an extraordinarily rapid march, and three days later, the King set out for Woodstock, leaving Will Legge behind him as Governor of Oxford. Danger was on every side. The Scots dominated the North; the West was falling rapidly away, and Cromwell's new army threatened that of the King. At starting, Charles had but 1,100 men, but before a month was past, Rupert had doubled their number. Digby and the Court party would fain have joined with Goring in the west, but Rupert, "spurred on by the northern horse, who violently pursued their desires of being at home," [2] was eager for the North. For the moment his star was in the ascendant, and, to Digby's disgust, the King yielded. "All is governed by Prince Rupert who grows a great Courtier," reported Arthur Trevor. "But whether his power be not supported by the present occasion is a question to

---

[1] Dom. State Papers. Bard to Rupert, Ap. 28, 1645.
[2] Walker's Historical Discourses, ed. 1705, pp. 126, 129.

ask a conjuror. Certainly the Lord Digby loves him not." [1]
At Evesham, which was reached on the 9th, Rupert gave
new offence to the Court by making Robin Legge, Will's
brother, Governor of that town, in defiance of the wishes
of the Council. Moving slowly northwards through the
Midlands, he took Hawkesly House near Bromsgrove; on
the following day he was at Wolverhampton. On the 27th
both he and the King were the guests of the Hastings,
at Ashby de la Zouch, and on the 29th Rupert "laye in
the workes before Leycester." [2] By his skill and energy,
this town was taken in two days, and the triumph not only
revived the drooping spirits of the Cavaliers, but won them
material advantages in the way of arms and ammunition.
It was believed that Derby would have surrendered on a
summons, but Rupert would not take the chance. Should
it refuse his summons, he maintained, "out of punctilio of
honour" he would be forced to lay siege to it, which he
had not means to do. [3] Willingly would he have pressed
on northwards, but Fairfax was threatening Oxford, and the
civilians, always anxious to keep the army in the south,
clamoured loudly of the danger of the Duke of York, the
Council, the Stores, and all the fair ladies of the Court. The
said ladies also "earnestly by letter, solicited Prince Rupert to
their rescue." [4] Reluctantly he faced southwards. But the
danger of Oxford was less imminent than had been represented; Fairfax retired from before it. Then the contest of Rupert
against Digby, the soldier against the civilian was renewed.
"There was a plot to send the King to Oxford, but it is undone," the Prince wrote to his "dear Will." "The chief of the
counsel was the fear that some men had that the soldiers would
take from them the influence they now possess with the King." [5]

[1] Carte's Letters, I. 90, May 25, 1645.
[2] Clarendon State Papers, Rupert's Journal, May 29, 1645.
[3] Walker, p. 128.
[4] Walker, p. 128.
[5] Warburton, III. p. 100. Rupert to Legge, June 8, 1645.

It was in accordance with the perversity of Charles's fate that just when the Parliamentary army had thrown off civilian shackles, he was ceasing to be ruled by the military counsels of his nephew. Rupert again urged a march to the North. Digby and the Councillors of Oxford, ever eager to keep the army in the South, recommended an attack on the Eastern counties. The King remained at Daventry hesitating between the two counsels, and in the meantime Fairfax and Cromwell were advancing towards him. Rupert's unaccountable contempt for the New Model Army prevented him from taking the proper precautions, and he remained absolutely ignorant of Fairfax's movements, until he was quartered eight miles from Daventry. Then the King decided to move towards Warwick, and that night he slept at Lubenham, Rupert at Harborough. On the same evening Ireton surprised and captured a party of Rupert's men, as they were playing at quoits in Naseby. A few who escaped, fled to warn the King, and the King hastened to Rupert. With unwonted prudence, Rupert advised retreat; reinforcements might be found at Leicester and Newark, and there was yet a hope that Goring might march to their aid. He did not know, as Fairfax knew through an intercepted despatch, that Goring was unable to leave the West. But Digby and Ashburnham were for fighting, and once again the civilian triumphed. On June 14th took place the fatal battle of Naseby.

Very early the royal army was drawn up upon a long hill which runs two miles south of Harborough. Here Astley intended the battle to be fought, resolving to keep on the defensive. But the enemy did not appear, and Rupert, growing impatient, sent out his scout master to look for them, about eight o'clock in the morning. The man returned, after a perfunctory search, saying that Fairfax was not to be seen. Then Rupert, unable to bear inaction any longer, rode out to look for him in person, with a small party of horse. At Naseby he found the whole army of the Parliament. It was just then engaged in shifting its position, and Rupert jumped to the conclusion that it was in full retreat. Lured on by this idea, he established himself on a piece of rising ground to the right, and summoned the rest of the army from its well-chosen position to join him there. This was perhaps the chief cause of the defeat that followed. Rupert and Maurice charged together on the right, and swept the field before them, till they reached the enemy's cannon and baggage waggons. Here Rupert was mistaken for Fairfax, for both were wearing red cloaks, and some of the Puritan reserve rode up, asking, "How goes the day?" The Prince responded by an offer of quarter, which was met by a volley of musket shot. But Rupert could not stay to complete his conquest. His part of the battle had been won, but behind him Cromwell had scattered the Royalist left, and was trampling the infantry of the centre in "a dismal carnage."[1] The King was turned from the battle too soon, his whole army was disheartened and overwhelmed, and Rupert returned too late, to find Cromwell in possession of the field. The Royal army was destroyed, and the war almost at an end. That night the King retreated to Ashby, and the next day, Sunday, he reached Lichfield, whence he hastened on to Raglan Castle. Rupert went on westward to the Prince of Wales at Barnstaple.

His departure from the King was due to a new quarrel with Digby, who attributed the disaster to the fault of the Prince. "Let me know what is said among you, concerning our last defeat," Rupert wrote to Legge, at Oxford; "doubtless the fault of it will be put upon me ... Since this business I find Digby hath omitted nothing which might prejudice me, and this day hath drawn a letter from the King to Prince Charles, in which he crosses all things that befell here in my behalf. I have showed this to the King, and in earnest; and if thereupon he should go on

[1] Sir Edward Southcote. Troubles of our Catholic Forefathers. Series I. p. 392.

and send it, I shall be forced to quit Generalship and march towards Prince Charles, where I have received more kindness than here."[1] At the same time, Legge received a long account of the battle from Digby himself, in which the Secretary, very cleverly, charged all the misfortune of the day to the Prince, while pretending to acquit him. "I am sure that Prince Rupert hath so little kindness for me, as I daily find he hath, it imports both to me and mine to be much the more cautious not to speak anything that may be wrested to his prejudice. I can but lament my misfortune that Prince Rupert is neither gainable nor tenable by me, though I have endured it with all the industry, and justness unto him in the world, and I lament your absence from him. Yet, at least, if Prince Rupert cannot be better inclined to me, that you might prevail with him so far that his heats, and misapprehensions of things may not wound his own honour, and prejudice the King's service. I am very unhappy that I cannot speak with you, since the discourse that my heart is full of is too long for a letter, and not of a nature fit for it. But I conjure you, if you preserve that justice and kindness for me which I will not doubt, if you hear anything from Prince Rupert concerning me, suspend your judgment. As for the particular aspersion upon him, which you mention, of *fighting against advice, he is very much wronged in it,* ... and for particular time, place and circumstance of our fighting that day, His Highness cannot be said to have gone against my Lord Astley, or any other advice; *for I am confident no man was asked upon the occasion,*—I am sure no council was called. I shall only say this freely to you, that I think a principal occasion of our misfortune was the want of you with us. .... But really, dear Will, I do not write this with reflection, for indeed we were all carried on at that time with such a spirit and confidence of victory as though he that should have said

[1] Warburton. III. pp. 119—121. Rupert to Legge, June 18, 1645.

"consider" would have been your foe. Well, let us look forward! Give your Prince good advice, as to caution, and value of counsel, and God will yet make him an instrument of much happiness to the King, and Kingdom, and that being, I will adore him as much as you love him." [1] But "Honest Will" was quite shrewd enough to read between the lines of this elaborate epistle, and he answered with a spirit and candour worthy of his character. "I am extremely afflicted to understand from you that Prince Rupert and yourself should be upon so unkindly terms, and I protest, I have cordially endeavoured, with all my interest in His Highness, to incline him to a friendship with your Lordship, conceiving it a matter of advantage to my Master's service, to have a good intelligence between persons so eminently employed in his affairs, and likewise the great obligation and inclination I had to either of you. But truly, my Lord, I often found this a hard matter to hold between you; and your last letter gives me cause to think that your Lordship *is not altogether free from what he accused you of*, as the reason of his jealousies. Which was that you both say and do things to his prejudice, *contrary to your professions, and not in an open and direct line, but obscurely and obliquely*; and this, under your Lordship's pardon, I find your letter very full of. For where your Lordship would excuse him of the particular and general aspersions, yet you come with such objections against the conduct of that business, as would, to men ignorant of the Prince, make him incapable of common-sense in his profession. For my part, my Lord, I am so well acquainted with the Prince's ways, that I am confident all his General officers and commanders knew beforehand how, and in what manner, he intended to fight; and when, as you say, all mankind were of opinion to fight, it was his part to put it into execution. Were any man in the army dissatisfied in his directions,

---

[1] Warburton. III. pp. 125—128. Digby to Legge. No date.

or in the order, he ought to have informed the General of
it, and to have received further satisfaction. And for the
not calling of a Council at that instant, truly, the Prince
having before laid his business, were there need of it, the
blame must be as much yours as any man's." And, after
a great deal more to the same purpose, Legge concludes
with the stout declaration, "and assure yourself you are
not free from great blame towards Prince Rupert. And no
man will give you this free language at a cheaper rate
than myself, though many discourse of it." [1]

[1] Warburton, III. pp. 128—131. Legge to Digby, June 30, 1645.

CHAPTER X

RUPERT'S PEACE POLICY. THE SURRENDER OF BRISTOL.
DIGBY'S PLOT AGAINST RUPERT. THE SCENE AT
NEWARK. RECONCILIATION WITH THE KING.
THE FALL OF OXFORD

AFTER the battle of Naseby, misfortunes crowded thick upon the Royalists. Garrisons surrendered daily to the Parliament; Goring suffered a crushing defeat; and the King seemed in no way to raise another army. Rupert retired to his city of Bristol, and summoned Maurice to his side. But the younger Prince was at Worcester, which was threatened by the Scots, and could not quit the place with honour. "I hope when you have duly considered my engagement herein, you will be pleased to excuse me for not observing your orders to be personally with you,"[1] he wrote humbly to his brother.

After a three weeks' stay at Raglan, the King himself thought of joining his nephew at Bristol. But the Prince's enemies opposed the idea, and Rupert, though enough inclined to it, declared that he would not be responsible for what he had not advised. And the rallying loyalty of the Welsh, combined with continued misfortune in the West, caused Charles to change his mind. In Rupert's eyes the King's final decision was a matter of indifference; defeat was inevitable, and all the Prince's efforts were directed towards peace. This complete change of attitude is an evidence of Rupert's strong common-sense. In 1642 he had been regarded as one of the obstacles which made peace impossible; but in 1642 there had been hope, even

---

[1] Warburton. III. p. 133. Maurice to Rupert, July 7, 1645.

probability, of victory. In 1645 defeat and ruin stared the Royalists in the face, and Rupert would not, like the King and Digby, shut his eyes to disagreeable fact. On July 28th he wrote to Richmond a plain statement of his views. "His Majesty has now no way left to preserve his posterity, Kingdom, and nobility, but by a treaty. I believe it a more prudent way to retain something than to lose all. If the King resolve to abandon Ireland, which now he may with honour, since they desire so unreasonably; and it is apparent they will cheat the King, having not 5,000 men in their power. When this has been told him, and that many of his officers and soldiers go from him to them (*i. e.* to the Parliament), I must extremely lament the condition of such as stay, being exposed to all ruin and slavery. One comfort will be left,—we shall all fall together. When this is, remember I have done my duty. Your faithful friend, Rupert." [1]

On the same day he wrote to Legge:

"I have had no answer to ten letters I wrote, but from the Duke of Richmond, to whom I wrote plainly and bid him be plain with the King, and to desire him to consider some way which might lead to a treaty, rather than undo his posterity. How this pleases I know not, but rather than not do my duty and speak my mind freely, I will take his unjust displeasure." [2]

This advice was in fact exceedingly displeasing to the King. Richmond, who fully concurred in Rupert's opinion, showed the letter to his master "with as much care and friendship to Rupert" as possible; and the King read it graciously, saying that his nephew had "expressed as great generosity as was all his actions;" [3] but, for all that, he firmly forbade him to write in such a strain again. "Speaking as a mere soldier or statesman," he acknowledged that

---

[1] Warburton. III. p. 149. Rupert to Richmond, July 28, 1645.
[2] Ibid. p. 151. Rupert to Legge, July 28, 1645.
[3] Add. MSS. Richmond to Rupert, Aug. 3, 1645.

Rupert might be right; but, "as a Christian, I must tell you that God will not suffer rebels and traitors to prosper, nor this cause to be overthrown; and whatever personal punishment it shall please Him to inflict on me must not make me repine, much less give over this quarrel; and there is little question that a composition with them at this time is nothing less than a submission, which, by the grace of God, I am resolved against, whatever it cost me. For I know my obligation to be, both in conscience and honour, neither to abandon God's cause, injure my successors, nor forsake my friends. Indeed I cannot flatter myself with expectation of good success more than this, to end my days with honour and a good conscience; which obliges me to continue my endeavours, as not despairing that God may yet, in good time, avenge his own cause. ...I earnestly desire you not in any way to hearken after treaties, assuring you, low as I am, I will not go less than what was offered in my name at Uxbridge. Therefore, for God's sake, let us not flatter ourselves with these conceits; and believe me, the very imagination that you are desirous of a treaty will lose me so much the sooner." [1]

But noble and earnest as were the King's words, they could not alter his nephew's mind. Rupert had little faith that a miracle would be vouchsafed to save the royal cause; and he could never be made to understand that the questions at issue were such as admitted of no compromise. Digby of course seized the opportunity of widening the breach between King and Prince. Ever since Marston Moor, he had intrigued with increasing success against his rival, and Rupert struggled vainly in his meshes. "I would give anything to be but one day in Oxford, when I could discover some that were in that plot of Herefordshire and the rest. But I despair of it!" [2] the Prince had written in the March of this year. In June he had sent Langdale to Ormonde in

<hr>

[1] Rushworth, VI. 132. King to Rupert, Aug. 3.
[2] Warburton, III. 73. Rupert to Legge, Mar. 31, 1645.

Ireland, as a counterfoil to O'Neil, and Digby hastened to let the Lord Lieutenant know that Langdale was "a creature of Prince Rupert, and sent over not without jealousy that Dan O'Neil may be too frank a relater of our military conduct here."[1] And, July 21st, 1645, it is entered in the Prince's diary: "Ashburnham told the Prince that Digby would ruin him."[2] By that time Rupert had become convinced that Digby would succeed in his endeavours. A week later he wrote passionately to Legge, from Bristol: "You do well to wonder why Rupert is not with the King! When you know the Lord Digby's intention to ruin him you will not then find it strange."[3]

Digby's chance was close at hand. Throughout July and August Rupert busied himself at Bristol, circling about the country, pacifying and winning over the Clubmen and trying to supply the deficiencies of the Bristol stores. This town was now the most important garrison of the King. It was the key of the Severn. It alone held Wales and the Marches loyal, and its loss would also terribly affect the Royalists in the south-west. Rupert had assured the King that he could hold the place four months, and great was the horror and dismay when he surrendered it after a three weeks' siege.

The truth was that he had found the town insufficiently supplied, greatly undermanned, and full of despondency and disaffection. He had done his best to remedy these evils; he ordered the townspeople to victual themselves for six months, imported corn and cattle from Wales, and he started manufactories of match and bullets within the town. All the recruits he could gain were "new-levied Welsh and unexperienced men," and even of these there were but few. "After the enemy approached, His Highness never could draw upon the line above 1,500," and this to defend a

---

[1] Carte's Ormonde, VI. 303. Digby to Ormonde, June 26, 1645.

[2] Warburton, III. p. 145.

[3] Ibid. p. 156. Rupert to Legge, July 29, 1645.

stretch of five miles![1] Moreover, all his Colonels assured him that the wall was not tenable against a vigorous assault. The one chance was that, if they repulsed the first storm, the enemy might be discouraged, and the approaching winter might save the city for yet a little while.

On September 4th Fairfax sat down before Bristol, and summoned Rupert to surrender, in rather peculiar language. The summons was a private exhortation to the Prince himself, and a personal appeal to his sense and humanity, "which," says Fairfax, "I confess is a way not common, and which I should not have used but in respect to such a person, and such a place."[2] He proceeded to explain that the Parliament wished no ill to the King, but only his return to its care and Council, and entreated Rupert to end the schism by a surrender without bloodshed. The Prince only replied by demanding leave to send to ask the King's pleasure. This Fairfax refused to grant, and Rupert entered into a treaty, hoping thereby to spin out time until relief could come. But the patience of Fairfax was soon exhausted. On September 10th he assaulted the city, about 2.0 a.m., entered the lines at a spot held by some new recruits, and was, by daybreak, in full possession of line and fort. Thus the enemy was already within the city, and Rupert had no hope of relief, for, since Naseby, the King had had no army in the field. Moreover, since the siege began, no word had come to the Prince from any quarter. Three courses now lay open to him. He might, with his cavalry, break through Fairfax's army, leaving behind him just sufficient men to keep the castle; this plan was rejected as exceedingly dangerous and unsatisfactory. Secondly, he might retreat to the castle, which could be held for a long time; but the castle would not contain all the cavalry, and thus a large portion of it, together with the "nobility, gentry and well affected of the town," would

[1] A Narrative of the Siege of Bristol. Warburton, III. pp. 166—180.
[2] Warburton, III. pp. 172—174.

be left to the mercy of the conquering foe. [1] Thirdly and lastly, he could surrender on honourable terms; and this was the course chosen by the Council of War. Rightly or wrongly, Rupert entered into treaty, and a cessation of arms was agreed on. But the cessation was violated by Fairfax's men, and Rupert thereupon declared that he " would stand upon his own defence, and rather die than suffer such injuries." [2] Fairfax hastened to apologise and make amends; Rupert was pacified, and the treaty concluded. The terms were good and honourable; the garrison were to march out with the honours of war, a charge of bullet and powder was granted to each of the Prince's guards, the sick were to stay uninjured in the city, and no private person was to be molested. It must also be noted that Rupert yielded only at the second summons, and after the city had been entered by the enemy. Relief was "as improbable to be expected as easy to be desired," and though he could certainly have held the castle longer, "the city had been thereby exposed to the spoil and fury of the enemy, and so many gallant men who had so long and faithfully served His Majesty, (whose safeties His Highness conceived himself in honour obliged to preserve as dearly as his own) had been left to the slaughter and rage of a prevailing enemy." [3] It may be that Rupert mistook his position. Perhaps he should have held the castle entrusted to him at all costs, and suffered no other considerations to cross his military councils. But his unwillingness to desert the townspeople and his beloved cavalry, can hardly be counted to his discredit.

On September 10th the Royalist garrison marched out of Bristol, and was escorted by Fairfax himself for two miles over the Downs. Rupert had dressed himself carefully for his part, and there was nothing of the broken down Cavalier about his attire. " The Prince was clad in scarlet,

[1] Narrative of Siege of Bristol. Warburton, III. pp. 168—169.
[2] Ibid. p. 178.
[3] Narrative of Siege of Bristol. Warburton, III. p. 180.

very richly laid in silver lace, and mounted upon a very gallant black Barbary horse; the General (Thomas Fairfax) and the Prince rode together, the General giving the Prince the right hand all the way."[1] The courtesy on both sides was perfect; the Puritans showed no unseemly triumph over their fallen foe, and the Prince bore himself towards his conquerors as a soldier and a gentleman should. "All fair respects between the Prince and Sir Thomas Fairfax," reported a Puritan witness; "much respect from the Lord General Cromwell. He (the Prince) gave this gallant compliment to Major Harrison, 'that he never received such satisfaction in such unhappiness, and that, if ever in his power, he will repay it.'"[2]

Truly Rupert shone more in evil fortune than in good, and he seems to have completely won the hearts of his enemies. His request for muskets for his men was readily granted, on his promise to deliver them up to the Parliamentary convoy, at the end of his journey, "which every one believes he will perform,"[3] said an adherent of the Parliament. And the Puritan Colonel Butler, who convoyed him from Bristol to Oxford, wrote of him to Waller, with enthusiasm. "I had the honour to wait upon His Highness Prince Rupert, with a convoy from Bristol to this place, and seriously, I am glad I had the happiness to see him. I am confident we have been much mistaken in our intelligence concerning him. I find him a man much inclined to a happy peace, and he will certainly employ his interest with His Majesty for the accomplishing of it. I make it my request to you that you use some means that no pamphlet is printed that may derogate from his worth for the delivery of Bristow. *On my word he could not have held it, unless it had been better manned.*"[4] Changed in-

---

[1] Narrative of Siege of Bristol. Warburton, III. p. 181.
[2] Pamphlet, Sept. 10, 1645. Warburton, p. 183.
[3] Ibid.
[4] Nicholas Papers, I. p. 65. Camden Society. New Series. Butler to Waller, Sept. 15, 1645.

deed was the Puritan attitude towards the mad Prince, and more than one officer of the Parliament was eager to justify his conduct. "I have heard the Prince much condemned for the loss of that city, but certainly they were much to blame," wrote another. "First let them consider that the town was entered by plain force, with the loss of much blood. And then the Prince had nothing to keep but the great fort and castle. Perchance he might hold out for some weeks, but then, of necessity, he must have lost all his horse, which was in all, 800; and he had no expectation of any relief at all. Let all this be considered, and no man can blame him." [1]

But the advocacy of the Parliament was not likely to allay Royalist indignation; nay, it was but another proof of Rupert's collusion with the enemy! The Queen spoke "largely" of her nephew, giving out in Paris that he had sold Bristol for money; [2] and the story gained colour from the fact that the Elector really did receive a large sum from the Parliament at this time. The loss of Shrewsbury was brought up against Maurice, and it was rumoured that the younger Princes were in league with the Elector; though they had never once written to him, since he had chosen to identify himself with the Parliament. Here was Digby's opportunity; and the King, overwhelmed by the unexpected catastrophe, listened to his representations. On his arrival at Oxford, Rupert received, from the hands of Secretary Nicholas, his discharge from the army, a passport to leave the country, and a letter from the King, desiring him "to seek subsistence somewhere beyond seas." [3] Further, Nicholas was directed to deprive Legge of the Governorship of Oxford, and to place him under arrest.

With deep reluctance Nicholas obeyed orders; and both Legge and Rupert behaved themselves with quiet dignity.

[1] Carte's Original Letters, I. p. 134.
[2] Domestic State Papers. Honeywood, Oct. 7—13, 1645.
[3] Warburton, III. p. 185.

"According to your commands, I went immediately to the Lord Treasurer," wrote Nicholas to the King. "We thought fit to send for Colonel Legge thither, who willingly submitted himself prisoner to your commands. This being despatched, I went to Colonel Legge's house, where Prince Rupert dined, and desiring to speak with him privately in the withdrawing room, I presented to him first his discharge, and then after that your letter; to which he humbly submitted himself, telling me that he was very innocent of anything that might deserve so heavy a punishment. ... Your Majesty will herewith receive a letter from Prince Rupert, who will, I believe, stay here, until he hears again from you, for that he cannot without leave from the rebels go to embark himself, and without Your Majesty's license, I hear, he will not demand a pass from the rebels." [1]

Rupert's letter consisted of a grave and calm protest, and a demand for a personal interview with his uncle. "I only say that if Your Majesty had vouchsafed to hear me inform you, before you had made a final judgment,—I will presume to present this much,—you would not have censured me, as it seems you do." His first duty was, he admitted, to give an explanation to the King, but, since the opportunity was denied him—"In the next place I owe myself that justice as to publish to the world what I think will clear my erring in all this business now in question from any foul deed, or neglect, and vindicate me from desert of any prevailing malice, though I suffer it. Your commands that I should dispose myself beyond seas be pleased to consider of, whether it be in my power, though you have sent me a pass, as times now are, to go by it." [2] In accordance with this statement he published a detailed account of the state of Bristol, and all that had passed there, and continued at Oxford, awaiting the King's pleasure. "I must not omit to acquaint Your Majesty," wrote the faithful

[1] Domestic State Papers. Nicholas to King, Sept. 18, 1645.
[2] Ibid. Rupert to King, Sept. 18, 1645.

Nicholas, "that I hear Prince Rupert hath not £50 in all the world, and is reduced to so great an extremity as he hath not wherewith to feed himself or his servants. I hear that Colonel Legge is in no more plentiful condition." [1]

The loss of Rupert's military experience was soon felt in the Royalist ranks; and would have been felt more severely had there been any serious undertaking on hand, or any army to execute it. As it was, when the first moment of panic was past and men could consider the question calmly, he appeared to have been hardly dealt with. To seriously suspect him of treachery was absurd; he was, in effect, the victim of Digby's malice; and the arrest of Legge, for no other crime than that of being the Prince's friend, favoured this view. Digby of course pretended that he could furnish proofs of Legge's contemplated treacheries, "as soon as I can come at my papers, which were left with Stanier, and all my other necessaries, at Worcester," and insisted that, so long as Rupert were in England, it would he unsafe to set his friend at liberty. [2] Equally, of course, no one—except the King—believed him; for Legge's loyalty and integrity were above suspicion. He was, says Clarendon, considered "above all temptations," [3] and the indignation felt at this injustice greatly favoured the Prince's cause.

Digby had no mind to face "the fury of the storm" [4] which he had raised. Before Rupert could reach Oxford the Secretary had hurried the King away to Newark, a place which would be very difficult of access for the Prince. Personally, Charles had inclined to Worcester, but Digby would not hear of it. Not only was Worcester within easy distance from Oxford, but Maurice was Governor there; and Maurice had, as Digby knew, "a very tender sense

<hr>

[1] Dom. State Papers. Nicholas to King, Sept. 18, 1645.
[2] Ibid. Digby to Nicholas, Sept. 26, 1645.
[3] Clarendon, Bk. IX. 91.
[4] Walker, p. 142.

of the severity his brother had undergone, and was ready to revenge it."[1]

The younger Prince was only just recovering from a second severe illness. As before, his recovery had been despaired of, and his death freely reported by friends and foes. "Maurice is very sick at Worcester of the plague; some say he is dead, and the malignants are very sorrowful at the news,"[2] said a Puritan pamphlet. While he was still too ill to take any active share in the dispute, the King had written to him, telling of Rupert's dismissal, but adding kindly: "I know you to be so free from his present misfortune that it noways staggers me in that good opinion I have ever had of you; and so long as you be not weary of your employment under me, I will give you all the encouragement and contentment in my power."[3] But Maurice was far too devoted a brother to be soothed by such words. Ill though he was, he made a copy of the King's letter in his own hand to send to Rupert, and by all possible means he showed "sensibility" of the injury done to his brother. Worcester was full of his partisans, and Digby knew better than to venture into his power. At Newark, the Secretary felt himself safe, and there he continued to inflame the King against his nephew. The task was not difficult. The King was shaken and despairing, and Digby had calumnies ready to his hand.

"It hath been the constant endeavours of the English nation—who are naturally prone to hate strangers—to seek, with false calumnies and scandalous accusations, to blast and blemish my integrity to my uncle and to his Royal family," declared Rupert himself, a few years later. "Neither hath the abuse laid on me by my uncle's pretended friends been sufficient, but the gross lies and forgeries of that rebel nest at Westminster have branded me with the worst

---

[1] Clarendon, Bk. IX. 121. Walker, 142.
[2] Warburton, III. p. 183.
[3] Ibid. p. 188. King to Maurice, Sept. 20, 1645.

of crimes that possible any man might be charged with.
... The command which His Majesty had been graciously
pleased to confer on me—as I shall answer at the day
of judgment—I did improve to the best of my power,
without any treachery, deceit, or dissimulation. And for
my unfortunateness, I hope it was excusable, it being not
only incident where I had command, but in all other places
where my uncle had any power of soldiers; yet, notwithstanding, I was the butt at which envy shot its arrows,
and all my uncle's losses were laid to my charge." [1] This
was not an unfair statement of the case. It is the way of
all nations and parties to blame some one for their misfortunes, and the foreign prince made a convenient scape-
goat for the Royalists. The libels originated in the "rebel
nest" were taken up and cherished by the foes of Rupert's
own household. As early as February 1644, there had
appeared a pamphlet which stated plainly that Rupert was
aiming at the English Crown. He was not, it was suggested, "so far from the Crown, but, if once the course of law,
and the power of the Parliament be extinguished, he may
bid as fair for it, by the sword, as the King; having possessed himself of so much power already under colour of
serving the King; and having, by his German manner of
plundering, and active disposition in military affairs, won
the hearts of so many soldiers of fortune, and men of prey.
He is already their chieftain and their Prince, and he is
like enough to be their King. ... This whole war is managed
by his skill, labour and industry; insomuch as, if the King
command one thing and he another, the Prince must be
preferred before the King. Witness Banbury, which was
secured from plundering under the King's own hand; but
that was slighted, and the town plundered by Prince Rupert
vilifying the King's authority, and making it a fault of his
unexpertness, saying, ' His Uncle knew not what belonged

[1] Pamphlet. Brit. Mus. "Prince Rupert: his Declaration", March 9, 1649.

to war.' ... Neither shall Prince Rupert want abettors in his
cursed design; for many of our debauched and low-fortuned
young nobility and gentry, suiting so naturally with this
new conqueror, will make no bones to shoulder out the
old King." [1] Eagerly did Rupert's Royalist foes catch at
the libel. We have already seen that, before Marston
Moor, Digby, Percy and Wilmot ventured to assert openly
that the victory of Prince or Parliament was a matter of
indifference. And even after that battle had broken his
power, Sir George Radcliffe wrote to Ormonde of "the
great fear some have of Prince Rupert, his success and
greatness." [2]

The formation of Rupert's peace-party in 1645 put the
finishing touch to Digby's hatred of him, and also afforded
means of exciting the King's distrust. The sanguine and
unpractical Secretary, ignorant of military details, did not
know that the King was beaten and could never draw
another army into the field. He had a thousand schemes
for gaining over the Scots, for obtaining help from Ireland
or France, and he would not, and could not, believe that
the game was lost. Consequently he resented the suggestion
of compromise even more hotly than did the King. "Alas!
my Lord!" he wrote to Jermyn in August, "I do not
know four persons living, besides myself and you, that have
not already given clear demonstration that they will purchase
their own, and as they flatter themselves, the Kingdom's
quiet, at any price to the King, the Church, and the faithfullest of his party... The next news that you will hear,
after we have been one month at Oxford, will be that I,
and those few others who may be thought by our Counsels
to fortify the King in firmness to his principles, shall he
forced or torn from him. You will find Prince Rupert,

---

[1] Pamphlet. Brit. Mus. "A Looking-glass wherein His Majesty may see his
Nephew's Love."
[2] Carte's Ormonde, VI. 167, 18 July, 1644.

Byron, Gerard, Will Legge, and Ormonde [1] are the prime instruments to impose the necessity upon the King of submitting to what they, and most of the King's party at Oxford, shall think fit." [2]

But though he thus posed as a martyr, Digby had no intention of letting his rivals prevail. Ormonde he tried to gain over, of course without success, by the suggestion that he might supplant Rupert as Commander-in-Chief; and he had already laid a deliberate and ingenious plot for ruining the reputations of Rupert and Legge. By means of his agent, Walsingham, he obtained incriminating letters which represented both the Prince and his friend as deeply involved in intrigue with the Parliament. The letters, which are anonymous, were apparently the work of some spy in the opposing camp, who was willing to supply any information desired,—for a consideration. The Secretary was scarcely so insane as to believe in the accusations which they contained, but it suited his purpose to feign belief. Certainly it seems strange that Digby, who was undoubtedly a gentleman, and by no means devoid of honour and generosity, could have stooped to such baseness; but he had a versatile mind, and he probably persuaded himself that Rupert's peace policy was as dangerous to the King's interests as actual treachery could be, and that any means were therefore justifiable to overthrow its authors.

As early as August 8th, Walsingham forwarded to his patron an anonymous letter which stated the absolute necessity of deposing Rupert from the chief command. "I have not been silent heretofore concerning Prince Rupert and his assistant, Will Legge. ... Many did suppose, and those none of the weakest men, that upon the late defeat (Naseby), his Majesty would seriously take to heart the many great

---

[1] The names are so printed in the Calendar of State Papers. But in the original MS. they are so blotted that only "Rupert" and "Legge" are really distinct. Professor Gardiner adds Culpepper.

[2] State Papers. Digby to Jermyn, Aug. 27, 1645.

and irregular errors hitherto admitted." [1] Four days later, Walsingham himself wrote from Oxford, hinting at a design to betray Bristol, and proposing that Digby should get Legge supplanted at Oxford by Glemham. "Legge is pleased daily to show his teeth plainer to you and yours. ... Prince Rupert salutes him daily from Bristol with epistles beginning 'Brother Governor', which are communicated to the Junto you know of, ... Prince Rupert is now in general obloquy with all sorts of people, except Will Legge, and some few others of that stamp. Now every one desires his absence and discarding. His Majesty has had experience both of his wilfulness and ignorance, *if of no worse*. Now is the time to take the bridle out of Phaeton's hands, and permit him not a third time to burn the world... Something extraordinary is on hand is evident from the daily letters which pass between here and Bristol. 'Tis sure time to provide for the safety of Oxford; for I am certain many things are done which will not bear examination, both within and without the line." [2]

On the sixteenth, Walsingham wrote by Lady Digby's command, that Lord Portland had joined the "Cumber-landers," as Rupert's party was now called, and must be banished at all costs. The "Cumberlanders" were endea-vouring also to win Ashburnham, but some thought him "a slippery piece, and dangerous to build upon." To this was added a hint that the Prince was leaguing with the Irish rebels,—the last thing he was likely to do as he had just urged the King to abandon them; but Walsingham added cautiously that he held "only the skirts" of the story, and could say nothing certain. [3]

On September 10th Bristol fell. That the very thing should happen at which they had so darkly hinted, was luck beyond what the conspirators had hoped; and Wal-

---

[1] State Papers. Anon. to Walsingham, Aug. 8, 1645.
[2] Dom. State Papers. Walsingham to Digby, Aug. 12, 1645.
[3] Ibid. Aug. 16, 1645.

singham's anonymous friend wrote to reproach him for "making no better use of my frequent informations concerning Prince Rupert and his creature, Legge." Further, he stated that Oxford was also sold to the Parliament and would speedily share the fate of Bristol. "I have seen the transactions for the bargain already, and there is no prevention but by an immediate repair of His Majesty thither, changing the Governor, and putting the city into the hands of some worthy man. The same I say for Newark (?); for, believe me, we esteem ourselves masters of both already. But whilst His Majesty is solicitous for this, I would not, by any means, have him neglect his personal safety, upon which he will needs have an extraordinary watchful eye; for I hear a whisper as if something ill were intended him, and to your master for his sake."[1] This extraordinary document apparently constitutes the "proofs" against Legge of which Digby wrote to Nicholas.

The arrival of Rupert at Oxford, on September 16th, gave some uneasiness to the conspirators. "Prince Rupert is hourly expected with his train, which will so curb the endeavours of all honest men that it will be mere madness to attempt anything,"[2] wrote Walsingham! But two days later he had gained courage from the Prince's quiet acceptance of his disgrace, to declare that now was the time to restore prosperity to the Kingdom, "by weeding out those unhappy men that poison all our happiness." Also, he related an incident intended to give colour to the reports of Rupert's ambition. "As even now I came through the garden of Christchurch, a gentleman met me, and took me into the inner garden, and told me that he would show me our new ruler. Fancy! When I came there, I found Prince Rupert and Legge, with the Lord — walking gravely between them, on the further side. I seemed to take no notice of the gentleman's meaning, but came away, resenting

[1] Dom. State Papers. Δ to Walsingham, Sept. 14, 1645.
[2] Ibid. Walsingham to Digby, Sept. 14, 1645.

to see the nobility and gentry stand there bare at a distance, as if His Majesty had been present." [1] A second letter, bearing the same date, and sent at Lady Digby's desire, states that Rupert had declared that to treat was "the only thing His Majesty hath now to do." But this desire for peace Walsingham represented as a mere pose to mask the Prince's real aims. "Observe but this popular and perilous design!... Assure yourself, my Lord, that though this be Prince Rupert's aim here pretended 'tis but the medium to his real one; yet it is so plausible that you would bless yourself to see how it is here cherished by all that are either malcontent, timorous, or suspected... Surely there is no way left for His Majesty to recover, prosper, and give life to his discouraged party, but by expressing his high dislike and distrust to Prince Rupert." [2]

But notwithstanding Walsingham's hints, Rupert's desire for a treaty was perfectly sincere and disinterested. Personally he had less to gain by it than most of the Cavaliers, and certainly he had nothing to save, for he had no stake in the country. And the perfect integrity of his party is sufficiently guaranteed by the very fact that it counted Richmond, Legge, and Philip Warwick among its members.

By October Rupert's patience was exhausted. He could not quit the country without the leave of the Parliament, he had no money to support himself, or his servants, and Legge was still a prisoner on his account. He resolved, at all hazards, to see the King. Fain would he have had Richmond accompany him, but the Duke, though still his faithful friend, would not leave Oxford.

"The Duke of Richmond goes not hence upon many considerations, though Prince Rupert much desired it. They are very good friends, and both much for peace, though not for particular ones," [3] reported a Cavalier from Oxford.

<hr>

[1] Dom. State Papers, Sept. 16, 1645.
[2] Ibid. Sept. 16, 1645.
[3] Ibid. Oct. 11, 1645.

On October 8th Maurice met Rupert at Banbury, and together they set out for Newark. The journey was attended with much danger, for Newark was surrounded by a large army of the Parliament, and the Parliament had warned its officers to intercept the Princes. But Rupert in prosperity had always been faithful to his friends, and he now found that they would not forsake him in adversity. A troop of officers volunteered to escort him, and Maurice brought an addition of strength, making about 120 in all.

The enemy had posted about 1,500 horse at various places, to intercept the Princes' march, but all were skilfully evaded. Near the end of their journey, however, the Princes found themselves stopped at Belvoir Bridge, by Rossetter with three hundred horse. There was no choice but to charge through them. Two attempts failed, and Rupert turned to his men, saying cheerfully: "We have beaten them twice, we must beat them once more, and then over the pass, and away."[1] The third charge, carried them through the enemy, as he promised, and then they divided into two parties. The larger troop went on, with the baggage, to Belvoir; but the Princes, with about twenty more, proceeded by a short cut, which Rupert remembered passing ten years before when a boy, "shooting of conies." Here they were hotly pursued by a body of horse, and the enemy, thinking the Prince trapped, offered him quarter. His only answer was to direct his friends to follow him closely, and, breaking through the hostile ranks, they came safely to Belvoir Castle.[2]

Digby had not awaited the Prince's arrival, but had fled north, on the pretext of leading a force to join Montrose; and it was thought, on all sides, that he had done wisely. The King no sooner heard of his nephews' arrival at Belvoir than he sent to forbid their nearer approach. "Least of all I cannot forget what opinion you were of when I was at Cardiff," he wrote to Rupert, "and therefore must remember

---

[1] Warburton, III. p. 194.
[2] Ibid. pp. 194—5.

you of the letter I wrote to you from thence, in the Duke of Richmond's cipher, warning you that if you be not resolved to carry yourself according to my resolution, therein mentioned, you are no fit company for me." [1]

In defiance of this prohibition, Rupert came on next day to Newark. Within the town there existed a considerable party in his favour, headed by the Governor, Sir Richard Willys. Two days earlier Willys had received the King at the city gates, but he now rode out a couple of miles, with a large escort of horse, to meet the Prince. The accounts of the scene that followed are many, but all agree in the main points. Rupert walked straight into the presence of the King, and, without any apology or ceremony, abruptly informed him "that he was come to render an account of the loss of Bristol." [2] The King made no reply,—he probably did not know what to say,—and immediately went to supper. His nephews followed, and stood by him during the meal; but, though he asked a few questions of Maurice, he still would not speak to Rupert. After an embarrassing hour the King retired to his bed-chamber, and the Princes went to the house of Willys.

On the next morning Rupert was permitted to lay his defence before a court-martial, which acquitted him of any lack of "courage or fidelity," though not of indiscretion. [3] The verdict, though qualified, was in effect a triumph for Rupert, and completely vindicated his honour. As to the relief which the King fancied he had intended to send to Bristol, Sir Edward Walker, no friend to Rupert, admits that "it was a very plausible design on paper, ... and I fear it would have been a longer time than we fancied to ourselves, before we made both ends to meet." [4] Here the matter should have ended, and had it done so, the whole

---

[1] Add. MSS. 31022. King to Rupert, Oct. 15, 1645.
[2] Walker, pp. 136—137.
[3] Warburton, III. 201—203.
[4] Walker, 137.

affair would have been little to Rupert's discredit. Unfortunately his passionate temper now put him completely in the wrong.

The King had resolved to quit Newark, and, remembering Willys's frequent quarrels with the Commissioners of the County, and also his recent display of partisanship, he judged it unwise to leave him behind. For this reason he ordered him to change posts with Bellasys, who, since the death of Lord Bernard Stuart, had commanded the King's guards. This was promotion for Willys, but a very unwelcome promotion, for which he perfectly understood the King's motives. Moreover, Bellasys was Digby's friend, and the whole military party rose in protest against this new evidence of Digby's power. It was agreed that Willys should demand the grounds for his removal, and a trial by court-martial. The stormy scene which resulted has been rather confusedly described by Walker, Clarendon and others, but the best account is to be found in the diary of Symonds, though he unhappily repented of having written it, and tore a part of it out of his book.

The King had just returned from church, and sat down to dinner, when Rupert, Maurice, Gerard, Willys and some other officers entered the room. Rupert "came in discontentedly, with his hands at his sides, and approached very near the King." Charles thereupon ordered the dinner to be taken away, and, rising, walked to a corner of the room. Rupert, Gerard and Willys followed him. Willys spoke first, asking, respectfully enough, to be told the names of his accusers. Rupert broke in impatiently: "By God! This is done in malice to me, because Sir Richard hath always been my faithful friend!" Gerard then launched into a protest on his own account, and Rupert again interrupted, saying: "The cause of all this is Digby!"—"I am but a child! Digby can do what he will with me," retorted the King bitterly.—A long and violent altercation followed. Rupert referred to Bristol, and the King sighed, "O nephew!"

and then stopped short. Whereupon Rupert cried, for the third time: "Digby is the man that hath caused all this distraction between us!" But the King could endure no more: "They are all rogues and rascals that say so!" he answered sharply, "and in effect traitors that seek to dishonour my best subjects!" There was no more to be said; Gerard bowed and went out. Rupert "showed no reverence, but went out proudly, his hands at his sides."[1]

That evening the Princes and their party sent in a petition to the effect that: "Many of us trusted in high commands in Your Majesty's service, have not only our commissions taken away without any cause or reason expressed, whereby our honours are blemished to the world, our fortunes ruined, and we rendered incapable of command from any foreign prince,—but many others, as we have cause to fear, are designed to suffer in like manner."[2] They repeated their demand for trials by court-martial, and desired that, if this were refused, they might have passes to go over seas. The King answered that he would not make a court-martial the judge of his actions, and sent the passes. Next morning about ten o'clock, the two princes and Lord Gerard came privately to the bed-chamber to take their leave. Gerard "expressed some sense of folly,"[3] but the Princes offered no apology, and, with about two hundred officers, they rode off to Belvoir, "the King looking out of a window, and weeping to see them go."[4]

As an instance of the way in which stories are exaggerated, Pepys's account of the affair, written some twenty years after, is instructive: "The great officers of the King's army mutinied and came, in that manner, with swords drawn, into the market-place of the town where the King was. Whereupon the King says, 'I must horse,' and

---

[1] Symonds Diary. Camden Society, 268—270, also Walker, 145—148.
[2] Evelyn's Diary, ed. 1852. IV. 165—166.
[3] Walker, p. 148.
[4] Pamphlet. Merc. Brit. Warburton, III. 206, *note*.

there himself personally; when every one expected they should be opposed, the King came, and cried to the head of the mutineers, which was Prince Rupert,—'Nephew, I command you to be gone!' So the Prince, in all his fury and discontent, withdrew; and his company scattered." [1]

This was the climax of the long-continued strife between the military and civilian parties; the civilians had triumphed, and the princes now resolved to leave the country. In great indignation, a large number of officers prepared to follow them. "This is an excellent reward for Rupert and Maurice!" declared Gerard wrathfully. [2]   Rupert himself wrote to Legge: "Dear Will, I hope Goodwin has told you what reasons I had to quit His Majesty's service. I have sent Osborne to London for a pass to go beyond seas; when I have an answer you shall know more. Pray tell Sir Charles Lucas that I would have written to him before this, and to George Lisle, but I was kept close here. ... If I can but get permission, I shall hope to see you and the rest of my friends once more; and in particular to bid farewell to my Lord Portland. I forgot to tell you that Lord Digby is beaten back again to Shipton. Alas, poor man!" [3]

Osborne, whom Rupert had sent to London to obtain from the Parliament a pass and safe convoy to a sea-port, found his mission greatly facilitated by Digby's new defeat, and the consequent capture of his papers. It was characteristic of the Secretary, that, though his love-letters were carefully preserved in cipher, all those of political importance were written in plain language. Among these papers was found a copy of the King's answer to Rupert's advice to treat, and the Parliament was moved thereby in Rupert's favour. A pass was granted, but on condition of a promise given never again to bear arms against the Par-

[1] Pepys Diary, 4 Feb. 1665.
[2] State Papers. Gerard to Skipworth, Nov. 2, 1645.
[3] Dom. State Papers. Anon. to Legge, Nov. 3, 1645.

liament. This promise the Princes would not give; and, as they could not possibly leave the country without the Parliament's good will, they fought their way back to Woodstock.

A few weeks later Charles returned to Oxford, and at once released Legge from his confinement. Rupert was still at Woodstock, and his faithful friend lost no time in attempting to mediate between him and the King. "My most dear Prince," he wrote, November 21st, "the liberty I have got is but of little contentment when divided from you..., I have not hitherto lost a day without moving His Majesty to recall you; and truly, this very day, he protested to me he would count it a great happiness to have you with him, so he received the satisfaction he is bound in honour to have. What that is you will receive from the Duke of Richmond. The King says, as he is your Uncle, he is in the nature of a parent to you, and swears that if Prince Charles had done as you did he would never see him again, without the same he desires from you.... you must thank the Duchess of Richmond, for she furnished a present to procure this messenger—I being not so happy as to have any money myself." [1] And four days later, he wrote again: "I am of opinion you should write to your Uncle—you ought to do it—; and if you offered your service to him yet, and submitted yourself to his disposing and advice, many of your friends think it could not be a dishonour, but rather the contrary, seeing he is a King, your Uncle, and, in effect, a parent to you." [2]

But Rupert sulked, like Achilles in his tent, and his other friends took up the protest. "This night I was with the King, who expresses great kindness to you, but beleevs y[r] partinge was so much the contrary as Y[r] Highnes cannot but think it finill," wrote an anonymous correspondent, "Now truly, Sir, His Majesty conceiving it soe, in my

[1] Warburton, III. p. 211. Legge to Rupert, Nov. 21, 1645.
[2] Ibid. p. 212. Legge to Rupert, Nov. 25, 1645.

opinion, 'tis ffitt you should make sume hansume apply-
cation, for this reason; because my Lord Duke and others
here, are much your servants, and all that are so wish
your return to courte, though it be but to part frindlye.
But I think it necessary you should prepare the way first
by letters to the Kinge. Sir, I have no designes in this
but your service, and if you understand me rightlye, that
will prevayle so far as you will consider what I saye before
you resolve the contrarye. I knowe there be sum that are
your enemies, but they are such as may barcke, but I am
confident are not able to fight against you appeare. Therefore, Sir, I beseech you, do not contrybute to the satisfaction of your foes, and the ruyne of your friends, by neglect-
ing anything in your power to make peace with fortune.
If after all your attempts to be rightlye understood you
shall fayle of that, yet you cannot waynt honor for the
action. 'Tis your Uncle you shall submit to, and a King,
not in the condition he meryt! What others may saye I
knowe not, but really, soe may I speak my opinion as a
person that valews you above all the world besydes. I am
confident you know how faithfully my harte is to your
Highness!"[1] Also from Lord Dorset came a pathetic appeal:
"If my prayers can prevail, you shall not have the heart
to leave us all in our saddest times. If my advice were
worthy of following, surely you should not abandon your
Uncle in the disastrous condition these evil storms have
placed him in."[2]

These exhortations and entreaties at length prevailed;
the Prince suffered his natural generosity to overcome his
pride, and was induced to write the required apology: "I
humbly acknowledge that great error, which I find your
Majesty justly sensible of, which happened upon occasion
at Newark."[3] Several letters passed, and Charles then sent

[1] Pythouse Papers, p. 27.
[2] Warburton, III. 213. Dorset to Rupert, Dec. 25, 1645.
[3] Ibid., p. 222. Rupert to King. No date.

his nephew, "by Colonel Legge, a paper to confess a fault." Rupert returned a blank sheet with his signature subscribed, to signify his perfect submission to his Uncle's will: "the King, with tears in his eyes, took that so well that all was at peace ... The Prince went to Oxford, and the King embraced him, and repented much the ill-usage of his nephew." To this account of the reconciliation, is appended the marginal note, "ask the Duchess of Richmond," but the information that she was able to supply was never filled in. [1]

Rupert was now restored to the favour and the counsels of his Uncle, but not to military command. The war was practically over, and though the King would have had his nephew raise a new life-guard, the Oxford Council quashed the design. Then Charles confided to Rupert his intention of taking refuge with the Scottish army. The Prince distrusted the Scots, and strongly combated the idea; but, finding that he could not move the King's resolution, he obtained from him a signed statement that he acted against his nephew's advice. For one mistake, at least, the Prince would not be held responsible. April 27th, 1646, the King left Oxford secretly, rejecting Rupert's companionship on the grounds that his "tallness" would betray him. [2]

Oxford was now almost the last town holding out; on the first of May, Fairfax sat down before it, and the end was not long in coming. A little skirmishing took place, but the Royalists had no real hope of success. On one occasion Rupert, Maurice and Gerard went out against the Scots, with "about twenty horse, in stockings and shoes." In mere bravado, they charged three troops of the enemy, and Maurice's page, Robert Holmes, of whom we shall hear more hereafter, was wounded. Rupert also was hurt, for the first time in the war; "a lieutenant of the enemy shot the Prince in the shoulder, and shook his hand, so

<hr>

[1] Warburton, III. pp. 195—196.
[2] Ibid. p. 196.

that his pistol fell out of his hand; but it shot his enemy's horse." [1]

Rupert had previously demanded of the governor, Sir Thomas Glemham, whether he would defend the town, but Glemham replied that he must obey the Council, and Rupert therefore interfered no more in the matter. On May 18th a treaty was opened with Fairfax, but broken off on a disagreement about terms. But by June 1st, all the water had been drawn off from the city, and surrender was inevitable. The treaty was renewed, and Rupert prudently came to the Council to demand a particular clause for the safety of himself and his brother. This occasioned a quarrel with Lord Southampton, who retorted that "the Prince was in good company," and was understood by Rupert to imply disrespect to his person. He sent Gerard to expostulate with Southampton, who offered no apology, but, saying that his words had been unfaithfully reported, repeated them accurately. Rupert was not satisfied, and sent Gerard again, with a message that he expected to meet Southampton "with his sword in his hand," and at as early a date as possible, lest the duel should be prevented. The Earl cheerfully appointed the next morning, and selected pistols as his weapons, acknowledging that he was no match for the Prince with the sword. But fortunately the suspicion of the Council had been roused; the gates were shut, the would-be combatants arrested, and a reconciliation effected. "And the Prince ever after had a good respect for the Earl." [2] There was no surer way of winning Rupert's esteem than by accepting a challenge from him.

After this episode, the special clause by which the Princes were to have the benefit of all the other articles, and free leave to quit the country, was inserted in the treaty, and accepted by Fairfax. Indeed the Parliament showed the Princes a greater leniency than might have been expected. They

[1] Warburton, III. p. 197.
[2] Clarendon's Life, ed. 1827, vol. III. p. 235.

were permitted to take with them all their servants, and to remain in England for six months longer, provided they did not approach within twenty miles of London. But on their quitting Oxford, June 22nd, Fairfax gave them leave on his own authority to go to Oatlands, which was within the proscribed distance of the capital. The reason for their move thither, was their desire to see the Elector, who was then in London; but it greatly excited the wrath of the Parliament. Notwithstanding the express permission of Fairfax, it was declared that the Princes had broken the articles, and they were ordered to leave the country immediately, on pain of being treated as prisoners. In a letter curiously signed "Rupert and Maurice," they answered, meekly enough, that they had acted in all good faith, believing the general's pass sufficient, and that in coming to Oatlands they had regarded the convenience of the house more than the distance from London, "of which we had no doubt at all." [1]

But the Parliament refused to be pacified, and insisted that the Princes must depart within ten days. A long correspondence ensued, relating chiefly to passes for various servants, "whom we would not willingly leave behind." The list forwarded to the Parliament by Rupert, included a chaplain, some seven or eight gentlemen, footmen, grooms, a tailor, a gunsmith, a farrier, a secretary, "my brother's secretary's brother," and "a laundress and her maid." [2] On July 4th the brothers reached Dover, whence Rupert took ship for Calais, and Maurice for the Hague. Rupert's "family," as his train was called, followed more slowly, and rejoined him on July 23rd, at St Germains. "Blessed be God, for his and our deliverance from the Parliament," [3] piously concludes the journal of his secretary.

So ended Rupert's part in the Civil War; a part played, on the whole, creditably, and yet not without serious faults

---

[1] Cary's Memorials of Civil War, ed. 1842, vol. I. pp. 114—115.
[2] Warburton, III. pp. 234—235, *note*. Cary, I. 121—122.
[3] Prince Rupert's Journal. Clar. State Papers.

both of temper and judgment. In the earlier days of the war, while possessed of the King's confidence, the Prince had been almost uniformly successful. Later, when he had to struggle against plots and counter-plots, a vacillating King, false friends, and open enemies, he failed. That Digby had laid a deliberate scheme for his overthrow is evident; yet he had made Digby his enemy by his own faults of temper, and his own indiscretions had placed the necessary weapons in the Secretary's hands. That he was unjustly treated with regard to Bristol there can be no doubt, but he ruined his own cause by his hopeless loss of temper. Nothing could justify the mutinous scene at Newark, and Rupert afterwards confessed himself ashamed of it. That the King's affairs would have prospered better had Digby's influence been less and Rupert's more, seems probable. Faults and limitations, Rupert had, but he understood war as Digby did not. His fidelity was irreproachable, and could never have been seriously doubted. But he knew when the cause was lost, though the sanguine secretary failed to perceive it, and his advice to make peace was reasonable enough. It was unfortunate that the position was such as made that reasonable advice impossible to follow.

CHAPTER XI

THE ELECTOR'S ALLIANCE WITH THE PARLIAMENT. EDWARD'S MARRIAGE. ASSASSINATION OF D'EPINAY BY PHILIP

BEFORE their departure from England, Rupert and Maurice had received a visit from their brother, the Elector. The Thirty Years' War was drawing to a close, and the Peace of Munster which was to restore Charles Louis to the Palatinate, was already under consideration. But the Elector could not make terms with the Emperor without the consent of his brothers, and therefore June 30th, 1646, he wrote to the Parliament:

"Having received information from Munster and Osnaburgh, that in whatsoever shall be agreed at the general treaty concerning my interests, the consent of all my brothers will be required, I am desirous to confer with my brothers Rupert and Maurice, afore their departure out of this kingdom, about this, and other domestic affairs which do concern us. Whereby I do not at all intend to retard my said brothers' journey; but shall endeavour to efface any such impressions as the enemies of these kingdoms, and of our family beyond seas, (making use of their present distresses,) may fix upon them, to their own and our family prejudice." [1] The desired interview was permitted by the Parliament, and on July 1st the Elector met his brothers at Guildford. What reception he had we do not know, but it cannot, in the nature of things, have been very cordial.

With all their faults, which were many, Rupert and Maurice were incapable of the meanness to which Charles

---

[1] Cary's Memorials. Vol. I. p. 120.

Louis had descended, and for which he did not conceal the mercenary motive. During the King's prosperity he had lived much in England; and from the King he had received nothing but kindness and affection, though the Queen apparently gave him cause of complaint. In 1642 he had accompanied the King to York, but, finding war inevitable, he had quitted the Court at a moment's notice, and returned to Holland, just when Rupert and Maurice were hastening to their uncle's assistance. The Parliament "expressed a good sense" of this desertion, pretending to believe that Charles Louis had discovered secret designs of the King to which he could not reconcile his conscience. [1] And for some time the Elector watched events from a distance, taking care to detach himself from all connection with his brothers by declarations, and messages to the Parliament.

By 1644, it appeared to him that the Parliament was likely to have the better in arms, as it certainly had in money, and in the August of that year he suddenly arrived in London. In a very long, and very pious document he stated his reasons for his conduct. The Puritans, as "the children of truth and innocency who are not changed with the smiles or frowns of this inconstant world," were, he declared, his "best friends, and, under God, greatest confidants," and he wound up with a direct attack on Rupert. "Neither can His Highness forbear, with unspeakable grief, to observe that the public actions of some of the nearest of his blood have been such as have admitted too much cause of sorrow and jealousy, even from such persons, upon whose affections, in respect of their love and zeal to the reformed religion, His Highness doth set the greatest price. But, as His Highness is not able to regulate what is out of his power, so is he confident that the justice of the Parliament, and of all honest men, will not impute

[1] Clarendon. Hist. Bk. VII. p. 414.

to him such actions as are his afflictions, and not his faults." [1]

Princes were scarce with the Puritans, and Charles Louis was well received, lodged in Whitehall, and granted a large pension. [2] In recognition of this he took the Covenant, and begged leave to sit in the Assembly of Divines, then debating on religious "reforms". His request was readily granted, and it is to be hoped that he suffered some weariness from the long-winded debates to which he thus condemned himself.

The King regarded his conduct with quiet indifference, only remarking that he was sorry, for his nephew's sake, that he thought fit to act in such a manner. It has been suggested that he willingly connived at this hypocrisy as the only means by which the Elector could obtain money, but Charles Louis' own letters to his mother disprove that view. In 1647, when the King was a prisoner, he often received the visits of his eldest nephew, and the Elector thus described their mutual attitude to Elizabeth: "His Majesty, upon occasion, doth still blame the way I have been in all this time, and I do defend it *as the only shelter I have*, when my public business, and my person, have received so many neglects at Court. Madame, I would not have renewed the sore of his ill-usage of me since the Queen hath had power with him, but that he urged me to it, saying that I should rather have lived on bread and water, than have complied with the Parliament, which he said I did '*only to have one chicken more in my dish*'; and that he would have thought it a design more worthy of his nephew if I had gone about to have taken the crown from his head. These and such-like expressions would have moved a saint. Neither do I know of anyone, but Our Saviour, that would have ruined himself for those that hate one." [3]

[1] Rupert Transcripts. Declaration of the Prince Elector.
[2] Whitelocke, 85, 101.
[3] Forster's Eminent Statesmen. 1847. Vol. VI. pp. 80—81.

The King seems to have entertained no suspicions of actual treachery on the part of his nephew, but it is by no means unlikely that Charles Louis really did cherish some vague design of "taking the crown from his head". If the King were deposed, and his children rejected as the children of a Roman Catholic Queen, then the Elector, after his mother, was the Protestant heir to the throne. Probably the aspersions cast upon Rupert would have better fitted his elder brother, and the French Ambassador did not hesitate to assert plainly in 1644: "Some entertain a design for conveying the crown to the Prince Palatine".[1] But, whatever his degree of guilt, the political conduct of Charles Louis could be regarded only with contempt by Rupert and Maurice, though concerning their "domestic affairs" they seem to have been of one mind with him.

During the years of turmoil in England the Palatines on the Continent had not been inactive. Edward and Philip, clinging together as did Rupert and Maurice, had resided chiefly in Paris, where they seem to have led a very gay life, if Sir Kenelm Digby is to be credited. "All my conversation is in the other world, and with what passes in the Elysian fields," wrote that romantic personage to Lord Conway; "gaieties of Paris, gallantries of Prince Edward, his late duel with Sir James Leviston, who extremely forgot his duty. In a word, it was impossible for a young man, and a noble prince, to do more bravely than His Highness did."[2]

A month later, Edward, inspired probably by Queen Henrietta, wrote to Rupert to suggest that he also should come over to fight for his uncle's cause. "I have a letter from my brother in France who desires my order to come to me; if it be His Majesty's desire I should send word presently," Rupert wrote to Legge in April 1645; and he

---

[1] Von Raumer's History of England in 17th Century. III. p. 330.
[2] Cal. Dom. State Papers 13/23 Feb. 1645. Carl I. DVI. f. 43.

added a postscript curiously indicative of the haste and
want of thought with which he must have written. "Since
I wrote I remember the King was contented, and therefore I will send an express for my brother."[1]

The express was sent: "This day arrived a gentleman
from Prince Rupert to fetch his brother Edward into England," wrote Jermyn to Digby.[2] But ere the messenger
could arrive Edward had eloped with a fair heiress, for
whose sake he joined the Roman Church. Jermyn hastened
to inform Rupert of the event. "Your Highness is to
know a romance story which concerns you here in the
person of Prince Edward, who is last week married privately
to the Princess Anne, the Duke of Nevers' daughter. This
Queen,[3] the thing being done without her consent, hath been
very much offended at it, and, notwithstanding all the
endeavours of your brother's friends, he hath received an
order to retire himself into Holland, which he hath done, ...
But there will come no further disadvantage to him than
a little separation from his wife. She is very rich, £6,000
or £7,000 a year is the least that can fall to her, maybe
more; and she is a very beautiful young lady."[4]

Edward's bride, Anne de Gonzague, was in fact a very
distinguished personage,—famous already for her startling
adventures, and destined to become more famous as a
political *intrigante*.[5] The displeasure of the Queen Regent
was speedily softened by the intercession of Queen Henrietta, and still more by Edward's conversion, which went
far to palliate his fault. On his own family it had precisely
the opposite effect. His mother was furious; and the Elector,
moved by fear of the English Parliament's disapproval,
wrote indignantly that Edward could not be really "persuaded

<hr>

[1] Warburton, III. p. 75.
[2] Cal. Dom. State Papers. Jermyn to Digby, 12 May, 1645.
[3] Anne of Austria, Queen Regent of France.
[4] Warburton, III. p. 82. 5 May, 1645.
[5] Memoirs of Anne de Gonzague. Ed. Sénac de Meilhan. Memoirs of
Cardinal De Retz, and of Mademoiselle de Montpensier.

of those fopperies to which he pretends."[1]   He also ordered
Philip to quit Paris, where "only atheists and hypocrites"
were to be found, and he exhorted his mother to remove
a Roman Catholic gentleman from attendance on the boy,
and to lay her curse upon him should he ever change his
religion.[2]

Philip had no sooner returned to the Hague than he
distinguished himself in a way which won him the affectionate admiration of all his brothers, and the lasting displeasure
of his mother. Elizabeth's favourite admirer, at that period,
happened to be the Marquis d'Epinay, a French refugee,
remarkable for his fascinating manners and disreputable
character. The young Palatines detested him, but the man,
notwithstanding, became intimate at the Court, and was
soon acquainted with the Queen's most private affairs. The
intimacy produced scandal without, and dissension within
the household. D'Epinay boasted of his conquest, and
Philip, a boy of eighteen, could not endure his insolence.

On the evening of June 20, 1646, D'Epinay, and several of
his countrymen encountered Philip alone. They greeted him
by name, insulting both him and his mother, but eventually
fled before the fierce onslaught of the youngest Palatine.
The affair could not end thus. On the following morning,
as he drove through the Place d'Armes, Philip caught sight
of his enemy. Without a moment's thought he sprang from
his curricle, and rushed upon D'Epinay. D'Epinay was armed,
and received Philip on the point of his sword, wounding
him in the side. Philip had no sword, but he was a Palatine,
and he plunged his hunting-knife deep into the Frenchman's
heart. D'Epinay fell dead, and Philip, flinging his knife
from him, regained his curricle and drove off to the Spanish
border.[3]

Then arose a mighty storm. The Queen, passionately

[1] Bromley Letters, p. 127, 28 Nov. 1645.
[2] Bromley, pp. 129—131.
[3] Soeltl's Elizabeth Stuart, 1840. Bk. IV. Chap. 7, pp. 402—403.

bewailing her misfortune in having such a son, vowed that she would never look on Philip's face again. But Philip's brothers and sisters rose up in his defence. The Princess Elizabeth boldly averred that "Philip needed no apology,"[1] and, finding her position in her mother's house untenable, retreated to her Aunt at Brandenburg. And both Rupert and the Elector warmly espoused Philip's cause. "Permit me, madame," wrote Charles Louis, "to solicit your pardon for my brother Philip,—a pardon I would sooner have asked, had it ever entered my mind that he could possibly need any intercession to obtain it. The consideration of his youth, of the affront he received, and of the shame which would, all his life, have attached to him had he not revenged it, should suffice."[2] Rupert wrote, in the same strain, from Oatlands, and his letter was accompanied by a second from the Elector, in which he declared that the very asking pardon for Philip would "more justly deserve forgiving than my brother's action."[3] The Queen ultimately accorded a nominal pardon to the unfortunate Philip, for in July 1648, he was again at the Hague, under the protection of Rupert and Maurice, whom he accompanied to a dinner at which Mary, Princess of Orange, entertained her two brothers and three cousins.[4]

He had, in the meantime entered the Venetian service, rather to the annoyance of the Elector, who wrote: "I could wish my brother Rupert or Maurice would undertake the Venetian business, my brother Philip being very young for such a task."[5] But neither of the other two brothers had any intention of deserting the Stuart cause, and the Elector obtained leave from the Parliament for Philip to raise a thousand men in England. For this purpose, Philip

<hr>

[1] Strickland's Elizabeth Stuart, p. 209.
[2] Ibid.
[3] Bromley Letters, p. 134.
[4] Queen's Princesses, VI. p. 149.
[5] Bromley Letters, p. 136. Elector to Elizabeth, Jan. 9, 1646—7.

visited his eldest brother in London, but stayed only a few weeks. [1] Returning to Holland, he completed his levies in the states, with some assistance from Maurice; [2] and in the autumn of 1648 he departed to Italy, whence he wrote to Rupert that the Venetians were "unworthy pantaloons." [3]

Rupert was, meanwhile, watching over the Stuarts in France, and Maurice remained quietly at the Hague with his mother and sisters. We find him with no more exciting occupation than the paying of visits of compliment on behalf of his mother; or walking meekly behind her and his sisters, when they met distinguished visitors in the garden of the Prince of Orange. Perhaps his health had suffered from his two severe illnesses in England, and he needed the long rest. But, whatever the reason, at the Hague he stayed, until May 1648, when he was summoned by Rupert to join the Royalist fleet.

[1] Whitelocke, p. 306.
[2] State Papers, 20 April, 1647.
[3] Rupert Transcripts, Sept. 30, 1648.

CHAPTER XII

COMMAND IN THE FRENCH ARMY. COURTSHIP OF MADE-
MOISELLE. DUELS WITH DIGBY AND PERCY

SOMETIME before the end of the war the Queen of England had fled to France, and had set up her court at that
home of Royal exiles,—St. Germains! There she had been
joined by her son, the Prince of Wales, and by many English Cavaliers; and thither went Rupert in July 1646. "If
thou see Prince Rupert," wrote King Charles anxiously to
his wife, "tell him that I have recommend him unto thee.
For, albeit his passions may sometimes make him mistake,
yet I am confident of his honest constancy and courage,
having at the last behaved himself very well." [1] Henrietta,
convinced by her husband's words, or forgetful of the
reproaches she had so recently heaped upon her nephew,
received Rupert graciously, and to the Prince of Wales he
was of course very welcome.

Nor was his reception at the French court less cordial.
The Queen Regent, impressed by his romantic history and
famous courage, showered marks of her favour upon him ;
and Mazarin, the true ruler of France, at once offered him
a command in the French army, "upon whatever conditions
of preferment or advantage he could desire." [2] Rupert
hesitated to accept the flattering offer, without his Uncle's
sanction. "Prince Rupert had several assurances by the
mouth of the Duke of Orleans, Cardinal Mazarin and others,
of the charge of the foreign forces mentioned in my last,"
says a letter in the Portland MSS., "but I am informed

---

[1] Letters of Charles I. p. 58. Camden Society. 1st Series. King to Queen,
5 Aug. 1646.

[2] Warburton, III. p. 236.

he defers to accept the commission of it, until he hears his Uncle, the King of Great Britain, doth approve it; which deference is well taken here." [1]

Apparently Charles expressed approval of the arrangement, for Rupert finally entered the French service, reserving to himself the right of quitting it whenever his Uncle should need him. He was immediately given the rank of Field-Marshal, with a regiment of foot, a troop of horse, and a commission to command all the English in France. The Cavaliers, exiled and destitute, eagerly embraced the opportunity of serving under their Prince, and Rupert had no difficulty in raising a large corps, more especially as the conditions of service were exceptionally good. Among those who applied for a commission was the ever plausible Goring, but he found himself promptly refused, and thereupon took service under Spain.

The summer of 1647 found Rupert fighting his old enemies the Spaniards, in Northern France, and on the borders of Flanders. The campaign was a desultory one, in which little was effected, owing partly to the jealousies of the French officers, who were little more in concord than those of the English army had been. The two Marshals, Rantzau and Gassion, detested each other, and Gassion, at least, was exceedingly jealous of Rupert's reputation. His conduct throughout the campaign was, if not treacherous, extremely eccentric, and he seems to have deserved the name of "that madman" bestowed on him by Rantzau.

They marched first to the relief of Armentières, and, on their arrival near the town, Gassion invited Rupert to come and "view the enemy," accordingly they set out alone, and advanced some way down the river, concealing themselves behind the sheltering hedges. Then Gassion, directing the Prince to stay behind until he called him, proceeded alone to a little house on the river bank. In the meantime some

---

[1] Hist. MSS. Com. Rept. 13. Portland MSS. III. p 150.

Spanish soldiers came down in a boat, and landed by the house. Rupert saw them clearly, but dared not warn his comrade lest they should hear him sooner than could Gassion. Luckily the French Marshal was equal to the emergency. He was wearing a Spanish coat, and when he came face to face with the Spanish soldiers, he had the presence of mind to address them in their own language, and as though he were one of their officers. This so surprised them that they stood still, staring; and Gassion, with more prudence than dignity, took to his heels. In spite of the enemy's fire, he regained the hedge, and Rupert, coming to meet him, pulled him over the ditch. "Mort Dieu!" gasped the Marshal. "Ça m'arrive toujours!" To which Rupert retorted in the dry manner which he seems to have usually assumed towards Gassion, "Je n'en doute point, si vous faites souvent comme ça." Both got safely away, but the battle intended to relieve Armentières never took place.[1] The Spaniards numbered three times as many as the French: and when Gassion began to draw out his troops next day, Rantzau flew to exhort Rupert to stop such madness. The Prince thereupon urged Gassion to give up the idea of battle; the army was withdrawn to Arras, and Armentières fell to the Spaniards.

On the retreat to Arras, Rupert was attacked by Piccolomini, in great force. Again and again Rupert repulsed his charge, retreating slowly all the time. Gassion, actuated by jealousy, sent an order to the Prince to remain where he was; but Rupert, retorting fiercely that it was the other Marshal's day of command, continued his retreat. After that he despatched a formal complaint of Gassion's conduct to the Queen Regent, who rebuked Gassion with the curious question—"Was he a general or a Croat?"[2]

The Spaniards marched next to La Bassée, and Gassion there invited Rupert to take another survey of their forces,

[1] Benett MSS. Warburton, III. pp. 238—9.
[2] Ibid. p. 240.

asking, "Are you well mounted, Sir? Shall we go see the army?" Rupert assented, and they started—not this time alone, but with three or four others in their company. They had not gone far when they fell into an ambush of foot soldiers, and perceived that a troop of Spanish horse was following to cut off their retreat. Seeing this, they wheeled round, and two of Rupert's gentlemen, Mortaigne and Robert Holmes, beat back a troop of Spaniards who were crossing the rivulet between them and the French. Both were hurt, Mortaigne in the hand and Holmes in the leg. Mortaigne retired, but Holmes lay upon the ground, exposed to the sweeping fire of the enemy. Rupert was retreating with the French, but, seeing Holmes in this predicament, he turned and went calmly back through the Spanish fire, with Mortaigne following him. With great danger and difficulty he lifted Holmes on to his own horse, and brought him safely off, "not a man of the French volunteers coming to his assistance. [1]

In this inglorious campaign there seems to have been little save retreats to record. An attempt to relieve Landrécies failed as that at Armentières had done, chiefly through the mistake, or treachery of a guide. Rupert was told off to secure the retreat with three German regiments and one of Croats. Continually skirmishing with the Spanish horse, he had got through the first pass, when Gassion returned to him, in great distress, saying that the cannon was stuck fast in the mud, and would have to be abandoned. Rupert replied that, if he might have the Picardy guards and a regiment of Swiss, he would not only make good the retreat, but would also bring off the cannon. Gassion willingly sent back the required troops, and Rupert made good his promise, without losing a single man. This done, "he thought to have lain down and refreshed himself," but an order came to march on to La Bassée, and

---

[1] Benett MSS. Warburton, III. p. 241.

he at once set out with the horse, leaving the foot to follow. At La Bassée he won the only success that fell to the French in the campaign. Reaching the town that night, he found that a relief of some four hundred men, under Goring, had just been despatched thither by the Spaniards; the opportunity was more than welcome. All Goring's men were captured by Rupert's guards, and most of them, being English, transferred their services to the Prince.[1] That same night Rupert began his line round the town, and in less than three weeks it was his.

Gassion was furiously jealous. During the whole course of the siege, he had refused to lend any aid whatever, and when the town was taken in spite of him, his jealousy led him to play the Prince a very treacherous trick. He invited him one morning to "take the air," and Rupert, for the third time, agreed to accompany him. They went out attended by a guard of eighty horse; but a peasant warned the Spaniards of their whereabouts, and an ambush was laid to intercept their return. As they came back, Rupert noticed a dog sitting with its back towards him, and staring into the wood. The circumstance roused his suspicions; he took off his cloak, threw it to his page, and pressing after Gassion who was some yards ahead, cried: "Have a care, sir! There is a party in that wood!" As he spoke the hidden enemy fired a smart volley. Setting spurs to their horses, the French party broke through it, losing only Rupert's page, who was taken, but courteously released next day. No sooner were they through the fire than Gassion faced about, saying: "Il faut rompre le col à ces coquins-là.—Pied à terre!" He took his foot from his stirrup; and Rupert, naturally understanding that they were to attack the ambush, dismounted. A few officers followed his example, and thereupon Gassion marched off with their horses, leaving them to face the difficulty as best

[1] Benett MSS. Warburton, III. p. 243.

they could. A sharp skirmish followed, in which Rupert received a shot in the head, but he contrived to retreat after Gassion, who was calmly waiting at some distance. The French General then expressed polite regret for the accident: "Monsieur," he said, "je suis bien fâché que vous êtes blessé!" To which Rupert replied, with crushing brevity: "Et moi aussi!" [1]

This little skirmish ended an uneventful campaign, and Rupert returned to St. Germains, "where he passed his next winter with as much satisfaction as the tenderness he felt for his royal uncle's affairs would permit." [2] King Charles was then a prisoner at Hampton Court, whence he wrote a very affectionate letter to his nephew, sympathising with him for his recent wound, and assuring him that, "next my children, I say *next*, I shall have most care of you, and shall take the first opportunity either to employ you, or to have your company." [3]

Rupert was in the meanwhile, exerting himself in the service of the Prince of Wales. It was the ambition of Henrietta to unite her eldest son to her niece, the daughter of the Duke of Orleans, known as La Grande Mademoiselle. This lady, as heiress of the Montpensiers, had inherited an enormous fortune, which Henrietta desired to acquire for her son's benefit. But young Charles did not care for his pompous cousin, and, in order to avoid the trouble of love-making, declared that he could not speak French. Though Rupert himself had obstinately declined to mend his fortunes by marriage, he seems to have been very anxious to overcome his cousin's contumacy. He became his interpreter, in which *rôle* he was obliged not merely to translate, but to invent pretty speeches for the refractory Charles. The task was a difficult one, for Mademoiselle was not stupid, and observed that when her supposed lover

[1] Benett MSS. Warburton, III. pp. 244—247.
[2] Warburton, III. p. 246.
[3] Ibid. III. p. 248. King to Rupert, Sept. 27, 1647.

wished to discuss dogs and horses with the young King of France he could speak French well enough.[1] Moreover, neither Rupert nor Henrietta could make Prince Charles dance with his cousin if he did not choose to do so. Mademoiselle pointed out his neglect of her to Rupert, "who," says she, "immediately made me all the excuses imaginable."[2] But neither Rupert's excuses, nor Henrietta's protestations could bring the affair to the desired conclusion.

An occupation more natural and congenial to Rupert than making love on behalf of an unwilling lover, was the settling of old scores, for which he now found leisure and opportunity. It was not to be expected that he should meet Digby peaceably, and when the Secretary arrived in France in September 1647, a duel was universally expected. "My Lord Digby, at his coming from Rouen towards Paris, received news of Prince Rupert being, two nights before, come from the army to St. Germains," wrote O'Neil to Ormonde. "His Highness and his dependants being the only persons from whom his Lordship could suspect any resentment, his Lordship prepared himself by the best forethought he could for any accident that night happen to him in that way."[3]

The Queen was resolved to prevent any such "accident," and to keep a close watch over her nephew, to that end, but Rupert's prompt action took her by surprise. On the morning after his arrival, while he was yet in bed, Digby received the Prince's challenge. "About nine of the clock," says O'Neil, "I came to the Lord Digby's chamber, being sent for hastily by him. Who told me that Prince Rupert had, a little before, sent him word, by M. de la Chapelle, that he expected him, with his sword in his hand, at the

---

[1] Mémoires de Mademoiselle de Montpensier. Michaud's Collections. Vol. IV. p. 57.

[2] Ibid. pp. 35, 37.

[3] Carte's Letters, I. 152—156, 9 Oct. 1647.

Cross of Poissy, a large league off in the forest, with three in his company." Digby sent back word that he was "highly sensible of the honour," and would come as soon as he could get on his clothes, but feared that there would be an hour's delay, since he had no horse, and was lame "in regard of a weakness in his hurt leg." Rupert received this message "with much nobleness and civility," and at once placed his own horse at Digby's service. By that time rumours of the impending fray were afloat, and Jermyn was sent by the Queen to remonstrate with Digby. But the only result of Jermyn's intervention was to produce a quarrel between himself and Digby, which determined him to attend the duel on Rupert's side. The delay, however, had given the Queen time to act, and just as Digby set foot in the stirrup, he was arrested by her Guards. The Prince of Wales then rode into the forest, where he arrested Rupert and his seconds, Gerard, Chapelle and Guatier. That evening, the Queen held an inquiry into the cause of quarrel, which Rupert declared to be certain private speeches made by Digby, and not his actions as Secretary of State. The matter was therefore delivered to the arbitration of Culpepper, Gerard, Wentworth and Cornwallis; and " His Highness was so generous in not demanding or expecting from the Lord Digby anything that might misbecome him, that the business was concluded that night, in presence of the Queen and the Prince of Wales, much to the satisfaction of all parties. Since which reconciliation," adds O'Neil, "Prince Rupert has carried himself so nobly to the Lord Digby, and the Lord Digby is so possessed with His Highness's generous proceedings towards him, that I think, in my conscience, there is no man, at present more heartily affected to His Highness's person and service." [1]

Thus happily and unexpectedly ended the long feud. Rupert's resentment was hot and passionate, but he could

[1] Carte Letters, I. 152—156. 9 Oct. 1647.

always forego it graciously, provided that advances were made from the other side. Nor were Digby's protestations of friendship insincere; in proof of which he promptly fought with and wounded Wilmot, because that gentleman had maligned the Prince. [1]

Digby and Wilmot being thus disposed of, there remained Percy with whom the Prince had yet to deal. Of this duel Rupert was resolved not to be cheated, and he therefore dispensed with formality. Seizing his opportunity on a hunting expedition, he rode up to Percy, and laying a hand on his bridle, abruptly demanded "satisfaction." Percy retorted angrily that he was quite ready to give it, and that the Prince's hold on his bridle was unnecessary. Both then sprang from their horses and drew their swords. Rupert "being as skilful with his weapon as valiant," ran Percy through the side, at the second pass; they closed, and both fell to the ground, Percy's hand being wounded in the fall. Upon this, one of Prince Charles's gentlemen came in and separated them, and so the affair ended, with advantage to Rupert. Report said, afterwards, that the Prince had had the longer sword, but as in French duelling law there was no rule about length of weapon, that fact could not be held to affect the case in any way. [2]

This was the last of Rupert's adventures in France. Within a few weeks an event occurred which recalled him to Holland, and gave him, once more, the opportunity of serving his uncle, King Charles.

[1] Carte Letters. I. 152—156. 9 Oct. 1647.
[2] Hamilton Papers, p. 178. Camden Soc. New Series.

CHAPTER XIII

RUPERT'S CARE OF THE FLEET.   NEGOTIATIONS WITH
THE SCOTS.   RUPERT'S VOYAGE TO IRELAND.   THE
EXECUTION OF THE KING.   LETTERS OF
SOPHIE TO RUPERT AND MAURICE

By May 1648 a Royalist reaction was setting in in
England. The King had been two years a prisoner, and
the people, already weary of the Army and the Parliament,
began to think with favour of their unfortunate sovereign.
Royalist risings took place in Kent and some of the Eastern
Counties, and a large portion of the fleet, encouraged by
this, revolted from the Parliament and came over to Holland.
Thither Rupert and the younger Charles hastened to meet
it. The French, eager to detain Rupert in their service,
again and again offered him "any conditions" to remain
with them, but he adhered firmly to the Stuart fortunes. [1]
And well was it for young Charles that he did so; for, as
even his enemies acknowledged, no other man could, or
would have competed successfully with the terrible difficulties which they had now to encounter. Fortunately, his
experience in England had not been wasted. He was learning to cultivate patience, tolerance and self-control, and
never were such qualities more needed. A letter, dated
August 9, 1648, bears witness to the change in the Prince's
manners.—"Let me assure you, Sir, that Prince Rupert's
carriage was such at Calais, and throughout the journey
thither, that, I protest, I was overjoyed to see it, both
for the public, and for the Prince's (Charles) happiness in
his company ... Certainly, Sir, he appears to me to be a

[1] Bennett MSS. Warburton, III. p. 250.

strangely changed man in his carriage; and for his temperance and his abilities, I think they were never much
questioned."[1]

His abilities were about to be taxed to the uttermost.
The small fleet was in a most unsatisfactory state. Provisions were scarce, the sailors mutinous, and the loyalty
of the Commanders—their recent revolt notwithstanding—
exceedingly doubtful. As usual, counsels were divided.
Batten and Jordan, the two officers who had brought over
the fleet from the Parliament, were for sailing to Scotland;
others desired to relieve Colchester, which had been seized
for the King; Rupert wished to make for the Isle of Wight,
where the King was confined; the sailors desired to hover
about the Thames and capture returning merchant vessels.
Consequently, all that could be done was to hang about
the Downs, capturing a few prizes and making occasional
assaults upon the English coast. An attack on Deal resulted
in the death of Captain Beckman, but the sailors were still
unwilling to return to Holland. On the approach of the
Parliamentary fleet, commanded by Lord Warwick, it was
resolved to fight, but the engagement was prevented,—once
by a sudden storm, and again by the contumacy of Batten,
who refused to follow Rupert.

Finally, in September it was decided to return to Holland;
but Warwick followed the Royalist fleet closely, and there
ensued a curious race for the possession of the Helvoetsluys
harbour. Warwick gained, and seemed likely to win the
day; but a Captain Allen, who happened to be on the
shore, came to the aid of the Royalists. As Warwick's
ship drew near, Allen signed for the line to draw him in,
and, when it was thrown to him, contrived to let Warwick
slip back, so that Rupert's ship came in before him. After
that, Rupert successfully hauled up all the rest of his fleet,
except the "Convertine," which came in with the next tide;

<hr>

[1] Nicholas Papers, I. 95. Camden Soc. New Series. Hatton to Nicholas,
Aug. 9, 1648.

nevertheless Warwick followed him into the harbour, and for more than a month the hostile fleets remained in this curious position; so close that the sailors could shout to one another, and yet unable to proceed to hostilities, because they were in a neutral harbour. [1] Sometimes the sailors met on shore, and then brawls arose amongst them. But much worse was the frequent desertion of Rupert's men. Warwick spared no pains to win them over, and once he even sent an officer to the Prince, with a request that he might speak to his men. Rupert's reply was characteristic: "The Prince told him, 'Yes, in his hearing; but, if he spake anything amiss he would throw him overboard'." Needless to add, the man retired without speaking at all. [2]

Yet in spite of Rupert's vigilance, bribes and other temptations drew some of the ships over to the enemy, until only nine remained. Thereupon the Prince manned the "Convertine" with his most loyal men, furnished her with cannon, and laid her athwart the rest of his fleet. The Dutch remonstrated against this warlike action, but Rupert answered that if they promised him protection, he would rely on their word; if not, he would himself protect the fleet entrusted to him by the King. And the Dutch, who seem to have been very compliant towards the young Prince who had grown up amongst them, let him have his way.

The Hague was now the head-quarters of the Prince of Wales, and thither flocked all his old Councillors, besides many other Cavaliers. Faction raged amongst them as violently as ever. "It was," says Clarendon, "no hard matter to get anything disliked that was resolved in the Council." [3] That the administration of affairs was bad was a point on which every one agreed, but they concurred in nothing else.

[1] Warburton, III. pp. 250—254.
[2] Ibid. p. 253.
[3] Clarendon, Bk. XI. p. 63.

Rupert had fallen under the influence of Sir Edward Herbert, the quarrelsome attorney-general, and Hyde and Cottington found themselves eagerly welcomed by these two, who "inveighed bitterly against the whole administration of the fleet." Batten, Rupert held for a coward or a traitor; Long, the secretary of the Prince of Wales, for a mere swindler, and, despite his "changed carriage", he had not renounced his old hatred of Culpepper. Their mutual animosity "infinitely disturbed councils," [1] and was in all respects unfortunate. Their policy was diametrically opposed. Culpepper was for conciliating the English populace, and when the Royalist rising took place in 1648, he was averse to permitting the young Duke of Buckingham to share in it, unless he would declare for the Covenant, "and such-like popular ways." Such views naturally did not find favour with the Prince, who adhered to the young Duke's cause.—"Prince Rupert stuck to itt," wrote Hatton, "and we carried it against him;" [2] that is, against Culpepper.

The disputes came to a climax over a question of supply. A cargo of sugar, captured at sea, had to be sold for the payment of the fleet, and Rupert proposed to employ a certain Sir Robert Walsh in the business. Culpepper protested such vehement distrust of the man in question that Rupert took his expressions as reflecting on himself, and haughtily demanded: "What exceptions there were to Sir Robert Walsh, that he might not be fit for it?" Culpepper returned, nothing daunted, that Walsh was "a shark, and a fellow not fit to be trusted." Whereupon, said Rupert: "Sir Robert is my friend, and you must not think to meet him but with your sword in your hand, for he is a gentleman and a soldier!" Culpepper, grown reckless of his words, declared fiercely that he would not fight with Walsh, but with the Prince himself, to which Rupert replied, very quietly, "It is well!" The Council rose in confusion; but the Prince

---

[1] Clarendon, Bk. XI. p. 127.
[2] Nicholas Papers, I. p. 96.

of Wales, who was greatly agitated, ultimately succeeded in soothing his cousin. Culpepper proved more implacable, and several days elapsed before he could be induced to offer an apology, which Rupert received graciously.[1]

The fleet was at this time formally given over to Rupert's command. For many reasons he accepted the charge reluctantly, and offered to serve nominally under the Duke of York. But of this Prince Charles would not hear, and Rupert was therefore invested "with all the command at sea that he formerly held on shore."[2] The facility with which the exiled Cavaliers took to the sea is strange to modern ideas, but in the seventeenth century the line between soldier and sailor was not very finely drawn. In Rupert's own case his education among the amphibious Hollanders probably stood him in good stead. Certainly he seems to have thoroughly understood all nautical matters, and on one occasion we read: "By the ill-conning of the mates the ship was brought to leeward, *which caused the Prince to conn her himself.*"[3]

Some of Rupert's friends would fain have dissuaded him from "an undertaking of so desperate an appearance,"[4] but he was determined to do his best, and the Prince of Wales frankly acknowledged that, but for his cousin's "industry and address" there would have been no fleet at all.[5] And Hyde, who, as we know, had never loved the Prince, wrote to Sir Richard Fanshaw, that the preservation of the fleet must be entirely ascribed to Prince Rupert, "who, seriously, hath expressed greater dexterity and temper in it than you can imagine. I know there is, and will be, much prejudice to the service by his being engaged in that command, but the truth is there is an unavoidable

---

[1] Clarendon, Bk. XI, pp. 128—130; Carte Letters, I. p. 192.

[2] Warburton, III. p. 257.

[3] Ibid. p. 386.

[4] Ibid. 255.

[5] Transcripts. Charles II to Rupert, 20 Jan. 1649.

necessity for it." And, after recounting the bad behaviour of Batten and Jordan, who had corrupted the sailors, and refused to put to sea, he adds: "In this distress Prince Rupert took the charge, and with unrivalled pains and toil, put all things in reasonable order.... And really I believe that he will behave himself so well in it that nobody will have cause to regret it." [1]

And Rupert did behave himself well. No toil proved too arduous for him, no undertaking too dangerous. Indeed, the labours involved in his task were so great and so many that it seems scarcely credible that they could be performed by one man. He became a merchant: he discussed the prices of sugar, indigo, tobacco, and other commodities, and personally conducted the sale of his prizes. He attended to his own commissariat; dispensing with the cheating commissioners, as "unuseful evils." [2] We find him gravely considering the quality of "pickled meat," or lamenting that peas and groats are both too dear to buy. [3] "Concerning the pork, he tells me he doth not think there can be so great a quantity provided suddenly," says a correspondent. "He hath not yet provided any shirts nor apparel for the men." [4] He was his own recruiting officer, and went from port to port in Ireland, persuading men to join his fleet. The conduct of each man was his personal concern; and, as in the war in England, he was overwhelmed with complaints and correspondence by his officers. One letter may serve as an example of the rest.

"According to the service and duty I owe unto your Highness," writes Thomas Price, "I am enforced to certify your Highness of the dangerous and unbeseeming carriage of Robert Pett, gunner of His Majesty's ship the Revenge,

---

[1] Clar. St. Papers. Hyde to Fanshaw, 21 Jan. 1649.
[2] Warburton, III. p. 295.
[3] Rupert Transcripts. Hyde to Rupert, Dec. 11, 1648. Mennes to Rupert, Jan. 12, 1649.
[4] Ibid. Ball to Rupert, 15 Dec. 1648.

who, upon Saturday night last, being the tenth of January, about nine o'clock at night, being very much in drink, would have taken tobacco over a barrell of powder, (being in his cabin, which is in the gun room and a great quantity of loose powder lying round about), had he not been prevented by Captain Payton Cartwright, who was called by some of the gun room for that purpose. The gunner, being something unruly, he was forced to go up to His Highness Prince Maurice to acquaint him with it. Upon which he was committed to the guard, for fear of further danger."[1]

Mutiny was unhappily only too frequent; but the Prince's presence usually sufficed to quell it. While the fleet was at Helvoetsluys, there arose some discontent in the "Antelope," beginning with "a complaint upon victuals." Rupert went on board, and promptly told the men that they were free to leave the service. To this they made no answer, but they were unappeased, and when, two days later, Rupert sent for twenty of them to help to rig up his own ship, they refused to come. The Prince then went again to the "Antelope," and "walked the deck, to see his commands obeyed." The sailors crowded about him, and one gathered courage to shout defiance. His example would have dis-astrously inspired the rest, had not Rupert acted with extra-ordinary promptitude. Seizing the mutineer in his arms, he held him as though about to drop him over the ship's side, which remarkable action "wrought such a terror upon the rest, that they forthwith returned to their duty."[2] Claren-don exaggerates this incident much as Pepys does the affair at Newark. The Prince, he says, "with notable vigour and success, suppressed two or three mutinies, in one of which he was compelled to throw two or three of the seamen overboard, by the strength of his own arms."[3] Since there

---

[1] Rupert Transcripts. Price to Rupert, 15 Jan. 1651.
[2] Warburton, III. pp. 262—264.
[3] Clarendon, Bk. XI. p. 152.

was frequently no money to pay the sailors, mutiny was of course to be expected. Nominally the men were paid 25s a month, but, unless prizes were taken, they did not get the money. Usually they acquiesced in the condition of affairs with admirable resignation. In 1648, a deputation of five sailors came from Helvoetsluys to Prince Charles at the Hague, with a request to be told whether he had or had not any money. Being truthfully answered that he had none, they expressed themselves satisfied with a promise of shares in the next prizes, and returned to the fleet, having, as Hyde informed Rupert, "behaved themselves very civilly."[1] And not only for money to pay his sailors, but for every other necessary Prince Charles was dependent on the prizes taken by Rupert. "Being totally destitute of means, we intend to provide for the satisfaction of our debts out of the proceeds of the goods in the ship lately taken," he wrote in 1650.[2] In short the fleet represented all the funds which the poverty-stricken Royalists could gather together, and for the next three years the exiled Court was supported by the exertions of Rupert.

While the fleet lay inactive in 1648 the Prince of Wales was engaged in negotiations with the Scots. In Scotland the Royalist reaction was stronger than it was in England; the Scottish Presbyterians were wholly dissatisfied with Cromwell and the English Puritans, and they now sought to make terms with their Sovereign. But one of their first conditions was that neither Rupert nor Maurice should set foot in Scotland, and this was exceedingly displeasing to the Prince of Wales. The Earl of Lauderdale, who had been sent to the Hague to negotiate the affair, reported that Rupert's power over the Prince was absolute, and that if he chose to come to Scotland come he would, in spite of the negative vote of the whole Council. Rupert himself proposed to accompany Prince Charles in a private capacity,

[1] Rupert Transcripts. Hyde to Rupert, Jan. 1649.
[2] Warburton, III. p. 308. Charles II to Rupert, Jan. 27, 1650.

taking no share in the affairs of State;[1] but the Scots, who knew his influence over his cousin, refused to entertain the suggestion. Prince Charles then, with his own hand, struck out the clause of the treaty which disabled Rupert from bearing him company; an arbitrary action which seriously annoyed Lauderdale.[2] Rupert, however, smoothed the matter over, saying that, provided his absence were not made a formal condition, he would remain in Holland. Altogether he "carried himself so handsomely"[3] as to win over Lauderdale, who finally declared that Rupert's coming to Scotland would be, after all, "of great advantage."[4]

But Rupert, in spite of his conciliatory behaviour inclined far more to the Royalism of Montrose than to that of Lauderdale and Argyle. The Marquess of Montrose, who had sustained the King's cause in Scotland with extraordinary heroism and brilliancy, was at that time at Brussels and quite ready to risk another venture on the King's behalf. He was, however, so obnoxious to the Presbyterian party that no hope of their union could be entertained. Charles had to choose between the two, and Rupert strongly inclined to the heroic Montrose. The character and achievements of the Marquess were well calculated to inspire admiration in the Prince. The two had met once in England, during the August of 1643, and a strong mutual esteem existed between them. Therefore, while Charles was leaning to Argyle, Rupert was conducting a voluminous correspondence with Montrose. The "noble kindness" of the Marquess, said the Prince, made him anxious to serve the King in his company, and he would very willingly join in any undertaking that he proposed.[5] Montrose replied with equal friendliness: "I will .. rather hazard to sink by you than

---

[1] Hamilton Papers, p. 219. Camd. Soc. June 24. 1648.
[2] Ibid. p. 245.
[3] Hamilton Papers, p. 246, Camden Soc. Lauderdale to Lanerick, Aug. 1648.
[4] Ibid. p. 249, Aug. 20, 1648.
[5] Warburton, III. pp. 254, 262, 267—270.

save myself aside of others." But, unfortunately, a meeting between them was impossible. The Marquess could not come to the Hague on account of the Presbyterian emissaries there assembled, and also because he was continually beset by spies, from whom he was anxious to conceal his alliance with the Prince. Rupert would fain have visited him at Brussels, but he was bound "by a heavy tie" to the fleet, and could only lament that "whilst I am separating the sheep from the goats I dare not absent myself without hazard."[1] Montrose was anxious to take the fleet to Scotland, where, he said, "there be so handsome and probable grounds for a clear and gallant design .. that I should be infinitely sorry that you should be induced to hazard your own person, or those little rests (remains) upon any desperate thrusts; for, while you are safe, we shall find twenty fair ways to state ourselves."[2] But both that scheme, and the negotiations with Lauderdale fell through, and it was finally resolved to take the fleet to Ireland, where the Marquess of Ormonde stood out for the King with as great a devotion as Montrose had shown in Scotland.

In October Rupert received a letter from the King, at the hands of Will Legge, who bore also an important message which the King dared not write. He had now laid a plan for escape from the Isle of Wight, and he required Rupert to send a ship thither, and to acquaint "no other mortal" with the matter, except the Prince of Orange.[3] Rupert would have gone in person, but was still detained by his care of the fleet. However, the Prince of Orange willingly sent one of his own ships, which was boarded and searched by a captain of the Parliament. For several days it lingered on the coast, under pretence of waiting for a wind, but, as we all know, Charles's

---

[1] Hist. MSS. Com. Rpt. II. Montrose MSS. p. 173.
[2] Warburton, III. p. 269.
[3] Ibid. p. 272.

attempt at escape was frustrated, and the vessel returned without him.

On November 21st Warwick sailed for England, and Rupert, freed from the surveillance of his foe, at once prepared his ships for action. Money of course was lacking, but Rupert sent out two of his ships to take prizes, which was successfully done, and the resources were further increased by the sale of the Antelope's ordnance; besides which, "the Queen of Bohemia pawned her jewels, or the work had never been done."[1] Lord Craven also added his contribution. "What I have in my power shall be at your service, unless your brother Edward in the meantime disfurnish me," he wrote to Rupert.[2]

A difficulty next arose about the use of the standard. Properly, only the Lord High Admiral could carry it, and that title the Prince of Wales had no power to confer. Yet Warwick made use of the standard, and it was therefore left to Rupert's discretion to hoist it if needful for the encouragement of his men.

Towards the end of January 1649, all was ready, and Rupert sailed for Ireland with three flag-ships, four frigates, and one prize; Maurice of course accompanying him. They were temporarily joined by three Dutchmen requiring consortship, a circumstance which proved very beneficial to the Royalists. At day-break, January 22, they sighted the Parliament fleet off Dover, and Rupert judging valour to be the better part of discretion, sailed straight for it. Terrified by this extraordinary boldness, and believing the Dutch ships to be in Rupert's pay, Warwick's fleet sought shelter beneath the forts; and the Prince, much encouraged by this success, passed unmolested to Kinsale.[3]

The usual endeavours to sow ill-will between Rupert and Ormonde had not been wanting. Digby, apparently

---

[1] Warburton, III. p. 273.
[2] Rupert Transcripts. Craven to Rupert, 29 Jan. 1649.
[3] Warburton, III. p. 282.

forgetful of his recent professions of friendship for Rupert, addressed the Lord Lieutenant in his old strain. "One thing I think it necessary to advertise you of, that Prince Rupert hath set his rest to command this expedition of the fleet, and the Council have complied with him in it, insomuch that if it arrives safe in Ireland you must expect him with it. I hope his aim is only at the honour of conveying the fleet thither, through so much hasard, and then returning to the Prince. But if he have any further design of continuing to command the fleet, or of remaining in that kingdom, I fear the consequences of it, knowing what applications have been made to him formerly, and how unsettled and weak a people you have there, apt to catch at anything that's new." [1] Hyde, on the other hand, warned Rupert that there would certainly be attempts to excite quarrels between himself and Ormonde, but added, with a confidence he did not feel: "Truly, Sir, I do not apprehend any danger this way. I know your Highness will comply in all things with him, as a person, besides his great merit, of the clearest and most entire approbation of any subject the King hath." [2] In similar terms wrote Jermyn at the Queen's behest, to Ormonde, who replied rather crushingly: "I am infinitely obliged to Her Majesty for her care to keep me in Prince Rupert's good opinion. I shall be, and have been, industrious to gain his favour, and my endeavour has hitherto been successful. Neither do I apprehend any danger of a change; his carriage towards me having been full of civility, as well in relation to my employment as to my person." [3]

There was in fact the best of intelligence between Rupert and Ormonde, and thanks to the Lord Lieutenant's noble and unsuspicious nature, nothing could destroy it. The "applications" to Rupert, mentioned by Digby, were made

[1] Carte's Ormonde, VI. 587. 27 Nov. 1648.
[2] Warburton, III. p. 277, Hyde to Rupert, Jan. 27. 1649.
[3] Carte Letters, II. p. 406. 29 Sept. 1648.

by the Roman Catholic rebels, who disliked Ormonde's steady hand and firm adherence to the established religion. They represented to Rupert that they were averse, not to the King, but to his Lord Lieutenant, and that if only he (Rupert) would consent to lead them "they would all join in one to live and die for His Majesty's service, under Your Highness's command; that being their greatest ambition."[1] Rupert's enemies at the Hague hastened to report these intrigues to Ormonde, colouring them, as much as possible, to Rupert's discredit. But Ormonde replied calmly that he had been already informed of them by Rupert himself, who had asked his advice as to the answers he should send. That he knew those who desired to divide the King's party "assumed encouragements from Prince Rupert, without warrant from him." That he, personally would willingly resign his charge to the Prince, if it were for the King's advantage; but that he knew it to be " impossible for the Prince to descend to what would look like supplanting one that hath endeavoured, with some success, to serve him in his charge."[2]

But though Ormonde refused to doubt Rupert's integrity, he did not derive from him the assistance he had hoped. Rupert had written, on his arrival at Kinsale, promising to follow Ormonde's advice in all things, and to give him all the aid in his power. But his want of men made it impossible for him to block up Dublin harbour, as the Lord Lieutenant desired,[3] and the necessity of capturing prizes, the sale of which supported the fleet, prevented any action of importance. The Parliament complained bitterly that no ship could leave the Bristol Channel by day without falling a prey to the Princes,[4] and yet Rupert seldom had money to send to Ormonde. "Your Lordship may be as-

[1] Rupert Transcripts. Talbot to Rupert, Nov. 7, 1648.
[2] Carte Letters, II. 427—430. 25 Jan. 1650.
[3] Ibid. II. 381. 29 May, 1649.
[4] Clowes Royal Navy, II. p. 120.

sured of all the supplies and assistances our ships can
afford you," he wrote in answer to one of Ormonde's frequent appeals for money. "But I must entreat your Lordship
to consider the great charge the fleet is at, and, if we lose
this opportunity, we may be hindered by a far greater
strength than yet appears. The least squadron we must
now send out must be of five ships. Three we can leave
behind, fitted with all but men, ready to do service here.
I intend, with the first opportunity, to go to Waterford.
... From thence I shall not fail to receive your commands.
Mr. Fanshaw can give you an account how low we are in
matters of monies." [1]

The want of men was even more serious than the want
of money. In the summer Rupert hoped to really fight the
Parliament fleet, and with that view he personally sought
recruits in all the neighbouring port towns. By great exertions he raised a considerable number, but, when the
task was accomplished, the Council of War hung back from
the risk of a battle, and the Prince, rather than incur the
charge of "vanity and rashness," dismissed his hard-won
recruits and retired into harbour. Changed indeed was the
man who had fought at Marston Moor! [2]

But in spite of all difficulties, Rupert contrived to take
prizes, to support the Royalists at the Hague, and even to
send some succour to the Scilly islands, which held out
for the King. "I believe we shall make a shift to live
in spite of all our factions!" [3] he wrote cheerfully. And
make a shift he did, through "a wearisome summer, passed
in anxiety and troubles." [4] Cromwell had arrived in June,
and was rapidly conquering Ireland. The King's army was
defeated near Dublin; the towns began to revolt to the
Parliament; the faithful garrisons were mercilessly massacred

<hr>

[1] Carte Letters, II. 375.
[2] Warburton, III. pp. 293—294.
[3] Ibid. p. 290. Rupert to Grenvile, Apr. 28, 1649.
[4] Ibid. p. 297.

by Cromwell; and Rupert only escaped the treachery of the Governor of Cork by a press of business which prevented him from accepting an invitation to hunt. "The Governor of Cork," says the historian of Rupert's voyages, "resolved to make himself famous by an infamous act, to which purpose, knowing His Highness loved hunting, he invited him to a chase of deer, close by the town; but Heaven abhorring such inhumanity, prevented that design, by providing importunate business to impede His Highness' intentions."[1] But though thwarted in this scheme, the Governor of Cork could and did surrender the city to the enemy, after which Kinsale was no longer a safe port for the Royalist fleet. If the ships were to be preserved, it was high time to quit the Irish coast. The Parliament had already sent a fleet to block the Prince up in the harbour, but again fortune favoured him. A friendly wind blew the Parliament fleet out to sea, and enabled Rupert to slip out past them. For want of men, he was forced to leave three of his ships behind him, and in November 1649, he began the world anew with seven sail.

Within a few days of Rupert's first arrival at Kinsale, the execution of Charles I had taken place. For some weeks Rupert remained ignorant of this final disaster, but in February a vague rumour reached him, and he wrote in great agitation to Ormonde: "I beseech your Lordship to let me know whether you have any certain news of the King's misfortune."[2] The dreadful rumour was only too soon confirmed. From the Hague he received dismal accounts of the general depression and confusion—"all men being full of designs to be counsellors and officers;" and he was entreated to write a few lines to cheer and encourage his young cousin, now Charles II.[3] Very shortly he received

---

[1] Warburton, pp. 297—8.
[2] Carte Papers. Irish Confederation, VII. 256. Rupert to Ormonde, Feb. 12, 1649.
[3] Warburton. III. pp 284—5. Hyde to Rupert, Feb. 28, 1649.

his commission as Lord High Admiral, which the new King had now power to grant, and he thereupon published a solemn declaration of his intention to fight the Parliament to the death.

"The bloody and inhumane murder of my late dread uncle of ever renowned memory hath administered to me fresh occasion to be assistant, both in Counsel and to the best of my personal power, to my dear cousin, now Charles II of England... I do protest and really speak it, it was ever my intention to do him service and employ my best endeavours for enthroning him, as bound by consanguinity, but more particularly engaged by reason of former favours received from his late royal father, my murdered uncle. Yet I do ingeniously confess it was never my desire to be employed in this great and weighty matter of His Majesty's Admiral. I should willingly have been satisfied with an inferior place, where I might have had the freedom, in part, to bring to condign punishment such great traitors and rebels who had a hand in the murder of my late uncle, and do still persist in their perverse way of rebellion and cruelty. And my reasons why I did not wish so great a command were these—namely, I know, and was ascertained, myself had been rendered odious to many English who did not rightly understand my real intentions, but only believed lies and forged reports of my enemies' framing. And I did likewise consider that my undertaking the admiralty might be a means to draw away the affections of His Majesty's subjects, by reason such rumours had been upon me. These, and many other reasons which now I will omit, did move me several times to refuse what, at length, His Majesty's Council of Lords, knights and gentlemen, who are now about him, did, in a manner, thrust upon me." [1] Rupert's greatness had been, in truth, thrust upon him, but having accepted it, he resolved to use it

---

[1] Prince Rupert: his Declaration. Pamphlet. British Museum. Mar. 9, 1649.

for avenging his uncle to the uttermost. "Prince Rupert," declared a sailor of the Parliament, who had been his prisoner, "is not ashamed openly to profess that, provided he may ruin and destroy the English interest, especially the estates of the merchants and mariners of London, he cares not whether he gets a farthing more while he lives than what will maintain himself, his confederates, and his fleet." [1]

Such being Rupert's attitude, it is worth while to note that of his brothers. Maurice was of course one with him. Edward also expressed himself as strongly as his two seniors could have wished. "I should die happy if I could steep my hands (quand j'aurai trempé mes mains) in the blood of those murderers." [2] That satisfaction was denied him, but he did his best by insulting the Ambassadors of the Parliament in the streets of the Hague. This affair produced great excitement in England, and the States of Holland were forced to request Edward to "keep a better tongue," or else to quit their territory. He had been just about to depart to Heidelberg, but, with true Palatine obstinacy, deferred his departure for another week, and went about boasting his status as a "freeborn Prince of the Empire." [3] The States, with their wonted prudence, let him alone until after he was safely departed, when they endeavoured to appease the English Parliament by a show of indignation. "The States here," wrote Nicholas, "have lately caused a summons publicly to be made, by ringing of a bell, requiring Prince Edward—who they know went hence to Germany three months since—to appear in the State House, by a day prefixed, to answer the affront he did to St. John and his colleagues; which is said to be only, as they passed him, to have called them a pack of rogues and rebels." [4]

[1] Dom. State Papers. Com. 24 fol. 60.
[2] Bromley Letters, p. 295. Edward to Elizabeth.
[3] Perfect Passages, April 11, 1651. Whitelocke, p. 49. Green, VI. 17—28. Mercurius Politicus, Apr. 3—10, 1651.
[4] Carte Letters, II. p. 2. 14 May 1661.

The conduct of Charles Louis contrasted strongly with that of the rest of his family. He, far more than Edward, had cause for gratitude to his Uncle, and yet he could write coldly of the King's trial:—"Others, (*i. e.* himself), who are but remotely concerned in the effects thereof, cannot be blamed if they do not intermeddle. Neither is it in their power to mend anything, for it hath been seen in all Governments that strength will still prevail, whether it be right or wrong."[1] Nevertheless he quitted England after the King's execution, chiefly, it is to be feared, because he had become convinced that he himself would not be elected to the vacant throne. Having renounced the cause of the Parliament, he was anxious to be reconciled to his brothers, and Sophie, evidently at his instigation, wrote to inform Rupert and Maurice of the Elector's changed views. Both her letters are dated April 13th, 1649, and that to Rupert is written in French.

"Dearest Brother,

"It is only through printed reports that we hear any news of Rupert le Diable, for no one has received any letters from you. My brother the Elector is now here, and cares no more for those cursed people in England, for he has paid his duty to the King, which he might easily have avoided, as business called him to Clèves. Here also are the Scottish Commissioners, who every day bring some new proposal to the King, full of impertinency. They would not that the King should keep any honest man about him, for which they are in great favour with the Princess of Orange, who declares herself much for the Presbyterians, and says that Percy is the honestest man the King has about him. But I believe you care not much to know of intrigues here, for which cause I shall not trouble you further; besides, you have other business to do

[1] Forster's Statesmen, VI. p. 82.

than read my letters.　Only I entreat you to take notice,
that I remain

　　　　　"Your most aff. sister and servant,

　　　　　　　　　　"Sophie." [1]

To Maurice, Sophie wrote in German, and in a more
familiar style.　Probably she was better acquainted with
him than with Rupert, for he had encouraged and laughed
at her childish tricks, during the years that he spent "in
idleness" at the Hague.

"Highborn Prince and Dear Brother,

　　　"I must write to you by all occasions, for I always
have something to tell you.　This time it shall be that
the Prince Elector is here, and that he is now altogether
against the Knaves, as we are.　The peace is made in
France.　My brother Edward says he has taken no employment yet.　Prince Ratzevil is deadly sick, they say that the
Marquis Gonzaga hath poisoned him; he is in Poland yet.
The States have forbidden all their Ministers to pray for
any Kings in the Church, but the French will not desist.
I am so vexed with you for not writing to me that I do
not know how to express it.　I hope you have not forgotten me, seeing that I am

　　　　　"Your faithful sister and humble servant,

　　　　　　　　　　"Sophie." [2]

To this letter the Elector added a short postscript.

"My service to you, brother Rupert and brother Maurice; more I cannot say, being newly arrived, and visitations
do hinder me.　Carl Ludwig."

What effect this judiciously-worded composition might have
had it is impossible to say.　Both letters fell into the hands
of the Parliament and never reached their proper destination.
It was many years before Rupert and the Elector met again.

---

[1] Domestic State Papers.　Commonwealth, I. fol. 53. Sophie to Rupert,
Apr. 13, 1649.

[2] Domestic State Papers.　Commonwealth, I. fol. 54, Sophie to Maurice.
Apr. 13, 1649.

CHAPTER XIV

THE FLEET IN THE TAGUS. AT TOULON. THE VOYAGE TO
THE AZORES. THE WRECK OF THE "CONSTANT REFORMA-
TION." ON THE AFRICAN COAST. LOSS OF MAURICE
IN THE "DEFIANCE." THE RETURN TO FRANCE

ON quitting Ireland in November 1649, the Royalist
fleet sailed straight for the Spanish coast. Hyde was then
at Madrid, as the Ambassador of Charles II, and he pressed
the Spaniards to grant the Prince free ports. This they
would not do, but they allowed him to clean and victual
his vessels upon their shores, until the arrival of the Parliament fleet changed their attitude. [1] The Parliament had
despatched their Admiral Blake in pursuit of the Royalists,
and Blake's ships were better manned, better fitted up,
and more numerous than those of Rupert. In fear of
Blake, the Spaniards ordered Rupert to leave their coasts,
and he took refuge in the Tagus. There he found a
generous reception. The King of Portugal, "a young man
of great hope and courage," sent an embassy to invite the
two Princes to Lisbon, and they were conducted, with
much state, to Court. Further, the King promised them
all the protection in his power, gave them supplies and
provisions, the free use of his ports, and purchased their
prizes. "The King of Portugal gives Rupert all kind of
assistance, and is extreme kind and civil to him and Maurice. I pray you tell your Lord this," wrote the Queen
of Bohemia to her "dear cousin," the Duchess of Richmond. [2]
For a brief period the adventurous Princes enjoyed a

[1] Clarendon State Papers. Hyde to Rupert, Oct. 19, 1650.
[2] Cary's Memorials, Vol. II. p. 164.

prosperous tranquillity, but it was not to last. Good though
were the intentions of the young King, his Ministers feared
the English Parliament as much as did the Spaniards.
Consequently, when Blake arrived at the mouth of the
Tagus and demanded the surrender of the Princes and
their fleet, dissension arose in the Court of Lisbon. The
young King was so indignant that he would fain have
gone on board Rupert's vessel to fight with Blake in person.
This rash design was prevented by the Queen Mother, and
the King, yielding to his Ministers, demanded three days'
start for the Princes if they should put to sea. This condition Blake would not grant, and the King therefore
refused to close his ports to the Royalists. The Count
de Miro, who headed the faction hostile to the Princes,
then tried to embarrass Rupert by all means in his power.
He ordered the Portuguese merchants to pay for the prizes
purchased in goods and not in money, he tried to prevent
Maurice from gaining an audience with the King, and he
actually succeeded in preventing him from making an attack
on Blake. "Hearing that Prince Maurice intends to sail
from our ports, with letters of marque against Parliament
ships, I beg it may not be done," was the concise and
explicit note received by Rupert. [1]

The Prince meanwhile gained allies against De Miro by
an appeal to the priests, who responded readily, preaching
everywhere "how shameful a thing it was for a Christian
King to treat with rebels." He also won the hearts of the
populace, by hunting daily amongst them with all confidence, and by his "liberality and complaisance to all
sorts of people." His exceeding popularity with priests and
people intimidated the hostile court faction, so that De
Miro dared no longer urge compliance with the demands
of Blake. [2]

For some time Rupert remained in the Tagus, with Blake

---

[1] Warburton, III. p. 306, *note*.
[2] Ibid. p. 303.

awaiting him outside. Occasionally, as in Holland. the sailors met on shore, and with more fatal results. An ambush laid by Blake for the capture of Rupert while hunting, resulted in the defeat of the Parliamentarians, with the loss of nine of their men. In revenge, Rupert attempted to blow up one of Blake's ships, sending one of his sailors, disguised as a Portuguese, with an infernal machine to the Vice-Admiral. But the man unwarily exclaimed in English, and so was discovered and his design prevented. These actions were very differently represented by Royalists and Parliamentarians, and both parties "complained to the King of Portugal." [1] Blake stigmatised Rupert as "that pyrate"; and Rupert declared the Parliamentarians to be only "tumultuous, factious, seditious soldiers and other disorderly and refractory persons," and Blake a "sea-robber." [2]

After this the King forbade any more Parliament ships to enter his harbour, and Blake in revenge attacked the Portuguese fleet returning from Madeira. The King, thus justly incensed, ordered his own fleet to sail with Rupert, against Blake. But the Portuguese Admiral was in the pay of De Miro, and "was so careful of his person" as to give Rupert no assistance. On Rupert's complaint he was deprived of his command, but his successor proved no more efficient. [3] The attack therefore failed, but Rupert was able to write cheerfully to Charles II that his "entertainment" was still "all civility," and that every facility had been afforded for the disposal of the goods taken in his prizes, which realised about £40,000. A part of this sum he sent to Charles, with the rest he fitted up his prizes as men of war, and victualled his ships for four months. [4]

He was now ready to force his passage through Blake's

---

[1] Warburton, III. pp. 304—305. Whitelocke, 458. Thurloe's State Papers, I. 145—146.
[2] Thurloe, I. 141. Dom. State Papers. Commonweath, IX. fol. 38.
[3] Warburton, III. pp. 306, 310.
[4] Ibid. pp. 310—312. Add. MSS. 18982. f. 210.

fleet, or "perish in the attempt."   But meanwhile Blake had
captured the Portuguese fleet coming from Brazil, and the
poor King, not knowing whom to trust, came in person to
Rupert to beg him to rescue it. The Prince willingly agreed,
but Blake was not anxious to fight just then, and the mists
and contrary winds prevented the Royalists from coming
up with him. The King thanked Rupert for his efforts,
but the continued misfortunes which the presence of the
Royalists was bringing on Portugal forced them to leave
Lisbon. From that time, September 1650, the Princes were,
in truth, little more than pirates. The small number of
their ships prevented them from ever engaging the fleet
of the Parliament, and they could only carry on a depreda-
tory warfare, injuring English trade, and at the same time
supporting the exiled court, by the constant capture of
merchantmen. Any English vessel that refused to own
Rupert as Lord High Admiral of England was a fair prize,
and from the time that Spain allied herself with the English
Commonwealth, Spanish vessels also were fair game in the
Princes' eyes. And thus, says one of the Royalist captains,
"our misfortunes being no novelty to us, we plough the sea
for a subsistence, and being destitute of a port, we take
the Mediterranean sea for our harbour; poverty and despair
being our companions, and revenge our guide." [1]

On leaving Lisbon, Rupert returned at first to the coast
of Spain. Off Estepona he crippled, but could not take,
an English vessel. At Malaga he found some more English
ships, but was peremptorily forbidden to attack them by
the Spanish Governor. To this order he only replied that
he would not shoot, but that, since one of the vessels in
question was commanded by a regicide, he could not
possibly forego this opportunity of revenge. In accordance
with this declaration, he sent a fire-ship by night, which
successfully burnt the ship of the regicide, Captain Morley.

[1] Warburton, III. p. 313.

The anger of the Spaniards forced him to put to sea at once, and he next came to Montril, where he attacked and destroyed three English ships, in spite of the efforts made from the Spanish forts to defend them. [1] Between Cape de Gatte and Cape Palos, he took several prizes, and from there he stood for Tunis. But most of his captains disobeyed orders, and entered Cartagena, where they hoped to find booty. There the Spaniards allowed Blake to attack them, and, to escape capture, they ran their ships ashore and burnt them. Rupert and Maurice, unaware of the disaster, left letters for their missing captains, under a stone, on the coast of Tunis, and sailed for Toulon. But a sudden storm separated the Princes, and Maurice arrived at Toulon alone with his prizes; not knowing what was become of his brother, and fearing the worst. [2]

The condition of Toulon was somewhat disturbed, for the wars of the Fronde were then raging in France, and the town, at that moment, was for the Prince of Condé against the court. Maurice was therefore warned by the French Admiral commanding in the port, to be very careful of himself and of his ships. But happily both the magistrates of the town and the officers of the forts showed themselves well-disposed to the Prince. They hastened to visit him, offered all the aid they could give him, and pressed him daily to come on shore. Maurice, "through grief for that sad separation from his brother," [3] declined their invitations, and refused, for several days, to leave his ship. At last the twofold necessity of disposing of his prize goods, and of purchasing a new mast, determined him to land; but before the appointed day arrived, he was relieved from anxiety by the appearance of Rupert himself in the port. The meeting was rapturous. "I need not express the joy of their embraces, after so long and tedious

<hr>

[1] Hist. MSS. Com. Rept 14. Portland MSS. Vol. I. p. 548. 26 Dec. 1650.
[2] Warburton, III. p. 318.
[3] Ibid. 320.

absence, with the uncertainty of either's safety," says a witness of it, "wanting expressions to decipher the affectionate passion of two such brothers, who, after so long time of hardship, now found themselves locked in each others arms, in a place of safety." [1]　The brothers, thus reunited, went on shore together, where they were received with great enthusiasm, and were "magnificently treated" [2] at the house of the French Admiral.

Soon after this the captains who had lost their ships at Cartagena arrived to explain themselves, and each by accusing the others endeavoured to excuse himself.　Being in a foreign port, Rupert would not hold a court-martial, but finally the flight of one captain seemed to declare his guilt, and clear the rest, though they did not escape without a severe reprimand for disobeying orders.

The delay at Toulon lasted for a considerable time, and in the interval Rupert received a summons to Paris from the Queen Regent and Queen Henrietta, who offered him important employment in France, if he would leave the command of his fleet to Maurice.　But Rupert did not believe his brother capable of managing the fleet alone, and he was resolved not to abandon the desperate undertaking to which he was pledged. [3]　The fleet was then reduced to three sail, the "Constant Reformation," (Admiral,) and the "Swallow," (Vice-Admiral,) and Maurice's prize; and Rupert strained his slender resources to the utmost in order to purchase a new ship, which he named the "Honest Seaman." About the same time he was joined by a Captain Craven with a vessel of his own, which made up the number to five sail.　At last, after much delay and trouble, the prize goods were advantageously disposed of, the ships were supplied from the Royal Stores of France, and the Princes were ready to seek new adventures.　The Channel and the

---

[1] Warburton, III. 320.
[2] Ibid. p. 321.
[3] Carte Letters, II. p. 3. 14 May, 1651.

coast of Spain were now so well guarded by the Parliament ships as to be unsafe for the Princes' little fleet. Rupert saw that he must now seek distant seas, and after putting his enemies off his track by inquiring of suspected spies the best advice for sailing to the Archipelago, he slipped quietly away to the coast of Barbary. "I infinitely pity the poor Prince, who wanted all manner of counsel and a confident friend to reveal his mind unto," [1] wrote Hatton to Nicholas.

The first prize taken in the Straits was a Genoese vessel, bound for a Spanish port, which was taken, partly in reprisal for the stealing of one of Rupert's caravels by the Genoese, and partly because the sailors clamoured for her capture. A Spanish galleon was next taken, and her crew put on shore, after which Rupert made for Madeira. This island was possessed by the Portuguese, and the Princes were received with all kindness. The Governor, with all his officers, came on board the Admiral, and the Princes afterwards paid a return visit to the fort, when they were courteously received, and "accompanied to the sight of all that was worthy seeing on the island." [2]

Rupert's secret intention was to make for the West Indies, but no sooner did his mind become known, than the plan was vehemently opposed by most of his officers. The true cause of their opposition was the belief that the idea had originated with Fearnes, the captain of the Admiral, who seems to have been very unpopular with the rest of the fleet. So high did the dissension run that Rupert felt himself compelled to call a council, the members of which, with two exceptions, voted to make for the Azores, alleging that the Admiral, which had lately sprung a leak, was unfit for the long voyage to the West Indies. Moved by his new-born anxiety to avoid the charges of "self-will and rashness," Rupert yielded to the voices of the majority,

[1] Nicholas Papers, I. 249. May 1651.
[2] Warburton, III. p. 325.

against his better judgment. To the Azores they went, and, as the Prince expected, disaster followed.[1] No prizes were taken, there was found no convenient harbour where the Admiral's leak might be stopped, and so bad was the weather that, for long, the ships could not approach the shores to get provisions. When, at last, they made the island of St. Michael—also a Portuguese possession—they were as well received as they had been at Madeira, and here also the Governor conducted the Princes "to all the monasteries and place of note."[2] Next Rupert stood for Terceira, but the Governor of that island belonged to the faction which had opposed the Royalists at Lisbon, and showed himself unfriendly. Still, he permitted Rupert to purchase wine and meat, and, the bargain arranged, the fleet returned to St. Michael. On the way the Admiral sprang a new leak, which could not be found, nor was there any harbour where she could be safely unloaded that it might be discovered. Rupert again proposed the voyage to the West Indies, but the suggestion nearly produced a mutiny, which the Prince only quashed by promptly breaking up the meetings of the disaffected.

While affairs were in this state, and the supply of provisions yet uncompleted, stormy weather drove the ships out to sea. The leak in the Admiral increased rapidly, and her boat, which was too large to be hoisted in, was washed away from her. On the same day, the Vice-Admiral, attempting to hoist in her own boat, sunk it at her side. The storm raged without abatement for three days, at the end of which the Admiral's condition was hopeless. By continually firing her guns she had contrived to keep the other ships near her, and by constant pumping the disaster had been deferred. But on the third morning, September 30th, 1651, at 3 a.m., the ship sprang a plank, and though a hundred and twenty pieces of raw beef were trodden down

[1] Warburton, III. p. 327.
[2] Ibid. p. 329.

between the timbers, and planks nailed over them, it was without avail. The sails were blown away, and by ten o'clock of the same morning, the water was rushing in so fast that the men could not stand in the hold to bale. In this desperate condition, the whole crew behaved with real heroism. Having thrown the guns overboard, in the vain endeavour to lighten the ship, they resigned all hope, and resolved to die together. The storm was so violent that none of the other ships dared to approach the Admiral, lest they should perish with her. Once the "Honest Seaman" ran across her bowsprit, in the hope that some of the crew might save themselves on her, but none made the attempt. Rupert then signalled Maurice to come under his stern, that he might speak his last words to him. Approaching as near as possible, the two Princes tried to shout to one another, "but the hideous noise of the seas and winds over-noised their voices." [1] Maurice, frantic with distress, declared that he would save his brother or perish; but his captain and officers, less ready to sacrifice their lives, "in mutinous words" refused to lay their ship alongside the Admiral. Seeing his orders given in vain, Maurice next tried to send out a little boat which he had on board, but, though his men feigned to obey him, they delayed, as long as possible, getting the boat ready. "The Captain of the Vice-Admiral cannot be excused," says an indignant letter, "for when he saw the ship perishing he made no action at all for their boat to help to save the men, but walked upon the deck, saying: 'Gentlemen, it is a great mischance, but who can help it?' And the master never brought the ship near the perishing ship, notwithstanding Prince Maurice's commands, and his earnestness to have it done." [2]

At last it occurred to the crew of the Admiral that their Prince, at least, might be saved in their one small boat, and they "beseeched His Highness" to make use of it.

---

[1] Warburton, III. p. 334.
[2] Ibid. pp. 533—535. Pitts to —. No date.

But of this Rupert would not hear. He thanked the men for their affection to him, and declined to leave them, saying that they had long shared his fortunes, and he would now share theirs. Then they represented to him that, supposing he could get on board another ship,—a very remote chance in such a sea,—he might, by his authority, cause something to be done to save the rest of them. Seeing that he still hesitated, they wasted no more time in parley, but promptly overpowered him, and placed him forcibly in the boat, "desiring him, at parting, to remember they died his true servants." [1] By a miraculous chance, as it seemed then, the little boat reached the "Honest Seaman" in safety, and, having put the Prince on board her, returned at once to rescue some others. Only Captain Fearnes accepted the offered rescue. M. Mortaigne, whom Rupert especially entreated to come to him, preferred to die with the rest, and after this second journey, the little skiff sank. Rupert, now as frantic as Maurice had been before, ordered the "Honest Seaman" to run towards the Admiral, and enter the men on her bowsprit. The Captain obeyed to his best ability, but could not accomplish his aim, be-cause the Admiral, having lost her last sail, and being heavy with water, could not stir. The gallant crew signalled their farewells to their Prince, and were then invited by their Chaplain, who had remained with them, to receive the Holy Communion. For some hours longer the ship remained above water, but at nine o'clock at night she sank with all on board, the crew burning two fire-pikes as a last farewell to their Admiral.

Rupert, for once in his life, was utterly crushed by the weight of misfortune. He was taken next day into his brother's ship, and there he remained for some time, "over-laden with the grief of so inestimable a loss", and leaving everything to the care and management of Maurice. The

---

[1] Warburton, III. p. 335.

loss of the treasure on board the Admiral had been enormous, amounting to almost the whole of the year's gains; but, wrote Rupert to Herbert, "it was not the greatest loss to me!"[1] Of the Prince's own enforced rescue we have three separate accounts. "The Prince was unwilling to leave us, and resolved to die with us," reported the Captain.[2] And says another writer: "His Highness would certainly have perished with them, if some of his officers, more careful of his preservation than himself, had not forced him into a small boat and carried him on board the 'Honest Seaman.'"[3] It is also noted in the common-place book of one Symonds, a manuscript now preserved in the British Museum: "It is very remarkable of Prince Rupert that, his ship having sprung a plank in the midst of the sea.... he seemed not ready to enter the boat for safety, nor did intend it. They all, about sixty, besought him to save himself, and to take some of them with him in the boat to row him; telling him that he was destined and appointed for greater matters."[4]

Misfortunes, as usual, did not come singly. Making for Fayal, with Maurice still in command, the "Swallow" and the "Honest Seaman" fell in with the other three ships, from which they had been separated, but only in time to witness the wreck of the "Loyal Subject." This time the Portuguese were far less friendly than before. Apparently they feared lest the English should appropriate a Spanish vessel which had just surrendered at Pico, and when Maurice sent to offer his assistance, they fired upon his envoys. Maurice's officer insisted upon landing and was promptly arrested, without a hearing. The "Honest Seaman" and the "Revenge" thereupon fired on the Portuguese, but without effect, and the whole fleet stood away to Fayal, where they found

---

[1] Warburton, III. p. 349.
[2] Rupert Transcripts. Captain Fearnes' Relation.
[3] Warburton, III. p. 540.
[4] Harleian MSS. 991.

that the officers whom they had left on shore to secure supplies, had also been arrested. The necessity for action roused Rupert from his melancholy. He guessed that the changed attitude of the Governors must be due to a peace made between Portugal and the English Commonwealth, and saw that he must act with decision. He therefore sent to the Governor of Fayal, saying that Prince Rupert was in his harbour, on board the " Swallow," and that unless his men were at once released, and things placed on the former friendly footing, he would free his men by force, and would also write to the King of Portugal "a particular of the affronts he had received." Evidently Rupert was a much more awe-inspiring person than Maurice, for the Governor, terrified by the unexpected discovery of his presence, at once released his prisoners, and permitted the Princes to take in their stores unmolested. [1]

Rupert was determined now to go to the West Indies, and, in order to prevent factious opposition, he sent his secretary on board each ship in turn to require the opinion of each officer, in writing, as to what it would be best to do. By this device all collusion was prevented, and consequently the majority decided with the Prince, for the West Indies. The only two dissentients were the Captain and Master of the Vice-Admiral, who had behaved so badly at the wreck of the Admiral. These two were for going to the mouth of the Channel to take prizes. But their advice was generally scouted, as it was evident to all that the ships could not live in the northern seas. The dissentient Captain thereupon quitted the fleet, "pretending a quarrel he had with Captain Fearnes," [2] and Rupert willingly let him go.

Distrusting the Portuguese in the Azores, the Princes sailed towards the Canary Islands, hoping to meet with prizes from which they might obtain new rigging and other

[1] Warburton, III. p. 340.
[2] Ibid. p. 537, Pitts to —. No date.

necessities, for all the ships were in a terribly damaged condition. Stress of weather forced them to put in at Cape Blanco, in Arguin, on the coast of Africa, where, finding a good harbour, they resolved to refit. A Dutch vessel, which had also taken refuge there, supplied them with pilots, and with planks and other necessaries for the repair of their ships. Having obtained these things, they set up tents on land, in which they stored their cargoes, while they brought the ships aground.

The repairs involved a considerable delay, and Rupert wished to employ the time in procuring new provisions. Fish was to be found in great abundance, but no cattle could be purchased on account of the timidity of the natives, who fled at the approach of Europeans. This timidity was exceedingly annoying to Rupert, and on January 1st, 1651, he marched inland with a hundred men, being resolved to get speech with the natives. A fog favoured him, so that he came upon an encampment before the people were aware of his neighbourhood. Nevertheless no sooner did they see him than they took to flight, leaving behind them their tents, and their flocks of sheep and goats. In a final attempt to detain them Rupert shot a camel, but the act naturally did not reassure them, and the rider mounted another and fled, "but for haste left a man-child behind, which by fortune was guided to His Highness, as a New Year's gift. The poor infant, embracing his legs very fast, took him for his own parent." [1] Child and flocks being carefully secured, Rupert marched on after the natives, dividing his men into small companies, that they might appear the less alarming. This plan succeeded so far that at length two natives came back with a flag of truce, desiring to treat for the recovery of the child and the sheep. To this the Prince readily consented; whereupon the men promised to come to him in two days' time, and he returned to his fleet.

[1] Warburton, III. p. 345.

According to promise, the African envoys appeared on the shore, Jan. 3rd, and desired a hostage. Rupert, doubtful of their good faith, refused to order any man to risk his life; but one volunteered, and was allowed to go. Then the Africans, making no offers of trading with the Prince, demanded the child's surrender, "expressing great sorrow for the loss thereof." This increased Rupert's suspicions, and he ordered his men to keep well within their own lines. One sailor, disobeying, went out upon the cliff, and was immediately killed by the natives, who, having thus broken truce, killed their hostage also, and fled. Rupert pursued in great fury, but without being able to overtake them. A second expedition, led by Robert Holmes, had no better result, and the child remained in Rupert's possession.[1] In 1653, "an African lad of five" is mentioned by one of Cromwell's spies, as "part of the prey the Prince brought over seas;"[2] and reference is made to "the little nigger"[3] in several of Robert Holmes's letters to Rupert.

The Dutch vessel from which the Prince had obtained his planks, now sent him supplies of water from the Island of Arguin, and seeing her thus well-disposed, he chartered her to carry his prize cargo of ginger and sugar to France. He also took the opportunity of sending a brief account of his adventures and misfortunes to the King, and to Sir Edward Herbert. The copy of his letter to Charles II is headed: "What our ship's company desired me to say to the King," and is as follows.

"Sire,—By several ways I have given your Majesty a general account of our good and bad fortunes, since we left Toulon, but fearing some, if not all, may have had worse fortune than I am confident this will, I have made a more particular relation to Sir Edward Herbert of both, to which I could

[1] Warburton, III. pp. 346—7.
[2] Thurloe State Papers, II. 405.
[3] Rupert Transcripts. Holmes to Rupert, May 3 and 19, 1653.

add more particulars to shew your Majesty how I have been hindered in a design to do your Majesty eminent service, but, Sire, I shall leave this until I have the happiness to be nearer your Majesty. In the meantime I have sent an order on Mr. Carteret, with some goods, to pay the debts of your Majesty I made at Toulon, and some others, which belong to me, my brother, and the seamen, the proceed of which I have ordered to be put into Sir Edward Herbert's hands for yourself, or your brother's necessities; be pleased to command what you will of it. In such a case, I dare say, there will be none among us will grumble at it. All I humbly beg is that Sir Edward Herbert may receive your Majesty's commands by word of mouth, or under your own hand, and that your Majesty be pleased to look upon us, as having undergone some hazards equal with others. Had it pleased God to preserve the 'Constant Reformation' (the Admiral), I had loaded this vessel with better goods." [1]

To Herbert the Prince wrote at greater length, giving an account of the wreck of the Admiral, and of the factious opposition he had encountered among his officers. He explained also that the shares of each man in the prizes taken had been adjudged by the chaplain, Dr. Hart, and he concluded: "If His Majesty or the Duke of York be in necessity themselves, pray dispose of all to what they have need of, for their own use; I mean *after the debts I made at Toulon for the fleet are satisfied*. I wrote word so to His Majesty." [2] Some eight years later, at the Restoration, those debts which weighed so heavily on Rupert's conscience were still unpaid, and the fact is worth remembering in connection with the quarrel that the Prince had with the King on his return to France.

<hr>

[1] Warburton, III. p. 348.

[2] Ibid. p. 349. This letter is supposed by Warburton to be written to Hyde, but it is without address; and the three references of Rupert to Herbert in the letter to the King seem to imply that the accompanying letter was intended for Herbert, and not Hyde.

The cargo being despatched and the ships repaired, the Princes made for the Cape Verd Islands, where they took in water and "one thousand dried goats."[1] From there they went to Santiago, which they found inhabited chiefly by negroes. There was, however, a Portuguese Governor, Don Jorge de Mesquita de Castello Baranquo, who overwhelmed them with attentions, and presents of fruit. Rupert returned his civilities with such presents as his cargo afforded, and wrote to the King of Portugal gratefully acknowledging the kindness of Don Jorge. The letter bears date March 2nd, 1652.[2] When the Princes had been some days in the harbour, Don Jorge informed them that certain English vessels, bound for Guinea, were at anchor in the River Gambia, and offered pilots to take the Royalists up the river. This offer Rupert eagerly accepted, but the pilots proved inefficient, and mistook the channel, forcing the "Swallow," now the Admiral, to anchor in very shallow water. Rupert went out in his boat to sound for the channel, and while thus occupied, came upon a ship belonging to the Duke of Courland, on the Baltic. The Courlanders at once told the Prince the whereabouts of the English vessels, and offered to pilot him up to them. With their help, the Admiral weighed anchor, found the channel, and captured an English ship, the "John." On board this ship was a negro interpreter, known as Captain Jacus, and the son of the Governor of Portodale. To these two Rupert showed much kindness, freely giving them their liberty, an action for which he soon reaped an ample reward. That night Rupert's fleet anchored by the Courlander, which continued professions of friendship and offers of aid, for which the Prince returned grateful thanks.

On the following morning, Rupert took a Spaniard, but failed to get into the tributary of the Gambia, where lay an English ship. With the next tide Maurice succeeded in

[1] Warburton, III. p. 541, Feb. 1st 1652.
[2] Ibid. p. 366.

getting in, and as soon as it was light, began the attack. The Englishman quickly surrendered, on a promise of quarter, and freedom for the Captain. Then, too late, the crew remembered that no terms had been made for the merchant whom they had on board. A dispute arose as to the fairness of the agreement already made, and Maurice, in true sporting spirit, offered to free the captured ship, and fight it out over again;[1] but the English crew, declining the quixotic offer, accepted his former terms, and Maurice boarded them, still in exuberant spirits. "See what friends you have of these Portugals!" he cried in youthful triumph. "But for them we should never have come hither and taken you."[2] Altogether three English ships, the "Friendship," the "John," and the "Marmaduke," had been captured in the river, besides the Spaniard. Rupert distributed the crews of the prizes among his own ships, and Maurice, re-naming the largest of the prizes, the "Defiance," made her the Vice-Admiral.

The natives of the country, thinking to please Rupert, and anxious, possibly, to gratify old grudges, murdered several sailors of the Parliament who had landed. But Rupert, "abhorring to countenance infidels in the shedding of Christian blood," took care to intimate his deep displeasure.[3] Thereupon the brother and son of the native King came to visit him. He received them with all due courtesy, offering them chairs to sit upon, which, however, they gravely declined, saying that only their King was worthy of such an honour.

But notwithstanding the friendly disposition of the natives Rupert could not prolong his stay in the river. The time of the tornadoes—May to July— was drawing near, and preparation was necessary. The Princes therefore broke up

---

[1] Warburton, III. p. 359.

[2] Domestic State Papers. Commonwealth, 41. fol. 34. 8 Oct. 1653. Report of Walker.

[3] Warburton, III. p. 360.

their Spanish prize, as unfit for service, bequeathed her guns to the Courlanders, and sailed for the Cape de Verd Islands. By the way some of their ships were missed, and they anchored on the coast to await them. During the delay, the natives stole away one of Maurice's sailors, and Maurice, finding fair words unavailing, sent a force, under Holmes, to recover him. The two boats, in which Holmes and his men were embarked, were overturned in the surf, and lost at their landing, but happily, the liberated negro, Jacus, came to their help with a party of his friends. Then Maurice sent a third boat to bring his men back, but with orders not to land unless Jacus advised it. Holmes and his force were safely re-embarked, when the captain of the boat, mistaking Maurice's orders, declared that they were to take Jacus back with them. On hearing this, Holmes went once more on shore, to speak to Jacus, and, during the delay involved, the hostile negroes began to attack the crew. The sailors shot a negro, and captured one of their canoes, which so incensed the rest that they seized upon Holmes and another man who had accompanied him. The men in Maurice's boat saw themselves outnumbered, and returned in all haste to their ship, with the bad news. Both Princes were "extremely moved," and, swearing that they would rescue their comrades or perish in the attempt, they went ashore to treat with the natives. The negroes declared, through Jacus, that they would release Holmes if their canoe were returned, and the men in her set at liberty. Rupert at once signalled to the Vice-Admiral to free the canoe, but no sooner was it done than Jacus came running down to the shore, with the news that his countrymen intended treachery, and would not release their prisoners. It proved too late to re-take the canoe, but the Prince fired on the natives, who were gathering round him, and signalled all his ships to send men to his aid. The natives fought with much courage; and Rupert himself was wounded by a poisoned arrow, which he instantly cut out with his knife.

While he engaged the attention of the hostile negroes, Jacus and his friends contrived to free Holmes and his comrade, and to embark them safely in Maurice's pinnace. This done, the Princes retreated to their fleet; but they did not show themselves ungrateful to Jacus, "whose fidelity," says one of the crew, "may teach us that heathens are not void of moral honesty." On the day following, Rupert sent his thanks, and an offer to take Jacus with him and "to reward him for his faith and pains." But Jacus, wishing the Princes all good luck, declined their offer; he was, he said, not in the least afraid to remain with his own tribe. [1]

The missing ships being come up, the Princes continued their voyage towards the Cape Verd Islands, taking a large English prize on the way. Two smaller English vessels were captured by the "Revenge" at Mayo, and Maurice took a Dane, but was promptly ordered to release her, by his brother. Then most of the ships went with Maurice to St. Iago, taking a present of 900 hides out of the spoil, to the Governor; the Admiral and the "Revenge" went on to Sal. The "Revenge," as it happened, was largely manned by the sailors taken in the prizes. These men, being naturally disaffected to the Princes, overpowered their officers in the night, and stole away to England. They reached home in safety, and were able to give a very edifying account of Rupert and his crews to the Parliament: "For their delight is in cursing and swearing, and plundering and sinking, and despoiling all English ships they can lay their talons on." Still the report of the Royalists' condition must have been very encouraging to their enemies. "The 'Swallow' and the 'Honest Seaman' were so leaky that they had to pump day and night, and consequently cannot keep long at sea. They had not above three weeks' bread, and nothing but water, at the time when they took the three ships in the River

---

[1] Warburton, III. pp. 363—367.

Gambia," said the escaped prisoners. [1] Rupert, on missing the "Revenge," guessed what had happened, but he touched at Mayo to ask if she had been sighted. His presence there so terrified a Spanish crew that they landed all their cargo, which was at once seized by the Portuguese. Rupert then returned to Santiago, where he took in water and provisions, bestowed the hulk of a prize on "the Religious people of the Charity," made "a handsome present to the Governor, in acknowledgment of his civilities," and took a final leave of the Island. [2]

The Princes were now fairly on their way to the West Indies; but, near Barbadoes, the Admiral sprang a leak, and had to put into Santa Lucia, in the Caribbees, the men "being almost spent with extreme labour." [3] Four days later, the leak being stopped, they proceeded towards St. Martinique, meeting on the way some Dutch men-of-war, with the officers of which they exchanged visits and civilities. The French Governor of St. Martinique proved very hospitable, and, moreover, sent the Princes a timely warning that all the English possessions in the West Indies had surrendered to the Parliament. Having returned grateful thanks for this information, the Royalists proceeded to San Dominique, where the natives brought them fruit, in exchange for glass beads. On the day before Whit Sunday they reached Montserrat, where they seized two small ships, but one, proving to be the property of Royalists, was released. At Nevis they found a large number of English vessels, which, like a flock of frightened animals, "began to shift for themselves," some endeavouring to escape, and others running ashore. [4] A brief engagement took place, in which Rupert's secretary was shot down at his side,

---

[1] Domestic State Papers. Commonwealth. Vol. XXIV. f. 60. June (?), 1652. Coxon's Report.

[2] Warburton, III. p. 370.

[3] Ibid. p. 371.

[4] Ibid. p. 376.

but no prizes could be taken, because the enemy's vessels were so fast aground that they could not be brought off.

After a brief visit to La Bastare, the Princes went to the Virgin Islands, intending to unload and careen the Admiral, and on the way thither, they added to their numbers by purchasing from a Dutch man-of-war a prize she had taken. They had hoped to find cassava roots in the islands, but these proved scarce, and consequently they suffered greatly from want of food. Rupert was even forced to reduce his men's rations, but, seeing that their Princes shared equally with them in all hardships, the sailors bore the privation with cheerful courage. The scarcity of food caused them to leave the Virgins as soon as the leaky ships were repatched, and, having burnt three small prizes as unseaworthy, they sailed southwards.

Now came the crowning misfortune of the unhappy Prince who had been so long "kept waking with new troubles."[1] Not far from Anguilla the fleet was caught in a most terrible hurricane. So strong was the wind that the men could not stand at their work; so thick the weather that no one could see more than a few yards before him. For two days the ships ran before the wind, the Admiral escaping wreckage on the rocks of Angadas by a miracle. On the third day the hurricane abated, and the Admiral found herself alone at the uninhabited island of St. Ann, in the Virgins; the "Honest Seaman" had been cast ashore at Porto Rico, and the Vice-Admiral had totally disappeared. "In this fatal wreck," says Pyne, "besides a great many brave gentlemen and others, the sea, to glut itself, swallowed Prince Maurice, whose fame the mouth of detraction cannot blast; his very enemies bewailing his loss. Many had more power, few more merit. He was snatched from us in obscurity, lest beholding his loss would have prevented others from endeavouring their own safety;

---

[1] Warburton, III. p. 337.

so much he lived beloved and died bewailed." [1]   Rupert's grief was beyond words.   He had lost the only member of his family to whom he was bound by close ties of affection, the most faithful and devoted of his followers, his favourite companion, his best-loved friend.   From the very first he accepted the situation as hopeless, and he bore his sorrow in grim silence, not suffering it to crush him as his grief for the loss of the "Constant Reformation" had done.   There was no Maurice now to fall back upon, and the needs of the ship could not be neglected.   Alas, one ship, the "Swallow," was all that remained of the gallant little fleet, and Rupert, finding himself thus alone, resolved to return to France.   First he paid a farewell visit to Guadeloupe, where he was kindly received, and supplied with wine.   There also he took an English prize, naively likened by the writer of his log to "Manna from Heaven." [2] But well might the crew rejoice at the capture, seeing that their rations were now reduced to three ounces per diem.   Touching at the Azores, they were surprised to be received with bullets, and not suffered to approach within speaking distance of the land.   Rupert therefore sailed straight for Brittany, stopping at Cape Finisterre for fresh provisions.   His health was completely broken down, and the food on board both scarce and nasty, and we read : "His Highness had not been very well since he came from the West Indies, and fresh provisions being a rarity, a present of two hens and a few eggs was very acceptable." [3]

But the Prince was nearing the end of his hardships, if not of his troubles.   Early one morning in the March of 1653, he came into the Loire and anchored at St. Lazar. The next day, in attempting to get higher up the river, he ran his ship aground.   The crew were anxious to leave her to her fate, but Rupert had not come through so many

[1] Warburton, III. p. 382.
[2] Ibid. p. 384.
[3] Ibid. p. 546.

difficulties only to succumb to the last, and by his "industry and care" he brought her safely off. Having secured his prizes, he sent the "Swallow" back to the mouth of the river to refit. "Here, however, like a grateful servant, having brought her princely master through so many dangers, she consumed herself, scorning, after being quitted by him, that any inferior person should command her." [1]

Thus closed the most singular episode in a much chequered career. The morality of Rupert's proceedings during his three years' wanderings on the high seas has been much debated. In theory he was a loyal Admiral holding his own against a rebel fleet, but in fact, it must be owned, he was little more than a pirate, or at best, a privateer. He was never able to meet the fleet of the Parliament in battle, and could only wage war by crippling the trade of the hostile party. Moreover, though his desire to injure the trade of the enemy was both earnest and sincere, he was still more anxious to gain merchandise, by the sale of which he could support his destitute sovereign and his fleet. Yet he kept within the limits he had set himself, and made prizes only of ships belonging to adherents of the Commonwealth or to its Spanish allies. The capture of a Genoese vessel has been admitted, but that was in the nature of a reprisal, and it has been seen how a Danish and a Royalist ship taken by mistake were set free. That the Prince endured hardship, difficulties and dangers out of a loyal devotion to his cousin, is shown by the readiness with which he renounced his private share of the spoil in Charles's favour, when he sent home the cargo of 1652. The devotion evidently felt for him by his crew speaks well for his character as a commander, and all his recorded dealings with the natives of Africa and the various islands, show a humane and enlightened spirit in which there is nothing of the buccanneer. Indeed the various logs which bear record of his voyages

[1] Warburton, III. p. 388.

are marked by a tone of great decorum. In them the chaplain figures frequently, and on one occasion it is noted, "The second day being Sunday, we rode still, and did the duties of the day in the best manner that we could; the same at evening." [1]   And even granting that the decorous tone of the logs is forced and exaggerated of set purpose, the fact remains that no specific charge of cruelty was ever brought against the Prince by his enemies or any one else. This, when it is remembered how lawless were the high seas in those days, is no slight praise. But, whatever may be thought of the ethics of the case, it will be universally acknowledged that to keep the seas as Rupert kept them for three years, with no previous experience in nautical affairs, with never more than seven, and usually only three ships at his command, with those ships hopelessly leaky and rotten, and continually beset by every possible form of danger and disaster, was a feat deserving of wonder and admiration.

[1] Rupert Transcripts. Journal, Feb. 26, 1651.

Photo E. Dosseter.

PRINCE RUPERT ABOUT 1654.
From the Engraving by Bernard in the British Museum.

Face page 265.

CHAPTER XV

RUPERT AT PARIS. ILLNESS. QUARREL WITH CHARLES II.
FACTIONS AT ST. GERMAINS. RUPERT GOES TO GERMANY.
RECONCILED WITH CHARLES

RUPERT'S return was eagerly hailed by all parties in the exiled Court of England. Wrote the King:

"My Dearest Cousin,

' "I am so surprised with joy in the assurance of your safe arrival in these parts that I cannot tell you how great it is; nor can I consider any misfortunes or accidents which have happened, now I know that your person is in safety. If I could receive the like comfort in a reasonable hope of your brother's, I need not tell you how important it would be to my affairs. While my affection makes me impatient to see you I know the same desire will incline you, (after you have done what can only be done by your presence there,) to make what haste to me your health can endure, of which I must conjure you to have such a care as it shall be in no danger."[1]

Hyde expressed himself with almost equal warmth. "For God's sake, Sir, in the first place look to your health, and then to the safety of what you have there, and lose no minute of coming away. I do not doubt you will find the welcome that will please you with the King, the Queen, and the Duke of York."[2]

And Jermyn added the assurance of his own "infinite joy," and the Queen's constant friendship, concluding with

---

[1] Warburton, III. p. 418. Charles II to Rupert, Mar. 22, 1653.
[2] Ibid. p. 419. Hyde to Rupert. No date.

the appropriate prayer: "God of Heaven keep you in all your dangers, and give you at length some quiet, and the fruits of them."[1]

The King gave proof of his affection by the zeal with which he prepared for his cousin's reception in Paris; an honour apparently disputed with him by Rupert's brother Edward. "The King is very active in preparing a lodging for you," writes one of the Prince's friends. "If I be not deceived he would have liked well to have it left to him, of which the Prince, your brother, as I understand, gives you some account. I will send you more by the next, knowing no more as yet, but that the King hath it in his love for you to have you near him, which certainly is fitter than to have thought of another lodging, without his knowledge."[2]

But, alas! the Rupert who returned was not the Rupert who had sailed away three years before! He had, as Hyde expressed it, "endured strange hardness,"[3] and the "hardness" had left its mark upon him. He came back from his long voyage a changed and broken-hearted man. "His Highness's fire was pretty much decayed, and his judgment ripened," says Campbell; but the change went deeper than that. The Prince had failed in his undertaking; he had lost the greater part of his hard-won treasure, his ships, his men, above all his best-loved brother—and these losses had carried with them a part of his old self. The high spirits and buoyant hopefulness of earlier days were gone for ever. Gone too was something of the youthful generosity; Rupert was embittered now, harder, colder, more sardonic; a man, said Colbert, "with a natural inclination to believe evil!"[4]

His health too, that best inheritance from his mother, had been ruined by bad climates and insufficient food. On

[1] Warburton, III. p. 390. Jermyn to R., Feb. 6, 1653.
[2] Rupert Transcripts. — to Rupert, 1653.
[3] Clar. State Papers, 1089. Hyde to Nicholas, Apr. 18, 1653.
[4] Cartwright. Madame: A Life of Henrietta of Orleans, p. 359.

his arrival at Nantes he fell dangerously ill, nor was he ever again wholly free from suffering. His illness created no small consternation among the Royalists, and much sympathy was poured out upon him. "Think of your health," urged one friend, "and if you dare venture on your old apothecary you may, from whom you will receive some drugs, well meant, if not well prepared." [1] This tempting offer was probably declined. The Palatines had ideas of their own upon the subject of medicine, a profound distrust of doctors, and a very reasonable aversion to the then universal practice of bleeding. "Pray God she fall not into the Frenchified physician's hands, and so let blood and die!" [2] Rupert wrote of a fair friend, at a later date, On the present occasion he recovered from his illness, with or without the aid of physicians, and in April hastened to join his cousin, King Charles.

At Paris he met with as warm a reception as he could have desired. Not only the English exiles, but the French Court also hastened to do him honour. The Queen Regent and Mazarin had always been his good friends, and now his strange adventures had fired the imagination of the young King Louis, who "complimented him in an extraordinary manner." [3] Indeed Rupert, with his romantic history, his striking personality, gigantic stature, and supposed magical powers, [4] not to mention his accredited wealth, his monkeys and "blackamours," made a considerable sensation in the excitable world of Paris. Many were the anonymous letters addressed to him by fair hands; but for some time his bad health and his sorrowful heart made him indifferent to the adulation bestowed on him. "Prince Rupert goes little abroad in France, and is very sad that

[1] Warburton, III. p. 420.
[2] Ibid. p. 454.
[3] Memoir of Prince Rupert, ed. 1683, p. 35.
[4] Evelyn, IV. 282. He was supposed to have cured Jermyn of a fever, with a charm. "His Highness, it seems, has learnt some magic in the remote islands."

he can hear nothing of his brother Maurice,"[1] was the report made by Cromwell's spies. And wrote Hyde, April 25, 1653: "Prince Rupert is not yet well enough to venture to go abroad, and therefore hath not visited the French Court, but I hope he will within a day or two. Of Prince Maurice we hear not one word."[2]

But as his health improved, Rupert relaxed his austerity and joined his Stuart cousins in their amusements. He was often to be seen in the hall of the Palais Royal, playing at billiards with the King and the Duke of York,[3] and sometimes he swam with them in the Seine. On one such occasion he was very nearly drowned; he was seized with cramp, and had already gone under water, when one of his train rescued him by the hair of his head. "The River Seine had like to have made an end of your black Prince Rupert," wrote one of the Puritan spies who watched all his actions, "for, some days since, he would needs cool himself in the river, where he was in danger of drowning, but, by the help of one of his blackmores, escaped."[1]

The same spy related another adventure which, if true, illustrates the singularly lawless state of Paris, and also suggests that Rupert was not quite indifferent to the overtures of the ladies who courted him. As he returned from hunting, one Sunday, accompanied only by Holmes, he was overtaken by two gentlemen, riding in great haste towards Paris. No sooner had they passed the Prince, than, wheeling suddenly round, they both fired at him. Both missed, and Rupert promptly returning the shots, wounded one and killed the other. A third gentleman then coming up, was about to fire on the Prince, but seeing him prepared, changed his mind and called out that he was the husband of the Maréchal de Plessy Praslin's daughter. Rupert retorted that he did

---

[1] Whitelocke, p. 556.
[2] Clar. State Papers. Hyde to Nicholas, 25 Apr. 1653. Printed Vol. II. p. 163.
[3] Cartwright. Madame: Duchess of Orleans, p. 50.
[4] Evelyn, IV. 282, *note.* Thurloe, I. 306.

not believe him, but, since he said so, would let him alone. So the matter passed," concludes the narrator of the story coolly, "and the gentleman killed, the worse for him!"[1]

In the midst of these adventures Rupert did not neglect business. He had to dispose of the guns and other fittings of his ship, which it was impossible to render sea-worthy again; and he also had a considerable quantity of goods to sell, the nature of which we learn from the letters of Holmes, who had gone back to Nantes in May 1653. From Nantes, Holmes sent samples of sugar, copper, tobacco, various kinds of woods, and elephants' teeth to the Prince at Paris. He also sent, at Rupert's express desire, "the little nigger," and promised to search among the ballast for two elephants' teeth which Rupert particularly required.[2] His search was very successful, and May 24 he reported, "I met, in tumbling over the ballast, 21 elephants' teeth, 36 sticks of wood, a chest of white sugar, and a small chest of copper bars."[3] It was time that some steps were taken for the disposing of these commodities. The officers of the ships were "much destitute of money." Fearnes refused to give Holmes any proper account of the stores, and the sailors were mutinying for pay. Holmes encountered them with drawn swords in their hands, but pacified them with "gentle mildness";[4] and Rupert came himself to Nantes to attend the sale of his treasures. In this matter, Mazarin lent all assistance in his power, and Cromwell who claimed the Prince's goods as stolen from English merchants remonstrated with the French court in vain.

"What should His Excellency the Lord General Cromwell expect from the Cardinal but a parcel of fair promises?" protested an agent of the Commonwealth. "I assure you the King and the Cardinal are resolved not to

---

[1] Thurloe State Papers, II. 186. 1 April, 1654.
[2] Rupert Transcripts. Holmes to Rupert, May 3, May 17, 1654.
[3] Ibid. May 24, 1654.
[4] Ibid. May 17, June 24, 1654.

deliver Prince Rupert's merchandizes. The merchants, having given a good deal of money to some ministers here, thinking to corrupt them,—a thing very easy to be done, in any other occasion but this,—find now that it is but so much money cast into the sea. Prince Rupert was somewhat affrighted, by reason of the bribes, but there is given him by the Queen, Cardinal, and Council such assurances as his mind is at rest. I protest they laugh at you, and think your demands so insolent as nothing more." [1]

In fact, while the English merchants lavished money, and Cromwell protests, Rupert was quietly selling the disputed goods at Nantes, and also the "Swallow" and her guns. He had no sooner accomplished this than he hastened back to Paris, in obedience to an urgent letter received from Charles.

"Dearest Cousin,

"According to your desire I sent the warrant to sell the 'Swallow' and her guns. I have little to say to you, only to put you in mind to make all the haste you can hither, when you can do it without harm to your business. For, besides the great desire I have of your company, I do believe there is something now to be done which I cannot do without your presence and assistance. I have no more to say until I see you, but to assure you that I am entirely, dearest Cousin,

"Your most affectionate Cousin,

"Charles R." [2]

After this very cordial letter it is rather surprising to find a violent quarrel between the two cousins immediately following Rupert's return to Paris. The truth was that Charles had expected to gain much wealth on the return of the fleet, which would, he hoped, enable him to leave

---

[1] Thurloe State Papers, I. p. 344. 19 July, 1653.
[2] Rupert Transcripts. Charles II to Rupert. Nov. 1654.

France, of which he was as weary as France was of him. But before Rupert's first coming to Paris he had sent such an account as ought to have convinced Charles that he had little to expect. That he had gained treasure of great value the Prince confessed, but most of it had been lost with Maurice, or in the wreck of the "Constant Reformation." What remained would scarcely suffice to pay off the sailors and discharge the old debt at Toulon. Moreover, the ships were so worm-eaten that there was no possibility of again sending them to sea.[1] Bitter as was this disappointment to the King, he still hoped to gain something by the sale of the guns, and when he found that Rupert laid claim to half the money thus obtained, it was more than he could endure. Hyde, who had never loved Rupert, easily persuaded the King that his cousin was dealing unfairly, and induced him to demand an exact account. The Prince, hotly resenting Hyde's insinuations, refused to offer any explanation more explicit than that already made.

When it is remembered how devotedly Rupert had exposed his person and all that he had in Charles's service, how his mother's jewels had helped to fit out the fleet, and how freely he had surrendered his private share in the prizes to the King, it is scarcely credible that he could have put forward an unjust, or even a selfish claim. Campbell corroborates the Prince's own statement that the sale of the goods did not realise enough to pay off all the sailors; and there still remained the debts at Toulon, which Charles had been begged to pay two years before. Nor were they paid now; in 1662, one Guibert Hessin petitioned Charles II for 29,480 livres tournois, being the debt for victualling the fleet at Toulon in 1650, of which Rupert had ordered payment in 1654.[2] It is therefore fairly evident that Rupert did not claim the money for

---

[1] Clarendon, Bk. XIV. p. 71. Campbell's British Admirals. 1785. Vol. II. p. 243.

[2] Domestic State Papers. March 1662. Petition of Guibert Hessin.

his own use, but in order to satisfy the just claims of others. The payment of his debts was a point on which he was particularly sensitive, but the practice may well have failed to commend itself to Charles. An important witness on Rupert's side is Hatton, who, a little before the quarrel, had written to Nicholas: "I am sure they now owe Prince Rupert £1,700, . . . and that will, at the day of reckoning, breed ill-blood." [1]

The day of reckoning came in February 1654, and all happened as Hatton had predicted.

"You talk of money the King should have upon the prizes at Nantes!" wrote Hyde indignantly. "Alas, he hath not only not had one penny from thence, but Prince Rupert pretends that the King owes him more money than ever I was worth." [2] The quarrel raged for a month before Rupert would give any explanation of his claims. At last, in March, he condescended to give the King "a little short paper, not containing twenty lines," which he charged his cousin not to show to Hyde. But Charles of course suffered Hyde to see it, charging him, in his turn, to conceal his knowledge of it from Rupert. [3] The result was a worse quarrel than ever. Seeing that the King was not going to acknowledge his claim, Rupert prompted his creditors to arrest the guns. Charles remonstrated,—"kindly expostulated," Hyde phrased it,—whereupon Rupert lost his temper, and declared passionately that "justice would have justice," speaking, said Hyde, "with insolence enough." [4] The affair was "exceedingly taken notice of," [5] and it was rumoured that Rupert would leave his cousin's service. Mazarin, who realised that the sooner Charles got some money, the sooner he would leave France, enabled him to

---

[1] Nicholas Papers. Camd. Soc. New Series. Vol. II. p. 33. 9/19 Dec. 1653.
[2] Clarendon State Papers, Hyde to Nicholas, Feb. 27, 1654.
[3] Ibid. March 13, 1654.
[4] Ibid. April 10, 1654.
[5] Ibid.

rescue the guns from the creditors' clutches; but Queen Henrietta gave all her support to her nephew. "It is not possible to believe how much, in so gross a thing, the Queen and Lord Jermyn side with Prince Rupert," complained Hyde.[1] Probably Henrietta and her favourite cared little whether the creditors were paid or not; but more than a mere question of debts was at stake, the exiled Court was as factious as ever. In the King's Council, Henrietta, the Duke of York, the Duke of Buckingham and Lord Jermyn opposed themselves violently to the policy of Ormonde, Rochester (Wilmot), Percy, Inchiquin, Taafe, and Hyde. Hyde's party was then in the ascendant, and the Queen was anxious to secure Rupert's adherence to her own party. He was not without a considerable following of his own, and there was a definite design to represent him "as head of the Swordsmen, making it good by little insignificant particulars."[2] The most influential of his friends was the Attorney-General, Herbert, recently made Lord Keeper, to whom Henrietta had hastened to pay court as soon as she heard of Rupert's arrival at Nantes. Herbert, though distinguished neither for tact nor for wisdom, possessed great influence with the Prince. "The Lord Keeper is so extreme vain and foolish in his government of Prince Rupert that he does more towards the ruin of that Prince than all his enemies could do,"[3] declared Hyde. And though Charles declared that he could cure his cousin of his infatuation, he failed to do so. Lord Gerard, a man of fertile brain, who "could never lack projects,"[4] was not much wiser than Herbert. Between them, they concocted a thousand schemes "to make Prince Rupert General in England, Scotland, and Ireland, and Admiral of two or

---

[1] Clarendon State Papers, Hyde to Nicholas, April 10, 1654.
[2] Nicholas Papers. Camden Society. Vol. II. p. 91, 25 Sept. 1654.
[3] Clarendon State Papers, Hyde to Nicholas, June 13, 1653.
[4] Ibid. Apr. 24, 1654.

three fleets together," not to mention other projects, all contrived for the benefit of the unlucky Prince, who, Hyde might justly say, would "have cause to curse the day he ever knew either of them." [1]

The Queen, on her part, was doing her best to destroy Hyde's power with the King, that being the chief obstacle to the exercise of her own influence. The Chancellor had no lack of enemies, but the charges brought against him were so absurd that he could afford to laugh at them. "I hope you think it strange to hear that I have been in England, and have had private conference with Cromwell; and that you are not sorry that my enemies can frame no wiser calumny against me," [2] he wrote to a friend. The inventor of this extraordinary story was the King's secretary, Long, who was backed up by the Queen and her partisans. They expected the support of Rupert, but he, much as he detested the Chancellor, was too honest to lend himself to any such plot. "They are much disappointed to find Prince Rupert not of their party," declared Hyde triumphantly. "He indeed carries himself with great discretion." [3] Nor did the Prince content himself with discretion, he even actively defended Hyde's character. A dispute on the subject had arisen between Ormonde and Herbert, the latter having remarked that "it was strange the King should make such a difference between Mr. Chancellor and Mr. Long, whereas he held Mr. Long as good a gentleman as Mr. Chancellor." Rupert, who was standing by, retorted sharply that the King "made not the difference from their blood, but from the honesty of the Chancellor and the dishonesty of Long." Herbert vehemently protested that he believed Long as honest as Hyde; to which replied Ormonde, "Ay, but the King thought not so, and perhaps

---

[1] Clarendon State Papers, Hyde to Nicholas, Jan. 2, 1654.
[2] Evelyn, IV. 298, 27 Dec. 1653.
[3] Clarendon State Papers, Hyde to Nicholas, 16 Jan. 1654.

there were times when his Lordship thought not so." And
a very pretty quarrel ensued. [1]

In the meantime Sir Marmaduke Langdale, a man of
more sense than Gerard or Herbert, seriously proposed that
Rupert should take a new expedition to Scotland. To this
plan the Queen lent a willing ear. The Scots, though still
resolved that only those "eminent for righteousness" should
enter Scotland with the King, were willing to include Rupert,
Ormonde, Nicholas, Gerard and Craven under that head. [2]
The scheme therefore seemed feasible, but Rupert and
Henrietta were of one mind in wishing that James of York,
rather than the King, might be the nominal leader of the
enterprise. The wish was natural enough, for the life led by
Charles in Paris was not calculated to commend him to his
serious-minded cousin. James, on the contrary, seemed full
of promise, practical, conscientious, and energetic. [3] Negotiations with the Scots were seriously opened, but they
were not all agreed concerning Rupert; and a letter shown
to James by his secretary, Bennet, created considerable stir
in the Palais Royal. This letter stated that the Scots still
cherished a strong aversion to Rupert, and earnestly hoped
that he would not appear in their country. James hastened
with the letter to his cousin, who "would needs know"
the name of the writer. This, Bennet refused to divulge,
until the writer himself arrived on the scene, in the person
of Daniel O'Neil, who, seeing the excitement he had caused,
"told plainly he wrote it, and said further that most of the
friends of the English and Scots were of that opinion." [4]

Eventually the whole scheme fell through, as a hundred
others had done, but not before Charles's anger and jealousy
had been excited against James. The result of the negotiations was therefore to produce a coldness between the

---

[1] Nicholas Papers, Vol. II. p. 50, 16 Jan. 1654.
[2] Clarendon State Papers. News from London, May 27, 1653.
[3] Thurloe State Papers, Vol. II. p. 179.
[4] Thurloe, II. 140—141, 14 May, 1654.

Stuart brothers, a further breach between Charles and Rupert, and a definite quarrel between the King and the Queen mother. Henrietta reproached her son violently with his conduct towards Rupert, Herbert and Berkeley; and Charles retorted angrily, that, after their behaviour to him, they should "never more have his trust nor his company."[1]

Upon this, Rupert resigned his office of Master of the Horse—a mere empty title—and departed for Germany, notwithstanding Henrietta's entreaties that he would remain.[2] He had hardly declared his intention of going, when the good-natured Charles half-repented of his share in the quarrel; and a reconciliation was accomplished, so far as the debt was concerned.[3] But Rupert adhered to his resolution of visiting Germany, saying that he had affairs of his own to look after, to obtain some appanage from his brother, and to demand the money due to him from the Emperor, under the treaty of Munster. Charles therefore wrote an apologetic letter to his aunt, the Queen of Bohemia, explaining that his cousin had not quitted his service, and that, though he did not deny having "taken some things unkindly" from Rupert, he trusted that they might soon meet again, "with more kindness and a better understanding," for, in spite of all that had passed, he continued to "love him very much, and always be confident of his friendship."[4]

Rupert went first to his brother at Heidelberg, with "a great train and brave," consisting of twenty-six persons,—three negroes and "the little nigger" included.[5] At Heidelberg he remained for about a month, but his real destination was Vienna, whither he went to demand the money

---

[1] Thurloe, II. 312.
[2] Clar. State Papers, 1 May, 1654. Printed, III. p. 236.
[3] Thurloe, II. p. 327.
[4] Clarendon State Papers. Charles II to Elizabeth of Bohemia, May 29, 1654.
[5] Thurloe, II. 327, 9 June, 1654.

owed him by the Emperor. He arrived there in September, and was received with great cordiality. He had been a *persona grata* to the Austrians ever since he had won their hearts as their prisoner; and Cromwell's spies commented, in great disgust, on the honour shown him, and the alacrity with which dues were promised to him. "His Imperial Majesty hath commanded an assignation to Prince Rupert Palatine of 30,000 rix dollars, of a certain sum due since the Treaty of Munster. Prince Rupert has also obtained money for Charles Stuart, and more is promised," they reported. [1]

It is here seen that not Rupert's private affairs alone had taken him to Vienna, nor was his separation from Charles of long duration. France had now concluded a treaty with Cromwell, so that the exiled King was forced to quit that country. The money obtained through Rupert enabled him to leave France with ease, and he proceeded to Cologne. A rumour arose that he intended to throw himself upon the hospitality of the Emperor, and perhaps Rupert's visit to Vienna had been partly designed to ascertain the possibility of this move. But the idea did not commend itself to the Austrian Court, and the Elector Charles Louis wrote hastily to Rupert, October 1654: "I have ventured to send M. Bunckley to the King of Great Britain, to warn him that he would be unwelcome at Vienna. Doubtless you will be able to confirm this, concerning which I have received an express messenger from his Imperial Majesty." [2] Probably Rupert did confirm his brother's message, for Charles stayed at Cologne, awaiting his cousin's "much longed for" return. Rupert rejoined him there in January 1655, but did not stay long. Hyde was still all powerful, and Rupert was never a man who cared to take the second place. "I need not tell you," wrote one of the ubiquitous spies, "by whom Prince Rupert was turned from Court; yet perhaps you

---

[1] Thurloe, II. 580, 567, 644, 1 Sept., 8 Sept., 13 Oct. 1654.
[2] Bromley Letters, p. 315, Elector to Rupert; also Thurloe, II. p. 644.

have not known that Hyde offered Charles Stuart that 50,000 men should be in arms in England, before a year went about, if he would quit the Queen's Court, and the Prince's party. By the last letters it doth seem as if Prince Rupert had an intention to see Cologne before Modena, and, if he can break Hyde's neck here, it may alter his design, and make him stay with the King, which he hath most mind of." [1]

The last sentence alludes to an engagement entered into by Rupert to raise men for the Duke of Modena. In May 1655 he was busy with his levies, and he had offered commands in his force to Craven, Gerard, and the once Puritan Massey. [2] The French Court patronised the Duke of Modena, and Mazarin promised Rupert the command of 2,000 men chosen from the best troops of France, 1,000 Swiss, and three other regiments. The arrears of pay due to the Prince for his services to France in 1648, were less readily conceded. Fortunately Rupert had a friend at court in the person of Edward's wife, Anne de Gonzague. This lady, being a very powerful person in France, obtained a promise of speedy payment, the more readily since Rupert declared that without the money he could not equip himself for the enterprise, and without himself his levies should not go. [3] Yet, in the very next month, he quietly renounced the whole scheme, sent his troops to Modena, and returned to Heidelberg. The reason for this sudden change of plan was the anxiety of Charles, who, fearing to lose his cousin altogether, had "abruptly begged him to quit all employments," and serve himself only. Rupert, loyal as ever, answered with equal abruptness that he would serve his cousin "with all his interest, either in men, money, arms, or friends," provided that he could effect "a handsome conjuncture," *i.e.* an honourable arrangement,

<hr>

[1] Thurloe, III. 459, 1 June, 1655.
[2] Thurloe, III. 414, 591, 8 May, 8 July, 1655.
[3] Bromley Letters. pp. 196—202. De Choqueux to Rupert, June 23, 1655.

with Modena.[1] This done, he joined the King at Frankfort, whence we find Ormonde writing to Hyde: "When
to-morrow we have been to a Lutheran service, and on
Monday have seen the fair, I know not how we shall con-
trive divertissements for a longer time, unless Prince Rupert,
who is coming, find them."[2]

Whether Rupert found them or not is unrecorded, but
he certainly made friends with the King, in whose company he remained until October. Charles had still some
hopes of the Scots, and it was rumoured that Rupert
endeavoured to win the Presbyterians by stating—with
perfect truth—that he had been bred a Calvinist.[3] It was
said also that he had countenanced the plot of 1654 for
Cromwell's assassination, and had even introduced the author
of it to the King. Whether the accusation be true or
false it is hard to say.[4] The only allusion to the plot
found in the Prince's own correspondence is in a letter
written from Heidelberg, which narrates the fate of the
conspirators; "the Diurnal says Jack Gerard is beheaded,
and another hanged, and that the Portugal ambassador's
brother was beheaded at the same time, and another
English gentleman hanged about that business, but says
little of any design. I have not yet received one line, so
I cannot give your Highness any further account."[5] This
letter may, or may not imply a previous acquaintance
with the design. It certainly assumes that Rupert knew
all about it, but the affair was then public property. Still
there is nothing absolutely impossible in the Prince's com-
plicity. Cromwell was regarded by the Royalists at that

---

[1] Thurloe, III. 659. 28 June, 1655.

[2] Clar. State Papers. Ormonde to Hyde, Sept. 25, 1655.

[3] Dom. State Papers. Commonwealth. Vol. XCIX. fol. 33. 10—20 July,
1655.

[4] Dom. State Papers. Gerard's Trial. Common. Vol. 72a. Clarendon State
Papers. Aug. 1654. Henshaw's Vindication.

[5] Rupert Correspondence. Job Holder to Rupert, July 25, 1654. Add.
MSS. 18982.

time, as a being almost beyond the pale of humanity. He was "the beast whom all the Kings of the earth do worship;"[1] and, though Rupert's known words and actions fit ill with assassination plots, it may be that the crime of murder looked less black to him when the intended victim happened to be the English Lord Protector.

In October 1655, the Prince was suddenly called away to Vienna, where he seems to have acted as Charles II's informal ambassador. The rumours as to his intended actions were many and various. At one time he was expected to command the Dutch fleet against the fleet of the Commonwealth, some said that he would take service with the Swedes, others that he would adhere to the Emperor.[2] But his real intention was, as we know, to serve his cousin, and Cromwell, evidently convinced of this, deputed the traitor Bampfylde to watch the Prince's movements. Concerning this same Bampfylde there is a rather amusing correspondence extant. Jermyn, on whom he had successfully imposed, recommended him to Rupert's patronage, as a man "suffering and persecuted" for his loyalty.[3] Rupert referred the matter to the King, who expressed himself "astonished" at Jermyn's letter, saying that he had already warned him of Bampfylde's treachery.[4] Bampfylde, in his turn, wrote to Cromwell, begging to be sent into Germany; "for I know the Duke of Brandenburg, the Prince Elector and Prince Rupert, and could give you no ill information. I would conceal my correspondence with you, and only pretend that I wished to see Germany and to seek employment in the wars there."[5] And when Cromwell had granted his desire, the spy found that he had walked into the clutches of Rupert, who was fully

---

[1] Elizabeth of Bohemia, 4 Jan., 1655. Evelyn IV. p. 222.
[2] Thurloe, II. 327. III. 683. IV. 697.
[3] Domestic State Papers, Jermyn to Rupert, Aug. 30 1657.
[4] Ibid. Nicholas to Rupert, May 16, 1658.
[5] Ibid. Bampfylde, June 24, 1657.

aware of his intended treachery. "I have obeyed to the utmost your commands about Colonel Bampfylde," wrote the Prince to the King. "You will receive particulars from your factor, Sir William Curtius, and from the Elector of Mayence. No impartial merchants being present, we could do no more, and could not have done so much, had not Bampfylde consented to a submission in this Imperial town. I will obey any further commands you may send me, in these parts."[1]

Rupert's loyalty was, in spite of everything, inextinguishable, and the tone which he now assumed towards his young cousin was singularly deferential. "Wyndham writes to my servant, Valentine Pyne, conjuring him to come with all possible speed to the King," he wrote, in 1658, to Nicholas. "I owe my person, and any of mine to his service; but represent to him that it would be a great obligation if Pyne could stay with me, till there be some great business in hand. Meantime he can study things in these parts, fit to use for some good design."[2] Even his advice was couched in an apologetic form. Thus he advised against attempting a Spanish alliance in 1656: "Sir, I received your Majesty's of the 16th of December, but at my arrival at this place. With great greefe I understand the continuation of the news that was whispered at Vienna, before my departure, of the Spaniards tampering for a peace with Cromwell. Yet I am so confident that they will come off it, that I wish the King of England would not be too hasty in offering himself to Spain. If the business between them and England break, they will be sure to take the King of England by the hand; if not, all will be vain. I humbly beseech Your Majesty to pardon this boldness, which proceeds from a very faithful heart to serve Your Majesty."[3]

<hr>

[1] Clar. State Papers. Rupert to Charles, Nov. 21, 1657.
[2] Dom. State Papers. Common. 179 fol. 13, 20 Jan. 1658.
[3] Thurloe, I. 694, 6 Feb. 1656.

This humble submission is indeed a contrast to the "insolence" described by Hyde. Possibly the increased deference corresponds to a decrease of friendship. What Rupert could do for Charles's service he would do; but, though they were reconciled and, to all appearance, on excellent terms, it is probable that the intimate friendship which had existed between them, previous to their quarrel in 1653—4, was never fully restored. Rupert was no longer the elder cousin, but the faithful servant, and he evidently meant to mark his change of position. In the early years of the Civil Wars, he had exercised a paramount influence over Charles, but his three years' absence had lost that for ever. With James he retained his influence longer. We find him expressing "astonishment" at the contents of a letter written by the younger of his royal cousins, and James meekly replying that he does not remember what he said, but is sure he did not mean it. "Je parlai à son Altesse (James) de l'étonnement qu'avait la votre de ce qu'elle avait reconnu en sa dernière lettre; qu'il me dit ne se point ressouvenir ni avoir fait à dessein; au contraire, qu'il fera toujours son possible pour la service et contentement de Votre Altesse, à laquelle il me dit vouloir en écrire pour s'en excuser."[1] In the differences between the Stuart brothers Rupert seems to have sympathised with James. "My godson (James) I am sure will take very well what you have answered for him," wrote his mother to the Prince; "I am extremely glad you did it."[2]

<hr>

[1] Bromley Letters, p. 201. De Choqueux to Rupert, June 23, 1655.
[2] Ibid. p. 294, Elizabeth of Bohemia to Rupert.

CHARLES LOUIS, ELECTOR PALATINE.

From the Engraving in the British Museum after a Portrait by Vandyke.

Face page 283.

CHAPTER XVI

RESTORATION OF CHARLES LOUIS TO THE PALATINATE.
FLIGHT OF THE PRINCESS LOUISE FROM THE HAGUE.
RUPERT'S DEMAND FOR AN APPANAGE. QUARREL
WITH THE ELECTOR

THE Peace of Munster, concluded October 24th, 1648, between Austria, France and Sweden, had terminated the long exile of the Palatines. By it Charles Louis was recognised as Elector Palatine, ranking henceforth as last among the Electors, instead of first, as his ancestors had done; and he was also restored to the Lower Palatinate, though still excluded from the upper. He immediately took up his residence at Heidelberg, and his mother expected, not unreasonably, that his restoration would, at least, ameliorate her sufferings. But Charles Louis entered upon a country exhausted by war, and grievously in need of cherishing care. He had, of course, no money to spare, and he was far too selfish to forego any of his schemes, or to sacrifice himself for the sake of his unhappy mother. He went so far as to invite his two sisters, Elizabeth and Sophie, to Heidelberg, thereby relieving his mother of the burden of their support, but the coming of the Queen herself he carefully discouraged. Worse still, he refused to send her even a portion of her jointure. "The next week I shall have no food to eat, having no money nor credit for any; and this week, if there be none found, I shall neither have meat, nor bread, nor candles," she complained to Lord Craven.[1] That faithful friend was quite unable to assist her, having been himself ruined by his services rendered

---

[1] Strickland's Elizabeth Stuart, p. 218; also Green's Princesses, VI. 38—41.

to the Stuarts; and how the hapless Queen existed it is hard to say, until, in 1657, the States generously granted her a pension of 10,000 livres per month.

Nor were her poverty and the callous indifference of of her favourite son her only troubles. Her third daughter, the fair Henriette, had died, after a three months' marriage with the Prince of Transylvania, and the eldest and youngest having departed to Heidelberg, she was left alone with the artist, Louise. Next to the Elector, Louise had been her mother's favourite child, and great was the shock to Elizabeth when this last remaining daughter suddenly professed herself a Roman Catholic, and fled secretly to France. For several days no one knew what had become of her; and the mother, sufficiently distracted by her daughter's abrupt desertion, found her grief enhanced by the circulation of scandalous rumours. The escapade was well calculated to produce them, for the Princess had fled from the Hague alone, and on foot, at seven o'clock on a December morning. Not till the day following, was the letter which she had pinned to her toilet table discovered; and its contents were not very consolatory to Elizabeth. From it she learnt that Louise, being convinced that the Roman was the one true Church, had acted thus strangely because she dared not attend the Anglican Celebration of the Holy Communion on Christmas Day.[1]

Rupert, who seems to have been much moved by his mother's distress, wrote to the States of Holland, begging their care and consideration for the Queen, and demanding "the satisfaction that is due to us in regard of the slanders that so greatly augment the injury;" and he added a passionate protest of gratitude for all that the States had done for his family.[2] They complied with his request by depriving the Princess of Hohenzollern, the supposed perverter of Louise, of all her privileges at Bergen. But

<hr>

[1] Green's Princesses, Vol. VI. 55—58.
[2] Thurloe, VI. p. 803, 24 Feb. 1658.

though the Princess of Hohenzollern bore the blame, the responsibility probably belonged as much to Louise's brother Edward as to any one else. "Ned is so wilful!" complained his mother, in reference to his conduct in this affair.[1] He came to meet his sister at Antwerp, where she had taken refuge in a Carmelite convent, and conducted her thence to Paris. She was, of course, kindly received by the French Court, and the joy of Henrietta Maria over the repenting heretic was very great. The English Queen wrote to Elizabeth that she would care for Louise as her own daughter, and begged forgiveness for her. "But," said Elizabeth to Rupert, "I excused it, as handsomely as I could, and entreated her only to think what she would do, if she had had the same misfortune."[2] It was not long before Henrietta had a somewhat similar misfortune, in her failure to convert her youngest son, Henry of Gloucester. The boy took refuge in Holland, and Elizabeth had a pleasing revenge in receiving her young nephew. King Charles and his sister, Mary of Orange, both visited Louise, and reproached her for her "unhandsome" flight from her mother; but she only answered that, though sorry for Elizabeth's displeasure, she was "very well satisfied" with her change of faith.[3] Subsequently she entered a convent and became abbess of Maubuisson, where she lived long enough to see the second exile of the Stuarts, of whom she was ever a warm partisan.

Elizabeth, thus left alone in her poverty, seems to have turned to Rupert with more affection than she had ever before shown him. She wrote him long letters, full of Hague gossip, of complaints of the Elector, and professions of affection for himself. "I love you ever, my dear Rupert," or, "I pray God bless you, whatever you resolve to do."[4]

[1] Bromley Letters, pp. 285—288. Elizabeth to Rupert, March 4, 1658.
[2] Ibid. p. 289.
[3] Bromley, pp. 287—288.
[4] Bromley Letters, pp. 189, 295, Elizabeth to Rupert.

Occasionally she relapsed into her old jesting manner.
Thus, she told him of a present of oranges forwarded
to him from Spain: "My Lord Fraser sent you a letter
from Portugal from Robert Cortez. He sends you two
cases of Portugal oranges, two for the King, and two for
me.... I believe my Lord Craven will tell you how much
ado he has had to save your part from me. I made him
believe I would take your cases for my niece and the
Prince of Orange. I did it to vex him." [1] She was still of
her "humour to be merry," though she had more cause
than ever for sadness.

Philip had fallen in 1650 at the siege of Rhetel, fighting
for France against Spain, but no allusion to his death
from the hand of his mother or brothers has been preserved.
Edward, who lived nominally in France, but was generally
to be found at the Hague and at Heidelberg, was on
friendly terms with Rupert, though he could not be to him
as Maurice had been. From time to time disquieting rumours
of Maurice's reappearance were afloat, and in 1654 the
story was very circumstantial. "Here is news of Prince
Maurice, who was believed to be drowned and perished,
that he is a slave in Africa. For, being constrained at
that time that he parted from Prince Rupert to run as far
as Hispaniola in the West Indies, he was coming back
thence in a barque laden with a great quantity of silver,
and was taken by a pirate of Algiers. The Queen, his
mother, hath spoken to the Ambassador of France, to the
end that he may write on his behalf, to the Great Turk." [2]
Rupert, personally, was convinced that his brother had
perished in the hurricane, but he would lose no chance of
recovering him, however slight, and he urged the Elector
to investigate the matter with all speed. "Concerning my
brother Maurice," wrote Charles Louis to his mother, "my
brother Rupert, who is now here, thinks the way by the

[1] Bromley Letters, p. 286, March 4, 1658.
[2] Thurloe, II. 362, 19 June, 1654.

Emperor's agent at Constantinople too far about for his liberty, if the news be true, and that from Marseilles we may best know the certainty, as also the way of his releasement."[1] But the news was not true, and Rupert's inquiries left him more hopeless than ever.

The Prince deprived at once of his chief companion and of his occupation, now bethought him of marrying and settling down. But in order to do this, it was necessary to have some visible means of subsistence, and therefore, in June 1654, he required a grant of land, as a younger brother's portion, from the Elector. He was, at that time, the guest of his brother at Heidelberg. The brothers had not met for eight years, and had parted last in England, when their relations, all things considered, cannot have been very cordial. Now they appeared to have buried the past, and were perfectly friendly. Even Rupert's modest claim to some few miles of land was not abruptly rejected by the Elector, and it was confidently reported in England, that Prince Rupert would "settle on his plantation, his brother having given him lands to the quantity of twenty English miles in compass."[2] But this grant was never finally completed. During Rupert's absence in Vienna the affair seemed to be progressing favourably, and his agent, Job Holder, wrote to him from Heidelberg: "This day Valentine Pyne made an end of measuring the Cloysture and Langessel. The circumference which is given to the Elector, is ten English miles,—reckoning 1,000 paces to the mile,—and 90 paces. This morning I waited upon Mr. Leslie from Langessel to Heidelberg, who gave H. H. the Elector an account of what was done, and desired H. H. to confirm those lands upon your Highness, with the full freedom and prerogatives thereof. But His Highness defers it until the draught thereof be finished; it will be, I believe, next Tuesday before a further account can be had from

---

[1] Bromley, p. 167. Elector to Elizabeth, June 27, 1654.
[2] Thurloe, II. 514, 12 Aug. 1654.

hence. Mr. Leslie says there is a necessity of having the
house speedily repaired; after two months winter comes on,
which will be unseasonable for the purpose. In the meantime he intends to go on with the Paddock, in observance
of Your Highness's commands, and to make it as large
as the highways will permit. Her Highness, the Princess
Elizabeth, commanded me to write that my Lady Herbert
was coming to the Hague with 30 English gentlemen." [1]
But a couple of months later the Elector declared himself
dissatisfied with the management of Leslie, and desired
Rupert to have no more to do with him. [2]

The business remained unfinished, but the Elector's
letters to his brother were still in a most friendly and affectionate strain; addressed always to his "très-cher Frère," and
signed "très-cher frère, votre très affectionné, et fidèle frère
et serviteur," they are full of good-will, and wishes for
"une prompte et bonne expédition" in Rupert's affairs.
Occasionally they assume the old tone of jesting familiarity;
in one letter Charles laments that the poems—"nos
poësies"—forwarded to his brother have miscarried; and in
another, remarks, in the true polyglot style of the Palatines,
"Le Duc de Simmeren nous a vu à Hort, en passant pour
être au baptême d'un fils de Madame la Landgrave de
Cassel, où je suis prié aussi; but I do not love to go a-
gossipping." [3] In August he anticipated a petty war with
the Bishop of Speyer, but he hastily declined Rupert's
prompt offer of assistance. "I am deeply obliged for the
offer you make me, but I should be desolated to think
that you neglected your own more pressing business for a
dispute of so little consequence." [4] In truth, the less his
brother interfered in Palatine politics, the better pleased
was the Elector. Rupert, he once wrote to his sister Sophie,

---

[1] Add. MSS. 18982. Job Holder to Rupert, Aug. 1, 1654.
[2] Ibid. Oct. 14, 1654.
[3] Bromley Letters, pp. 170, 173, 315, 25 Aug., 25 Sept., Oct. 1654.
[4] Bromley Letters, p. 171, 25 Sept. 1654.

might suit very well with those who cared "to propagate the gospel by the sword," but he, for his part, loved "peace and concord." [1]

His concord with Rupert was not of long duration, and this time the *causa belli* was a woman. The Elector had married, in 1650, Charlotte of Hesse Cassel, but the marriage was not a happy one. The Electress was of a violent temper, jealous and unreasonable to the last degree, and Charles Louis, wearying of his attempts to win her affections, permitted his wandering fancy to dwell on a certain Louise Von Degenfeldt, a girl not only beautiful, but clever enough to write her love-letters in Latin. Most unfortunately, the Baroness Louise also fascinated—quite unconsciously—the Elector's brother Rupert. At the same time the Electress conceived a violent admiration for her gallant brother-in-law, and the situation was, as may well be imagined, somewhat critical. The explosion was caused by a letter which Rupert wrote to Louise, complaining bitterly of her coldness towards him. The letter, which was without superscription, fell into the hands of the Electress, who, believing it intended for herself, received it with delight. It was her chief desire, just then, to appear to Rupert the most fascinating person in her court, and, encouraged by his letter, she assured him publicly that he had no cause to complain of lack of affection on her part. Rupert, who had evidently not learnt to command his countenance, was overcome with confusion, and blushed so furiously as to show the Electress her mistake. Thenceforth the Electress abused and persecuted Louise for having endeavoured to win the Prince's love, of which crime, at least, she was perfectly innocent. [2]

The affair came to the Elector's ears, and jealousy sprang up between the brothers. The Elector's manner changed;

---

[1] Briefwechsel der Herzogin Sophie mit ihrem Brüder Karl Ludwig, p. 309. 5 Jan. 1678. Publication aus der Preussischen Staats Archiven.

[2] Memorien der Herzogin Sophie, p. 57.

he refused the promised appanage, he treated Rupert with marked coldness, and finally retired to Alzei, where there was little accommodation for his court. Rupert followed him thither, and was denied a sufficiency of rooms for himself and his servants; then, as usual, he lost his temper.[1] There was a quarrel, and the younger brother departed in a rage, taking with him all his movables—which cannot have been many.[2] He went first to Heidelberg, but the Elector, either wishful to insult him, or really fearful of his violence, wrote, ordering that he should be refused admittance to the city. To his surprise and indignation, Rupert found the gates closed against him. He demanded to see the order by which this thing was done. The order was shown him, written in the Elector's own hand. It was too much! Then and there Rupert raised his hat from his head, and swore, with tears in his eyes, that he would never more set foot in the Palatinate.[3] Twenty years later, when it seemed to the Elector that his race was about to die out, he would have given much to recall his ill-used brother. But all the entreaties which he lavished on Rupert, produced but one answer: "Ich habe auf Euer Liebden Veranlassung ein feierliches Gelübde zu Gott gethan, die Pfalz nie wieder zu betreten; und will, bei dem wenn auch bedauerlich beschwornen Vorsatze beharren." "Your Belovedness,"—a curious Palatine substitute for Your Highness,— "has caused me to take a solemn oath to God that I will never more set foot in the Palatinate; and my sworn, if regretable, oath I will keep."[4] Rupert, like his father before him, was "a Prince religious of his word."

After his quarrel with his brother, Rupert wandered back to Vienna, and is said to have served in the wars in Pomerania and Hungary. In 1657 it was stated in England

---

[1] Haüsser's Reinische Pfalz, II. p. 643.
[2] Thurloe, V. p. 541.
[3] Reiger's Ausgelöschte Simmerischen Linie, ed. 1735. p. 182.
[4] Sprüner's Pfalzgraf Ruprecht, p. 134.

that "Prince Rupert hath command of 8,000 men, under the King of Hungary, who will owe his empirate to his sword."[1]   And a German authority describes him as leading in the capture of the Swedish entrenchments at Warnemünde, 1660.[2]   But the truth of these reports is very doubtful, and he seems to have resided between 1657 and 1660 chiefly with his friend the Elector of Mainz.   At Mainz he lived in tranquillity, but in great poverty.   "He looks exceedingly poverty-stricken," wrote Sophie of another Cavalier, "and I fear that Rupert will soon do the same, judging by his ménage."[3]

But to Rupert poverty was no new thing, and he now enjoyed, for the first time since his captivity in Austria, leisure to devote himself to art, philosophy and science. In these years he first studied the art of engraving, in which he was afterwards so famous.   He is popularly supposed to have invented the process of engraving by Mezzotint, the idea of which he is said to have conceived from watching a soldier clean a rusty gun.   But the process was, as a matter of fact, communicated to him by a German soldier, Ludwig von Siegen.   In 1642 von Siegen had completed his invention, and had sent a portrait, produced by his new process, to the Landgrave of Hesse, with the announcement that he had discovered "a new and singular invention of a kind never hitherto beheld."   In 1658 he met Rupert in Vienna, and, finding in him a kindred spirit, disclosed his secret.   They agreed only to reveal the process to an appreciative few, and it is probable that, but for Rupert's interest in it, the invention would have died with the inventor.[4]   To the Prince belongs the credit of introducing it into England.   "This afternoon Prince Rupert shewed me, with his own hands, the new

<hr>

[1] Hist. MSS. Com. Rept. V. App. I. p. 152, Sutherland MSS.
[2] Allgemeine Deutsche Biographie, XXIX, 745.
[3] Briefwechsel der Herzogin Sophie, p. 4, 21 Oct. 1658.
[4] Challoner Smith, Mezzotint Engraving, Part IV. Div II. pp. xxvi—xxx.

way of engraving," says Evelyn in his diary, March 16, 1661. [1] And in his "Sculptura" he says, after describing the process, "Nor may I without ingratitude conceal that illustrious name which did communicate it to me, nor the obligation which the curious have to that heroic person who was pleased to impart it to the world." [2] Rupert himself worked hard at his engravings, assisted by the artist, Le Vaillant; and Evelyn refers with enthusiasm to "what Prince Rupert's own hands have contributed to the dignity of that art, performing things in graving comparable to the greatest masters, such a spirit and address appears in all he touches, especially in the Mezzotinto." [3]

While at Mainz, Rupert developed other inventions, among them the curious glass bubbles known as "Rupert's Drops," which will withstand the hardest blows, but crumble into atoms if the taper end is broken off. He also prepared to write his biography. This he intended as a vindication against all the calumnies which had been associated with his name. But long before the vindication was compiled the need for it had vanished. The Restoration of 1660 changed Rupert's fortunes as it changed those of his Stuart cousins. He found himself "in great esteem" [4] with the whole English nation, and he therefore abandoned the idea of writing his history. All that remains of the projected biography are a few fragments relating to his childhood and early career.

[1] Evelyn's Diary, I. p. 346.
[2] Evelyn's Sculptura, 1662, Chap. VII. p. 145.
[3] Sculptura, p. 147.
[4] Campbell's Admirals, 1785, Vol. II. p. 245.

CHAPTER XVII

RUPERT'S RETURN TO ENGLAND, 1660. VISIT TO VIENNA.
LETTERS TO LEGGE

CHARLES II, so often accused of ingratitude, did not prove forgetful of the cousin who had endured so much in his service. No sooner had the Restoration established him in his kingdom, than he summoned Rupert to share in his prosperity, as he had formerly shared his ill-fortune. The summons found Rupert with the Emperor, and suffering from an attack of the fever, which had clung about him ever since his return from the West Indies.

"Your friend Rupert has not been well since he came into his quarters," wrote the Queen, his mother, to Sir Marmaduke Langdale. "He had like to have a fever, but he writes to me that it left him, onlie he was a little weak. As soon as he can he will be in England, where I wish myself, for this place is verie dull now, there is verie little company."[1] Her position at the Hague was, in truth, a sad and lonely one, but she was still able to write in her old merry style, rejoicing greatly in a mistake made by Sir Marmaduke, who had inadvertently sent to her a letter intended for his stewards, and to the stewards a letter intended for the Queen. "If I had you here, I would jeer you to some tune for it!" she said; and so, no doubt, she would have done. But in her next letter she confessed that she had herself "committed the like mistake manie times," and added more news of Rupert, who had gone away for change of air.[2] In a third letter she expressed

[1] Strickland's Elizabeth Stuart, p. 268.
[2] Ibid. p. 268.

satisfaction at the King's affection for Rupert, who was then at Brandenburg with his sister Elizabeth.[1] Before coming to England, the Prince also visited his youngest sister at Osnabrück, and it was late in September when he arrived in London.

His coming had been for some time anxiously expected, though he was evidently regarded as still in the Emperor's service. "For ambassadors," it was said, "we look for Don Luis de Haro's brother from Spain, with 300 followers; Prince Rupert, with a great train from the Emperor; and the Duc d'Epernon from France, with no less State."[2] Rupert came, however, in a strictly private capacity; and September 29th, 1660, Pepys recorded in his diary: "Prince Rupert is come to Court, welcome to nobody!"[3] How the Prince had, thus early, incurred the diarist's enmity is puzzling; later, the causes of it are perfectly understandable.

But though unwelcome to Pepys, Rupert was very welcome to many people, and not least so to the Royal family, who received him as one of themselves. In November the Royal party was augmented by the arrival of Queen Henrietta; her youngest daughter, Henrietta Anne; and the Palatine, Edward, from France. The young Princess Henrietta was already betrothed to the French King's brother, Philippe of Orleans; and Rupert, who had a just contempt for the character of the intended bridegroom, vehemently opposed the conclusion of the match. He could, he declared, arrange the marriage of his young cousin with the Emperor, who would be at once a greater match and a better husband.[4] But both the Queen mother and Charles were anxious for the French alliance, and the marriage took place notwithstanding Rupert's opposition. When, after ten years of unhappiness, the poor young Duchess died a tragic

[1] Strickland's Elizabeth Stuart, p. 269.
[2] Hist. MSS. Com. Rept. V. App. I. p. 173. Sutherland MSS., 4 Aug. 1660.
[3] Pepys Diary, Sept. 29th, 1660.
[4] Cartwright. Madame: A Life of Henrietta of Orleans, pp. 70—71.

death, Rupert was in a position to say "I told you so," and he always maintained that her husband had poisoned her. "There are three persons at court say it is true," wrote the French Minister, Colbert: "Prince Rupert, because he has a natural inclination to believe evil; the Duke of Buckingham, because he courts popularity; and Sir John Trevor, because he is Dutch at heart, and consequently hates the French." [1]

On New Year's Day, 1661, Anne Hyde, the clandestine bride of James of York, was formally received at court. Rupert and Edward dined with the rest of the Royal family, in public; and on this occasion there was a most unseemly contest between the Roman chaplain of the Queen mother, and the Anglican chaplain of Charles II, for the honour of saying grace. In struggling through the crowd assembled to see the King dine, the Anglican priest fell down, and the Roman gained the table first and said grace. His victory was greeted by the disorderly courtiers with shouts of laughter. "The King's chaplain and the Queen's priest ran a race to say grace," they declared, "and the chaplain was floored, and the priest won." [2]

Rupert, soon after his arrival in England, had resigned his title of President of Wales and the Marches, granted him by Charles I, on the grounds that he would hold only of the reigning King. [3] He had, however, found himself so cordially received, and so generally popular, that he resolved to accept Charles's invitation to remain permanently in England. "Prince Rupert," says a letter in the Sutherland MSS., dated March 1661, "is the only favourite of the King, insomuch that he has given him £30,000 or £40,000 per annum, out of his own revenue, for his present maintenance; and is resolved to make him Lieutenant

---

[1] Cartwright's Madame, p. 359.

[2] Strickland's Henrietta Maria, Queens of England, VIII. p. 232. From MSS. of Père Cyprian Gamache.

[3] Hist. MSS. Com. Rept. V. App. I. p. 200. Sutherland MSS. 3 Nov. 1660.

General of all Wales, and President of the Marches. Mean-time he is preparing to go to Germany to take leave of that court and to resign his military charge there, and so return to England. I am told that the King went into the Palatinate with an intent to have procured some money of the Palsgrave, which was refused. Prince Rupert, being then there, seeing the unworthiness of his brother in this particular, made use of all the friends he had, and procured his Majesty a considerable sum of money, which was an act of so much love and civility as his Majesty was very sensible of then, and now he will requite him for it." [1] But Charles's intentions towards Rupert, though doubtless good, were far less magnificent than here represented. The claims on his justice and bounty were far too numerous, and his means far too small, to permit of his rewarding anyone so lavishly.

Rupert was still in high favour at the Austrian court, and the "temptations to belong to other nations" were real ones; but he preferred England and the Stuarts to any of the allurements held out to him by France or Germany, and therefore resolved to "remain an Englishman." In accordance with this decision, he set forth for Vienna in April 1661, partly to wind up his affairs there and to take leave of the Emperor, and partly to transact business on behalf of Charles II. His absence from England lasted nine months, and his doings and movements during that period are chronicled in letters addressed to his "Dear Will." The old friendship of the Prince and the honest Colonel had not cooled, though tried by time and long years of separation; and, on his departure, Rupert appointed Legge his "sufficient and lawful attorney, to act, manage, perform and do all, and all manner of things" in his behalf. [2]

The greater part of his letters to Legge are printed in

<hr>

[1] Hist. MSS. Com. Rept. V. App. I. p. 170. 2 Mar. 1661.
[2] Collins Peerage, Dartmouth, Vol. IV. p. 107, *passim*.

Photo Walker & Cockrell.

COLONEL WILLIAM LEGGE.   BY J. HUYSMAN.

From the Picture in the National Portrait Gallery, London.

Face page 297.

Warburton, but with some omissions and inaccuracies. They are also to be found, in their original spelling, in the Report of the Historical MSS. Commission on Lord Dartmouth's Manuscripts; but they are, in their frank, familiar, somewhat sardonic style, so characteristic of the Prince as to merit quotation here.[1]

The first letters are dated from the Hague, whither he had gone to visit his solitary mother. "I found the poor woman very much dejected," he informed his friend. And after mentioning disquieting rumours of war ,he concluded, with evident triumph :—

"I almost forgott to tell you a nother story which be plesed to acquainted (sic) the Duke of Albemarle with. You have doubtlesse seene a lame Polish Prince, some time at Whitehall with passe ports a beggin. This noble soule is tacken and in prisoned at Alikmare; hath bin butt twice burnt in the bake befor this misfortune befell him. The Duke I am sure will remember him, and what my jugement was of the fellow.

"I am your most faithful friend for ever,

"Rupert."

Europe was at that time swarming with impostors, who impersonated all imaginable persons of distinction. Only a few months earlier a "Serene Prince" had been visiting the Elector, who wrote of him much as Rupert might have done. "His Highness was graciously pleased to accept from me three ducats for his journey, besides the defraying. I doubt not but he and the counterfeit Ormonde and Ossory will come to one and the same end one day."[2]

In the beginning of May Rupert had reached Clèves, where he found the little Prince of Orange. Rumours of war met him on all sides; both Swedes and Turks were arming against the Emperor, and the Dutch declared loudly

---

[1] See Hist. MSS. Com. Rept. on Dartmouth MSS. Vol. I. pp. 1—9,

[2] Bromley Letters, p. 209, Aug. 11—21, 1660.

that they would defend their herring fisheries against England,
with the sword. "I told some that butter and cheese
would do better," wrote the Prince; little thinking what
stout antagonists he was to find those despised Hollanders
at sea. He was anxious to recommend to Charles' service
an engineer, "the ablest man in his profession that ever I
saw... If the fortification of Portchmouth go on, I wish
his advice may be taken, for noen fortifies so well, and
cheap, and fast as he. He has a way of working which
noen has so good. Pray neglect not this man, and tell
Sir Robert Murray of him, with my remembrances; also
that I met with camphor wood, which smells of it, also
with a distilled pure raine water which dissolved gold."

After a short visit to his friend, the Elector of Mainz,
who, he said, "assured me to be assisting in all things,"
Rupert reached Vienna. There he was very cordially received by the Emperor, though the Spanish Ambassador,
for political reasons, saw fit to ignore his arrival. The
Austrians were still loth to let him leave them; and on
June 22, he wrote to Legge: "A friend of mine, att my
coming, assured me that there were but twoe difficulties
whiche hindred my advancement to the Generallship of the
Horse. The one was my being no Roman, the other that
the Marquess of Baden and Generall Feldzeugmeister de
Sanch might take ill if I was advanced before them. And
he thought both these small impediments might easily be
overcome, but especially the first, on whiche, he assured
me, most ded depend." He had not yet forgotten his *rôle*
of Protestant martyr! To this letter he added, as usual, a
hurried and incoherent postscript.

"I almost forgott to tell you how that Comte Lesley's
cousin, (I forgott his name, but I remember that his sister
was married to St. Michel,) this man ded me the favor to
send over a booke to Comte Lesley, entitled 'The Iron
Age,' in whiche it speekes most base languiage of me and
my actions in England. It is dedicated to Jake Russell,

but I am confident if honest Jake had reade the booke, he would have broke the translator's head... One Harris translated it; pray inquire after the booke, and juge if it were not a Scotch tricke to sende it... Moutray is the name I forgott."

By July the Spanish Ambassador had deigned to visit the Prince, and to reveal the true cause of his long delay— namely, the rumours of Charles II's approaching marriage with the Infanta of Portugal, which was likely to produce a war with Spain. For this same reason, joined with their resentment at Rupert's refusal of the Generalship of the horse, the Austrian Ministers also treated him with coldness, though the personal kindness of the Imperial family was never abated. "In the meantime be pleased to knowe that Rupert is but coldly used by the Ministers here," wrote the Prince; "they would have him demand the Generallship before there is an appearance of subsistence,— nay, before what is oweing in arreare, by the Peace of Munster, be made sure unto him; to whiche Rupert doth no waies incline, especialy since he had the intimation given him that his religion was an obstacle to his advancement in the warr. The Emperor, Emperatrice and Archduc are extreamly kind to Rupert; but noen of the Counsellors have done him the honor of a visit. The reason is, I believe, the marriage aforesaid... For God's sake, if there be any likelihood of a breach with Spaine, lett us knowe it by times; it concerns us, Ile assure you."

In August matters were much in the same condition, and Rupert was still struggling for the arrears of the debt due to him. "Monys is comodity in greate request in this court, and scarce enough!" he confessed. Notwithstanding his refusal to enter the Austrian service, he identified himself with the Empire sufficiently to write of "our commander," when referring to the war then waged by the Emperor against the Turks. In the next month the Elector had played him "a brotherly trick," and the letter which he wrote to Will was as full of fury, as any he had indited during the Civil War.

"Dear Will,

"I am not able to writt you of any subject but of one, which, I confesse, doth troble me in the highest degre, and dothe concerne our master as well as myself. The stori is this. The Elector Pallatin hath bin plesed to writt to a Prive Consellor of this Court, in these terms—what the King of England's ambassador doth negotiate with the Porte Elector Pallatin knowes not, nor what is intended by him against the house of Austria, but Prince Rupert, whoe is intimate with Kinge of England and his Prive Consellor, can tell, if he plese.—All this is a brotherly tricke you'l saye; but I thancke Gode they heere doe little beleeve what he saies ... By Heven I am in suche a humour that I dare not writt to any; therefore excuse me to alle, for not writting this post ... Faire well, deare Will!"

Five days later Rupert had recovered himself, and could write in his ordinary sarcastic fashion: "By the last I writt you the kinde usage of my brother the Elector to me, as alsoe the good office he ded the Kinge in this Court. I thanke Gode he hath not realised his barbaros intentions!" But the letter was broken off abruptly, because the Emperor was waiting for Rupert's hounds to hunt a stag. By the next post the Prince had to lament the loss of one of these hounds, and his keen regret shows plainly that his love for dogs was as strong as ever.

"I am glad that Holmes hath given the King satisfaction ... Pray give him thankes for remembering his ould master. Pray remember my service to the General (Monk); tell him I am glad to heere of his recouvrey, it was before I knew he had been sicke. If my Lord Lindsay be at court, the same to him, with the doleful news that poore Rayall att this instant is dying, after having ben the cause of the death of many a stagge. By Heven, I would rather loose the best horse in my stable."

Rupert was now preparing to return to England, and was very busy purchasing wines for the use of the English Court. A considerable quantity, presented to him by the Elector of Mainz, he had already forwarded to Legge, to dispose of as he pleased. By November 22 he had reached Cassel, whence he wrote to Legge, "I am making all the haste I can to you." But at Cassel he found his eldest sister, and he remained with her some weeks, not returning to England until the beginning of 1662.

His mother, in the meantime, had obtained her much desired summons to England, and had taken up her abode in a house placed at her disposal by the ever faithful Craven. For a brief period she enjoyed rest and peace, rejoicing in the return to her native land, and in the affection of her Stuart nephews, who, she said, showed her more kindness than any of her own sons had ever done. Eighteen months after her arrival in England, she died, in the arms of the King. Her pictures she bequeathed to Lord Craven, and her papers and jewels to Rupert, thereby establishing a new cause of contest between her two eldest sons.[1] For the Elector denied his mother's right to leave the jewels—which were, he declared, heirlooms—to a younger son. Rupert held tenaciously to his possessions, and the dispute raged long and bitterly.

[1] Will of Elizabeth of Bohemia. Wills from Doctors Commons, p. 109. Camden Society.

CHAPTER XVIII

RUPERT AND THE FLEET. PROPOSED VOYAGE TO GUINEA.
ILLNESS OF RUPERT. THE FIRST DUTCH WAR. THE
NAVAL COMMISSIONERS AND THE PRINCE. SECOND
DUTCH WAR. ANTI-FRENCH POLITICS

RUPERT received a warm welcome on his return to
England, and was at once sworn a member of the Privy
Council. It was but natural that he should turn his attention
to naval affairs. The growth of the sea power of England
had received an impetus during the years of the Commonwealth, due indirectly to Rupert himself; for had not the
Commonwealth been forced to protect itself against the
pirate Princes, it would probably have cared less for its
navy.[1] Charles II, like a true Stuart, cared for his fleet
also, and took a keen interest in ship-building and other
matters connected with the navy. In October 1662, he
appointed Rupert to the Committee for the Government of
Tangiers, together with the Duke of York, Albemarle,
Sandwich, Coventry, and Pepys of famous memory. If Pepys
may be credited, the Prince did not take the business at
all seriously: "The Duke of York and Mr. Coventry, for
aught I see, being the only two that do anything like men.
Prince Rupert do nothing but laugh a little, with an oath
now and then."[2]

But if Rupert was indifferent about Tangiers he was keenly
interested in the African question. The quarrels of the English and Dutch traders on the African coast had produced
much ill-feeling between the two nations, and, in August

---

[1] Campbell's Admirals, II. p. 242.
[2] Pepys Diary, 4 June, 1664.

1664, Rupert offered to lead a fleet to Guinea, to oppose
the aggressions of the DutchAdm iral, De Ruyter.   A fleet
of twelve ships was accordingly fitted out.   On September
3, wrote Pepys: "Prince Rupert, I hear this day, is going
to command this fleet going to Guinea against the Dutch.
I doubt few will be pleased with his going, he being accounted an unhappy man;"[1]—a view which contrasts
strangely with the terror which Rupert's mere name had
roused in earlier days.   Two days later Pepys had encountered Rupert himself: "And, among other things, says
he: 'D— me! I can answer but for one ship, and in that
I will do my part, for it is not as in an army where a
man can command everything.'"[2]

A royal company had been formed for the promotion
of the enterprise, and a capital was raised of £30,000, in
which the Duke of York held many shares.[3] Eighty pounds
was laid out on "two trumpets, a kettle-drum, and a drum-
mer to attend Prince Rupert to sea;"[4] and, after a farewell
supper at Kirke House, Rupert went down the river at
three o'clock on an October morning, accompanied by the
King, Duke of York, and many Courtiers.   With the next
tide he embarked, but the weather was very rough, and
for some days he was wind-bound at Portsmouth.   His
crews numbered two hundred and fifty in all, besides fifty-
four supernumaries in his train.[5]   As was invariably the
case at this period, the fleet was badly and insufficiently
provisioned; but the delay at Portsmouth enabled Rupert
to have this rectified, and thus, for the first time, he came
into collision with Pepys, the victualler of the navy.

For some weeks the Prince hovered about the Channel,
waiting for an expected Dutch fleet; but the Dutch out-

[1] Pepys Diary, Sept. 3, 1664.
[2] Ibid. Sept. 5, 1664.
[3] D. S. P. Sept. 13, 1664.
[4] Dom. State Papers, Sept. 23, 1664.
[5] Ibid. Oct. 8, 15, 24, 1664.

witted him. By promising to keep within harbour, they persuaded the King to recall Rupert, and, in the meantime, privately ordered their Mediterranean fleet to sail for New Guinea. Thus nothing was done by the English, and the only warfare waged by Rupert was with his chaplain, of whom he wrote bitter complaints to Lord Arlington, the then Secretary of State.

"Sir,

"I beseech you, at the delivery of this inclosed leter, to acquaint the King and the Duke of York that, after I had closed their leters, the spirit of mutiny entered our parson againe, so that there was no rest for him, until I commanded him to his cabin, and withal to make readdy for prayers this next morning, which he had neglected yesterday. Att this instant I receave this inclosed, by whiche you may see his humor. After this stile he talked, till ten last night, abusing the captain most horribly. In consideration of my Lord of Canterburie, whoe recommended him, I strained my patience very much; but if this felow shoulde continue longer on bord, you may easily imagine the troble he woulde put us to. If I had any time I would writt to my Lord Archbishop, giving him the whoele relation of what passed. I am now sending all our captains present to indevor the hastening down to the Downes. If nothing hinder, I hope, God willing, to sayle to-morrow. Minne is not yet abord, but I expect him the next tide. I will be sure give you notice what our motions will be from time to time, and rest

"Your affectionat frend to serve you,

"Rupert.

"Oct. 8, Lee Rd.

"Pray to doe me the favor as to acquaint my Lord Archbishop of Canterburie with this, and my respects to him."[1]

---

[1] Domestic State Papers. Oct. 8 1664. Carl II. 103. f. 27.

His next letter, of October 11, shows that the Prince had been relieved of his militant chaplain. "Our ship, by wanting Levit, is very quiet. God send us another (chaplain) of a better temper. Hitherto we have not trobled Him much with prayers."[1] But the matter did not end there, and October 30, Rupert wrote again: "Our late parson, I heere, plaies the devil in alle companies he comes; raising most damned reports of us alle, and more particularly of me." This letter is devoid of all complimentary phrases, and ends simply, "Yours, Rupert." An apologetic postscript explains these omissions. "His Majesty has given me direction to write to him thus, without ceremony, and it will be easier for us all to follow. I have therefore begonne, and desire you to do the like."[2]

The fleet never reached its destination. A war was imminent nearer home, and Charles was probably unwilling to send so many ships out of the Channel; but the reasons for their abrupt recall were a subject of much discussion. "This morning I am told that the goods on board Prince Rupert's ship, for Guinea, are unlading at Portsmouth, which makes me believe that he is resolved to stay and pull the crow with them at home," says a letter among the Hatton papers. "But the matter be so secretly carried that this morning there was not the least intimation given what to depend on, even to them that are commonly knowing enough in affairs of that kind."[3]

An additional reason for the collapse of the expedition was the severe illness of Rupert. The old wound in the head, which he had received through Gassion's treachery, had never properly healed, and now an accidental injury to it had very serious results. The Duke of York, much concerned by the accident, immediately sent a surgeon to

---

[1] Dom. State Papers. Carl II. 103. f. 40.
[2] Ibid. Oct. 11. 1664. Carl II. Vol. 103. f. 153.
[3] Hatton Correspondence, Vol. I. p. 37. Camd. Soc. New series. Lyttleton to Hatton, Oct. 19, 1664.

the fleet, and wrote with friendly solicitude to his cousin:
"As soon as Will Legge showed me your letter of the
accident in your head, I immediately sent Choqueux to
you, in so much haste as I had not time to write by him.
But now, I conjure you, if you have any kindness for me,
have a care of your health, and do not neglect yourself.
I am very glad to hear your ship sails so well. I was
yesterday to see the new ship at Woolwich launched, and
I think, when you see her, (which I hope you will do
very quickly, under Sir John Lawson,) you will say she
is the finest ship that has yet been built." [1]

The surgeon operated upon the Prince, who wrote
November 6, to the King: "I could not go from shipp
to shipp to hasten the work, since Choqueux will not let
me stir, to which I consented the rather, since he promises
to have me quite well and whoele in a few days." [2] But
the promise was not made good, and a very dangerous
illness ensued. "Prince Rupert, by a chance, has bruised
his head, and cannot get cured," says one of the Hatton
correspondents in December. "He is gone up to London
to endeavour it there ... He is mightily worn away, and in
their opinion that are about him is not long-lived. He would
fain go to Guinea, and is endeavouring to be despatched
there; he believes the warmth of that clime would do him
good." [3] Life, apparently, still held attractions for Rupert.
According to Pepys, he was "much chagrined" at the idea
of dying, but recovered his spirits wonderfully when assured
of convalescence. "Since we told him that we believe he
would overcome his disease, he is as merry, and swears,
and laughs, and curses, and do all the things of a man
in health as ever he did in his life." [4]

The illness lasted a long time; but though he was ex-

---

[1] Bromley Letters, 283—284. 27 Oct. 1664.
[2] Domestic State Papers. Rupert to King, Nov. 6, 1664. Carl II. 104. 42.
[3] Hatton Correspondence, Vol. I. p. 44. 10 Dec. 1664.
[4] Pepys. 15 Jan. 1665.

ceedingly weak, Rupert did not fail to take his part in the first Dutch war. The formal declaration of war was made in February 1665, to the great joy of the English nation, whose commercial heart had been stirred by colonial jealousies. "What matters this or that reason?" cried the honest Duke of Albemarle (General Monk). "What we want is more of the trade which the Dutch now have!"[1] France, for equally selfish reasons, threw in her lot with the Dutch, but delayed coming to their assistance; and the first engagement did not take place till June 13, 1665.

The English fleet was divided into three squadrons, Red, White and Blue. In the Red commanded the Duke of York, as Lord High Admiral; Rupert was Admiral of the White, and his rival, Lord Sandwich, led the Blue. On the twenty-first of April they sailed to the Texel, hoping to blockade the Zuyder Zee, meet De Ruyter on his return from Africa, and cut off the home-coming vessels. The English commanders, Rupert excepted, believed that the Dutch would at once come out and fight. But Rupert proved right, the Dutch made no sign, and within a fortnight, want of provisions drove the English back to Harwich.

In the meantime the Dutch sent forth a fleet of 103 men-of-war, 7 yachts, 11 fire-ships, and 12 galiots. This was divided into seven squadrons, and placed under the joint command of Evertsen and Opdam. By May 13th they were at sea, and immediately captured some English merchantmen coming from Hamburg. There was an outcry of indignation in England, and the fleet hurried to sea. On June 3rd the rival fleets met in Southwold Bay. The English, who had 109 men-of-war and 28 fire-ships and ketches, were numerically superior to their enemy. Opdam was, besides, hopelessly hampered by imperative commands from the States to fight at once, and by a want

---

[1] Mahan's Sea Power, p. 107.

of military pride and *esprit de corps* throughout his fleet. The action began with Rupert in the van, York in the centre, and Sandwich in the rear. Rupert "received the charge" of the Dutch fleet, not firing until close to it, and then shooting through and through it. [1] Having thus met, the two fleets passed each other, and then turned to renew the encounter. Sandwich, getting mixed up with the Dutch, cut their fleet in two and a general *mêlée* ensued. In the Dutch centre the Junior Admiral was killed, and his crew, in a panic, carried their ship out of action. Twelve or thirteen other vessels imitated this ungallant conduct, and when,—after a desperate encounter with the Royal Charles,—Opdam's ship blew up, the fate of the battle was decided. Evertsen and Tromp, each believing the other killed, both took command and issued contrary orders. Three or four of their vessels ran foul of one another, and were burnt by an English fire-ship; by 7 p.m. the whole Dutch fleet had begun a disorderly retreat. [2]

The Dutch losses had been very heavy, those of the English comparatively slight; but the English fire-ships were expended, and the wind blew hard for the coast of Holland, which made a too vigorous pursuit of the flying foe dangerous. Nevertheless, the Duke of York ordered the chase to be continued, and retired to rest. Sir William Penn, who was on board the "Royal Charles" as first Captain of the fleet, also went to sleep, leaving the ship in the charge of Captain Harman. During the night one of the Duke's gentlemen, Brouncker, came and urged Harman to slacken sail, in consideration of the danger to which the Duke was exposed. This, Harman refused to do; but when Brouncker returned later, with an order purporting to come from James himself, he reluctantly yielded. Next morning the enemy was out of sight, and James expressed both

[1] Dom. State Papers. Hickes to Winson, June 10, 1665.
[2] See Clowes' Royal Navy, II. pp. 256—266. Campbell, II. 93—98.

surprise and displeasure at the discovery, denying that he had ever ordered the chase to be given up. The affair was hotly discussed, and Bishop Burnet plainly implies that the Duke had used this cowardly device to save both his person and his reputation.[1] But James was no coward, and it is exceedingly unlikely that he would have stooped to such a trick. Rupert and Albemarle, who hated Penn, would fain have blamed him as "a cowardly rogue who brought all the roguish fanatic captains into the fleet."[2] But Penn declared that he had been in bed at the time, and knew nothing about the matter. The statement elicited from Brouncker, in a Parliamentary inquiry, that he had acted on his own responsibility, out of anxiety for the Duke's safety, was probably the real truth.

Rupert, though in an extremely weak state of health, had shown his usual courage and energy in the action. The official reports did not give satisfaction to his admirers. "Not a word is said of Prince Rupert, though the seamen say that none excelled him in valour and success," they complained.[3] The Prince himself wrote cheerfully to Arlington, though, as his letter confesses, he was again on the sick-list. "My greatest joy is to have ben so happie as to have bin a small instrument in this last encounter, to chastise so high an insolency as that of the Dutch. I hope, with his Majesty's good liking, to continue so, till they be brought to their duty; which work will be very easy if we linger not out the time, for which this place is not unfitt and will give a thousand excuses for delays. What this day will be resolved on in the Council I know not, being laid by the leg, by a small mistake of the Surgeon, of which I shall not trouble you. This

---

[1] Burnet Hist. of his own Times. ed. 1838. p. 148 and *note*. Campbell, II. pp. 99—100. Clowes, II. 265. Pepys Diary, 20 Oct. 1666.

[2] Pepys, 6 Nov. 1665.

[3] Dom. State Papers, June 10, 1665.

is writt abed, as you may see by the ill caracter, which I desire you not to take ill."[1]

Though the Dutch had been defeated with great loss, the war was by no means over, and it was necessary to put to sea again, as soon as refitting had been accomplished. This time the Duke of York was forced, much against his will, to stay at home. Charles at the instigation of the Queen mother, forbade his brother again to risk his life, and offered the joint command of the fleet to Rupert and Sandwich. Rupert was supposed to have a personal aversion to Sandwich, which may or may not have been well grounded.[2] Sandwich's character has been variously represented, and, whether justly or not, his honesty was certainly suspected. His own creature, Pepys, a little later confided to his diary his concern for his lord in "that cursed business of the prizes," and his vehement disapproval of the whole affair.[3] On the other hand, both Evelyn and Clarendon esteemed Sandwich highly.

But be the reason what it may, Rupert was averse to sharing the command with him, and hesitated to accept it. A conference with the King at Hampton Court at last won him over; he submitted "very cheerfully," and forthwith made ready to sail.[4]

Unfortunately Coventry, who disliked Rupert "for no other reason than for not esteeming him at the same rate he valued himself," says Clarendon, succeeded in persuading the King that the result of such a union must be disastrous. When all was ready, and Rupert's "family" on board, the King affectionately informed his cousin that he could not dispense with his society that summer. Rupert, "though wonderfully surprised, perplexed, and even broken-hearted," offered no resistance. He quietly dis-

[1] Dom. State Papers, Carl II. 124, 46. Rupert to Arlington, June 13, 1665.
[2] Ibid. 2 July, 1665.
[3] Pepys. 11 Oct., 31 Sept. 1665, 12 Jan. 1666, 23 Oct. 1667.
[4] Clarendon Life, II. 402.

embarked his retinue, and returned, "with very much trouble," to Court.[1]

Some consolation he may have found in the fact that Sandwich did nothing all the summer, and, on his return, fell under a cloud on charges of peculation. Rupert seems to have treated him with great kindness, giving him his countenance and support,[2] but the sympathies of the Parliament were evidenced by a proposal to vote to Rupert a gift of £10,000, and to Sandwich half-a-crown.[3]

His rival being thus disposed of, the command of the fleet was offered in 1666 to Rupert, in conjunction with the Duke of Albemarle. To this new colleague Rupert had no objections, and there was, happily, "great unanimity and consent between them." True, Rupert would fain have sailed in a separate ship, but, it being represented that this might cause confusion in orders, he yielded to the argument. Albemarle left much to Rupert's management, "declaring modestly, upon all occasions, that he was no seaman;" and this was doubtless very pleasing to the Prince, who loved to rule. As both Admirals were "men of great dexterity and indefatigable industry," the outlook was exceedingly favourable.[4]

The sailors welcomed Rupert gladly; and, on February 13, "several sea-captains who had served under Prince Rupert, invited him to dinner, and spoke cheerfully of going against the Dutch again together."[5] On May 23 they sailed from the Nore, with 58 ships and 9 fire-ships. Rupert was in excellent spirits and, reported his secretary, went "most cheerfully" on the expedition.[6]

Unfortunately the King and his Council committed at the outset a strategic blunder for which neither of the Admirals

[1] Clarendon Life, II. 403.
[2] Pepys. 25 Oct. 1665.
[3] Ibid. 6 Nov. 1665.
[4] Clarendon's Life, III. 69.
[5] Dom. State Papers, Feb. 16, 1666.
[6] Ibid. May 27, 1666.

was responsible. It was rumoured that a French fleet was coming from Belle Isle, under the Duke of Beaufort, and Rupert was ordered to sail with 24 ships to intercept it before it could join with the Dutch. The sailors grumbled loudly at this separation. "Nothing was to be heard among the seamen but complaints about the dividing of the fleet, and the sending away Prince Rupert."[1] But orders had to be obeyed, and Rupert sailed away, leaving Albemarle with only 56 ships to meet De Ruyter's 85.

In the Prince's absence, Albemarle fell in with the Dutch in the Downs, and the famous four days' battle began, June 1st. The wind was with Albemarle, but he had only 35 ships well in hand, the rest straggling behind. With great ingenuity he made his attack so that only a portion of the Dutch fleet could engage with him, and the fight was continued, with immense gallantry and varying fortune, from 9 a.m. till 10 p.m. On the second day the English returned in good order, but, though the Dutch were crowded and confused, Albemarle was too weak to press his advantage. Each side lost about three ships. On the third day Albemarle held off, hoping for Rupert's arrival. This did not take place till late in the afternoon, and the blame of this long delay was due to home authorities. As soon as firing was heard in the Downs, Coventry had signed an order for Rupert's recall, and sent it to Arlington, expecting that he would at once despatch it. But Arlington happened to be in bed, and his servants dared not wake him; "a tenderness not accostumed to be in the family of a secretary," says Clarendon, with just severity.[2] Consequently Rupert never received the order until he himself had heard the noise of battle, and turned back to Albemarle's aid, on his own responsibility. A contrary wind delayed him yet longer, and it was 3 p.m. on Sunday, June 3, before he reached the scene of action, where he was received by

[1] Dom. State Papers, Clifford to Arlington, June 6, 1666.
[2] Clarendon's Life, III. 72.

the sailors with shouts of joy. In the confusion of joining the fleets, the " Royal Prince " ran aground, and was burnt by the Dutch; a misfortune " which touched every heart, for she was the best ship ever built, and like a castle at sea." [1] The fight was not resumed until the next morning. All order had been lost, and both sides were in confusion. There was two hours' furious firing, and the Dutch centre passed right through the English centre, where the fight was very hot. Finally the exhausted Dutch suffered the English to draw away, and Albemarle, rallying his scattered fleet, beat an honourable retreat. [2]

Rupert's arrival had not turned defeat into victory, but it had saved Albemarle from imminent disaster. The losses of the English had been extremely heavy, but those of the Dutch had been also severe, and all the moral prestige belonged to the English, who had sustained the fight against great odds, with extraordinary gallantry. The credit was due, in a great measure, to the skill and valour of the admirals, but not a little, also, to the good discipline and seamanship of the men and officers. Dryden who celebrated the event in a long poem, while giving the admiral's their due, did not forget the rest.

> " Thousands there were, in darker fame shall dwell,
> " Whose deeds some nobler poem shall adorn,
> " But. though to me unknown, they sure fought well,
> " Whom Rupert led, and who were British born." [3]

As before, Rupert's admirers thought that "the good prince" had not received his due in the official reports of the action. His secretary, James Hayes, wrote to Arlington's secretary to expostulate. "Give me leave to suggest that,

[1] Dom. State Papers, Clifford to Arlington, June 6, 1666.
[2] Campbell. Vol. II. 107—111. Mahan's Influence of Sea Power on History, 118—126. Clowes' Royal Navy, II. 267—278.
[3] Dryden, Annus Mirabilis. 1666.

since in the Dutch gazette those lying words speak dis-honourably of the Prince, it will offer an occasion of a word or two in yours, more to his merit; in whom I did indeed discover so extraordinary courage, conduct and presence of mind in the midst of all the showers of cannon bullet, that higher I think cannot be imagined of any man that ever fought. I observed him with astonishment all that day."[1] This letter produced the following note, added to the official gazette: "The writer of this letter could not think fit to mingle in his relations any expressions of His Royal Highness's personal behaviour, because it was prepared for his own sight. But it is most certain that never any Prince, or it may be truly said, any private person, was, in an action of war, exposed to more danger from the beginning to the end of it. His conduct and presence of mind equalling his fearless courage, and carry-ing him to change his ship three times, setting up his Royal standard in each of them, to animate his own men and brave the enemy."[2] For this tribute Hayes returned grateful thanks. "You have done right to a brave Prince, whose worth will endure praise, though I find his ears are too modest to hear his own."[3]

Rupert was far more engaged with his smouldering wrath against the Commissioners of the Navy, than in con-sidering what the gazette did, or did not say of himself. A month earlier he had written to the King that "unless some course" were taken with the victualler—viz. Pepys—the whole fleet would be ruined.[4] Now, when the fleet came in to refit, the first thing he did on meeting the King, was to reiterate his complaints. "Which," wrote Pepys, "I am troubled at, and do fear may in violence break out upon this office some time or other, and we shall

<hr>

[1] Dom. State Papers. Carl II. 159. f. 3. Hayes, 15 June, 1666.
[2] Ibid. Vol. 159. 3 (1).
[3] Ibid. 159. 55. Hayes, June 21, 1666.
[4] Ibid. Carl II. 156. 100. 22 May, 1666.

not be able to carry on the business."[1] But Rupert's time on shore was short, and the storm was deferred.

By July 22 the fleet was again at sea. Severely as it had suffered, the refitting had been conducted with remarkable celerity, and the King and the Duke of York themselves showed such an active interest in the preparations, that Rupert swore that they were the best officers in the navy. The fleet went out "in very good heart," Rupert's ship boasting "a dancing-master and two men who feign themselves mad and make very good sport to a bag-pipe."[2] Unluckily, the very day after putting to sea, came a violent thunderstorm, which damaged the ships so severely that the Prince declared himself more afraid of the weather than of the enemy.

On July 25 they fell in with the Dutch fleet, commanded by Tromp and De Ruyter, off the North Foreland. The Dutch line was uneven, the van and centre crowded; the English line presented a remarkable regularity. The fight began at 10 a.m., and Tromp immediately engaged the English rear, carried it away with him, out of sight, and was eventually shattered by it. This independent action on the part of his subordinate, greatly embarrassed De Ruyter. His van was speedily over-matched, and at 4 p.m. his centre gave way. At night the English renewed the attack in a desultory fashion, and Rupert appears to have run some danger, for he afterwards promoted a gunner who had saved his life at the risk of his own.[3]

On the day following, the Prince added insult to injury by sending his little yacht "Fan-Fan," which had been built the week before, to attack De Ruyter. Rowing under the great ship, the little vessel plied her valiantly with her two small guns. This game continued for an hour, to the intense amusement of the English, and the indignation of

---

[1] Pepys. June 20, 1666.

[2] Dom. State Papers, Clifford to Arlington, July 5, 1666.

[3] Ibid. Geo. Hillson, Gunner of Ruby, to Pepys, Nov. 30, 1666.

the Dutch, who could not bring their guns to bear on the yacht, by reason of her nearness to them. At last they contrived to hit her, and she was forced to retreat to the protection of her own fleet.[1] De Ruyter then effected a masterly retreat, his enemies fearing to follow on account of his proximity to his own shores.

The English had won a brilliant victory with very little loss—only one ship and two or three fire-ships at most. Of the Dutch fleet at least twenty ships had perished, and it was quite unable to renew the fight. The coast of Holland was now exposed to a triumphant enemy, and a renegade Dutchman, Laurens van Heemskerk, offered to guide the English to the islands of Vlieland and Ter Schelling, where lay many merchant vessels and all kinds of stores. The enterprise was entrusted to Robert Holmes, with orders to destroy all that he found, and to carry away no booty. In the harbour he discovered 170 merchant-men and two men-of-war, and he did his work so thoroughly that the affair was called in England, "Sir Robert Holmes, his Bonfire."[2]

Van Heemskerk afterwards fell into great poverty in England, and was evicted from his house for non-payment of rent; upon which he petitioned the King for some reward for his services, stating that, but for the great goodness of Prince Rupert, his wife and children must inevitably have starved.[3]

During August the fleet lingered about Sole Bay, hoping that wrath for the burning of their harbour would bring the Dutch out again. But Rupert laid Albemarle a bet of "five pieces" that they would not come, and won his money.[4] The sailors, inspired by their late success, were anxious for further action, and would fain have attacked

---

[1] Dom. State Papers. Clifford to Arlington, July 27, 1666.
[2] Dom. State Papers. Rupert to King, Aug. 11, 1666. Clowes, II. 278—285. Mahan, 131. Campbell, 112—117. Clarendon Life, III. 79.
[3] D. S. P. 1670. Carl II. 281 a 173.
[4] Ibid. Clifford to Arlington, Aug. 16, 1666.

the East India fleet at Bergen; but want of provisions held the commanders back. Rupert wrote furiously to the King that his men were all sick for want of food; the beer was bad, each barrel was short of the proper quantity, and all his remonstrances only produced from Pepys accounts of things already sent.[1] Fearing the weather, he came into the Downs, and there took a French vessel. The French Vice-Admiral on board at once demanded to be taken to Rupert, whom he knew. The Prince treated him "as a gallant person ought to be," and restored to him all his personal possessions.[2] On board the same vessel was found the engineer, La Roche, with whom Arthur Trevor had battled in earlier days at Oxford. Rupert had, however, pardoned, or forgotten, his contumacy, and released him in consideration of the services he had formerly rendered in England.[3] Finally, on October 2nd, the fleet anchored in the Thames, and immediately afterwards burst the storm which Pepys had long expected.

It is indisputable, even on Pepys' own showing, that peculation, bribery, and corruption were the causes of the neglect from which the fleet had suffered. The Naval Commissioners, in order to make their own profit, cheated and starved the sailors; they falsified the quantities of food that they sent, and what they delivered was bad. Rupert had just cause for his wrath, and he did not hesitate to express it. Five days after the return of the fleet, Pepys and his colleagues were called upon to answer for their conduct. They endeavoured very ingeniously to defend themselves by transferring the blame to the Prince. Thus Pepys describes the interview. "Anon we were called into the green room, where were the King, Duke of York, Prince Rupert, Lord Chancellor, Lord Treasurer, Duke of Albe-

---

[1] Dom. State Papers, Rupert to King, Aug. 27, Sept 24, 1666.

[2] Clarendon's Life, III. 83.

[3] Dom. State Papers, 19 Sept. 1666, 19 and 20 Oct. 1666. Carl II. 175. f. 111, 112.

marle, and Sirs G. Carteret, W. Coventry, Morrice. Nobody beginning, I did, and made, as I thought, a good speech, laying open the ill state of the Navy, by the greatness of the debt, greatness of the work to do against next year, the time and materials it would take, and our own incapacity through a total want of money. I had no sooner done, but Prince Rupert rose up in a great heat, and told the King that, whatever the gentleman said, he had brought home his fleet in as good a condition as ever any fleet was brought home; that twenty boats would be as many as the fleet would want, and that all the anchors and cables left in the storm might be taken up again ... I therefore did only answer that I was sorry for His Highness's offence, but what I said was the report I had received. He muttered and repeated what he had said, and, after a long silence, no one, not so much as the Duke of Albemarle, seconding the Prince, we withdrew. I was not a little troubled at this passage, and the more, when speaking with Jack Fenn about it, he told me that the Prince will now be asking who this Pepys is, and will find him to be a creature of My lord Sandwich, and that this was therefore done only to disparage him." [1]

In consequence of this dispute, Batten was sent down to view the fleet. He had been Rupert's enemy of old, and he now made a very unfavourable report, which he intended to present to the Duke of York. To this end he obtained an audience, but great was his dismay when he found Rupert in the company of his cousin. "It was pretty to see," says Pepys, with malicious glee, "how, when he found the Prince there, he did not speak out one word, though the meeting was of his asking, and for nothing else. And when I asked him, he told me that he knew the Prince too well to anger him, and that he was afraid to do it." [2]

[1] Pepys, Oct. 7, 1666.
[2] Ibid. Oct. 10, 1666.

But the King showed himself apathetic in this matter; it was doubtless true that the Commissioners lacked funds, and the charges against them were not, just then, further pressed. Probably the plague and the great fire of London threw all other affairs temporarily into the shade. The Prince was with the fleet when informed of the great fire, and is said to have merely remarked that, "Now Shipton's prophecy was out,"[1]—the burning of London having been one of the events foretold by the reputed prophetess, Mother Shipton. Evidently Rupert had ceased to be surprised, whatever might happen.

In January 1667 he was again very ill. The old wound in his head broke out afresh, and his life was despaired of; but in February he consented to an operation, which gave him some relief and enabled him to sleep. A second operation brought him fairly to convalescence, and after this he "diverted himself in his workhouse," where, amongst other curious things, he made instruments with which the surgeons were able to dress his wound quickly and easily.[2] Owing partly to this illness and partly to the King's poverty and home policy, the fleet was neglected throughout the whole year—only two small squadrons were fitted out; and in May, the Dutch took an ample revenge by entering the Medway, and burning the country near Felixstowe.

Rupert had, before this, urged the fortification of Harwich and Sheerness; and the King, now roused from his nonchalance, sent him to superintend the fortification of these and other places, which would secure the Medway from invasion,—and the Prince also had command of all the troops quartered in these places.[3] With his usual care for his subordinates, he demanded the deferred pay of his captains, and attended a Council meeting in order to press the

[1] Pepys, 20 Oct. 1666.
[2] Dom. State Papers, Feb. 21, 1667.
[3] Ibid. June 13, July 6, Nov. 23, 1667.

matter.[1] The empty condition of the treasury occasioned a quarrel with Arlington, and the report ran that Rupert had, in Council, dealt Arlington a box on the ear, which had knocked off his hat and wig.[2] This was an exaggeration, but Rupert was always on bad terms with the cabal of which Arlington was a member. The known integrity of the Prince made him very popular with the nation at large, and he was requested by Parliament to draw up a report on the causes of the late naval disasters. Few things could have pleased him better than such an opportunity of airing his grievances. He drew up a long narrative, beginning with the separation of the fleet in June 1666, and going on to the "horrible neglects" of the overseers, workmen, and above all, the victuallers of the navy. "The next miscarriage I shall mention was the intolerable neglect in supplying provisions during the whole summer expedition, notwithstanding the extraordinary and frequent importunity of our letters ... I remember also we did then complain that great quantities of wood-bound casks were staved, and much of the provisions proved defective; also that the gauge of the beer barrels was 20 gallons in a butt short of what it ought to be, and the bills of credit came with the pursers of the fleet, instead of provisions. This want of provisions did manifestly tend to the extraordinary prejudice of his Majesty's service in that whole summer, but most especially after the victory obtained in July fight, when we had carried the fleet on the enemy's coast, and lay there, before the Vlie Island, in the way of all their merchant ships. We were enforced, merely for want of provisions, to quit out to Sole Bay."[3] The Parliament, upon receipt of this report, appointed a committee to inquire into the neglect mentioned, and voted thanks to Rupert and Albemarle for their conduct of the war.

[1] Dom. State Papers, July 25, 1668.
[2] Ibid. Sept. 12, 1668.
[3] Prince Rupert's Narrative, see Warb. III. p. 480.

The manning of the fleet caused nearly as much discussion as did the victualling, and about this period Rupert and James of York were by no means of one mind concerning it. Rupert dismissed James's men as cowards, and James rejected Rupert's "stout men" as drunkards. "If they will turn out every man that will be drunk, they must turn out all the commanders in the fleet," cried the exasperated Prince. "What is the matter if a man be drunk, so, when he comes to fight, he do his work?"[1] But the dispute ran high; James declared he "knew not how" Colonel Legge's son had been made a captain after a single voyage, and, though he liked Colonel Legge well, he insisted that the boy must serve a longer apprenticeship. "I will ask the King to let me be that I am—Admiral!" he declared wrathfully, when Rupert combated his decisions.[2] The King listened to all these disputes with his usual lazy good nature. "If you intend to man the fleet without being cheated by the captains and pursers, you may go to bed and never have it manned at all," he said.[3] But James had his way in so far that Sir William Penn was appointed to command the summer fleet, in spite of Rupert's aversion to him. "I do pity Sir William Penn," quoth Pepys, naively.[4]

Owing to the representations of Rupert "and other mad, silly people," as Pepys phrased it,[5] no large fleet was fitted out in 1668; and, so far as the navy was concerned, no events occurred until 1672, when the second Dutch war broke out.

This war was as unpopular as the first had been popular. In the interval between them Charles II had made the secret Treaty of Dover with Louis XIV, and he now

---

[1] Pepys, Jan. 2, 1668.
[2] Pepys, Jan. 28, 1668.
[3] Ibid. Mar. 18, 1668.
[4] Ibid. Mar. 20, 1668.
[5] Ibid. May 28, 1668. Campbell, II. 121—122.

entered into this war solely to assist Louis' ambition. Therefore instead of the English opposing the Dutch and French, as formerly, the French and English were now allied against the Dutch. Rupert and Ormonde vigorously opposed the declaration of war, and perhaps it was on account of his dislike to the whole business that the Prince remained at home, while the Duke of York took command of the fleet. Nevertheless Rupert was put in command of all naval affairs on shore, and he resolved that the fleet should not suffer as it had before done, for the want of all necessary supplies.

His first act in his new capacity was to summon Pepys, and his colleagues to give an exact list of the fleet, the station and condition of each ship, and an account, "particular, not general," of all their stores, great and small. [1] He diligently superintended the fortification of the coast, inspected the regiments there stationed, and kept a watchful eye on the necessities of the fleet. But, in spite of this efficient assistance on shore, James accomplished nothing of moment, and the battle of Southwold Bay, fought May 28, left the honours to the Dutch, though both sides claimed the victory.

Before the next campaign, the Test Act had been passed, by which Roman Catholics were prevented from holding any office under the Crown. This forced the Duke of York to resign his command of the fleet, and Rupert was appointed to take his place.

Rupert's position was a difficult one. He detested the secret policy of Charles, and consequently the French, who were his allies. With the Cabal, as the home Ministry was then called, he was also at enmity. The Ministers, therefore, in order to make him as inefficient as possible, manned the fleet with adherents of the Duke of York, who were told—though falsely—that detracting from the Prince

[1] Dom. State Papers, May 4, 1672.

would please the Duke. Therefore "they crossed him in all that they could, and complained of all that he did." In short, Rupert had to contend with intrigues at home, limitation of his proper powers, want of men, ammunition and provisions, the deceit of the Naval Commissioners, insubordination among his officers, and defection of his allies. [1]

As his second in command, he begged to have Holmes, with whom his connection had been so long and intimate. Thanks to the favour of both Rupert and the Duke of York, Holmes had risen high in the navy, and was now an Admiral, and Governor of Sandown Castle, in the Isle of Wight. His promotion seems to have excited some jealousy, and Marvell described him bitterly, as "First an Irish livery boy, then a highwayman, (a pirate would be nearer the mark,) now Bashaw of the Isle of Wight, the cursed beginner of the two Dutch wars." [2] The last sentence alludes to Holmes's exploits in Africa in 1664, and his attack on the Smyrna fleet in 1672, which were the immediate causes of the wars of 1665 and 1672 respectively. But in both cases Holmes only obeyed orders for which he was not responsible. Pepys hinted darkly, concerning him, that "a cat will be a cat still," [3] but then Pepys had private reasons for disliking him. He was a good soldier, and an experienced sailor, and the Cabal Ministry had no better reason for refusing to let him go with Rupert than the fact that he was the Prince's friend. Instead of Holmes they forced Rupert to take Sir Edward Spragge, with whom he was not, then, on good terms. [4]

The long delay in setting out the fleet tempted the Dutch to repeat their descent upon the Medway, and this

---

[1] Campbell, II. 246. Letters to Williamson, I. p. 195.
[2] Andrew Marvell. Seasonable Argument, 1677. Letters to Williamson. II. 63, *note*.
[3] Pepys, 24 Jan. 1666.
[4] Campbell, II. 149. Clowes, Vol. II. 309—310.

they would undoubtedly have done, but for the personal energy of the Prince. Collecting together a few ships, he "made a demonstration", and sailed through the Channel, to the great surprise of the Dutch, who immediately retired. [1]

By May 20th the English fleet was ready to sail, and it was at once joined by the French, under Admiral D'Estrées. About a week later they fell in with the Dutch off Schoneveldt. Rupert sent a few vessels forward to draw out the enemy from their harbour, but De Ruyter came upon them so unexpectedly that they crowded back in confusion, each falling to the squadron nearest to her. The place was narrow, the wind for the Dutch, and some of the officers advised retreat. "But," said the English proudly," our Admiral never knew what it was to go back," [2] and Rupert insisted on fighting then and there. When De Ruyter attacked, the line of the allies was not ready, and the result was an indecisive battle, attended with great loss of life. [3] In his official report, the Prince acknowledged that all had done their best:—"All the officers and seamen generally behaved themselves very well, of which I shall send the particulars when I am better informed; in my squadron, more especially Captain Legge, Sir John Holmes, Captain Welwang, Sir Roger Strickland and Sir William Reeves. Sir Edward Spragge also, on his side, maintained the fight with so much courage and resolution, and their whole body gave way to such a degree, that, had it not been for fear of the shoals, we had driven them into their harbours. The case being thus, I judged it fit to stand off a little, and anchor where now I ride. I hope his Majesty will be satisfied, that, considering the place we engaged in, and the shoals, there was as much done as could be expected; and thus I leave it to His Majesty's

1 Campbell, II. 149. Clowes, II. 310.
2 Hatton Correspondence, I. p. 105. May 20, 1673.
3 Clowes, II. 311—315.

favourable construction, to whom I wish many happy years to come, this being his birthday."[1]

The Dutch were at home, and it was easy for them to refit, but the situation of the allies was more critical. Rupert made what preparations he could, and sat up the whole night of June 3rd, expecting an attack. But the carelessness of Spragge nullified this vigilance. Early on the morning of July 4th, Spragge came on board the Admiral. Rupert "said little", but told him to prepare for battle. Nevertheless he delayed his departure so long that De Ruyter came out before he had reached his own ship, and the whole of the Blue Squadron had to await his return.[2] The Red and White Squadrons weighed anchor very quickly; Rupert, in his impatience cut his cable, and some others followed his example.

But this second battle was as indecisive as the first. D'Estrées permitted the Dutch Admiral Banckert to hold him in check, and gave no effective aid. Rupert engaged with De Ruyter and "performed wonders," though his ship took in so much water that he was unable to use his lower tier of guns. Spragge opposed himself to Tromp. The loss of men was about equal on both sides, and no ships were lost at all. The allies pursued the Dutch from 10 p.m. to 6 a.m.; but they had gained no serious advantage, and were obliged to turn home to refit.[3]

Rupert came home in an exceedingly bad temper. "There goes a story about town that the Prince, at his first coming, when the Commissioners of the Navy came to wait upon him, fell into such a passion against them that he had like to have made use of his cane upon some of them. Certain it is that he is very angry with them for not having taken care to supply the fleet with neces-

---

[1] Campbell, II. 246. Memoir of Prince Rupert, p. 58.

[2] Hist. MSS. Commission, Rept. 15. Vol. III. pp. 9—13. Journal of Sir Edward Spragge, May 1673. Dartmouth MSS. Vol. III.

[3] Campbell, II. 151—153. Clowes, II. 314—315.

saries," [1] says one letter.   Another, dated June 13, shows that the King too came in for a share of his cousin's indignation : "The Prince, they say, storms exceedingly at the want of provision they had, and declares he shall never thrive at sea till some are hanged at land.   The King said merrily, the day before he went to see him, that he must expect a chiding, but he had sweetened him by letter all he could." [2] Rupert, however, refused absolutely to return to the fleet, unless he were given a new Commission, freed from all vexatious restrictions.   This was accordingly done, and July 9th, he was made General on sea and land, with power to make truce and grant articles; and he held the post of First Lord of the Admiralty from this date till May 1679.

It was now proposed to throw a land force into Holland, and the command of the army was given to Schomberg, a German soldier of fortune.   Unluckily, while the ships were refitting at Portsmouth, Schomberg irrevocably offended his chief, by ordering the "Greyhound" frigate to carry a flag on her main-top.   This order he gave that she might be the more easily distinguishable, but she had in reality no right to carry any such colours, and Rupert, when he beheld her coming through the fleet, was transfixed with amazement.   His peremptory orders for the hauling down of the flag being disregarded, he fired on it; whereupon it was taken down, and the Captain came on board the Admiral to explain that he had acted by Schomberg's direction.   Rupert arrested him for insolent language, but soon pardoned and released him.   Schomberg he would not forgive, and in revenge, as that General declared, he ordered him and his forces to Yarmouth, where they lay idle all the summer.   The feud raged for some

[1] Camden. Society. New Series. Letters to Sir Joseph Williamson, Vol. I. p. 48. May 6, 1673.
[2] Ibid. I. 39, June 13, 1673.

time, and Schomberg sent on a challenge to Rupert, but the duel was prevented by the King.[1]

A quarrel was also reported to have occurred between Rupert and the Duke of York, in which swords had been drawn, the Duke calling the Prince "Coward," and the Prince retorting with the epithet of "Traitor."[2] Another rumour, probably better grounded, was that D'Estrées would not sail with Rupert, and had refused to furl his flag[3] when the Prince came on board him. This was mere gossip, but it had a foundation, for the two Admirals were on very bad terms—a fact which increased Rupert's popularity at home, for the French were detested of the people, and the Prince was now "the only hero in their thoughts."[4]

At the beginning of August the allies put to sea, and on the 11th they met the Dutch off the Texel. The French were in the van, Rupert commanded the centre, Spragge the rear. The three squadrons engaged, as before, with Banckert, De Ruyter, and Tromp respectively. Rupert drew off, trying to lead De Ruyter from the coast. Spragge deliberately waited for Tromp, whom he had promised the King to take dead or alive, and, in the fierce personal contest that followed, lost his own life. D'Estrées simply allowed Banckert to run right through his squadron, and held off from the fight. Banckert was thus left free to join De Ruyter against Rupert, who, completely deserted by his van and rear, had to contend against fearful odds.[5]

"Does your Highness see the French yonder?" asked Captain Howard, standing at his side.

"Ay—Zounds, do I!" cried Rupert passionately.[6] The Dutch also noted D'Estrées' treacherous conduct. "The

<hr>

[1] Letters to Williamson, Vol. I. pp. 121, 124, 145, July 21, Aug. 4, Aug. 6, 1673.

[2] Hist. MSS. Com. Rept. 12. Fleming MSS. p.102, 22 July, 1673.

[3] Hatton Correspondence, Vol. I. p. 106.

[4] Letters to Williamson, I. p. 63.

[5] Campbell, II. 157—159. Clowes, II. 316—317.

[6] Letters to Williamson, Vol. I. p. 174. Aug. 18, 1673.

French have hired the English to fight for them, and have come to see them earn their wages," [1] was the saying passed amongst them. But one gallant Frenchman, at least, blushed for his countrymen. The Vice-Admiral, De Martel, putting himself into Rupert's squadron, fought valiantly at his side; on which, it was said, in bitter jest, that D'Estrées threatened to hang him "for venturing the King's ship." [2] Finally Rupert extricated himself and ran down to the rear, De Ruyter withdrawing about 7 p.m. The result of the battle was a victory for the Dutch, who thus opened their blockaded ports, and saved their coast from a second assault.

Possibly the French doubted the good faith of the English, and therefore acted thus strangely; but, be the motive for their conduct what it may, feeling ran high against them. Rupert, with difficulty prevented his own sailors from insulting D'Estrées when he came on board his ship, [3] and in England men spoke only of the French traitors.

Rupert's return was eagerly desired, and it was reported that he came back "very angry and raging and to do some extraordinary thing." He was in the zenith of his popularity, and was received "with the greatest dearness possible," both by King and people. [4] But it was no part of the King's policy to quarrel with the French, and he tried to smooth over the affair, saying that it was not foul play, but "a great miscarriage." [5] Rupert, however, would not hold his tongue, and wherever he went, he fiercely blamed D'Estrées, even stating plainly to the French Ambassador, his opinion of his countryman's conduct. [6] At the same time he was so scrupulously exact in his

[1] Campbell, II. 159.

[2] Letters to Williamson, Vol. II. p. 9. Sept. 5, 1673.

[3] Ibid. Vol. I. p. 185.

[4] Ibid. I. pp. 183, 191. Aug. 25, 1673.

[5] Ibid. II. p. 1.

[6] Ibid. I. p. 191. Aug. 29, 1673.

assertions that he would not publish his narrative of the battle, until he could find out what had been the exact way of the wind when he was off Camperdown.[1]

D'Estrées retorted with the declaration that Rupert, owing to his aversion to the war, had not pushed the first battle so far as he could have done.[2] But, said a contemporary, "it is as impossible to make any Englishman suspect the Prince's courage, as to persuade him that the French have any, at sea."[3] De Martel boldly seconded Rupert, and wrote to his own government: "If Count D' Estrées would have fallen with a fair wind upon De Ruyter and Banckert at their first engaging, when in numbers they much exceeded the Prince, they must, of necessity have been enclosed between His Highness and Count D' Estrées; and so the enemy would have been entirely defeated."[4] For this unwelcome candour he was sent to the Bastille, upon which Rupert swore furiously that Charles ought to defend him, by force of arms if necessary.[5] And the more the Prince raged and stormed, so much the more was he adored by the people, who admired him "to such a degree," said a cynical observer, "that it would be impossible for him to do anything amiss, so long as he opposes the French, or as they think he does."[6]

Ever since the Restoration he had been exceedingly popular, and as early as 1666 there had been rumours of an abortive plot to place him on the throne. The statement of the witness who revealed it, is as follows: "William Hopkins doth depose that he heard Edward Dolphin of Camphill, near Birmingham, say these words, or to that purpose, viz.: ' The Papists should be uppermost for a time...'

[1] Letters to Williamson, II. 13. Sept. 5, 1673.
[2] Clowes, II. 520—322. Campbell, II. 152. Hist. MSS. Com. Rpt. 12. Fleming MSS. p. 103.
[3] Hatton Correspondence, Vol. I. p. 114.
[4] Ibid. Vol. II. p. 1, *note*.
[5] Ibid. II. 20, Sept. 19, 1673.
[6] Ibid. I. p. 194, Aug. 29, 1673.

and said he could tell me more, for he cared not if he were hanged so he could serve the country. Then, speaking low, he said, (as I suppose,) 'The King and the Duke of York are Papists, and the King hath been at Mass underground within this week or fortnight, and I can prove it.' And when I contradicted him, he said the King's wife was a Papist, and that a royal G. should rule over us. And when I demanded if he meant not George Monck, he replied it was Prince Rupert he meant. Then I said he was no G., so he answered G. stood for a German, and Prince Rupert was a German Prince, and declared he meant Prince Rupert should be above the King, and said all should be willing to it, and venture lives and fortunes to vindicate the cause of the said Prince Rupert."[1] The whole plot probably existed only in the ravings of a lunatic, but insignificant though it is in itself, it is an indication of the country's feeling.

That Rupert would have listened for a moment to any disloyal scheme is, of course, incredible. Indeed the only time, after the Restoration, that he played any part in politics was in this year of 1673, when he was forced into the position of popular leader, and carried away by his wrath against the French. Feeling against "Popery" was, just then, keen, the nation having been stirred by the Duke of York's open adhesion to the Roman Church, and his marriage with a Roman bride, believed by the ignorant, to be the Pope's own granddaughter. "What will the Prince say?" was the popular cry, on all occasions;[2] and the position contrasts oddly with the attitude of the populace towards Rupert in the Civil War. Then he was "atheistical, popish, heathenish, tyrannical, bloodthirsty;" now the country turned to him as a true patriot, the staunch upholder of the Anglican Church, the defender of the rights of Parliament.

Shaftesbury, the prime mover of all the agitation against

---

[1] Dom. State Papers. Carl. II. 172. 13.
[2] Letters to Williamson, Vol. I. p. 143, Aug. 4, 1673.

James, hastened to ally himself with the Prince, and together they formed an anti-French party, which stirred up the Commons against the French alliance. "Prince Rupert and he are observed to converse much together, and are very great, and indeed I see His Highness's coach often at the door. They are looked to be the great Parliament men and for the interests of old England."[1]

The result of all this was, naturally, a coolness between Rupert and the King, but it was not of long duration. The Prince was really too loyal to suffer his connection with the country party to carry him to any great lengths, and it soon ceased altogether.[2] In the iniquitous Popish Plot he had no share, nor would he countenance the attempts to exclude James from the succession in favour of Monmouth. True he lent Monmouth his house at Rhenen, when that unsuccessful schemer had been forced to retire abroad, but the loan was entirely a private matter, and quite apart from politics.[3] Rupert had no liking for intrigues, and he held himself equally aloof from those of Shaftesbury, and those of the Cabal. To the members of the Cabal he was always hostile, which, says Campbell, was no wonder, seeing that they were "persons of the utmost art," and the Prince was "one of the plainest men that could be."[4] Yet, in spite of his objections to the King's ministers, Rupert always retained the King's friendship, steering his way amongst factions and intrigues so tactfully, and yet so honestly, that he was beloved and respected by all parties.[5]

---

[1] Letters to Williamson, Vol. II. p. 21, Sept. 19, 1673.
[2] Campbell, II. p. 247.
[3] Hist. MSS. Com. Rept. 12. Fleming MSS. p. 162.
[4] Campbell, II. p. 246.
[5] Ibid. II. 245. Memoir of Prince Rupert, Preface.

CHAPTER XIX

OF Rupert's later life in England, apart from his naval
career, there is not much to tell. In the dissolute court
of the Restoration there was no place for Rupert of the Rhine.
He represented the older Cavaliers. He had stood side by
side and fought on many a field with the fathers of the
men who adorned the Court of Charles II; but with the
sons, the children of the exiles, he could have no sympathy.
Much has been said and written contrasting those fathers
and sons, the men who died for Charles I, and the men
who lived with Charles II. But no contrast is stronger
than that of the two Kings themselves,—of the grave, dig-
nified, blundering, narrow, but ever earnest martyr-king,
with the dissolute, easy-going, but always shrewd, merry
monarch.

The Cavaliers of the Civil War were, as we have seen,
by no means free from faults and follies; but the real difference between them and their successors lay less in individual character than in ideal. In the first half of the
seventeenth century religious feeling had been strong in all
classes, and the tone of morality high. Devotion to duty
was strongly inculcated, and men believed it their duty to
sacrifice themselves for their King, or for their opinions as
the case might be. That most of the Cavaliers were willing to offer their sacrifices in their own way only, and
that many were desirous of gaining rewards for their services may be granted; but the fact remains that they did

PRINCE RUPERT.

From the Engraving in the British Museum after the Portrait by Sir Peter Lely.

To face page 332.

sacrifice themselves, and clung loyally to their Sovereign when all hope of reward was passed.

In 1660 the ideal of life was changed, or rather all ideal had perished, and the Courtiers imitated their master in his attempt to lounge through life with as much pleasure and as little inconvenience to themselves as possible. The relaxation of all moral restraint was due, in a great measure, to the inevitable reaction from Puritan rigidity and hypocrisy; but it was due still more to the years of exile, during which the Royalists had been "strangely tossed about on the fickle waves of fortune."[1] The Civil War had been a check on all education; it had released boys from school and students from college to throw them, at an early age, into the perils and temptations of a camp. At the same time, it had deprived ᴣm of the care and guidance of parents and guardians. Later, these boys, grown men before their time, had led a precarious existence on the Continent, living how and where they could, and snatching consolation for sorrow and privation in such illicit pleasures as came in their way. This life had ruined Charles II, and it is not wonderful that it ruined other men.

Rupert had been young too in those days,—he was only eight years Charles's senior, but the precarious life had not affected him in the same way. He had never drifted; it was not in his nature to drift, and his own strength and earnestness had kept him ever hard at work, with some definite end before him. Yet it cannot be denied that his character had suffered. The edge of it was, as it were, blunted. His ideals had perished in the stress of toil and anxiety. His chivalry had given place to common-sense. His hopefulness was gone, and his youthful eagerness had been replaced by a coldly sardonic view of life. "Blessed are those who expect nothing" was Rupert's motto now.

In all things he had grown coarser, and yet his standard

---

[1] Memoir of Prince Rupert, p. 75.

of life remained, for those times, high. He had imbibed
in his youth, says an admiring contemporary, "such beautiful ideas of virtue that he hath ever since esteemed it,
notwithstanding the contempt the world hath put upon it;
nor could he abhor the debaucheries of the age as he
doth, had not his prejudice against it been of long duration.
Such virtue is not formed in a day, and it is to his education that he owes the glory of a life so noble and so
christian." [1] Rupert had in truth too much self-respect, it
may be too much religion, to sink to the depths to which
Charles's court was sunk, and he held himself aloof with
lofty disdain. "Mon cousin", as the mocking courtiers
called him, in imitation of the King, was at once the object
of their fear and of their merriment. So great was their
terror of him that, mock though they might behind his
back, not one of them dared, as they owned, make him
the object of open satire, from which the King and the
Duke of York did not escape.

The royal brothers themselves stood in some awe of
their cousin. Sandwich told Pepys that he had heard
James laugh at Rupert in his absence, [2] but in his cousin's
presence James usually behaved to him with due respect.
As for the King, he confessed, in 1664, that he dared not
send for Sandwich to Court, lest his coming should offend
Rupert. [3] Occasionally there were quarrels and coolnesses
between the cousins, for Rupert was still sometimes irri-
table; yet he always retained the friendship of both Charles
and James. His position was somewhat anomalous, especially after the popular party had raised the no-Popery cry,
and looked to him as their natural head. Yet he steered
through that difficult course with satisfaction to all parties,
and infinite credit to himself. He showed, says one of his
admirers, "temperance and moderation in committing

[1] Lansdowne MSS. 817. fols. 157—168. British Museum.
[2] Pepys, 23 June, 1665.
[3] Ibid. 14 July, 1664.

nothing towards the present differences amongst us, nor adding any fuel to those unhappy heats, which he, supposing too high already, endeavoured rather to quench than to increase."[1]

He was not infrequently to be found in the King's company, notwithstanding his aversion to the court. In 1663, he accompanied Charles on a progress through the western counties. On the King's marriage he went with him to meet the bride at Dover; and, on this occasion, he scandalised the Portuguese by his rudeness. The Portuguese Ambassador took precedence of the Prince, whereupon Rupert took him by the shoulders and quietly put him out of the way. The King, much shocked, remonstrated with his cousin, and induced him to yield place.[2] In March 1669 Rupert was driving with the King on the occasion when the royal coach was upset in Holborn, and, as Pepys said, "the King all dirty, but no hurt."[3] Rupert was also of the party that received Henrietta of Orleans on her one brief visit to England in 1670; he is frequently mentioned as dining with the Royal family; and when the Prince of Tuscany visited England incognito, the Queen Mother decided that, according to etiquette, his first visit was due to Rupert.[4] Pepys tells how he went to see a tennis-match between Rupert and Captain Cook on one side, and May and Chichely on the other. The King was present as a spectator, and, says the diarist, "It seems they are the best players at tennis in this nation."[5] A trivial, yet characteristic anecdote is told by Coke. He was walking in the Mall with the King, when they were overtaken by Prince Rupert. "The King told the Prince how he had shot a duck, and which dog fetched it, and

<hr>

[1] Memoir of Prince Rupert, Preface.
[2] Strickland. Queens of England, VIII. pp. 303—304.
[3] Pepys, 8 Mar. 1669.
[4] D. S. P. Feb. 1669.
[5] Pepys, 2 Sept. 1667.

so they walked on, till the King came to St. James's House,
and there the King said to the Prince: 'Let's go and see
Cambridge and Kendal!'—the Duke of York's two sons,
who then lay a dying." [1]

One of Rupert's principal cares was the relief of the
distressed Cavaliers, who looked to him as their supporter
and representative. Charles II has often been blamed for
not relieving the wants of so many of those who had
suffered for his father. Probably he was callous to suffering which he did not directly witness, but it must be
confessed that his position was a hard one. He could
dispose of very little money, and he was much bound to
the Presbyterians who had restored him to the throne.
His pledges to them prevented him from upsetting much
of the existing arrangements, and consequently hampered
him in the relief of the Royalists. Such of these as were
in want turned to Rupert, sure of a hearing and of such
aid as he could give, whether it were in money, or in
intercession with the King. The State papers are full of
their petitions, which generally refer to Rupert as their
guarantor; indeed his certificate seems to have been regarded as the necessary hall-mark of their authenticity. In
1660 he came to the defence of 142 creditors of the late
King; [2] and we find him pleading for a certain Cary Heydon,
and other people, at the commission for indigent officers. [3]
One very striking instance of his justice and good memory
occurred just before his death. A certain member of
Parliament, named Speke, had been accused of conspiring
for Monmouth against the Duke of York, and was summoned
before the Council Chamber. He defended himself ably,
and quoted his former services to Charles I. Rupert suddenly
stood up, told the King that it was all true, "and added
one circumstance which Mr. Speke had thought it not

<hr>

[1] Knight's London, Vol. II. p. 374.
[2] Dom. State Papers, Nov. 1660.
[3] Ibid. Nov. 1668.

handsome to mention," namely, that when he, Rupert, had been in great want of money for the King's service, Speke had sent him "1,000 pieces"; and had been so far from asking repayment, that the Prince had neither seen nor heard of him from that day to this. The accusation was promptly dismissed; and on the next day Rupert invited Speke to dinner, when he "entertained him in the most obliging manner."[1]

In December 1662 Rupert became one of the first Fellows of the Royal Society, of which the King was also a member,[2] and their common interest in science formed an additional bond of union between the cousins. Rupert had both a forge and a laboratory in which he himself worked with great zeal. The King, with his favourite Buckingham, was wont to lounge in and sit on a stool, watching his energetic cousin, with keen interest. Sometimes the Prince would weary of their chatter, and he had a short and effectual way of ridding himself of them. He would coolly throw something on to the fire which exhaled such fearful fumes that the King and courtiers would rush out half-choked, vowing in mock fury that they would never again enter the "alchemist's hell."[3]

Rupert's inventions were many, and were connected chiefly with the improvement of weapons and materials of war. He made an improved lock for fire-arms; increased the power of gunpowder ten times; invented a kind of revolver; a method of making hail-shot; a means of melting black-lead like a metal; a substance composed of copper and zinc, and called "Prince's metal" to this day; and a screw which facilitated the taking of observations with a quadrant at sea. In 1671 he took out a patent "for converting edge-tools forged in soft iron, after forged; and for converting iron wire, and softening all cast or melted iron, so that

---

[1] Warburton, III. pp. 508—510.
[2] Campbell, II. 244.
[3] Treskow. Prinz Ruprecht, 210—211.

it can be wrought and filed like forged iron."[1] He also
had a patent for tincturing copper upon iron,[2] and he
built a house at Windsor for the carrying on of his works.

Besides his scientific works and studies, he had on hand
innumerable projects, adventurous and commercial. He was
deeply interested in African trade, and was a patentee of
the Royal African Company, formed for its promotion. In
1668 he had conceived a scheme for discovering the north-
west passage. The idea had been suggested to him by a
Canadian, and he forthwith demanded of the King a small
ship, the "Eagle," which he despatched on the quest.[3] As
a result of this, he became first President of the Hudson Bay
Company, to which the King granted in 1670 the sole
right to trade in those seas.[4] In the same year he was
appointed to the Council of trade and plantations. During
the Dutch wars he fitted out four privateers, the "Eagle,"
the "Hawk," the "Sparrow Hawk," and the "Panther."[5] In
1668 he petitioned, in conjunction with Henry Howard, for
the sole right to coin farthings, for which he had invented a
new model.[6] This petition was regarded with great favour
by the nation at large, for "every pitiful shopkeeper"
coined at his own pleasure, and the abuses of the system
were many. The farthings of Prince Rupert were "much
talked of and desired;"[7] and, in consequence of his petition,
he was empowered, with Craven and others, to examine
into the abuses of the Mint.[8] Later he started a project,
in partnership with Shaftesbury, for working supposed silver-
mines in Somersetshire.[9]

[1] Dom. State Papers, Apr. 22, 1671.
[2] Ibid. Nov. 17, 1671.
[3] Ibid. Feb. 7, 1668.
[4] Campbell, II. 249.
[5] Dom. St. Papers, 3 June, 1667 ; 3 May, 1672.
[6] D. S. P. 11 Mar. 1668.
[7] D. S. P. 11, 21 Nov. 1669.
[8] D. S. P. 28 Aug. 1668.
[9] Hist. MSS. Com. Rept. 9. App. III. p. 6a. Sackville MSS.

In September 1668 the Prince was made Constable of
Windsor, in November he was granted the keepership of the
Park, and in 1670 he became Lord Lieutenant of Berkshire.
From that time he lived much at Windsor, but we find
him still occasionally employed in the public service. At
the request of the Mayor and Aldermen of London he laid
the first stone of a new pillar of the Exchange. [1] In 1669
he was on the Committee for Foreign Affairs; and in 1670
he was authorised to conclude a commercial treaty with
the French Minister, Colbert. [2] In 1671 he was one of the
commission appointed to consider the settlement of Ireland;
and in 1679 various "odd letters and superscriptions"
taken on a suspected Frenchman, were handed over for
the Prince to decipher. [3]

But after the last naval action of 1673 Rupert retired
more and more from public life. The peacefulness of
Windsor suited him far better than the turmoil of the court,
and he devoted himself to the repairing and embellishing
of the castle, in which he took an "extraordinary delight." [4]
Evelyn, who visited Windsor in 1670, describes the castle
as exceedingly "ragged and ruinous," but Rupert had
already begun to repair the Round Tower, and Evelyn was
lost in admiration of the Prince's ingenious adornment of
his rooms. The hall and staircase he had decorated entirely
with trophies of war,—pikes, muskets, pistols, bandeliers,
holsters, drums, pieces of armour, all new and bright were
arranged about the walls in festoons, giving a very curious
effect. From this martial hall Evelyn passed into Rupert's
bedroom, and was immensely struck with the sudden contrast;
for there the walls were hung with beautiful tapestry, and
with "curious and effeminate pictures," all suggestion of
war being carefully avoided. Thus successfully had Rupert

[1] Hist. MSS. Com. Rept. 12. Fleming MSS. p. 54.
[2] D. S. P. 27 Oct. 1670.
[3] Hist. MSS. Com. Rept. 7. 496a.
[4] Memoir of Prince Rupert. 1683. p. 75.

represented the two sides,—martial and artistic,—of his nature.[1]

At this time he devoted himself more closely than ever to his scientific and mechanical studies, "not disdaining the most sooty and unpleasant labour of the meanest mechanic."[2] In such harmless and intelligent pursuits did he find his pleasures. He was not a person of extravagant tastes, which was fortunate, seeing that his means were not large, and that his purse was always open to the needy, so that he had no great margin for personal expenditure. From his trading ventures he doubtless derived some profits; and in 1660 he had been assigned a pension of £4,000 per annum. For his naval services he received no wages, but occasional sums of money offered as the King's "free gift."[3] As Constable of Windsor he had perquisites, and when he chose to live at Whitehall, an allowance of food was given him, at the rate of six dishes per meal.[4] But, after his appointment to Windsor, he was seldom seen at Whitehall, except when it was necessary to attend some State funeral, at which functions he was generally required to play the part of chief mourner.

Sometimes his solitude was disturbed by visitors. In 1670 he entertained the young Prince of Orange, who had come to marry his cousin, Mary of York.[5] In May 1671 the Installation of the Garter was held at Windsor, when the King of Sweden, represented by Lord Carlisle, and introduced by Rupert and James of York, received the insignia of the Garter.[6] At intervals the King paid private visits to his cousin; and in February 1677 he came down with the intention of spending a week at the castle, but his intention was changed by the wild conduct of his retinue.

[1] Evelyn's Diary, 28 Aug. 1670. Vol. II. p. 51.
[2] Memoir. 1683. p. 73.
[3] D. S. P. 1668.
[4] Ibid. Aug. 25, 1663.
[5] Hatton Correspondence, I. p. 59.
[6] D. S. P. May 29, 1671.

"On Wednesday night," says a letter in the Rutland MSS., "some of the Courtiers fell to their cups and drank away all reason. At last they began to despise art too, and broke into Prince Rupert's laboratory, and dashed his stills, and other chemical instruments to pieces. His Majesty went to bed about twelve o'clock, but about two or three, one of Henry Killigrew's men was stabbed in the company in the next chamber to the King .... The Duke ran speedily to His Majesty's bed, drew the curtain, and said: 'Sir, will you lie in bed till you have your throat cut?' Whereupon His Majesty got up, at three o'clock in the night, and came immediately away to Whitehall." [1]

To such visitors the Prince must infinitely have preferred his solitude. He was a lonely man; the last, in a sense, of his generation. Between him and the Courtiers of Charles a great gulf lay. Will Legge was dead, and most of his other friends had likewise passed before him. Lord Craven was left, and Ormonde absent in Ireland, but they were the last of the old régime. For companionship Rupert fell back on his own "gentlemen," the people of Berkshire, and his dogs. His "family" was devoted to him, but it seems to have been somewhat troublesome on occasion. Thus, soon after the Restoration, certain members of it caused the Lord Chamberlain to search Albemarle's cellars for gunpowder, a proceeding which naturally excited Albemarle's wrath. Rupert was so exceedingly annoyed at the occurrence, that he not only dismissed the servant in fault, but "offered to fight any one who set the design on foot." [2] Later, we find a petition from a Frenchman, complaining of an assault made upon him "by several scoundrels of the Prince's stables." [3]

Rupert's love for dogs had not abated with advancing years. In 1667 he lost a favourite greyhound, for which

---

[1] Hist. MSS. Com. Rept. 12. Rutland MSS. Vol. II. p. 38.
[2] Dom. State Papers. Jan 11. 1661.
[3] Ibid. Feb. 2, 1665.

he advertised as follows:—"Lost, a light, fallow-coloured greyhound bitch. She was lost on Friday last, about twelve of the clock, and whosoever brings her to Prince Rupert's lodgings at the Stone Gallery, Whitehall, [they shall be well rewarded for their pains."[1] But at Windsor it was a "faithful great black dog" which was his inseparable companion, and which accompanied him on the solitary evening rambles which won them both the reputation of wizards. The fact that he was so regarded by the country people troubled Rupert not at all, and he referred to it with grim amusement in writing to his sister Elizabeth.[2]

"And thus," says one of his gentlemen, "our noble and generous Prince spent the remainder of his years in a sweet and sedate repose, free from the confused noise and clamour of war, wherewith he had, in his younger years, been strangely tossed, like a ship, upon the boisterous waves of fickle and inconstant fortune."

The end came in 1682. For many years Rupert had been quite an invalid—"fort maladif", as the Danish Ambassador told the Princess Sophie; not only the old wound in his head, but also an injury to his leg caused the Prince acute and constant suffering during the last years of his life. He was at his town house in Spring Gardens, November 1682, when he was seized with a fever, of which he died in a few days. It was said that his horror of being bled led him to conceal the true cause of his suffering until it was too late to remedy it. "Yesterday Prince Rupert died," says a letter, dated November 30th. "He was not ill above four or five days; an old hurt in his leg, which has been some time healed up, broke out again, and put him into an intermitting fever. But he had a pleurisy withal upon him, which he concealed, because he would not be let blood until it was too late. He died in great pain."[3]

---

[1] Dom. State Papers, 1667. Carl II. 187 f. 207.
[2] Strickland, Elizabeth Stuart. Queens of Scotland. Vol. VIII. p. 280.
[3] Hatton Correspondence. II. p. 20, Nov. 30, 1682.

Rupert made his will, November 27th, appointing Lord Craven his executor, and guardian of his daughter, Ruperta; and not forgetting any of those who had served him faithfully. Two days later he died.[1] His funeral was conducted with all due state, Lord Craven acting chief mourner; and the King ordered a waxen effigy of the Prince to be placed, as was then the fashion, beside his grave. He lies in the chapel of Henry VII, in Westminster Abbey, but his effigy is not one of those that survive to the present day; and the verger who points out to us the tombs of George of Denmark and other insignificant people, passes by that of Rupert of the Rhine without remark.

[1] Wills from Doctor's Commons. Camden Society. p. 142.

CHAPTER XX

THE PALATINES ON THE CONTINENT. RUPERT'S DISPUTES
WITH THE ELECTOR. THE ELECTOR'S ANXIETY FOR
RUPERT'S RETURN. WANT OF AN HEIR TO THE
PALATINATE. FRANCISCA BARD. RUPERT'S
CHILDREN

THE oath which Rupert had sworn in 1658, he faithfully
kept; never again, in spite of changed circumstances, and
the earnest entreaties of his family, did he set foot in the
Palatinate. Yet he was not quite forgotten by his relatives.
The lively and voluminous correspondence of Sophie and the
Elector, from which we learn much of all family affairs,
contains many allusions to "mon frère Rupert," in whose
sayings and doings the brother and sister took a keen
interest.

Sophie had been married, October 17th, 1658, to Ernest
Augustus of Brunswick, one of the Dukes of Hanover, and
titular bishop of Osnabrück. In her new home she was
visited by Rupert, Sept. 1660, and she wrote of the visit
to Charles Louis, as most satisfactory. " My brother
Rupert made a great friendship with my Dukes," she said;
"they agree so very well in their amusements!"[1] Since
Sophie's Dukes were devoted to music and to hunting, it
may easily be understood that Rupert's tastes accorded
well with theirs.

Sophie wrote "Dukes" advisedly, for she had practically
married, not only Ernest Augustus, but his elder brother,
George William. These two were even more inseparable

---

[1] Briefwechsel der Herzogin Sophie mit Karl Ludwig von der Pfalz, p.
38. Sophie to Karl. 21 Sept. 1660.

than Rupert and Maurice had been, and their mutual affection caused considerable annoyance to the unfortunate Sophie. She had been first betrothed to the elder of the two, but George William being seized with a panic that marriage would bore him horribly, had persuaded his devoted brother Ernest to take the lady off his hands. Sophie acquiesced placidly in the arrangement; she desired chiefly to secure a good establishment, and if she had any preference, it was for the younger brother. But she was not allowed to keep her husband to herself. Neither brother could bear the other out of his sight; and when constant intercourse with his sister-in-law had roused George William's regret for his hasty rejection of her, the position of Sophie became exceedingly difficult. Worse still, her husband was possessed with so ardent an admiration for his brother as to fancy that everyone else must adore him as he did; and this idea kept him in a terror of losing his wife's affections. As he would endure separation from neither wife nor brother there was no remedy, and for months the hapless Sophie was led in to dinner by George William, without ever daring to raise her eyes to his face. Luckily for her the strain became too much at last, even for Ernest Augustus, and he consented to take an eighteen months' tour in Italy with his brother, leaving his wife to visit her own relations in peace.[1]

The eldest sister, the learned Elizabeth, had devoted herself, like Louise, to a religious life; and became first Coadjutrice, and afterwards Abbess of the Lutheran Convent of Hervorden. In this capacity she governed a territory of many miles in circumference, and containing a population of seven thousand. She was recognized as a member of the Empire, had a right to send a representative to the Diet, and was required to furnish one horseman and six foot soldiers to the Imperial army. Every Saturday she

---

[1] Memorien der Herzogin Sophie, pp. 64—67.

might be seen gravely knitting in the courtyard of her castle, while she adjudged the causes brought for her decision. For some reason or other she and her religious views were a subject of great mirth to her brothers and sisters. Rupert visited her more than once in 1660 and 1661, but, said Sophie, "Il se raille beaucoup de La Signora Grecque."[1] And Sophie herself usually alluded to her eldest sister with mild amusement, Charles Louis with evident irritation.

Louise seems really to have been the happiest of all the family, and to have lived with true contentment in her convent of Maubuisson. Sophie, who had the joy of visiting her there in 1679, wrote to the Elector:—"She has not changed. I find her very happy, for she lives in a beautiful place; her garden is large and very pleasant, which is one of the things I love best in the world."[2] In her next letter she remarked that Louise was very regular in her observance of convent rules, "which makes her pass for a saint;" and she added, with a little sigh of envy for the peace she witnessed, "I could easily accommodate myself to a life like that."[3] But the reply of Charles Louis was satirical and unsympathetic: "I know not if I dare ask you to make my very devoted 'baisemains' to my sister the Abbess of Maubuisson, provided that the offering of my profane lips, which still smack somewhat of the world, does not offend her abstracted thoughts, and that she can still spare some for her carnal brother, who is now only skin and bones. At least, I am always grateful that she asks of me nothing mundane."[4]

Louise lived to a cheerful and healthful old age, retaining to the last her interest in art. Her own chapel and many neighbouring churches were beautified by the produc-

---

[1] Briefwechsel des Herzogin Sophie mit Karl Ludwig. p. 35. Sophie to Karl, 1660.

[2] Ibid. pp. 371—3. 24 Aug. 1679.

[3] Ibid. p. 374. 4 Sept. 1679.

[4] Ibid. p. 371. 15 Aug. 1679.

tions of her brush; and in 1699, when she had reached
the age of seventy-seven, she was painting a copy of
Pousin's Golden Calf, as a gift for Sophie. Her life was
simple but peaceful: she ate no meat, slept on a bed "as
hard as a stone," sat only on a straw stool, and rose always at mid-night to attend chapel. [1] Yet she was never
ill, nor did she ever lose her high spirits. "She is better
tempered, more lively, sees, hears and walks better than I
do," wrote her niece Elizabeth Charlotte, the daughter of
Charles Louis, when Louise was eighty. "She is still able
to read the smallest print without spectacles, has all her
teeth complete, and is quite full of fun (popierlich), like
my father when he was in a good humour." [2]

Elizabeth Charlotte had been married to Philip of
Orleans, the quondam husband of her fair cousin, Henrietta Stuart, and Louise was her chief consolation in an
exceedingly unhappy life. "One cannot believe how pleasant and playful the Princess of Maubuisson was," she said,
"I always visited her with pleasure; no moment could
seem tedious in her company. I was in greater favour with
her than her other nieces, (Edward's daughters,) because I
could converse with her about everything she had gone through
in her life, which the others could not. She often talked
to me in German, which she spoke very well. She told me
her comical tales. I asked her how she had been able to
habituate herself to a stupid cloister life. She laughed,
and said: 'I never speak to the nuns, except to communicate my orders.' She said she had always liked a country
life, and fancied she lived like a country girl. I said:
'But to get up in the night and to go to church!' She
answered, laughing, that I knew well what painters were;
they like to see dark places and the shadows caused by
lights, and this gave her every day fresh taste for painting.

[1] Briefe der Prinzessin Elizabeth Charlotte von Orleans an die Raugräfinuen.
7 Aug. 1699. p. 43. ed. 1843.
[2] Strickland. Queens of Scotland, VIII. p. 403.

She could turn everything in this way, that it should not seem dull." [1]   But in spite of her flippant speeches, Louise was respected by all who knew her, adored in her own convent, and died in the odour of sanctity, attesting to the end her staunch adherence to the Jacobite cause.

Edward, with whom Rupert had more intercourse than with the other members of his family, died young, three years after the Restoration, and thus Rupert was left alone in England. Occasionally he wrote to his sisters, but not very often. "If you knew how much joy your letters give me I am sure you would have the good nature to let me receive them oftener than you do," [2] declared Eliza-beth. And Sophie complained likewise: "It is so long since I have heard from Rupert that I do not know if he is still alive." [3] With Elizabeth, Rupert had a common ground in the contests they both waged with "Timon" the Elector: "Timon is so finely vexed at the 6,000 rix dollars he has to pay me, out of a clear debt, that he will not send me my annuity," [4] declared Elizabeth in 1665. Rupert's own quarrels with "Timon" were more bitter. The unsettled dispute about the appanage had been aggravated by the struggle over their mother's will. The Queen had threat-ened, in her wrath, to bequeath her unsatisfied claims on the Elector to his brothers. This she had not done, but she had made Rupert her residuary legatee, leaving to him most of her jewels. The Elector, as we have seen, denied his mother's right to do this. Rupert refused to give up his legacy, and for years the sordid dispute dragged on.

In 1661 the Elector offered a sum of money in lieu of all Rupert's claims upon him; but the offer was rejected with scorn. The Elector professed himself much injured;

[1] Green's Princesses, VI. p. 61.
[2] Bromley Letters, p. 254. 20/30 May, 1665.
[3] Bromley. p. 226. 31 Oct. 1661.
[4] Bromley. p. 254. 20/30 May, 1665.

and Sophie, who sided entirely with her eldest brother, wrote consolingly: "Rupert does not do you much harm by rejecting your money." [1]   Next Charles Louis tried to put his brother off by assigning to him a debt which he pretended due to him from France; but neither would this satisfy Rupert. "Give me leave to tell you," he wrote to Arlington in 1664, "that the debt my brother pretends from France is a mere chimera. It was monys promised to Prince John Casimir to goe bake with his army out of France, whiche, you will finde, is not intended to be payed yett. As I assured His Majesty, I remitt the whoele business to him to dispose, and have given my Lord Craven order to satisfy His Majesty and yourself in all which shall be desired, in order to it. Soe you may easily believe I shall imbrace most willingly the offers you made unto me, assuring you that I shall repay the favor by possible meanes I can." [2]

But the mediation of Charles II did not bring matters to a peaceful end, and Rupert seems to have sought accommodation through Sophie. "It seems to me that Rupert never remembers my existence, except when he thinks of being reconciled with you," declared that lady to the Elector. [3] Nevertheless she did her best to produce the reconciliation. "I am very glad that you are anxious to do all you can to content Rupert," she wrote to her eldest brother; "I do not doubt he will be reasonable on his side, and that he will consider your present position, since he expresses a desire to be friends with you." [4] And in the next year, 1668, she was still hopeful. "I hope Rupert will be contented with what you offer him, for he seems to be in a very good temper." [5]

---

[1] Briefe der Herzogin Sophie. p. 48.
[2] Dom. State Papers. Carl II. 103. 40. Rupert to Arlington. Oct. 11, 1644.
[3] Briefe der Herzogin. p. 133.
[4] Ibid. p. 116.
[5] Ibid. 133.

But, in spite of Rupert's good temper, the affair was not concluded, and in 1669, even the indolent Charles II was roused to pen an expostulatory letter to Charles Louis, with his own hand.

"Most dear Cosin,

"It is well known to you that I have always expressed myself very much concerned for the differences that have been between you and my Cosin, Prince Rupert; and that I have not been wanting, in my indeavor to bring them to a good conclusion, and how unsuccessful I have been therein. But, being still desirous thereof, I cannot but continue my interposition, and, upon a due consideration of both sides, (and very tenderly the state of your own affairs,) I have thought fit to offer yet one more expedient towards the accommodating of the matter, which is this:—that my Cousin Rupert shall disclaim and discharge you from all arrears of appanage due unto him by a former agreement, which, according to your owne computation,—as I am informed,—by this time, amounted above the sum of £6,000 sterl. He shall alsoe lay downe all his pretensions as executor to the late Queene, my Aunt, contenting himself only with the moveables in his possession, which belong to the Palatinate house, and £300 sterl. by the year,—if he have no lawful issue—ad duram vitae; the first payment to be made forthwith, and the subsequent allowances at Easter Fair at Frankfort. The one halfe of whiche sum, if contented, to be obliggeded to lay out in comodities and wines of the growth of your country. And that you may have a more particular accompt of this last proposition, and the reasons inducing to it, I have thought fit to send unto you the bearer, James Hayes, Esq., my Cousin Rupert's secretary, as being best acquainted with this affair; to whom I desire you to give credence in this matter, and conjuring you to give him such a despatch as may finally dethrone this unhappy controversy. Wherein, if ye shall comply with my desire, ye shall give me a great satisfaction; but if other-wise, you must excuse me, if I use my utmost interest for the obtaining of that to my cousin, which I conceive so justly belongs to him. I am, with all truth, most dear cosin,

"Your most affecionat cousen,

"Charles R. [1]

"March 31, '69."

This letter does considerable credit to Charles's business capacities; but even so modest a settlement as he proposed was refused. Nor did the interference of Louis XIV of France, in July 1670, produce any better result. "As to the letter of the King of France about Rupert, I think it is easy to answer with very humble thanks, neither accept-ing nor declining his mediation," advised Sophie. [2]

But Rupert's revenge was not long deferred. About five years later the Elector found cause to repent his ill-usage of his obstinate brother, and would have given much to recall him to the home of his fathers.

The scandals rife at the Court of Heidelberg, in 1658, had by no means abated after Rupert's withdrawal. The dissensions of the Elector and Electress became a subject of public remark, and the Queen of Bohemia had herself written of them to Rupert, adding prudently—"I do not tell you this for truth, for it is written from the Court of Cassel, where, I confess, they are very good at telling of stories, and enlarging of them." [3] But, unluckily, matters were so bad that no embellishments from the Court of Cassel could make them much worse. The scandal—"accidents fallen out in my domestic affairs," Charles Louis phrased it, [4] —had come to such a pitch that the Electress, after boxing her husband's ears at a public dinner, and attempt-

---

[1] Dom. Entry Book. Record Office, 31. fol. 21.
[2] Briefe der Herzogin, 9 July, 1669, p. 141.
[3] Bromley Letters, p. 291.
[4] Ibid. p. 236.

ing to shoot both him and Louise von Degenfeldt, fled from Heidelberg, leaving her two young children, Karl and Elizabeth Charlotte,—or Carellie and Liselotte, as their father called them,—to the mercy of her husband.

Thereupon Charles Louis formally married Louise von Degenfeldt, who was thenceforth treated as his wife. By her he had no less than eight children, but as the marriage was not, of course, really legal, none of those children could succeed him in the Electorate. Carellie, his only legitimate son, was delicate, and his marriage childless; Elizabeth Charlotte had renounced all claim to the Palatinate on her marriage with the Duke of Orleans, and in 1674 the extinction of the Simmern line seemed imminent. This danger affected Charles Louis very deeply. He had been a bad son, an unkind brother, and an unfaithful husband, but he was, for all that, a good ruler and an affectionate father. "The Regenerator" he was called in the war-wasted country to which his laborious care had brought peace and comparative prosperity; and his name was long remembered there with reverent love. The prospect of leaving his cherished country and his beloved children to the mercy of a distant and Roman Catholic cousin, caused him acute suffering. Nor did he believe the said children would be much better off in the care of their eldest brother and his wife.

"What devours my heart is that, in case of my death, I leave so many poor innocents to the mercy of their enemies," he wrote to Sophie; "Wilhelmena (the wife of Carellie) shows sufficiently what I may expect of her for those who will be under her power after my death; since, particularly in company, she shows so much contempt for them. This also has some influence on Carellie, who treats them—with the exception of Carllutz—like so many strangers, as does Wilhelmena;.... the poor little ones are always in fear of her severe countenance."[1]

[1] Briefwechsel der Herzogin mit Karl Ludwig, p. 179. Karl to Sophie, 5 Mar. 1674.

With this depressing prospect before him, Charles Louis turned his thoughts to his neglected brother, showing his confidence in Rupert's generosity, by his readiness to entrust him with the care of his children. "George William says that the Prince Rupert ought to marry,"[1] wrote Sophie, quoting her troublesome brother-in-law, in Jan. 1674. Such was the opinion of the now regretful Elector, and he pressed his brother to return, promising to grant him all he could desire, if he would but come and raise up heirs to the house of Simmern. But Rupert remembered his oath, and answered as we have seen in a former chapter. Then Sophie tried her powers of persuasion, and bade Lord Craven tell Rupert how much the Elector would be pleased, if he would but yield. But Lord Craven showed himself, for once, severely practical. If Sophie would name to him some very rich lady willing to 'marry Rupert, he would be delighted to negotiate the matter, he said; if not, then he begged to be excused from interference. "And there I am stuck (je suis demeuré)," confessed Sophie, "for I do not know how he would support her."[2]

Nevertheless the family continued their solicitations, to which Rupert next retorted that the Elector had better get his cousin, the Elector of Brandenburg, and his sister Elizabeth to persuade Charlotte of Hesse to agree to a divorce; when, Louise being dead, he could marry again. "He must either be very ignorant of our intrigues here, or wishes to appear so," wrote the Elector bitterly.[3] He knew that Charlotte would never forego her vengeance by setting him free, and that neither his cousin nor his sister would interfere in such an affair. Elizabeth was, however, so far pressed into the service, that she, in her turn, exhorted Rupert to come over and marry. To her he only replied, "that he was quite comfortable at Windsor, and had no intention

---

[1] Briefe der Herzogin, p. 175. 24 Jan. 1674.
[2] Ibid. p. 315. 10 Feb. 1678.
[3] Ibid. p. 385, 28 Oct. 1679.

of moving; that Charles Louis had insulted him and might do what he pleased for an heir, he should not have him." [1] Such was his final word, and consequently the Palatinate passed, on the death of Carellie in 1685, to the Neuburg branch of the family.

Charles Louis died in 1680, and Rupert did not cherish the enmity he had borne him beyond the grave. On the contrary, he was anxious to do what he could for the benefit of his impecunious nephews and nieces. For Carellie he did not care, the young Elector had offended him by his neglect, [2] but it was not Carellie who needed his protection; it was rather against Carellie that he took up the cause of the Raugräfen, as Charles Louis' children by Louise were called. The circumstances of the case had left them completely dependent on their eldest brother, who bore them no great love. This was not due to the fact that their mother had supplanted his own. Carellie had never loved his mother; he had often told his father that he paid no heed to what Charlotte might say, and had himself urged her to consent to a divorce. [3] But he was of a peculiar temperament, jealous, fretful, difficult, and his dislike of the Raugräfen was really due, partly to the influence of his disagreeable wife, and partly to jealousy of the affection which his father had always shown to them, especially to Moritzien,—poor Moritzien, gifted with all the Palatine fascination and brilliancy, but ruined by a life of uninterrupted indulgence, so that he drank himself to death.

Promises of providing for these cadets had been wrung from Carellie by his anxious father, but these promises he showed himself in no haste to keep, and Sophie appealed, on their behalf to Rupert. He showed himself ready to assist them, and demanded a concise account of the whole busi-

---

[1] Strickland's Elizabeth Stuart. Queens of Scotland, VIII. p. 210.
[2] Briefe der Herzogin Sophie an die Raugräfen, etc. p. 32. 27 Dec. 1682.
[3] Briefwechsel mit Karl Ludwig, pp. 348. 329. 7 Feb. 1679 and 25 June, 1678.

ness, in order that he might be qualified to interfere.[1] "Not that he thinks the Elector will break his sacred promise to his father,"[2] declared Sophie. Nevertheless she urged the eldest Raugraf, Karl Ludwig, or "Carllutz," who had shortly before visited Rupert in England, to write very affectionately to his uncle, in gratitude for the interest shown in them.[3] But, unfortunately for the Raugräfen, Rupert did not long survive his brother; and only a few months later Sophie wrote to one of her nieces: "You have lost a great friend in my brother Prince Rupert. I am very much troubled and overwhelmed with the unexpected loss. I know the Electress Dowager will also bewail him."[4]

Considering that for more than twenty years Sophie had not seen her brother, her grief seems a little excessive, but doubtless she lamented him for many reasons. The memory of old days dwelt with her all the more as she advanced in years, and latterly she had drawn nearer to her brother. By his means a marriage had been projected between Sophie's eldest son George and the Princess Anne, the second daughter of the Duke of York. During the progress of this negotiation, Sophie sent George over to England, on a visit to his uncle. She had some misgivings about his reception, for, as she confessed, George was not "assez beau" to resemble a Palatine in any way, though her second son Friedrich, or "Gustien," as she called him, was tall and handsome,—"the very image of Rupert" (Rupert tout crâché).[5] Gustien had, moreover, not only Rupert's handsome face and gigantic stature, but also his resolute character. "If he would have changed his religion, he might have succeeded well at the Imperial Court,"

1 Briefe an die Raugräfen, p. 17. 14 Mar. 1680.
2 Briefe. p. 11. 20 Dec. 1680.
3 Ibid. p. 17.
4 Briefe an die Raugräfen, p. 32. 27 Dec. 1682.
5 Strickland. Queens of Scotland, VIII. p. 334. Briefwechsel der Herzogin mit Karl Ludwig.

wrote his mother; "but he has too much of his uncle Rupert not to be firm in his religion." [1]

However, George, if less favoured by nature, was still the eldest son, and therefore of necessity the bridegroom elect. Notwithstanding his want of good looks he was very kindly received, both by King Charles and Rupert. The King declared that he would treat him "en cousin," and lodged him in Whitehall. Rupert paid him daily visits when his health allowed of it, but he was very ill, and often confined to his bed. "I went to visit Prince Rupert, who received me in bed," wrote George to his mother; "he has a malady in his leg, which makes him very often keep his bed; it appears that it is so, without any pretext, and that he has to take care of himself. He had not failed one day of coming to see me." [2]

But though entertained with "extraordinary magnificence," [3] the Hanoverian was not favourably impressed with either England or the Princess Anne. The country was in a ferment over the alleged discovery of the Popish Plot, and George regarded the judicial murders then perpetrated with astonished disgust. "They cut off the head of Lord Stafford yesterday, and made no more ado than if they had chopped off the head of a pullet," he told his mother. [4]

But notwithstanding the averseness of the intended bridegroom, the project was not at once renounced; and Rupert's last letter to Sophie, written shortly before his death, contained definite proposals on the subject. "En ma dernière, chère sœur, je vous ai informé que cette poste je pourrai dire plus de nouvelles assurées de l'affaire en question. Saches donc, en peu de mots, on offre 40 mille livres sterl. assigné caution marchande, et 10 mille livres sterl. par an, durant la vie de M. le Duc, votre mari; et on souhaite

[1] Strickland. Queens of Scotland, VIII. p. 345.
[2] Strickland. Queens of England, X. p. 313.
[3] Memoir of Rupert, Preface.
[4] Queens of England, X. p. 313.

que donerez liberté à M. votre fils de demeurer quelques
temps en ce pays là, fin d'aprendre la langue, et faire
connaître au peuple; ce qu'on trouve nécessaire en tout
cas.   Voyez ce que j'ai ordre de vous dire, et de demander
un réponse pour savoir si l'affaire vous agrée; si vous avez
pour agréable, quelle en face, il sera nécessaire que M. le
Duc m'envoie un homme d'affaires, avec ses instructions,
et ses assurées que sera bien... de celui qui est à vous;
Rupert.

"Il faut vous dire si l'affaire se fait ou non vous avez fort
grand obligation à la Duchesse de Portchmouth;[1] elle vous
assure de toutes ses services en cette affaire."[2]

Apparently the offered terms were not acceptable to
the Hanoverians, for the negotiation closed with Rupert's
death.

Rupert died, to all appearance, unmarried, but he left
two children, a son and a daughter.   More than once he
had seriously contemplated matrimony.   In 1653 it had been
rumoured that he was about to wed his cousin Mary, the
Princess Royal, widow of the Prince of Orange.[3]   In 1664
he made proposals for a Royal lady of France, but the
said lady objected that he had been "too long and too
deeply attached to a certain Duchess."[4]   That obstacle was
removed in the same year by the Duchess of Richmond's
clandestine love-match with Thomas Howard; but the French
lady was long in coming to a decision, and in the meantime the young Francesca Bard crossed Rupert's path.

Francesca was the eldest daughter of Sir Henry Bard,
one of the wilder Cavaliers, who had been raised to the
Irish peerage as Viscount Bellamont; the same who had
pleaded so earnestly with Rupert for Windebank's life in
1645.   He had died during the exile, when on a mission to

<hr>

1 Renée de la Querouaille, Duchess of Portsmouth.
2 Hist. MSS. Com. Rept. 9, 18 Sept. 1682. Morrison MSS.
3 Clar. State Papers. Cal. Vol. II. Fol. 1271. News Letter, 8 July, 1653.
4 Bromley Letters, p. 252, 22 Mar. 1664.

Persia; and Francesca, on the death of her only brother, assumed the family title, as Lady Bellamont. Except a title her father had nothing to bequeath, and it was probably the urgent petitions for the relief of their poverty, addressed by the family to the King, that first brought Francesca into contact with Rupert. [1]

The Prince loved Francesca Bard, renounced his French alliance, and thenceforth turned a deaf ear to all entreaties that he would marry. A son was born to him, and christened "Dudley." Rupert seems to have cared for the boy, and he certainly conducted his education with anxious solicitude. He sent him first to school at Eton, where he could himself watch over him from Windsor. At Eton the boy was distinguished for his "gentleness of temper," and "the aimiableness of his behaviour," characteristics which he certainly did not inherit from his father. Nevertheless he had Rupert's martial spirit, and like his father before him, he early showed an aversion to study, and a passion for arms. Rupert observing this and remembering his own boyhood, removed his son from Eton and placed him under the care of Sir Jonas Moore at the Tower, in order that he might receive instructions in mathematics and other subjects necessary for a military profession. [2]

To Dudley, at his death, the Prince left his house and estate at Rhenen, the debts still due to him from the Emperor, from the Elector Palatine, and from all persons not natural born subjects of England. The English debts, which were considerably less, he destined to be divided amongst his servants. [3]

"Der armer Dodley," [4] as his Aunt Sophie called him, went to Germany to secure his property, and was received

---

[1] Cal. Dom. S. P. 1660, pp. 300, 331.

[2] Wood's Athenæ Oxoniensis. ed. 1815. Vol. II. Fasti I. p. 490. Campbell II. 250.

[3] Wills from Doctor's Commons, p. 142.

[4] Briefe an die Raugräfen, p. 33. 12 Mar. 1683.

with great kindness by the Palatines, though there was a difficulty about the house at Rhenen, that being entailed property.[1] In 1685 he was back again in England, fighting loyally for King James, as his father would have approved. In the battle of Norton St. Philip, where Monmouth fought an indecisive battle with Grafton, Churchill and Feversham, we find "Captain Rupert, the Prince's son," in command of the musketeers, and playing a prominent part.[2] But when the rebellion had been suppressed, Dudley returned to Germany, seeking employment in the wars waged by the Empire against the Turks. He had all his father's active spirit and dauntless courage, but he had not also his enchanted life. In August 1686 young Dudley fell, in a desperate attempt made by some English volunteers to scale the walls of Buda. His death is mentioned with deep regret in several contemporary letters and diaries. Though so young—he was only nineteen—he had already become famous for his valour, and exceedingly popular on account of his lovable character.[3]

Many believed him to have been Rupert's lawful son, and there seem to have been some grounds for the belief. He was universally known as "Dudley Rupert", and his mother maintained to the end of her days that she had been Rupert's wife. Her claim was practically acknowledged in Germany, where morganatic marriages were already in fashion; and even in England rumours of it were rife. "Some say Prince Rupert, in his last sickness, owned his marriage," says a letter in the Verney Correspondence, "if so, his son is next heir, after him, to the Palsgrave.[4] But no public acknowledgment ever took place, and Rupert styled the boy in his will, "Dudley

[1] Briefe an die Raugräfen, p. 49. Campbell. p. 250. Vol. II.

[2] Hist. MSS. Com. IX. 3. p. 36.

[3] Hist. MSS. Com. Rept. V. App. I. p. 187. Sutherland MSS. Aug. 1686. Autobiography of Sir John Bramston. p. 236. Camden Society.

[4] Hist. MSS. Com. Rept. VII. p. 479b. Verney MSS.

Bard." On the other hand, he bequeathed to him property entailed on heirs male, and the Emperor actually paid to Francesca, after her son's death, the sum of 20,000 crowns which he had owed to Rupert. [1]

It seems possible that there was some kind of marriage, but that such marriages were of rather doubtful legality. It could not have given Dudley royal rank, and hardly even a claim to the Palatinate, [2] for, had such a claim existed, Rupert would certainly have put his son forward when the House of Simmern was crying out for an heir. His niece, Elizabeth Charlotte of Orléans, declared that he had deceived Francesca with a false marriage. But the good Duchess was notoriously ignorant of her uncle's affairs, and added to her story several impossible circumstances which tend to discredit it, asserting, among other things, that Rupert had been lodging at the time, in Henry Bard's house, though Bard had been dead nearly ten years. [3] Moreover, such treachery is at variance with Rupert's whole character and all his known actions, and, though he cannot be said to have treated Francesca well, he may at least be acquitted of the baseness suggested by his niece.

During Rupert's life-time no mention is made of Francesca in letters or papers, public or private. Yet, after his death, we find frequent reference to her as to a well-known personage. Two reasons for her retirement suggest themselves. In the first place she was, as she herself asserted, too virtuous to care to have any dealings with the corrupt Court, and in the second place she was a devout Roman Catholic. Considering the prevalent horror of "Popery," the fanatical agitation concerning the second marriage of the Duke of York, and Rupert's position as the popular

---

[1] Add. MSS. 28898. fol. 21. Brit. Mus.

[2] Cf. Marriage of Geo. Wm. Duke of Hanover with Eleonore D'Olbreuse. His children were excluded from succession.

[3] Briefe der Prinzessin Elizabeth Charlotte. ed. Menzel. 1843. p. 86.

hero, it may be that Francesca's religion made him unwilling to bring her forward publicly. But, be the exact facts of his connection with her what they may, that bond was probably the true reason for his obdurate refusal to hear of any other marriage.

The later history of Francesca is sufficiently curious. In consequence of her own avoidance of the Court she had no powerful friends in England, and on Rupert's death, she sought refuge with his sister Sophie. The kindly Electress received her as a sister, though she quite realised the difficulty of proving her right to the name. "She says she was married to my brother," wrote Sophie, "but it will be very difficult to prove; and because she has always behaved herself honourably, she has no friends at Court."[1]

Of Dudley his aunt wrote as "the noble Dudley Rupert," and she actively assisted him to make good his claims to the property left him by his father.[2] After his death she endeavoured to get his possessions transferred to his mother, and wrote on the subject both to James II and to Lord Craven. "It will help her to enter a convent," she said, "for the poor woman will be inconsolable."[3]

But the lively Irish woman, devout though she was, had no taste for the cloister, and preferred to remain at Sophie's Court, where she was greatly beloved. "She is an upright, good and virtuous woman; there are few like her; we all love her!"[4] declared the Electress. In a later letter she refers to the lively wit of Francesca, "who makes us all laugh,"[5]

Evidently she accompanied Sophie on her visits to other potentates, and by William III she was accorded almost royal rank. In 1700 she went with Sophie to visit him at his Palace at Loo, and was there admitted to the royal

---

1 Briefe der Kurfürstin Sophië an die Raugräfen, p. 84. 12 Mar. 1680.
2 Briefe an die Raugräfen, p. 49. 9 Sept. 1686.
3 Briefe an die Raugräfen, p. 49.
4 Briefe an die Raugräfen, p. 152. 11 Feb. 1697.
5 Briefe an die Raugräfen, p. 269. 1 Oct 1704.

table. "The King ate in the back stairs, without an armchair, with only the two Electresses, the Princess, and the Irish Lady (Francesca), the Electoral Prince, and the Prince of Hesse," says an Englishman, writing to a friend. "The rest of the company dined at the other tables below." [1]

After the English Revolution of 1688 Francesca became a staunch and active Jacobite. [2] She made no secret of her views, and even stimulated Sophie's own sympathy for her exiled relatives. The envoys of William III and of Queen Anne inveighed bitterly against "one Madame Bellamont, a noted lady, who is in favour with the Electress, has been her chief confidante, and to her all the discontented politicians address themselves, Papists and Sectaries. She is of the former communion, and I may safely say she is one of the most silly creatures that ever was born and bred in it, to say nothing of the scandal her person hath so justly deserved." [3] The same writer asserted that Francesca was the only person who could speak English at the Electoral Court; and frequent references to her are found in the despatches of himself and his successor. "A Lady whom they call ye Lady Bellamont," says one, "whose character ye well know already. She was Mistress, and she pretends married, to Prince Rupert, and as she is a zealous Roman Catholic so she seems to be a faithful friend to the Court of St. Germains, but is nevertheless used here with much kindness and civility." [4]

In 1708 Francesca undertook a journey to France on Jacobite business, but, opposed though her actions were to Sophie's interests, they could not diminish that lady's love for her. The Electress, declared the enraged English envoys, was as much enamoured as her brother had been. [5]

[1] Hist MSS. Com. Rept. 12. App. 3. MSS. of Earl Cowper, II. p. 404.
[2] A Jacobite at the Court of Hanover. Eng. Hist. Review. F. F. Chance.
[3] Regencies. Record Office. 2. 3. 12 Sept. 1702.
[4] Regencies. 3. 19 Sept. 1704.
[5] Add MSS. 23908. fol. 82. Brit. Mus.

And so she remained until Francesca's death in August 1708, when she wrote mournfully to one of her nieces: "I have lost my good, honourable, charitable Madame Bellamont." [1]

Strange enough was the position of the Jacobite lady in the Hanoverian Court, but the situation was rendered yet more complicated by the presence of Rupert's daughter, Ruperta, as the wife of Brigadier-General Emanuel Scrope Howe, William III's "envoy extraordinary to the most Serene House of Brunswick Lunenburg." The mother of Ruperta was a far less reputable person than was Francesca Bard. Rupert had, as we have seen, kept himself apart from much of the wickedness of Charles II's court, but in the summer of 1668 he was unhappily persuaded to accompany his cousin to Tunbridge Wells. There he fell a victim to the charms of the actress, Margaret Hughes. [2] This woman obtained considerable influence over him, and he purchased for her a house at Hammersmith; also he left to her and his daughter, in equal shares, all that remained of his personal property, after the claims of Dudley and his servants had been satisfied. This, when all had been realised, amounted to about £6,000 each; not an extravagant provision, but then Rupert did not die rich.

Occasional mention of Mrs. Hughes is found in contemporary letters. In 1670 her brother, who was in Rupert's service, was killed by one of the King's servants, in a dispute over the rival charms of Peg Hughes and Nell Gwyn. [3] A little later, Sophie informed the Elector that the woman was in high favour at Windsor, and would, she feared, get possession of the Queen of Bohemia's jewels. "Ein jeder seiner Weis gefelt!" she concluded sarcastically. [4] In another letter she wrote that the Danish Ambassador thought Mrs. Hughes very modest. "I was going to say

---

1 Briefe an die Raugräfen, p. 285. 16 Aug. 1708.
2 Hamilton's Mémoires du Comte de Grammont. ed. 1876. pp. 242—243.
3 Hist. MSS. Com. Rept. 12. Rutland MSS. II. 17.
4 Briefwechsel mit Karl Ludwig, p. 194. 3 July, 1674.

the most modest of the Court, but that would be no great praise!"[1] She seems, however, to have put slight faith in the assurance, for she earnestly desired Ruperta's marriage, on the grounds that she could get no good from her mother.[2] It was said that Rupert, when dying, had sent his Garter to the King, with the request that it, together with the hand of Ruperta, might be bestowed on Charles's son, Lord Burford.[3] With this request the King did not comply; and about 1696 Ruperta married Emmanuel Howe, son of Mr. John Howe of Langar, in Nottinghamshire.

For some time the marriage was kept a secret, for Howe feared the displeasure of the then King, William III. At last, just before his departure to Hanover, he permitted the Duke of Albemarle to break the news to the King. William was pleased to be gracious, and even recommended Ruperta to Sophie's notice, saying: "She is very modest, and lives like an angel with her husband."[4] The husband in question met with Sophie's approval, for she thought him "a fine man, rich, and in a good position."[5] With Francesca he had a double cause of enmity, both public and private, and he wrote of her as virulently as his predecessors had done, declaring that she "has done her endeavours continually to cross my transactions here for the Queen's service;"[6] and again,—"She is indeed a very simple creature, but as malitious and violent as is possible for anything to bee."[7]

Nevertheless the large-hearted Electress made her niece almost as welcome as she had made her reputed sister-in-law, and the Jacobite *intrigante* and the Orange Ambassadress, both so closely connected with Rupert, seem to have

[1] Briefwechsel mit Karl Ludwig, p. 368. 6 July, 1679.
[2] Briefe an die Raugräfen. p. 149. 4—14 Dec. 1696.
[3] Hist. MSS. Com. Rep. 7. p. 480*b*. Verney MSS.
[4] Briefe der Kurfürstin Sophie an die Raugräfen, p. 183, 26 Oct. 1698.
[5] Ibid.
[6] Regencies. 4 Jan., Feb. 1706.
[7] Ibid. 4, 22 May, 1708.

contrived to reside in comparative peace, under the protection of the mother of the house of Hanover.

But for the bar sinister the claim of Ruperta to the English throne would have preceded that of Sophie's son, George I. It has sometimes been regretted that Rupert left no legitimate child who might have reigned in George's stead; but it may be safely conjectured that the fact would not have been a subject of regret with Rupert himself. He would have been the last person to wish that any child of his should supplant the house of Stuart, which he had so long and so faithfully served. Honest in all his dealings, faithful to his friends, and unswervingly loyal to his king he had ever been, and in his old age he would not have turned traitor. Loyalty and strength were the key-notes of his character. Never did he break his given word, with friend and foe alike he scrupulously kept faith, and whatsoever he found to do, he did it with all his might. In all things he had the courage of his opinions; and the rigid temperance which he practised from his earliest youth, in an age and a country where drinking was almost universal, shows an unusual independence of character, and an unusual degree of self-respect.

His private life, if judged by the standard of the present day, was far from virtuous, but it was virtue itself when compared with the practice of those who were his daily associates. His exceptional powers of mind raised him above the ordinary intellectual level; his personal valour surpassed all common courage! But, if his talents and virtues were in the superlative degree, so also were his failings. His consciousness of his own powers made him over-confident, impatient of advice, intolerant of contradiction. His jealous pride rendered him incapable of filling the second place. With advancing years these faults were somewhat amended,—for Rupert was too wise not to profit by experience; but, as his hot temper and youthful insolence had won him the hatred of Charles I's courtiers, so his cold cynicism and haughty disdain made him detested of the Court of Charles II.

In the coarse and witty memoirs of that brilliant Court, Rupert passes without notice, or with only an occasional satirical reference. One noble writer, Anthony Hamilton, has, however, left a description of him, which, though written in prejudice, is not without its value.

"He was brave and courageous to rashness, but cross-grained, and incorrigibly obstinate. His genius was fertile in mathematical experiments, and he had some knowledge of chemistry. He was polite to extravagance when there was no occasion for it; but haughty and rude where it was his interest to conciliate. He was tall and ungracious. He had a hard, stern expression even when he wished to please, and when he was out of temper his countenance was truly terrifying"—("une physiognomie vraiment de reprouvé"). [1]

Such was the view of a courtier; Rupert's friends and inferiors saw him in another light. Beneath the cynical exterior the Prince had a kind heart still; his personal followers loved him; the poor blessed him for his charity; the trades-people remembered with wondering gratitude his "just and ready payment of their bills;" the sailors looked to him as the "seaman's friend;" impecunious scholars and inventors sought, not in vain, his aid and countenance; the distressed Cavaliers appealed to him in well-founded confidence that they would be heard and helped. [2] "In respect of his private life," says Campbell, writing while the memory of the Prince still dwelt among the living, "he was so just, so beneficent, so courteous, that his memory remained dear to all who knew him; this I say of my own knowledge, having often heard old people in Berkshire speak in raptures of Prince Rupert!" [3]

<hr>

[1] Hamilton's De Grammont. ed. 1876. p. 242.
[2] Hist. Memoir of Prince Rupert. ed. 1683. Preface.
[3] Campbell's Admirals, II. p. 250.

INDEX

C

D

E

F

Fairfax—Lord, 146, 150; Thomas, 171—173, 181—183, 201—203.
Falkland, Lord, 71, 122.
"Fan-fan", The, 315.
Fanshaw, Sir Richard, 226, 235.
Faussett, Captain, 134.
Fayal, 251.
Fearnes, Captain, 247, 250, 251—252, 269.
Fenn, Jack, 318.
Ferdinand of Styria, (*see* Emperors,) 3—4.
Ferentz, Count, 37, 39—41.
Feversham, Colonel, 359.
Fielding, Colonel, 90,106—107, 170.
Fiennes, Nathaniel, 87, 114, 116—117.
Fleet, English. Revolts to the King, 222; unsatisfactory state of, 223—229; on Irish Coast, 232—236; in Tagus, 241—244; on Spanish Coast, 244—245; refits at Toulon, 245—246; sails for Azores, 247—248; wrecks, 249, 250, 251, 261; dissension in, 247, 252; damaged by storms, 253, 259—260; on African Coast, 253, 256—259; voyage to West Indies, 260—261; return to France, 261—2; expedition for Guinea, 303—305; in first Dutch War, 307—316; in second Dutch War, 322—329; neglected by victuallers, 303, 314—315, 317, 320, 325—6; quarrels concerning, 321.
Fleet, Dutch, 303—304, 307—308, 312—316, 324—328; enters Medway, 319; want of union in, 308.
Fleet, French, 325, 327—328.
Forth, Lord, 120.
Fox, Captain, 59.
Fraser, Lord, 286.
Frederick, Elector Palatine, (King of Bohemia,) 3—8, 12—14, 46, 72; letters of, 9.
Frederick Henry, Prince Palatine, 3—9, 10—13; letters of, 8, 9, 13.

G

Gambia, River, 256—257.
Gassion, Maréchal, 214—218, 305.
George of Denmark, 343.
George William; *see* Hanover, Dukes of.
Gerard Charles, (afterwards Lord,) 78, 137, 190, 196—198, 201, 202, 220, 273, 275, 278.
Gerard, Jack, 279.
Glemham, Sir T., 191, 202.
Gloucester, Siege of, 120.
Gonzaga, Marquis de, 240.
Goodwin, Ralph, 198.
Goring, George, 27, 34, 35, 76, 84, 103, 141, 145—6, 149—150, 154, 158—159, 161, 170, 172, 177, 214, 217; character of, 83—84; enmity to Rupert, 82—84, 124; reconciled to Rupert, 158—160; letters of, 27—28, 155, 158—159.
Grafton, Duke of, 359.
Grandison, Lord, 34, 75, 115, 116.
"Greyhound", The, 326.
Guatier, M. de, 220.
Guinea, 303—304.
Gustave, Prince Palatine, 18.
Gustavus Adolphus, King of Sweden, 14, 15, 35, 36, 66, 92.
Gwyn, Nell, 363.

H

Haesdonck, Jan von, 95.
Hague, Court at, 224—226.
Hamilton, Anthony, opinion of Rupert, 366.
Hamilton, Marquis of, 140.
Hampden, John, 109.
Hanover, Dukes of: Ernest Augustus, 344—345, 357; George William, 344—345, 353; Prince George of, 355—356, 365.

I

J

K

L

M

N

O

P

Palatinate, The, 8, 28, 35—40, 283.

Parliament, English, 7, 57, 71; negotiates with King, 98, 99, 102, 163; allies with Scots, 128; army of, 163; remonstrates with Rupert, 169; offers pass to Rupert, 198—199; obliges Princes to leave England, 203; approves conduct of Elector, 206—7; sends ships against the Princes, 241—245.

Peace Party, 128.

Penn, Sir W., 308—9, 321.

Pepys, Samuel, Diary of, 197—8, 294, 302, 303, 306, 310, 314, 315, 321, 323; as victualler of fleet, 303, 314, 317—319.

Percy, Henry, Lord, 76, 82, 113, 120—124, 133—4, 145, 155, 157, 189, 239, 273; letters of, 122—123; duel with Rupert, 221.

Pett, Robert, 227.

Philip, Prince Palatine, 15, 18, 35, 49, 208, 210, 286; kills d'Épinay,

210—211; enters service of Venice, 211—212.

Picolomini, 215.

Plymouth, Siege of, 119.

Poland, Casimir, Prince of, 43.

Poland, Ladislas, King of, 22.

Popish Plot, 356.

Porter, Endymion, 24.

Portland, Lord, 191, 198.

Portodale, Governor of, 256.

Portsmouth, Duchess of, 357.

Portugal, Ambassador of, 335.

Portugal, Infanta of, 299; King of, 241—244, 252; Queen of, 242; Princes in, 241—244.

Portuguese in the Azores, 247, 248, 251—252, 256, 262.

Powick Bridge, Battle at, 87—88.

Price, Thomas, 227.

Purefoy, Mrs., 86—87.

Puritans: in terror of Rupert, 62, 63; hang Irish soldiers, 64; violence of, 94—95; exultation of, at Marston Moor, 150—152.

Pyne, Valentine, 261, 281, 287.

R

Radcliffe, Sir George, 89, 189.

Rantzau, Maréchal, 214, 215.

Ratzeville, Prince, 240.

Raugräfen, 354—355.

Ravenville, Prince, 51.

Reading, 106—107.

Reeves, Sir W., 324.

"Revenge", The, 227, 251, 259—260.

Richelieu, Cardinal, 31, 49.

Richmond, Duchess of, 111—113, 199, 201, 241, 357.

Richmond, Duke of, 93, 112, 130, 193, 195, 199, 200; character of, 77—78; letter of, to Rupert, 124—5, 138—9, 140—144, 160—1, 178; letter of Rupert to, 178.

Rivers, Lady, 96.

Roe, Sir Thomas, 10, 16, 51—56; Letters of Elizabeth of Bohemia to, 40—41, 49—51, 56; of Rupert to, 52—54; of Sir W. Boswell to, 56. Letters to Elizabeth of Bohemia, 22—25, 28, 30; to the Elector, 64, 88.

Rossetter, Colonel, 194.

Roundway Down, 113.

"Royal Charles", The, 308.

Royalists. Dissensions in Army of, 68—70, 91—92; want of discipline among, 93, 100; want of supplies among, 100, 164—165; factions among, 124, 156, 224—225; plot of, to surrender Bristol, 103; revenge of, for breach of faith, 107, 116.

"Royal Prince", The, 313.

Raugräfen, The, 354—355.

Rupert, Prince Palatine. Letters to, 69, 70, 74—75, 100, 103, 106—108, 113, 122—127, 129, 130, 133—145, 147, 151, 155, 158—161, 164—6, 168—170, 177, 179, 194—5, 199, 200, 209, 218, 227, 230—1, 232—236, 239, 240, 265—6, 269, 270, 277, 279, 282, 285—288, 306, 348; letters of, 144, 166, 169, 178, 235, 251, 255, 284. Letters of, to Arlington, 304—5, 309, 324, 349; to

S

Y